BATTLE AT ZERO POINT

MACK MALONEY

2003
50TH
ANNIVERSARY

ACE BOOKS, NEW YORK

If you purchased this book without a cover, you should be aware that this book is stolen property. It was reported as "unsold and destroyed" to the publisher, and neither the author nor the publisher has received any payment for this "stripped book."

This is a work of fiction. Names, characters, places, and incidents either are the product of the author's imagination or are used fictitiously, and any resemblance to actual persons, living or dead, business establishments, events, or locales is entirely coincidental.

BATTLE AT ZERO POINT

An Ace Book / published by arrangement with
the author

PRINTING HISTORY
Ace mass-market edition / September 2003

Copyright © 2003 by Brian Kelleher.
Cover art by Michael Herring.
Cover design by Pyrographyx.

All rights reserved.
This book, or parts thereof, may not be reproduced
in any form without permission.
The scanning, uploading, and distribution of this book via the Internet or
via any other means without the permission of the publisher is illegal and
punishable by law. Please purchase only authorized electronic editions,
and do not participate in or encourage electronic piracy of copyrighted
materials. Your support of the author's rights is appreciated.
For information address: The Berkley Publishing Group,
a division of Penguin Group (USA) Inc.,
375 Hudson Street, New York, New York 10014.

ISNB: 0-441-01096-2

ACE®
Ace Books are published by The Berkley Publishing Group,
a division of Penguin Group (USA) Inc.,
375 Hudson Street, New York, New York 10014.
ACE and the "A" design
are trademarks belonging to Penguin Group (USA) Inc.

PRINTED IN THE UNITED STATES OF AMERICA

10   9   8   7   6   5   4   3   2   1

RESONANCE DEPARTING

It started at thirty. On a technician's cue, the entire UPF contingent assembled below began shouting out the descending numbers.

But strange things started happening again. The sky suddenly turned black, as clouds covered the sun. A darkness more acute than any twilight descended on Happy Valley. Never had it grown so dark before. Still, the countdown continued.

It reached fifteen seconds—and a sudden clap of thunder rolled through the valley. It was powerful enough to shake the Vanex door, as well as everything and everybody nearby.

Another clap of thunder, this one so powerful, High Hill itself actually began shaking.

"Someone does not want this to happen!" Xara yelled to Hunter.

The countdown reached five seconds . . . four . . . three . . . two . . . one . . . *zero!*

Also by Mack Maloney

STARHAWK
STARHAWK 2: PLANET AMERICA
STARHAWK 3: THE FOURTH EMPIRE

CHOPPER OPS
CHOPPER OPS 2: ZERO RED
CHOPPER OPS 3: SHUTTLE DOWN

For more information visit
www.MackMaloney.com

For those souls lost aboard
the shuttle *Columbia*

<u>PART ONE</u>

The Battle That Never Was

PART ONE

The Goblin That Never Was

1

Earth
Third Month, 7202 A.D.

The big air-chevy began its climb up to the floating
city shortly before dawn.

It was a cold, dreary morning. Fog had enshrouded the mile-
high aeropolis known as Special Number One, and the rain
had started up again. Bad weather was supposed to be a rarity
on Earth these days. Its atmospherics were controlled by the
Imperial Engineers, and usually they produced only warm and
sunny days. Lately, though, it had been little else but dark
clouds and heavy showers all around the planet.

The guards at the front gate of Special Number One spotted
the air car shortly after it launched. Its dark blue color identified it as belonging to the Space Forces; its muted gold trim
indicated it might be attached to one of the SF's intelligence
services, though there was no way to know for sure. In any
case, the guards had been told it was coming and that whoever
was inside had already been cleared to enter the aerial city.

When the air-chevy arrived at the front gate, the guards
simply waved it on through. It slowed down, folded in its
wings, and began creeping along the winding streets of the
enormous sky castle. Special Number One was home for
nearly a million people. Ten square miles around, it contained
thousands of ornate buildings, both old and new. Multiple

spires rose from the clutter of structures at its center; long, sloping passageways crisscrossed these spires like latticework. At night, each of the towers glowed with a different iridescent color. Some of the tallest held zaser beams on their pointed tops. When illuminated, these zasers were so bright, they could be seen out beyond the Solar System.

A labyrinth of very narrow streets surrounded the middle of the city, and it was through these alleys the air car now traveled. Some of the pavements in this, the old section of the aeropolis, were so dated, they were made of cobblestones. Many of these stones had long since worn away, though, and as no one was quite sure just how to make cobblestones anymore, the streets remained cratered and pockmarked.

The air-chevy soon reached a main thoroughfare, and here the roadways became wider and glistening and new. Between each of the soaring buildings along these avenues were small forests of perfectly manicured trees and multicolored tropical gardens, sometimes surrounding shimmering reflecting pools. Columns of Imperial Guards, wearing vividly colorful uniforms, could always be found marching up and down these middle-city streets, and this morning was no different. Weapons on shoulders, prerecorded martial music blaring, their formations followed each other so closely, they formed one long, endless parade. For many of these soldiers, this spectacle would consume their entire day. The pageantry never stopped up on Special Number One. It got tired, but it never stopped.

The air car passed several small armies of promenading soldiers and soon came in sight of the Imperial Palace itself. It was for the person who lived here that all the pomp and circumstance was about. The palace was the home of the Emperor O'Nay, Supreme Ruler of the Fourth Galactic Empire and the deified head of The Specials, the near-immortal upper class that had ruled the Milky Way for more than 500 years. Aloof to the point of nonexistence, O'Nay was rarely seen, even by members of his immediate family, and almost never heard to speak. Atop the palace was an immense tower, soaring 500 feet above everything else on the floating city, so high, clouds perpetually gathered near its peak. This is where

O'Nay could usually be found, in a small room at the top, gazing out on empty space, apparently thinking his great thoughts as the Galaxy spun around him and his pretty soldiers marched below.

The air-chevy turned right, moving away from the palace and finally settling on the edge of the city's main square. The rain had let up momentarily, and the passenger decided he would walk from here. He stepped out and straightened his uniform; the air car floated away. But then the cold rain began falling again. *Bad timing*, he thought. He pulled up his collar and started walking.

He was Captain Gym Bonz, Space Forces Intelligence. Six foot even and just 120 years old, he was ruggedly built, with a handsome, friendly face broken only by a pair of black, steely eyes and a slightly misshapen nose. No hideously long sideburns or ground-scraping mustaches for him, though these were the fashion of the day. Bonz kept his hair cut cool and his ray-gun juice dry. He moved with the assurance of a veteran military officer. A light greenish aura surrounding him told of many trips taken in space.

Bonz was considered among the best intelligence officers in the Empire; indeed, doing intelligence work had been in his family for thousands of years. But he hadn't always been a spy. He'd started his career as a skyfighter pilot for the Space Navy, seeing his first combat during the Ninth Fringe War back in 7109. After performing well in that conflict—fought against an alliance of space pirates known as the Blackships—he'd moved on to driving Starcrashers, the gigantic aerial battleships flown by the Empire's military forces. In countless actions, mostly out on the Four and Five Arms, his ships were used for both landing troops on enemy-held planets or massive orbital bombardments of the same.

Bonz quickly distinguished himself as a commander of great skill. It took talent wielding a two-mile-long spaceship around in the heat of battle, but Bonz was able to do so with ease. He also became known as a great leader of men. His piloting crew alone numbered more than 1,000, and during a combat invasion, he was responsible for up to 20,000 starship troopers riding back in his holds. He'd received so many citations and combat medals in his time at the helm, he couldn't fit them all on one uniform. In the yearly review of starship officers before the Emperor, Bonz always appeared near the front of the line.

About forty years before, he'd caught the eye of Space Forces Intelligence, and most especially, an ultrasecret unit known as SF3. These deep-space superspies were the elite of the Empire's secret agents. They were in charge of identifying potential trouble spots out on the Fringe, the catchall name for the wild and chaotic outer-galactic territory that served as the frontier for the realm. SF3 was always on the lookout for high-caliber officers who could think quickly and didn't rattle easily. Bonz fit their bill. They received permission from the Space Navy to recruit him.

Bonz turned them down, though, at least at first. He'd never seen himself as a spook. He preferred direct action against a problem; creeping around the edges just didn't appeal to him. Plus he knew intelligence work would take him away from his family for even longer periods of time than flying monstrous Starcrashers did. It took the most tragic event of his life to change his mind.

He'd moved his family from their home on Saturn's Titan to a military settlement closer to the Fringe called Boomtown 52. Also known as B-52, the three-star system was located at the bottom of the Four Arm, the fourth major spiral of the Milky Way. It was considered a secure place against the hordes of space pirates who were perpetually causing havoc further up the Arm, and Bonz had uprooted his family only so he could be closer to them between missions. It turned out to be a horrible mistake. While on an operation several hundred light-years away, an army of pirates raided B-52, immolating one planet and pillaging the other two. Bonz's beautiful wife and his two young daughters were killed.

That had been thirty-eight years ago. It took him almost ten years to get past the grief. The Space Navy sent him to a desk job close in to The Ball, that being the very peaceful center of the Galaxy. When he emerged from his dark place a decade later, he contacted SF3 to see if they were still interested in him. They were.

He'd been doing undercover missions for them ever since.

• • •

He walked down the long, nearly empty concourse now, the great plaza of aluminum and gold that served to divide this part of the floating city neatly in two. At one end stood the soaring, brightly lit headquarters of Space Forces Command. This was his destination.

Known as Blue Rock, the headquarters was an extremely futuristic building, climbing dozens of stories into the sky, with a jumble of moving walkways, flying bridges, and air tubes surrounding it like so many sparkling halos. This place served as the supreme operations center for the Space Forces, the largest of the Empire's holy trinity of military services. The Space Forces were the Emperor's front-line troops, nearly thirty billion regulars in all, with millions of spacecraft to get them where they needed to go. Invading and holding hostile planets was its specialty, and its soldiers enjoyed great élan. Comprised primarily of the Navy, the Army, and the Air Service, the SF was well trained, highly motivated, and very loyal to the Emperor. And as its roots went back more than 1,000 years, its members liked to think they were the real professionals of the Empire's vast military, and for many reasons, they were.

By contrast, hanging off the floating city's northern tip was another very futuristic building, this one made entirely of black superglass. Unlike the brightness of SF's Blue Rock, it was rare to see any light at all coming from this place. This was Black Rock, the operations center for the second service of the Empire's triad: the Inner Defense Forces, also known as the Solar Guards.

Essentially, the SG were the military police of the Empire. They were mainly responsible for security within the Pluto Cloud, as the boundary of the Earth's Solar System was called. Or at least that's how it was supposed to work. Truth was, the Solar Guards could be found in just about every corner of the Galaxy these days. Though not quite half as large at the SF, they still fielded nearly fifteen billion soldiers; maintained millions of precincts, outposts, and ports of call throughout the Galaxy; and had many shady mercenary armies serving in their employ as well. Their far-flung influence, built up since the

SG's inception three centuries before, was in contrast to the Space Forces who, by tradition, had many of its bases, repair stations, barracks, and training facilities much closer in to Earth. This meant SF patrols were always longer and their resources always more stretched out. Frequently, it took the SF more time to get to their destinations, while the SG, with its established presence just about everywhere in the realm, were rarely very far from the action. This disparity was one of the great ironies of the Empire.

The opposite-end location of the two headquarters atop Special Number One was no coincidence. The SF and the SG did not get along. They used different types of weapons and flew different types of starships. They had different orders of rank and different style uniforms—the Space Forces wore blue with yellow trim, the Solar Guards wore black with red. Their missions were nothing alike. While it was the job of the Space Forces to project military policies throughout the Empire, the Solar Guards cruised the Galaxy, unencumbered by long traditions, conducting countless "investigations," some of them legitimate (like tracking down tax outlaws and criminal armies) but many of them not. SG troops were also considered more specialized and better trained than those in the Space Forces—and far more ruthless.

A difference in philosophy fueled the main conflict between the two services. The Empire was incredibly vast. As the Galaxy was 100,000 light-years across, the realm encompassed more than 100 billion star systems, upwards of 500 billion planets, and trillions of citizens—no one was sure of the exact number. Three Empires and several Dark Ages had passed since humans first left Mother Earth more than 5,000 years before. During the First Empire, which ran from about 2100 to roughly 3200 A.D., every planet in the Milky Way had been discovered, explored, terra-formed, (or puffed, to use the common term) and made part of the realm. But with three successive imperial falls, billions of these planets became lost again, their populations in upheaval, some not even realizing that they were still part of a huge Empire. Indeed, after successive waves of time and history over 5,000 years, some planets' inhabitants weren't even aware that life existed beyond their own atmospheres. The fourth and current Empire had reclaimed about 85 percent of the Milky Way during its reign, and the process continued unabated. The Empire's starships and soldiers were still investing planets, bringing them back under the imperial rule, whether they liked it or not, at a rate of about 1,000 a day. This is where the clash in doctrine between the SF and the SG came in.

The SG believed the Empire's best path to success was to reclaim as many of these worlds as possible, as quickly as possible, no matter what the means. This included invading unsuspecting planets without prior warning, a hugely traumatic event for the inhabitants of the unlucky world. The Space Forces were dedicated to the same goal of reclamation but believed the best way to accomplish it was to go after the troublesome planets first—those millions of worlds inhabited by pirates, criminals, tax dictators, and other interstellar lowlifes—and bring the more peaceful, law-abiding planets back in gradually.

So, it was not a question of expansion—that was everybody's objective—it was how quickly and humanely that expansion should be carried out. It seemed to be such a simple point really, but it was the dividing line between the two enormous military branches, one just as wide as the concourse that separated them up here on Special Number One. No one in the Imperial Court dared favor one service over the other, at least not in the light of day, and Emperor O'Nay was characteristically mute on the subject.

So the SG conducted their own reclaiming operations—most times on very flimsy criminal evidence—and the SF conducted theirs. Thus, the SG fought its own wars and the SF fought theirs. Not once in their combined history had the two services joined forces and fought side by side against a common enemy.

In fact, more than a few times of the past three centuries, they'd come close to trading shots themselves.

None of this would be of any help for what was about to come.

• • •

The Fourth Empire was in turmoil, perhaps the worst since its rise to power 500 years ago. Things started going wrong about a month before, when an army of mysterious invaders suddenly swept down the Two Arm, the second of the nine major swirls that, along with the Ball, made up the Milky Way. Though the Empire had been at war for centuries with space pirates, outlaw merc armies and other space trash out on the Fringe, the realm itself had never been *invaded* before. Even worse, no one had any real idea who the invaders were. They had appeared as if from nowhere farther up the Two Arm and, despite their relatively small numbers, had created widespread panic in that part of the Galaxy, causing a flood of refugees in the sector that had still not slowed down.

For a while, it even seemed the invaders were heading for Earth itself. The Empire's Starcrasher warships traveled in the Seventh Dimension at speeds reaching two light-years a minute. This made a trip to the far end of the Galaxy possible in less than a month. Earth, on the other hand, was located about two-thirds of the way out on the One Arm. Thus, the Two Arm was only a few days' travel away. When news got around that the invaders had managed to steal six Supertime-capable cargo ships, a shock wave went through the Empire. The enemy was only forty-eight hours away from the mother world! The crisis produced enough concern that O'Nay was forced to cancel the Earth Race, the centuries-old contest that was the most important social and political event in the realm. That had never happened before, either.

The situation out on the Two Arm seemed to resolve itself, however, after a fierce battle on a crossroads planet called Megiddo, when the invading force, consisting of six ancient warships and the six stolen Starcrasher cargo haulers, was met head-on by a fleet of Solar Guard warships near a place called Thirty Star Pass. What happened next was still being hotly debated both inside the Imperial Court and throughout the Empire.

Simply put, the Solar Guards claimed they destroyed the enemy and its ships. Indeed, the SG force that met the invaders was the elite Rapid Engagement Fleet, probably the best-trained, best-equipped unit in the Solar Guards. The REF boasted three times as many vessels as the invaders, plus it had been armed with specially adapted antistarship weapons designed to home in on the stolen cargo 'crashers control circuits. When the battle was joined, the half-dozen stolen cargo ships were annihilated first, followed quickly by the invaders' six original warships.

Or at least, that's what the Solar Guards reported to the Emperor. But even though the official SG brief on the incident had been accepted by the Imperial Court with much relief, rumors soon surfaced that the battle did not go the way the Solar Guards had claimed. In fact, some whispered that there hadn't been a battle at all, that the invaders' entire fleet had vanished just microseconds before the SG force unleashed its barrage of antistarship weapons at it.

But how could a fleet of twelve enormous warships just disappear? Strange things happened across the Galaxy every day, but few things as strange as that. The lingering doubts, both in the Imperial Court and on the streets of billions of planets around the Empire, had caused the SG to close ranks and become more defiant than usual. Declaring the whole matter top secret, Black Rock started issuing decrees. Any SG soldier caught talking about the "Thirty Star Pass incident" would be thrown in prison. Any civilian found doing the same would suffer a similar fate. At one point, the SG's high commanders even considered ordering every enlisted man who'd been involved in the alleged encounter to undergo a brain wipe, this to cut down on the number of potentially loose lips. And indeed, hundreds of SG personnel who were on the periphery of the action were forced to have the painful procedure, including many lowly staff people who just happened to be on duty that day inside Black Rock.

All this served to shut a lot of mouths—but still, the question remained.

What really happened out there?

Bonz reached the huge SF headquarters and was immediately cleared to go inside.

The building was lit up as always, each of its many levels glowing brightly. A full shift was on duty within, more than

50,000 people, most of them lording over millions of superfast communications bubbles from which the reports of the nonstop comings and goings of the vast space service gurgled up.

He rode the air tube up to the ninety-ninth floor, stepping out into a long hallway with very subdued lighting. There was only one doorway here. It was marked Advanced Logistics, but this was just a cover. Behind the door lay the main offices of the Space Forces Special Intelligence Service, the unit better known as SF3. It was the Empire's most secret spy agency.

While SF3 had millions of branches throughout the Empire, this low-key place was the office of the Boss, the man who had summoned Bonz here, the Secretary-in-Charge of all Space Forces military intelligence.

Bonz cleared the last security beam and went through the door. The office beyond was made entirely of bright superglass. The view from here was spectacular, despite the dreary weather. He was greeted by a pretty SF aide. She was young and blonde and wearing a tight SF uniform. Nice shape, nice eyes. She asked Bonz how his trip up from Earth was; it was a customary question for all those visiting the floating city. He replied it had been fine. She led him down the hallway to an enormous glass room. Inside, the Secretary was sitting behind a huge hovering desk, looking blankly out at the gray clouds of the morning.

"With all the resources those damn weather engineers get," he was mumbling, "you'd think they'd be able to produce a nice day every once in a while."

The aide announced that Bonz had arrived and then disappeared with a smile. The Secretary spun around and gave Bonz a quick salute. Bonz returned the formality, then stepped forward and they shook hands. The Secretary was nearly fifth century—he was 488 years old, and had spent a huge amount of that time in the service of the Space Forces. He was still a tall man for his age, ruddy face, long white hair, which was the custom of the Space Forces' Old Guard, and wearing a long blue gown. He was highly respected both inside and out of the SF and was one of the few people on Earth who could have the Emperor's ear within a few days' notice.

He rarely smiled, though. And on this dark day, he seemed particularly glum.

He motioned for Bonz to sit down and then got right to the point.

"You've been following this Thirty Star Pass thing, I assume?" he asked.

"As much as I can," Bonz replied.

"Well, what are your thoughts on it? Do you believe a battle took place out there?"

Bonz shrugged. "I hate to take the SG's side—ever. But obviously *something* must have gone on."

"Maybe so," the Secretary grumbled. "But you know how they are. If it had been the all-out victory that they've claimed, the SG Central Command would have run its own victory parade up and down these streets for a week. Hell, the Imperial Guards wouldn't have been able to step off the curb without running into them. Yet no such festivity ever took place."

"A good point, sir—"

"Glad you think so. Here's another one. No signs of a battle were ever picked up on our superstring net; no disruptions in any of the ultra–radio frequencies near the alleged battle area. No spikes at all on any of our subspace scanner systems. A battle like that would have made a lot of noise. Yet I've seen the readouts myself. They are still top secret, but I can tell you they look like just another normal day on the Two Arm."

"But as long as the SG sticks to its official version of events, most people have no choice but to believe them," Bonz said.

"Precisely," the Secretary agreed.

Bonz leaned forward in his seat. "Has anyone done a subatomic particle sweep of the area? If this battle happened as the SG claims, at the very least there should be clouds of stuff floating around out there. Infinitesimally small stuff, certainly, but enough to register on a SAP string. With the right gear in the right place, just about anyone could collect a star-ton of data."

"That's a good idea—but there's a problem," the Secretary told him. "Late last night the SG issued another decree. They declared the entire sector off-limits to all space vessels, including many of its own. They're calling it a 'No-Fly Zone.' "

"You've got to be kidding. . . ."

The Secretary just shook his head. "They drew a box one hundred light-years around the alleged battle zone and are not allowing anyone inside—except for the Rapid Engagement Fleet. We've got reports this morning that the REF is evacuating all inhabited planets inside this zone, moving the people out, sometimes with less than an hour's notice. Now, they've been drastically restricting traffic into the area since whatever the hell happened out there took place. But last night they made it official. No one but them can get in or out."

"A No-Fly Zone?" Bonz said. "I've never heard of such a thing."

"Neither had we," the Secretary replied. "I think they just made it up."

"Well, what's the official reason they are giving for this?"

The Secretary retrieved a small document by snapping his fingers. "This is from the SG command staff to the Imperial Court, and I quote: 'So that the REF's science ships can better study the aftereffects of the battle against the invaders.' "

Bonz almost burst out laughing. "*Science ships?* When the hell did the REF get any science ships?"

"That's just it," the Secretary said. "They don't have any— and wouldn't know what to do with them if they did. My sources inside the Imperial Court tell me they know this is all just a cover story, and a bad one at that—"

"A cover story for what, though?"

"Well, then, that's the question, isn't it?" the Secretary said in a hushed voice. "But between you and me, some people up here think the SG is still trying to find those twelve invasion ships. That they didn't destroy them at all."

"So they *have been* lying then," Bonz said.

The Secretary just shrugged. "If they are, they're playing a very dangerous game. And a desperate one as well. Lying to the Emperor can carry very dire consequences. Plus, it would mean the whereabouts of those twelve ships is still unknown. Thirsty?"

The Secretary snapped his fingers again, and an instant later they were both holding goblets filled with crystal-H water, the slightly intoxicating drink that was considered acceptable for consumption in the early morning.

"There's more, if you want to hear it," the Secretary went on after sipping his drink.

"Absolutely, I do. . . ."

The Secretary took a moment to activate the room's hum beam. With the push of a floating button, the walls of the office began vibrating ever so slightly. This meant the room was now immune to physical intrusion or eavesdropping.

"We intercepted some string comms from the SG two days before anything took place out there," the Secretary told Bonz. "Did you know the kid, Joxx the Younger, was responsible for that battle on Megiddo?"

Bonz shook his head no. Joxx the Younger was an extremely famous, extremely heroic, but extremely arrogant SG space commander. His father, Joxx the Elder, was the Supreme High Commander of the Solar Guards. His mother was sister to the Empress, O'Nay's wife. Therefore, Joxx the Younger was in line to become Emperor some day.

"What the hell was the kid doing out there?" Bonz asked.

"The old man sent him out—alone—when the SG got the first reports of large refugee movements," the Secretary replied. "Frankly, no one had any idea what he was getting himself into. He found the situation very chaotic as soon as he hit mid–Two Arm. By the time he reached Megiddo and Thirty Star Pass, it was out of control. Millions of refugees were on the move, and the invaders were just on the other side of the Pass—and were about to hit Megiddo. Joxx scrabbled together some ships, put prisoners on them, and sent them out to meet the invasion fleet. At the time, he thought the invaders were flying more than a hundred ships . . . but of course, now we know it was only the original six."

"How could Little Joxxy make a mistake like that?" Bonz laughed. "I thought he was supposed to be smart."

"Well, he is, but he ran into someone who was smarter, or at least smart enough to fool him into thinking they had fifteen times as many ships as they actually did. And somehow those six ships were able to destroy Joxx's cobbled fleet. Then, while Joxx wrapped Megiddo in wall-to-wall blasters, expecting the sky to fall in on him, the invaders hit a place called TransWorld 800 instead. It's an SG supply dump about ten light-years from Megiddo. That's how they stole the six cargo 'crashers, which, I don't have to remind you, are unarmed but still have the ability to travel in Supertime."

"No wonder our friends at Black Rock are feeling cranky these days."

"There's even more," the Secretary said, pouring out another round. "Did you know the Emperor's daughter is missing?"

"*Xara? Missing?* Since when?"

"No one has seen her in more than a month. The Imperial Family has been very low-key about it; they claim she's way the hell out on the Seven Arm, 'visiting relatives.' But we know that's not the case—mostly because they secretly have half the Imperial Guard forces out looking for her. And many of the Earth Guards as well. But what's particularly disturbing is that it adds a whole new twist to this Thirty Star Pass affair."

"You mean they're connected somehow?"

The Secretary nodded. "It's being said around the Palace that Xara vanished at the very moment the invaders' fleet disappeared—or close enough to it. Even stranger, Captain Vanex is missing as well."

"Vanex? The Imperial Janitor? He's seven hundred years old! Certainly no one is thinking Xara ran off with *him?*"

The Secretary grinned, another rare occasion. "Well, I haven't heard that particular spin on it yet," he said. "But we do know that they both disappeared at just about the same time."

Bonz ran a hand through his hair. "This is getting very strange."

"Well, I'm glad I got your attention," the Secretary said. "Because it gets even stranger."

He snapped his fingers, and an image materialized in front of them. It was a 3-D portrait of a man in his early thirties, wearing the uniform of the Empire's third major service, the Expeditionary and Exploratory Forces, more readily known as the X-Force. The man was strikingly handsome, with a strong jaw and large, intelligent eyes. He also looked, well, a bit *different* than a typical citizen of the Galaxy, though just what that difference was could not be easily explained.

Bonz recognized the man right away. It was Hawk Hunter. *"He's alive?"*

The Secretary's right eyebrow went up. "We have reports that he just might be. . . ."

Everyone in the Empire knew about Hawk Hunter. He was what space legends were made of. He'd been found living alone on a desolate planet at the far edge of the Galaxy about two years earlier. His origins were unknown, even to himself. There was one theory that said Hunter was from a different time period, thousands of years before, when a people known as Americans ruled much of Earth and led the first tentative steps into outer space. If so, Hunter would have been the first person to ever show up from the past—or the future, for that matter. At least the first that anyone knew about.

Whoever he was, and wherever he came from, Hunter was brought to Earth shortly after being found, and with his very bizarre but incredibly fast flying machine, won the illustrious Earth Race—in record time. As a result, he was lavished with riches and praise, given a commission and a ship's command in the Empire's forces.

Hunter went missing soon after his first mission, however, and it turned out, his disappearance was all part of a scheme he and Princess Xara had cooked up to allow him to search for the remnants of the people he called the "Last Americans." But the rumors had it that shortly after Hunter went AWOL, he'd been tracked down and killed by an SG hit squad, all this taking place about a year before. Bonz was surprised to hear his name mentioned now.

"He found his lost relatives," the Secretary explained soberly. "Or so I was told. These Americans? They were living on a planet so far off the star roads it isn't even in the Milky Way."

"Is that possible?" Bonz asked.

The Secretary's other eyebrow went up. It was the official line of the Fourth Empire that every inhabitable star system existed within the Milky Way, and that none could exist outside of it. Furthermore, humans were the only intelligent life-form not just in the Galaxy but in the entire universe. Therefore, all life had to exist *within* the confines of the Galaxy.

"I was at a cocktail party in the Imperial Palace not long ago," the Secretary went on. "A friend of mine was a bit into the cups and was more talkative than usual—a real departure for him, I might add. In any case—and remember, I'm telling you this thirdhand—this person claimed that Hunter not only located his Last Americans way out there, he also came across evidence that the Earth was stolen from these Americans and the other original peoples who lived here several thousand years ago. He came to believe that this rather sinister aspect of history was woven into the fabric of all four Empires, or at least the Second *and* the present one."

Bonz was thankful the hum beam was securely in place. Very little of the history of the empires had survived the handful of Dark Ages that separated the realms. In fact, very little was known about the Galaxy prior to the rise of the Fourth Empire. But still, such talk as this—even in idle conversation—was pure sedition and probably punishable by death.

The Secretary continued anyway: "And so, the story goes, it was from this knowledge that Hunter and some of his confederates—a pack of old-timers, so I'm told—somehow raised an army, launched the invasion of the Two Arm, defeated Joxx on Megiddo, and then stole the six cargo 'crashers from TransWorld 800. It was only that they ran up against the REF and their antistarship weapons that they didn't march right up to the One Arm itself. Had that happened, who knows what could have come next. . . ."

"Are you telling me the buzz around the Imperial Court is that *Hawk Hunter* was the leader of the invasion fleet?" Bonz asked incredulously.

His boss nodded.

"And that somehow Xara was involved with him?"

The Secretary nodded again. "We know they've had a liaison in the past. If it's still true today, then the Princess Herself is in league with these invaders. Not something we would normally expect from the daughter of the Emperor."

Bonz sat back in his chair. "Well, at least the story has a

romantic spin to it," he said. "Who told you all this, if you don't mind me asking?"

The Secretary sat back in his chair as well. "An Imperial Court spy."

Bonz rolled his eyes. By strict definition, he was a military intelligence officer; he gathered information that might affect the Space Forces in time of war or peace. He was, in fact, a soldier first, a spy second. The Imperial Court spies were different. They were civilians, strictly cloak-and-dagger types who were more interested in Palace intrigues than seeking out intelligence that might help the Empire. There was an unknown number of them, but certainly more than a hundred just here on Earth. They could usually be seen in their long capes and floppy black hats, skulking around the floating city's old section, entering or leaving the rambunctious Imperial Court by hidden doors, or deep in hushed conversations with the high court officers in the back rooms of the immense palace.

"Those guys spin more tales than witches these days," Bonz said.

The Secretary nodded. "But that doesn't necessarily mean they aren't true."

They both sipped their drinks in silence.

"What does Kid Joxx say about all this?" Bonz asked. "After all, he's supposedly in the middle of it."

The Secretary frowned, the most natural expression for him. "Young Joxx is not talking. In fact, we have information indicating he's been acting rather irrationally since all this occurred."

"Irrationally? How?"

"My source claimed he's been spotted carrying a silver dagger in his belt. . . ."

Bonz gasped. A silver dagger was supposed to be the traditional weapon for would-be imperial assassins. Why would Joxx be carrying one of those?

"What's more," the Secretary went on quietly, "my source claims Hunter had actually been captured by the SG at one point in all this. But he went missing again, somehow managing to disappear from his jail cell at the bottom of an SG warship even as it was speeding to an isolated planet where he was due to be executed and buried in an unmarked grave."

"And Kid Joxx was involved in that?"

The Secretary drained the last of his drink. "It's a deep secret, but some people think the kid helped Hunter escape just hours before his execution. Just how Joxx aided him, we don't know, though we have one report that the jail cell Hunter was sitting in was at the bottom of Joxx's own ship, the *ShadoVox*. In any case, Kid Joxx has refused all orders and has dropped completely out of sight."

Another silence; the rain began beating against the windows again.

"Well, we are certainly living in interesting times," Bonz finally said. "Though I understand that was meant as a curse, thousands of years ago."

"You know how superstitious people are across the Empire," the Secretary told him. "Rumors are already rife that things are not right here on Earth, and especially within the Palace. As word travels around about these invaders and Hawk Hunter and the disappearance of Xara, people are going to start asking what it all means. And you know to at least a few hundred billion of our citizens, it will mean nothing less than the first step in the fall of the Empire."

"Ask anyone down on the street of any planet," Bonz replied soberly. "Chances are they will say that the cracks have been showing for some time now."

"Well, we just can't have that kind of thinking," the Secretary said sternly. "It's not good for any of us. We need to get at the truth—whatever it may be—and make an informed report to the Court. After all, that's our job, whether the SG likes it or not. But we have to gather the evidence quietly. *Very* quietly. And that means someone has to infiltrate this No-Fly Zone and indeed set up a subatomic sweeper—and hopefully lead us to some answers."

He lowered his voice a notch. "We must find out three things: Did this battle take place out there or not? Is Princess Xara's disappearance connected with it somehow? And is this Hunter character involved in any of it? Again, we think it is wise to send someone out there and find out these things for ourselves."

He snapped his fingers, and a silver dish appeared in midair in front of him. On it lay a single bubble of clear fluid; a thought drop containing a multitude of information for anyone who put it on their tongue. The Secretary directed the hovering dish across the desk, away from him.

Then he said, "And that someone, Mr. Bonz, is you."

2

The small starship named *ZeroVox* **left Earth just af-**
ter midnight the following day.

It was 250 feet long and, just like everything else flying in
the Galaxy these days, was shaped like a wedge. But while
most ships leaving Earth were somewhat sleek and new, the
ZeroVox was anything but. Its fuselage was dented and
twisted. Its underbelly was patched with strips of atomic tape.
Its bubble-top canopy was cracked and scratched. Even its
stubby communications mast was leaning askew.

The ship's interior was no better. The rear quarter was home
to a very elderly looking star engine, one that appeared, at first
glance anyway, to be solely ion-ballast powered, as all civilian
ships in the Galaxy were. While still extraordinarily fast, ion-
powered vessels could travel at barely one-twentieth the speed
of Supertime-capable Empire ships—and that was only with a
very good power spike on a very good day. Not only did ion-
ballast ships have to stop to refuel frequently, they also broke
down a lot, especially when those power spikes gave out. This
meant extremely long-distance interstellar travel was usually
very uncomfortable in ion ships, or sometimes, if the distances
were too great, virtually impossible.

The *ZeroVox* had a battered cargo compartment, a pathetically small crew quarters, and a laughably old flight deck. Small and smelly, with only one seat for the pilot, its flight control panels were flame-scarred and leaking bubble fluids. The deck's half-dozen portholes were scraped and dirty, the floor panels thick with metal shavings and yellow atomic cigar ash. Everything visible to the naked eye up here led to only one conclusion: the *ZeroVox* was a space truck, used for hauling things between the stars. And a very old space truck at that.

But on this tiny ship, all was not as it appeared.

Hidden beneath its cracked flight control panel was an array of incredibly advanced, ultra–long-distance sensors that were so sensitive they could spot an approaching ship from fifty light-years away, or roughly twice the distance of a typical LDS. Ensconced below the stained floor panels was an LS2 life-sign detector, which allowed the operator to search an entire planet for signs of human life including heartbeats, breathing patterns, voices, footfalls, even DNA samples blowing in the wind. In the ship's nose, twisted and battered though it was, sat a four-pack of so-called XZ guns so powerful, they could send a bolt of destructo-beams more than five light-years in any direction. And what seemed to be a broken-down ion-ballast engine in the back was actually hiding a tiny but powerful prop-core power unit beneath it. This meant the *ZeroVox* could actually fly in two ways: ion power or in Supertime at close to two light-years a minute.

The *ZeroVox* was not a space truck at all. It was a brilliantly disguised, heavily armed spy ship.

And sitting at the helm was the SF3 secret agent, Gym Bonz.

He was carrying a crew of four clankers with him, robots that resembled human beings, but just barely, in that they had two arms, two legs, a torso, and a head, all made of metal. Their launch from Earth had gone off without a hitch. They had left from an isolated docking bay at the far end of Eff-Kay Jack, the enormous spaceport located next to Earth's capital, Big Bright City, and then fully kicked in the ion-ballast engine on leaving Earth's atmosphere. They were soon soaring past the Martian orbital plane.

While their destination was the mid–Two Arm, and specifically the Moraz Star Cloud, where the phantom battle supposedly took place, they would have to pass through the Pluto Cloud first. Made up of millions of artificial moons and heavily armed satellites stationed at roughly the same distance the ninth planet was from the Sun, the Pluto Cloud was a seventy-third-century version of a moat. No one got in or out of the Solar System, the Empire's inner sanctum, without passing through it and showing the proper authorization. Anyone caught trying to run the border crossing was usually executed on the spot.

This massive security swarm was under the command of the Solar Guards, and in this case, they usually did their jobs too well. The SG had a variety of ways to scan a ship, ID its passengers, rummage its cargo. One sniff of suspicion, and the SG border troops wouldn't think twice about tearing a ship apart, one electron bolt at a time. Even in the best of times, getting through their checkpoints could be troublesome. These days, it was bound to be more difficult.

Bonz was confident he could pull it off, however, though he knew he would have to be very careful. Leaving the Solar System with his undercover identity already in place was essential to his mission. At the very least it would prevent an SG stealth beam from attaching itself to his tail, as might happen if he'd passed through the Pluto Cloud in full SF uniform. But from all appearances, his ship was nothing more than a poky space lorry whose ID string would claim its one and only purpose was to pick up and deliver slow-ship wine to planets all around the Milky Way. All of the hidden exotic equipment was being concealed by holographic barrier beams, essentially modified spectrum rays that made things look like something they were not, from the subatomics up, and thus immune from most scanning units. Right down to the last detail, nothing on board the *Zero* could be linked back to SF3 or Bonz's true identity. He'd done this sort of thing many times before and had not been caught yet.

But shortly after passing through what was left of the asteroid belt, Bonz realized his masquerade might not go as smoothly as he'd planned. He hadn't been out of the Solar System since returning to Earth from his last mission about six weeks before. He was noticing now that in just that short time, things had changed drastically in the solar neighborhood.

On a typical ride out from Earth, the casual traveler was likely to pass a steady stream of passenger-carrying spaceships, both military and civilian, moving between the Pluto Cloud and the mother planet. Some were on their way out of the Solar System; others were traveling within it. Supply ships of all sizes were also a common sight, as were private vessels belonging to higher-up government officials or even members of The Specials, as the very-extended Imperial Family were known. It was also not uncommon to encounter sightseeing ships taking well-heeled joyriders on the famous nine-planets-in-an-hour tour, a breakneck spin around the original worlds of the Solar System, all of them puffed and populated some 5,000 years before.

But Bonz saw none of this frivolity now. The interplanetary travel lanes beyond Mars were devoid of anything but Solar Guard warships. From scouting vessels to monstrous Starcrashers, they seemed to be everywhere. And these weren't just single SG vessels flying about. There were hundreds of them traveling in single- or double-line formations—convoys, moving back and forth between Earth and the outer reaches of the Solar System. Even more disturbing, these SG ships were flying in full battle dress, meaning their gun doors were open, and their weapons were exposed, as if they were going in to battle—or trying to look as intimidating as possible. If it was the latter, they were doing a good job of it.

Bonz steered *ZeroVox* past the Jupiter Loop and then closer to Saturn, a pang of grief catching in his throat as he zoomed by the tiny jewel moon of Titan, once his happy home. He was heading for one of the main Pluto Cloud checkpoints for leaving the Solar System, a gigantic confluence of SG garrison moons known as the Saint Golden's Gate. But now his ultra–long-distance scans were telling him there was a major tie-up of ships at this heavily used border crossing; the traffic jam stretched for thousands of miles in all directions. Bonz keyed into some string comm chatter coming from the area, and the conversations confirmed what he had initially feared: the SG was not only stopping and questioning every vessel commander entering or leaving the Solar System, they were ultrascanning every ship, too.

This was not good news.

They reached the Pluto Cloud about a half hour later, taking their place in the long line of outward-bound ships. The queue was moving very slowly; as he watched the search process on his long-range viz scanner Bonz could see why. Essentially every ship had to pass through a gigantic gold ring, nearly a half mile in circumference, that the SG had set up next to the Saint Golden's Gate checkpoint. This was the ultraring, and, it could see all. The SF3 technicians who had presented Bonz with the *ZeroVox* for this mission had assured him that the disguised vessel would be able to go through a typical SG security beam with no problem. But this huge ring was about one hundred times more powerful, more invasive that the typical SG scanner.

Would *Zero* pass the test?

There was only one way to find out.

It took six long hours, but finally the *ZeroVox* reached the front of the line.

It was directed into the huge scanning ring, which had been set in place between two small artificial moons slightly beyond the Saint Golden's Gate. There were no less than 2,000 SG troops in the vicinity of the big scanner. Some were stationed in huge gun turrets on the two accompanying moons; others were manning the ultraring itself. Three SG *culverins* were also hovering nearby. This trio of small, swift warships was bristling with weapons, all of them pointed at a spot just beyond the exit point from the ultraring. The message was clear: anyone not passing muster would be blasted first, with questions asked later.

Bonz moved his ship inside the ultraring and crossed his fingers. He was immediately hailed by the SG officer in charge of the border crossing, his gruff, booming voice suddenly materializing inside the *ZeroVox*'s flight compartment. The voice demanded to know who Bonz was and where he was going. Bonz quickly keyed his intersystem communicator and identified himself as a wine hauler; destination: a backwater binary system on the lower Three Arm. He was to pick up a load of gold slow-ship wine for immediate shipment back to Earth. It was as good a lie as any, and SF3 had given him proper string documentation to back up the cover story.

The SG officer accessed this documentation, then broke off the communications link. Bonz called back to the clankers and told them to get ready to be scanned. Two seconds later, a bright blue, ghostly light penetrated the hull of the ship. It began moving slowly from stem to stern. Bonz stayed glued to his seat and began thinking about a particularly unattractive but busty girl he knew out on the Three Arm. She could drink him under the table and was a damn good cook. She would do anything for the right amount of slow-ship wine, and after all, that was his business. If only she took the time to wash her hair or actually bathe every once and a while . . .

The SG ultrascan could see, hear, and sense everything, including the thoughts of everyone on-board. It could penetrate every cell of a being, could capture memories, feelings, and inner thoughts. It was intrusive, demeaning, and intimidating— the Solar Guards' usual way of saying hello. The mind-scan part was the most tricky, though; it could not be easily fooled. But Bonz had done this sort of thing before, and he was good at it. Not only could he will away any of his own personal thoughts, he had cultivated thoughts that would be in the head of a typical space trucker—thus the dream about the loose woman out on the Three Arm. But generating the appropriate amount of false memories was only half the trick here. Bonz also had to maintain a slight modicum of reluctance to the scan, a hint of holding something back, as just about anyone would. As for the four robots on board, they'd had their brains wiped clean before leaving Earth.

The scan finished its initial sweep, then disappeared. Bonz fought back an almost involuntary sigh of relief, a dangerous emotion had it happened just seconds before. The holo-barriers had held, thank God, and his mind games had worked, too. If not, a small army of SG troops would have beamed aboard already. He waited a few seconds, then another tremor shook the ship back to front. This was the passport EMP, a marker that indicated the ship had been cleared by the SG security people at the Pluto Cloud. Bonz did breathe a sigh of relief now. The booming voice invaded the flight deck once again, telling Bonz he was free to go and strongly suggested that he do so "with all haste."

Then, strangely, the voice added, "And if you see any of our SG brothers out where you're going, tell them we said hello."

"Tell them we said hello?" Bonz wondered aloud. What the hell did that mean?

This puzzled him, but not for very long. It would be dangerous to linger here any more than he had to. So he thanked the SG officer, killed the transmission, and yelled back to the clankers to hold on. Then he hit the accelerator and left the SG checkpoint in a blur.

A few seconds later, the Solar System was far behind them.

Once he was certain no one was trailing him, Bonz settled down to begin the next part of his mission.

Working the few authentic controls on his dilapidated pilot's seat, he pushed his speed up slightly, though still only calling for a fraction of his available power. The idea was to ride on ion ballast until they got to the Two Arm, as traveling in Supertime in a space truck would tend to arouse suspicion, to say the least. Bonz inputted the set of coordinates SF3 wanted him to follow and then put the spy ship on automatic control. The new course would bring them right into the Moraz Star Cloud, which made up much of the mid–Two Arm, and then to the edge of the SG No-Fly Zone itself.

This done, Bonz poured himself a drink, shook it gently, and finally relaxed. The heavy lifting had been completed; now it was time to do his brain work. Among other things, the thought drop he'd ingested back on Earth contained a secret file filled with memory images and dossiers on a very unusual group of people. Bonz sipped his cocktail, then leaned back in his squeaky flight chair, closed his eyes, and began accessing this file. Hawk Hunter was the first image on the memory string. There was little information on the dashing yet enigmatic pilot that Bonz didn't already know. Indeed, at one point two years ago, Hunter was the best-known person in the Galaxy, next to the members of the Imperial Family. It seemed back then, *everyone* knew *everything* about him. Bonz certainly didn't have to dwell on him now.

Next in the synapse line were two pilots named Erx and Berx. Famous officers of both the SF and the X-Forces, they were middle aged and looked like human boulders with arms, legs, and extremely long *mustachios* attached. These were the men who'd rescued Hunter from the isolated planet called Fools 6 and eventually brought him to Earth. They'd been sent back out to the edge of space about a year ago by Princess Xara to find Hunter again after he'd so mysteriously disappeared, but they hadn't been heard from since, either.

Next came Petz Calandrx, the well-known space hero turned poet, who was both a personal friend of the Emperor and winner of the Earth Race more than a century before. He was a real oldster, rapidly approaching his fourth century. At one time, however, he'd been a brilliant soldier, and for a while, a regular on the Specials' ultraexclusive party list. He'd been sent with Erx and Berx on Xara's mission to rescue Hunter, only to go missing as well.

Then came a character named The Great Klaaz. Apparently a hero in the outer regions of the Fringe, this stooped and craggy old man was practically unknown to Earth's intelligence services. As he was approaching his sixth century, he seemed an unlikely candidate for what was afoot. Yet he, too, had apparently fallen in with Hunter and his band and was now wanted for questioning as well. After him came a short, mysterious, middle-aged man who went by the name Pater Tomm. Though he claimed to be a priest—and in the fuzzy image provided to Bonz on the mind drop, he was sporting a long cassock and bowl haircut similar to those worn by those of a religious bent—he hardly looked the part. Tax enforcer and knucklebreaker was more like it. The last member of this group was named Zarex Red, a gigantic individual with muscles bulging everywhere and a costume that looked like something out of a viz-screen movie. He was approaching his 150th year, Bonz estimated, and was known both for running weapons and discovering new or lost star systems out on the Fringe. He always traveled in the company of a huge robot.

Who were these people? They were as strange a collection of space rogues as Bonz had ever encountered, and most not so short on the tooth. Yet the SF3 believed this unlikely group was responsible for the mysterious invasion of the Two Arm and an equally mysterious disappearing act soon afterward. And because the people of the Empire were obsessed with putting a name on everything, a habit that was not discouraged inside the intelligence services, they had been christened by SF3 as The Hunter-Calandrx Gang, for their two most famous members.

In addition to his primary mission to the No-Fly Zone, Bonz was also supposed to look for this gang—or, more accurately, look for *signs* of them. Life clues, DNA debris, those sorts of things, anything that could place them at the scene of the crime, so to speak. He would also be searching for any clues to Princess Xara's whereabouts, and those of the Imperial Janitor, Vanex, though Bonz couldn't imagine them *all* being in the same place. No matter; it was all fine with him. Among his many undercover talents, he was also very adept at tracking down fugitives.

If it was his job to find them, then find them he would.

The rest of the thought drop consisted of a briefing on what else he had to do when he reached his secret destination. More specifically, it explained how the equipment packs hidden in the cargo hold would help him fulfill his bigger mission, looking for signs of the phantom battle. But these thoughts he would not have to access until the time came to put them into action. His brain work was done, at least for the time being.

Bonz drained his cocktail, double-checked the ship's controls, then walked back to the crew quarters where the robots were on their chargers. He checked over the prop core; it was running at such a low volume, the casing was barely warm. He then calibrated the ship's hidden hum beam; once activated, they would be fairly immune to any long-range deep space eavesdropping. Satisfied all was well, he returned to the flight deck and locked the door behind him. Then he reached into his pocket and pulled out a small white cube. It sparkled, emitting a tiny crackle of subelectricity. He set the cube on the battered control panel and tapped it once. There was a bright flash, and suddenly, three more people were in the control room with him.

Or so it seemed. Immediately his eyes began to water. His nose felt funny, and a lump formed in his throat. They looked so real. They were smiling, and waving, and trying to get him to join them, even converse with him. But they were not real. This was a projection; an old 3-D holographic image loop of his family—his wife and two daughters in matching SF flight suits—posing at the top of a peak on Ganymeade. It was taken during a vacation to Saturn's rings. The last image of all of them together.

The cube was actually filled with many holographs of his family; he was even in some of them, in uniform, his chest weighed down by all his medals. But this one Bonz liked the best. The girls, smiling and happy, his wife radiant. At just the right moment, he reached out and ran his finger down her face. She closed her eyes and smiled, just as she had that day so long ago.

Like every mission in the past four decades, Bonz's family would be making this trip with him as well.

It would take them five days to reach the bottom of the Two Arm. Another half-day's journey would get them to the edge of the Moraz Star Cloud.

Bonz's mechanical crewmen passed the time playing endless rounds of *diceo*. It was a three-dimensional game of chance in which markers could disappear into other dimensions at completely random and unexpected times. Huge swings of luck and money were frequent. Of course, the robots loved it. Most clankers were notorious gamblers, a quirk which, it was believed, had grown out of several thousand years of artificial intelligence being passed on to successive models and designs. The strange thing was, win or lose, the robots showed no emotion, no leaping about at gaining a big pot, no head-holding when a fortune in aluminum chips went down the drain. This gave the game a surreal edge, especially when the pots grew large and the tension in the air was thick.

Bonz drifted in and out of the game; he was smart enough not to play for too long with any robot, and these four seemed very up on their *diceo*. He spent most of his time up on the flight deck, driving the ship, catching up on his sleep, and keeping an eye on what kind of ships were flying around them. He'd been briefed on the horde of refugees that had rolled down the Two Arm in front of the mysterious invaders; their first movements had been a harbinger of the bad things to come. From Bonz's vantage point now, it was clear this mass exodus had not yet stopped. If anything, it had become worse. The usually busy space lanes linking the Two Arm with the rest of the Galaxy were brutally congested due to the uncertainty pervading the second swirl in the wake of the short-lived invasion and the forced evacuation of planets inside the SG's forbidden zone.

The rush of tens of thousands of ships an hour, hour after hour, became perversely fascinating to watch as the days wore on. Of course, all this traffic was heading away from the Two Arm, and in the opposite direction from Bonz. Millions were leaving the area—but for where? Worlds hundreds or thousands of light-years away? To find long-lost relatives and hope there was room to squeeze them in? Or maybe some of these people didn't have anywhere to go. Maybe some would be doomed to wander the stars forever. Suddenly the stability of the Empire—authoritarian as it was—seemed like something that really *was* slipping away.

A strange thing to miss, Bonz thought more than once.

Even more disturbing were the large numbers of SG ships mixed in with this tidal wave of the displaced. If someone had told Bonz that every SG warship in the Galaxy was now traveling in the vicinity of the Two Arm, he would have been hard-pressed not to believe them. From massive Starcrashers to the smaller, swifter *culverins*, to supply ships, cargo ships, scout ships, and even prison ships, the SG vessels were either mixed in thick with the high-speed traffic jam of refugee ships—*herding* was once the term for it—or flying above it all in Supertime, as detected by the *ZeroVox*'s top secret Ultra-

Distance Scanners. In any case, the Solar Guards were every-where.

So many SG ships made Bonz uneasy, especially when he seemed to be the only one heading toward the trouble zone and not moving away from it. At the moment, though, the SG appeared too preoccupied to notice one little old space truck going against the tide. Bonz could only hope it would stay that way until he got where he had to go.

The days went on, and the one-way stream of space vessels did not abate.

Until, that is, Bonz and his robots found themselves on the eve of the sixth day, at the foot of the Two Arm and about twelve hours from the edge of the Moraz Star Cloud. That's when the crowded space lanes suddenly dried up. A few strag-gling ships were still rushing by them in the opposite direction, but even that trickle petered out over the next few hours. When the sixth day finally arrived, no more ships—neither civilian nor SG—could be seen anywhere around them.

It seemed as if Bonz and his tin men were out here all alone.

Not a pleasant feeling.

They reached the edge of the Moraz Star Cloud on the morning of the sixth day.

The gigantic collection of star clusters stretched out before them like a brilliant, swirling ocean. Even the robots were impressed. This was one of the most beautiful parts of the Galaxy; some kind of celestial exotica could be seen wherever one looked. When the first explorers from Earth came here nearly 5,000 years before, they'd claimed that a strange but beautiful sound would envelop their ships—star music, they'd called it—and its resonance would stay with them even long after they left. But looking at the star cloud now, Bonz could hear nothing but silence. Dreadful silence. Strange things had been happening in those clusters of stars up ahead, so strange, even the star music had gone away.

Sitting alone on the flight deck, Bonz mixed himself another cocktail, shook it vigorously, then downed it in one long gulp.

Suddenly he couldn't wait to do the mission and get the hell back to Earth.

After another six hours of travel, they reached the border of the No-Fly Zone.

Once again, there were no ships around, either civilian or SG. Bonz could hear no chatter on his long-range comm sets, no indications at all that anyone was out here but him and his mechanical crew.

Odd as it was, their apparent isolation was a good thing, at least for the moment, as the real talent of the *ZeroVox* was about to be put to the test. Bonz signaled the robots to tie down, then belted down himself into the tiny pilot's seat. He rechecked all his systems controls, and everything came back green. He snapped his fingers, and a small, hovering control panel came into view; it had a large red switch surrounded by several smaller ones. Bonz took a deep breath and then hit the red switch.

The ship's tiny prop core instantly became hot, as it fully tapped into the omnipotent power of the Big Generator and allowed the ship to enter Supertime. Suddenly, the *ZeroVox* was moving at tremendous speed. The stars outside took on the look of long, straight lines, sparkling with dazzling colors. Within seconds they were deep inside the No-Fly Zone, traveling at blinding velocity. There was no need to steer or maneuver here. Bonz simply set the controls for the upper reaches of the Moraz Star Cloud and sat back to watch the light show. And what if he should find himself dead on the path of an approaching star, with little or no time to stop or alter course? No matter; the ship would go right through it with barely more than a ripple.

That's why they called them Starcrashers.

But only Empire ships could travel this interstellar highway, and this was where the *ZeroVox's* ultra–long-distance scanners would come into play. Bonz knew these sensors were so juiced up, they would let him see an SG ship coming long before the SG ship would see him, an invaluable aid for what he was about to do. But suppose the forward scans *did* pick up an SG ship coming toward him, then what? Bonz would simply drop out of Supertime and look for someplace to hide, not that difficult out here. And if he was caught anyway? He would quickly boost power to the ship's holographic barriers, order the clankers to dummy up, and then assume the role of a slow-thinking captain of a lowly ion-ballast-powered vessel, who somehow never got the word about the imposition of SG's No-Fly Zone.

As a veteran spy, Bonz knew playing dumb was a talent in itself.

They passed several key star systems in their dash through the forbidden zone.

One was Moog-SRX, with its one and only planet, the up-scale party world called Cubes. A favorite of Empire flight crews, Cubes featured thousands of drinking clubs, casinos, exotic eateries, and holo-girl houses. But the place was abandoned now. Bonz had turned the life-sign detector on the planet and cranked it up to full power; he received not a single reading in return, not even a blip. On the viz screen, Cubes looked dead, lifeless. Certainly no Solar Guards or anyone in the Hunter-Calandrx Gang was anywhere near it.

Next they streaked by the Stygnus-Malone twin star system, a place also known as S&M-2. Thirteen planets orbited the binary suns; at one time they'd held more people than any other system in this part of the Two Arm. Bonz once again used the life-sign detector, this time to scour the entire star system; he was sure there were more than a few places for someone to hide on the thirteen different worlds. But again the scanner came up empty. It found no inhabitants, civilians, outlaws, Solar Guards, or missing princesses anywhere. He proceeded to his next station, a star system called Gyros 6. But it was more of the same here. Lifeless, deserted planets.

Next came the artificial moon, TransWorld 800, the place were the mystery invaders stole the six SG cargo 'crashers. It was basically a large silver ball with induced gravity, a bare atmosphere, and no vegetation, just hangars and bunkers. The Secretary had told Bonz he privately suspected the Hunter-Calandrx Gang might be using the big silver ball as a place to hide. But like everywhere else the *ZeroVox* had passed so far, TW800 was empty. No people, no cargo, no cargo ships.

Just empty.

Bonz made another forty-four-light year leap, reaching the system known as Starry Town, the last populated area in the mid–Two Arm and very close to the infamous Thirty Star Pass. The only planet revolving around Starry Town's sun was Megiddo, the place where Kid Joxx had made his imaginative if misguided stand against the invaders. It was lifeless, too, but unlike the other empty planets, it was decimated as well. In fact, many parts of the planet were still billowing smoke, even now, more than a month after the titanic battle.

Bonz dropped out of Supertime and went into a low orbit around the planet. He scanned it top to bottom, and twice around the equator. The readings began flowing back immediately. No heartbeats, no voices, no breathing. Nothing but destruction—and lots of corpses. He couldn't imagine Xara or Hunter or anyone else ever wanting to come near this place. There was just too much death and misery here. Plus, the smoldering rock looked a little too much like the planet in system B-52 where his family had died. He didn't want to stick around here any longer than he had to.

He began to move the ship out of orbit, when suddenly every alarm on the flight deck went off.

The autopilot didn't even wait for him to react. It jerked the tiny ship out of orbit and engaged the prop core. Just like that, the *ZeroVox* was going top speed again, but the quick acceleration lasted only a fraction of a second. Then the controls shut down, and just as suddenly, all was still again.

"What the hell was that?" Bonz yelled, surprised at the intensity of his own voice.

Alarmed, the robots had rushed into the control room and began praying over the ship's control panels.

"The collision-avoidance system engaged itself," one robot told him, his slightly effeminate, mechanical voice rising above a bit of static. "Had we left orbit by regular egress, we would have flown right into a debris cloud."

A debris cloud?

Bonz had to think a moment. His ship was small and quick, and unlike the gigantic Starcrashers he used to fly, debris clouds were usually not a problem because the autopilot would routinely find a pathway through them.

Unless the debris cloud was enormous . . . like from a gigantic space battle. . . .

The robots gathered around the main sensor screen; Bonz preferred the bubble-top canopy window. What he saw was just as astonishing whether on-screen or on eyeball.

It was indeed a debris cloud, one of enormous proportions. And it was wreckage, indeed from a battle in space. Scans told Bonz that he was looking at the remains of dozens of warships. They were all in pieces, large and small, floating en masse, like a ragged saturn ring around the ghost planet of Megiddo.

But there was an even more grisly aspect of this. There were bodies floating among the debris, too. Lots of them. Bonz ordered the scanners to magnify. The sensor screen was quickly filled with a cluster of these corpses. They were skeletons in spacesuits, moving aimlessly among the violently twisted pieces of reionized steel that were once spaceships. Bonz had never seen anything like it. Even the robots were shaken.

Could this really be it? he wondered now. *Had they actually found what they'd come out here looking for? Had they found the remains of the mysterious invaders?*

It took a few more moments for them to realize what they were looking at here, but then the answer came back as *no*. These were not the remains of the mystery battle between the invaders and the SG's Rapid Engagement Fleet. Rather, the scans told him this was the wreckage of the fleet Kid Joxx had patched together, with prisoners as the crews, to meet the invaders deep inside Thirty Star Pass, another battle few people back on Earth had heard about. The overriding clue: the amount of debris indicated at least 100 ships had been involved in whatever happened here, and probably as many as 120, many more than had been reported in the battle between the invaders and the SG.

It had simply taken the better part of a month for the debris—both human and metal—to make its way through Thirty

Star Pass and reach Megiddo. It was now locked in eternal orbit around the devastated planet.

"Rather appropriate," was how one of the robots put it. "Death above. Death below."

Bonz could not disagree.

They took a few more readings, and then Bonz prepared to bump the spy ship back up into Supertime. But suddenly, the bells and whistles started going off again.

The ship's control panel lit up, this time with bright red and yellow lights. The Long-Distance Scan array was pulsating madly. The life-sign detectors were blaring, too. Even the long-range Z-beam gun in their nose clicked on.

All this could only mean one thing: a ship was heading for them. An SG ship.

Bonz almost laughed. Well, at least he knew all the spy equipment was actually working. He would have thought he'd run into at least a dozen SG vessels in the No-Fly Zone by this time. But it was almost as if the Solar Guards were taking their own no-fly edict to heart themselves. Until now, that is.

Bonz magnified the LDS signal, expecting to get an indication of an SG ship flying in Supertime but still some distance away; one that would simply pass on by. But he was in for a surprise: his scanner screen was telling him the SG ship was not flying in Supertime but rather was down here in regular time with them. In fact, it was coming right up on their tail.

Bonz pushed his rear-projection viz-screen button, and there it was. It was a *culverin*, a kind of pocket cruiser, about three times the size of the *ZeroVox*. Oddly, it was not a type flown by the SG's Rapid Engagement Fleet; they only flew Starcrashers.

Nevertheless, within seconds, it was flying right next to them.

Bonz hurriedly initiated the holo-activate string to secure all his spy gear again, then pushed his engine's idle output down to near zero. This would, he hoped, mimic a faulty star engine. Next he climbed into a very dirty flight suit and called the robots forward. Just in time, too. The SG boarding party beamed over just seconds later. No hail, no prior warning.

They were just suddenly there: six of them, all heavily armed.

But these weren't regular SG troopers. Their uniforms were light brown as opposed to the black satin and red-trim outfits regular front-line SG troops wore. These men were SG support troops, soldiers who flew the repair ships, the ammo ships, and sometimes, the hospital ships. One was an officer.

"We are authorized to destroy this ship and execute the crew," the officer said. "You have violated a standing military order by flying into this restricted area."

Bonz stayed cool. Regular troops or not, the SG modus operandi was to always come on strong at first. These guys did not disappoint.

"A million apologies, sir," Bonz replied. "But we did not fly into this area; we have been here since catastrophe struck Megiddo."

The officer seemed baffled. "You were here . . . during the battle below?"

"We were in the pass, but close by," Bonz lied. "All the subatomics skewed our power spike. We've fixed it as best we could and have been creeping along ever since. But it has been a long five weeks."

The clankers began squeaking on cue. Suddenly it seemed as if all of them were in dire need of a good oiling. "As for any executions," Bonz went on. "I'm afraid I am the only mortal soul on board."

The officer nodded to his soldiers, and they quickly went about searching the rear areas of the ship. Several tense minutes went by as they tossed everything from the engine compartment on forward. Finally they returned, carrying only a few bottles of slow-ship wine with them. They'd found them in the galley; it was Bonz's personal supply.

The officer took one bottle, popped its top, and took a sniff. He smiled, displaying a set of gold teeth.

"You have a remarkably good nose for vintage," he told Bonz. "For a space bum, that is—"

"In our best days, we deliver the finest wine around," Bonz replied, seeing an opening for a bribe. "So, please, consider those a gift."

The officer looked around the dilapidated cabin and shook

his head uncertainly. He, too, was dirty and disheveled as were his men. They all seemed as lost as Bonz was pretending to be. Finally the officer nodded to the boarding party. They began blinking out, one by one, Bonz's booze supply going with them.

The officer was the last to go, but before he'd faded out, he halted his transfer for a last question.

"By the way, space bum," he said to Bonz. "Have you encountered any more of our ships out here? Vessels belonging to the regular Solar Guards?"

Bonz shook his head. It was an odd question to ask.

"No, we haven't," he replied truthfully. "Not a one."

He might have added that there were plenty outside the star cloud but none so far within it. But of course, he said no more.

A funny look came over the officer's face. "Neither have we," he said, almost to himself.

Now came another awkward silence, as the partially dissolved officer looked at Bonz, and Bonz looked back at him.

"Very well then," the officer finally said, as he slowly faded away for good. "You must be gone from this area immediately. And take my advice: for your own good, go as fast as that claptrap engine will take you."

3

The planet was called Doomsday 212.

It couldn't have had a better name. It was located about four-fifths of the way up the Moraz Star Cloud, sixty light-years over from Megiddo and Thirty Star Pass, and just ten light-years from the wrecked cargo facility at TW800.

Its sun, Love Field 888, was 175 million miles away and failing, making the planet's days long, and dim. But this was the least of its problems. During the initial expansion to the stars by the First Empire, the so-called Ancient Engineers terra-formed just about every planet in the Milky Way. By puffing even the most despondent rocks floating about, they gave life to the Galaxy. They made billions of gas giants livable, too, usually by draining off the harmful vapors and then terra-forming the solid core beneath. Many of these old gas-bags were still habitable, despite enduring centuries of neglect as three subsequent empires rose and fell. But then, many were not so hospitable. Doomsday 212 fell into that category.

The millennia had not been kind to the planet, which was about ten times the size of Earth. Most of the breathable atmosphere was gone except for a thin layer very close to the surface. Below this air pocket were the remains of the craggy, disturbing core, a ball whose landscape was pockmarked with millions of meteor-impact craters, weirdly twisting dead river-beds, grotesquely shaped mountains, buttes, and mesas all carved out between miles of bottomless pits and valleys.

It got worse. At one time the planet had boasted a triple set of yellow, red, and green rings. They had been the rage of the star cloud many centuries before. But the only things orbiting the planet now were the angry swarms of rock fragments left over from these rings. Most were about the size of a boulder, but others were much larger. They made life on this bleak world extremely dangerous as they tended to fall through the planet's ultrathin atmosphere with great regularity, coming in at the speed of a small bomb and with enough kinetic force to ruin anyone's day. And those fire rocks remaining in orbit made navigating around the big planet a very dicey operation.

So why did SF3 want Bonz and his robots to come here? Simple. Doomsday 212 was the closest planet to that point in space where both the mysterious battle was supposedly fought and the mysterious invasion fleet supposedly disappeared.

For this spy mission to be a success, this was the only place to be.

It took more than four hours for Bonz and the clankers to maneuver the ship through the storm of orbiting fire rocks in order to get close enough to hand-scan the planet below. Their first priority was to find a safe place to set down.

A sanctuary of sorts was finally located under the face of a large mushroom-shaped butte about ten degrees above the dying planet's equator and on the side approaching morning. They could hide the ship here and hope to avoid any further encounters such as the one with the SG support ship just hours before. It was a wild ride down to the surface, but the *ZeroVox* landed smoothly enough, considering the terrain was so jagged and rocky. Now they got their first look at the planet from ground level. Bonz had never seen to a place like this. The landscape, so bare and barren. The sky, just brightening in the long dawn, was a palette of many odd colors—from the dim sun, to the leaks of bizarre leftover gases, to the never-ending meteor-like showers. It all combined for a kind of strange beauty, but forbidding as well.

In addition to all of Doomsday 212's bad points, it was also a graveyard planet, a place where old spaceships were crashed, on purpose, at the end of their useful lives. This was a custom throughout the Galaxy. Crashed ships could yield treasures big and small for salvage teams, and this was now the new disguise for the SF3 intelligence crew. It didn't take long for the robots to gather some nearby wreckage and scatter it around the ship and thus turn the spy ship's interior from space truck to typical-looking junker's scow. The dented, greasy controls, the busted seats, the busted windows—it was just another kind of mess, and not that much different from the space-truck mask. Thanks to the holographic barriers, the prop core became disguised again, this time to look, feel, and smell like a burned-out ion-ballast bolt bucket that seemed older than some stars. To make the ruse even more believable, Bonz tweaked the ion drive unit so it would appear to be horribly broken, as if it had been stuck in dead-drive for weeks.

The deception then was complete. Not only were they dirty dregs of the star roads now working salvage on a graveyard planet, they were stranded here as well.

Bonz locked in the ship's new holo-projections and then told the robots to set up the subatomic particle array, which was hidden in the cargo compartment. Nicknamed the Star Sweeper, the device was about six feet across and made of ion-gold. It looked like a huge musical instrument, which in ancient days was called a *trumpeta*. It was surrounded by a trio of small geodesic domes; they seemed to hover around it but were actually tied together by a network of extremely thin atomic strings.

The Star Sweeper had one very important function: it could detect a wide range of subatomic particles within a radius of one hundred light-years. These quicks, quarks, and snarks could tell many tales. First, because Empire ship propulsion units left subatomics in their wake, the sweeper could monitor the comings and goings of all SG ships inside the No-Fly Zone. Second, because the SG used communications string bubblers, which produced a subatomic particle known as a *quick* during operation, the Sweeper could eavesdrop on SG messages, too. But for this mission, it had a third most crucial capability: on its most advanced setting, the device could track the last flickers of subatomic decay, from Z-beam weapons residue, to quicks, to Starcrasher wakes, even if the leftover particles had already disappeared into other dimensions. By calculating backward to determine where this residue originated, the sweeper could detect activity from the past, as far back as two or three months under some conditions. In other words, if there had been a fierce battle fought out here between the Rapid Deployment Fleet and the mysterious invaders as the SG claimed, the Sweeper could look back in time and still find evidence of it.

It took about an hour to assemble the device, then the clankers commenced its deployment. A spot had been selected about 250 feet west of the *ZeroVox*'s hiding place. The sweeper was light enough for two robots to carry. A third clanker acted as a guide for the installation, while the fourth stayed on the lookout for any incoming fire rocks. Once the device was in place, Bonz flipped a switch in the control room, and an energy-scrambler bubble encompassed the unit. Essentially, this made the Sweeper invisible, unless someone was standing right next to it. This would also protect it from the rain of fire rocks coming down all over. This done, he switched the device on and ordered it to begin sweeping the No-Fly Zone. All of the relevant information would be dumped into the *ZeroVox*'s tiny onboard bubbler for analysis later.

The installation complete, the clankers quickly returned to the ship, dodging fire rocks as they bounced along. Bonz was still wearing his torn and dirty flight suit. The robots took on their own greasy disguises as well. Then, with little else to do but wait, they set up a *diceo* board in the crew quarters. A fast and furious game started soon afterward.

Bonz watched the action for a little while but then returned to the control room and stretched out as best he could on his grubby little control seat.

It had been a hectic week.

But so far, so good.

• • •

Three days went by.

The clankers stayed in their quarters and played *diceo*, going outside to check on the Sweeper unit twice a day. Bonz remained in the control room most of the time, door usually closed, sometimes locked, monitoring the readouts from the surveillance unit and making sure his holographic projections stayed in place.

Time passed slowly. The *diceo* game proceeded unabated, with huge piles of aluminum coins moving back and forth across the table. Occasionally, the robots would hear voices coming from the control room; voices that did not belong to Bonz. Female voices. Sweet, haunting, and like the clankers themselves, slightly mechanical.

The robots were smart; they knew what was going on when they heard these things. Bonz had activated his family album holo-cube, and they were with him again, in there, moving about, talking, joking, laughing. Re-creating some long-lost time sequence they'd unintentionally acted out nearly a half century before, never realizing that they would be fated to recreate it over and over and over again.

At times like this, the clankers knew enough to leave the boss alone.

On the fourth day, the faraway sun had finally climbed above the horizon. Its pale light made this part of Doomsday 212 look even bleaker, yet more oddly beautiful, too. With the new light though, came a wind that swept across the barren terrain. It was strong enough to make some of the fire rocks fall sideways. A weird, haunting whistle also began to blow through the crags of the overhanging butte.

In the time they'd been here, the Sweeper had picked up absolutely nothing of interest. It had found no indications of subatomic battle debris. It had found no storm of communications chatter associated with huge battles. In fact, the detection monitors hadn't emitted so much as a burp on anything critical. The numbers didn't lie: no great space battle had been fought anywhere near this part of the star cloud. At least not the kind of battle the SG claimed.

But the Sweeper had found something even stranger—or,

more accurately, *didn't* find something. In its three days of operation, it had not detected any vessels moving through the forbidden zone. No Empire ships, no ion-ballast vessels. In fact, there was no evidence of SG warships anywhere inside the No-Fly Zone, nor had any been in here recently.

This made no sense. Why would the SG go through the outrageous exercise of declaring the No-Fly Zone so they could study the aftereffects of this supposed great battle, and then not even fly in it themselves? And whereas the SF's information indicated that only the Solar Guards' Rapid Deployment Fleet would be allowed to operate in the forbidden zone, where were they, if they weren't here?

Bonz was baffled by all this, even though the odd remarks by both the SG sentry officer at the Pluto Cloud and the support troops on the *culverin* now made a little more sense. But it was not up to Bonz to solve the mystery. He was just a spy. His job was to deliver the information safely to someone who could figure out what it all meant. And that's what he was about to do.

The mission was only supposed to last for ninety hours. They finally reached that time mark. The clankers left the ship and began the retrieval of the spy array. Meanwhile, Bonz had begun preliminary procedures for takeoff. He was about to deactivate the Sweeper unit when suddenly, the array lit up like a small sun. Right before his eyes, it began picking up indications on all three sensors.

The sudden burst of activity was startling, to say the least. Bonz shut down the ship's flight systems and began studying the readouts. What he saw first was a huge spike in temperature coming from a point in space just about in the center of the No-Fly Zone. In fact, this spike registered nearly *a billion* degrees—but only for a fraction of a microsecond. Then came a deluge of subatomic activity. Quarks, quicks, quirks, and about a dozen others, all signatures associated with SG Starcrashers, as many as thirty or more. But these were not the ghostly songs of some phantom battle—they were too acute, too close for that. Nor were they from weapons discharges. The indications were coming from prop-core activity, and they were growing in volume and intensity by the second.

In other words, no less than an entire SG fleet was coming their way.

Not a minute later, thirty-six Solar Guards warships appeared in orbit above Doomsday 212. Ten seconds after that, two of them were hovering right over the crying butte. Bonz found himself staring up at the pair of flying monsters through the bubble-top canopy. They were Starcrashers, unmistakable in size and shape. And they were, no doubt, part of the SG's Rapid Engagement Fleet. Their hull numbers identified them as being attached to the special operations force which had been involved in the battle that never was.

But there was something *very* odd about these ships. Unlike most other SG war vessels, which were usually bright white, these ships were fiery red in color.

They were down to the surface before the clankers could completely disassemble the Sweeper, so the robots used their heads and destroyed the spy array instead. But even before the resulting dust was blowing away, the SG ships were dispensing troops in armed shuttlecraft. These soldiers were wearing red uniforms as well . . . very peculiar. In seconds, a small army of SG troops was charging toward the butte and the small spy ship hidden beneath.

Bonz stayed cool. This was a problem, but not an unfamiliar situation for him. Deep down, even in the worst-case scenario, he knew it would be OK for one simple reason. He was a member of the Empire's military; these troops so madly rushing toward him were as well. In effect, they were his own blood. Brothers in arms. Rivals, yes. Antagonists, certainly.

But not deadly enemies.

Bonz came out of the control room, still in the greasiest, most worn, most disgusting uniform imaginable. The interior of the ship was just as shabby now, and smelled the same. The clankers hustled back to the engine room to begin their parody of trying to fix the ion drive. Smoke was filtered through the environmental systems, further stinking up the joint. By the time the SG soldiers began pounding on the main hatch, the ship looked like it had been banging around the Galaxy for a half-dozen centuries.

Bonz opened the hatch. A squad of Solar Guards stormed in. They were gigantic, much larger in height and girth than any SG trooper Bonz had come across. They were heavily armed and were wearing shiny combat uniforms and helmets with visors that covered their faces—and again, not the usual color of black, but bright red. A chill went through the hold.

"Who is in command here?" one of the soldiers barked. His voice sounded very strange, mechanical but also gurgling.

Bonz responded, "I am—and I want to thank you for rescuing us—"

The words were barely out of his mouth when one soldier grabbed him by the scruff of the neck and literally threw him out the open hatch. Bonz hit the ground hard, scraping his hands and face. He was instantly furious but remained calm. He tried to get to his feet only to have a boot land on his neck. He went down again, this time on his face. The ground felt like glass, cutting into his body right through his dirty uniform.

He heard four more bodies hit the ground with one massive *clank*. His robot crew had been forced facedown, just as he was.

It was time to start complaining.

"We are a salvage crew!" Bonz yelled through the gravel in his teeth. "We've been stuck here for six weeks! Why are our rescuers treating us like this? We are citizens of the Empire. We have our rights!"

There came no reply. Just the cry of wind screaming across the butte. Bonz could see more troops barging their way onto his ship. He prayed that the holo-disguises would hold. As before, he was certain the SG would not start probing too deeply. Everything within the ship had been made to look so gross, he couldn't imagine elite troops like the REF wanting to get their hands dirty for no good reason.

"You are in a forbidden zone," a voice above him suddenly growled. "The punishment for this be death."

"But we were stranded here," Bonz said again. "We didn't know anything about a forbidden zone."

"Words can only hurt you now!" the man with the boot on his back screamed at him. The voice was pure evil.

Bonz raised his intensity level. "Look at us!" he cried.

"What trouble could we cause you? We're just trying to squeeze a few coins out of the wreckage here. It is our honor to be rescued by the likes of you. . . ."

Bonz thought he detected a whiff of relenting in the air.

"We just need a boost in our power pack," he went on. "Just a boost, and we will clear out of the Two Arm and never come back forever!"

Suddenly another voice was in his ear. "You are a grub crew?" This voice asked in a curious, angry whisper.

"Yes, true. . . ." Bonz stuttered in reply.

"And you had no idea that you are within a forbidden zone?"

"No, none at all."

"And you swear you are not military—that you were not sent out here to spy on us?"

"I swear . . ."

Two strong hands jerked him to his feet. He was suddenly staring into the cold hard eyes of a REF officer. This man looked slightly deranged to him. His red uniform was the color of blood.

"Then," the officer said to him, "how do you explain this?"

He was holding something up to Bonz's eyes. It took a moment for his vision to clear before he realized it was a small white device.

His family holo-cube . . .

Playing within was the preview image of his kids wearing their Space Forces uniforms with him, in his own medal-laden uniform, standing right beside them.

Bonz tried to say something but couldn't. At almost the same moment, other SG soldiers had found all the hidden switches in the control room and began activating them. The holographic blanket disappeared, and in seconds the small vessel reverted back to its real state, that of an unmistakable SF3 spy ship.

This was not good.

After a quick, hushed discussion among the SG soldiers, Bonz was marched in front of the rock wall next to the *ZeroVox*. He was ordered to remove his fake salvager's flight suit, revealing his SF-issued body liner beneath. Bonz stood shivering in the early morning cold; already he was composing a message of protest he planned to send to SG headquarters as soon as he got out of this. There was much confusion around him now. The SG troops appeared very agitated, and their deep red uniforms seemed just too bizarre for words. Another officer appeared, and he began barking orders. A gaggle of SG soldiers standing twenty feet away from Bonz began spreading out in a ragged line. What were they doing? Forming an honor guard? Each man then raised his weapon toward him and twisted its power knob to on. That's when Bonz realized he was staring at a firing squad.

His heart froze. He tried to say something, but no words would come out. He was SF—and he'd been caught. But the SG weren't his enemies. They belonged to the same military, for God's sake. Was this some sort of a ruse, to make him talk?

Suddenly, the superior officer barked out another order, and the SG soldiers aimed their guns.

Before Bonz could react, the man gave the order to fire. Bonz saw the deadly green beams heading right for him. He let out a long cry—it was probably his wife's name. Then the rays hit him.

He looked down, in shock, to see a large, smoking hole in the center of his chest. He staggered forward, unable to catch his breath. Then he fell over.

He was dead before he hit the ground.

4

The Space Forces cargo ship, *JunoVox*, was passing twenty light-years from the bottom of the Moraz Star Cloud when it received the startling viz-screen transmission.

The message did not come in over the ship's primary communications array, nor did it appear on the vessel's secondary or auxiliary displays. It showed up—fuzzy, in black and white and full of static—on the ship's 2-IS, the internal imaging system that was essentially a closed-circuit broadcast of goings-on within the ship.

Why the stream of disturbing images appeared on the least advanced viz screen aboard the *JunoVox* was never really explained. Sometimes the cosmos did funny things. One thing was certain though: the primitive broadcast was coming from a very small viz camera located deep within the Moraz Star Cloud—and right in the middle of the Solar Guard's No-Fly Zone.

It was only by chance that the *JunoVox* was even in the area. It was returning to the One Arm after an extended resupply mission to several SF posts out on the edge of the sixth swirl. It had been a long trip, and the crew of 500—pilots, techs, cargo masters, plus a company of 70 Space Marines—was anxious to get back to their home base and some long-overdue R and R. All that changed, though, when the weird images started blinking onto a small 2-IS screen located in the rear hold of the mile-long cargo ship.

It was one of the *JunoVox*'s loading techs who saw the pictures first. He thought someone was playing a prank. The images seemed to show an SF officer being executed by a firing squad of Solar Guards. It was no secret that the SF and the SG were rivals. The two services never agreed on anything. And should two opposing crews enter in the same saloon on some distant planet, after multiple ingestion of slow-ship wine by both sides, it was not unheard of for a brawl or two to break out.

But actual *murder* between the rivals? That had never happened.

Until now.

The cargo tech immediately called up to the bridge, at the same time punching commands into the primitive 2-IS system to record the puzzling images. Soon there were a half-dozen officers looking over his shoulder. The ship's communication section had already pinpointed the signals as coming from a dead-end Two Arm planet known as Doomsday 212. And even though the shaky transmission seemed to be showing the same sequence over and over again—it was thirty-five seconds long and depicted the SF man being gunned down and then two SG soldiers firing bursts into his head to make sure he was dead—it was being broadcast in real time.

"It's coming from a clanker's headset," one of the officers finally declared after watching the broadcast a dozen times. "The robot recorded the sequence and jammed it on replay. See how the frame is slightly off-kilter? The clanker is probably lying on the ground nearby and adjusted its lens to the best vantage point it could get."

"Then, this is *real*?" one of the other officers asked.

No one there could say it wasn't.

"The clanker is hip," the first officer said. "It's obviously sending out these images to let someone know what's happening up there."

"Solar Guards executing one of our guys?" the lowly cargo tech blurted out. "But why?"

No one had a good answer for that one, either.

At this point, the ship's commander, an SF colonel named Jeepz Mannx, arrived in the cargo hold. Mannx was a 251-year-old veteran of the Space Forces and was known—as were many high-ranking SF officers—for his intense dislike of the Solar Guards.

Mannx watched the sequence several times, his anger building. Then he asked both the officers and the cargo tech if there was any way that the broadcast could be a mistake. He was assured that it could not. They had no idea who the SF officer was, or why the SG troops had murdered him, but the broadcast itself was definitely real.

"*Those bastards . . .*" Mannx whispered under his breath.

Then, suddenly, he was gone. Hurrying up to the bridge, he ordered his pilots to turn the huge cargo ship 120 degrees and set the controls for the heart of the Moraz Star Cloud, indeed to the very center of the SG's forbidden zone.

Next, he put out a high-priority call for any other SF ships in the region, telling them what he'd just seen and informing them that he was breaking course and heading for the scene of the incident "to assist our brother." He suggested they do likewise.

Then he called down to the billet where the ship's company of Space Marines was housed. He told their CO that his men should suit up for an "emergency rescue mission" and be ready for deployment, with weapons loaded, in fifteen minutes.

Two SF vessels received the *JunoVox*'s emergency call.

One was the *KongoVox*, a scout ship heading in toward the One Arm shipyards for an overhaul after nearly two years out on patrol. The other ship was the *VogelVox*, a two-mile-long Space Navy Starcrasher. It had just left the Three Arm after battling space mercs for the past six months.

The *KongoVox* was just twelve light-years from the *JunoVox*'s position when the call came in. Its CO immediately turned back toward the Moraz Star Cloud and headed for the trouble area at top speed. The small ship was carrying just fifty crew members and no Space Marines, but at just 750 feet long, it held a formidable arsenal. This included an array of destructo-cannons in its nose and several long-distance, space-to-surface atomic missiles under its fuselage. Its navigation team reported they would arrive over Doomsday 212 approximately ten minutes after the *Juno*.

The much larger *VogelVox* was another fifty light-years removed from the edge of the No-Fly Zone; it would take about a half hour to make the outer reaches of the star cloud and another forty-five minutes to fly to Doomsday. The SF Starcrasher was a planet-assault vessel. It was heavily armed with space cannons, destructo-ray turrets, and myriad space-to-surface weapons. It was also carrying a brigade of regular SF infantry, battle-hardened soldiers who'd been doing search-and-destroy missions against the notorious Bad Moon Knights mercenary army for half a solar year.

As it was hurtling through space, the smaller scout ship, the *KongoVox*, exchanged several communication strings with the cargo ship *JunoVox*. In one of these strings, a facsimile of the mysterious transmission was beamed to the scout ship. For the first time, its crew saw the images of what appeared to be an execution of the Space Forces officer. Now they knew the reason the commander of the *JunoVox* had acted so quickly.

The last transmission the *Kongo* received from the *Juno* indicated the cargo ship had made orbit around Doomsday 212, and its scanners had found the area where the puzzling transmission was coming from. A long-range viz sweep of the terrain in question had provided two things. There was indeed a dead SF officer lying on the ground beside what appeared to be a SF3 intell ship; four partially disassembled clankers were lying close by. And, as had been speculated, the mysterious transmission was coming from one of these robots, the one farthermost from the ship. Its advanced AI had told it something was not right, and it had to do something about it. Broadcasting the grisly execution over and over again was its solution to the problem.

The crew of the *Kongo* then heard from the *Juno* that it was about to launch a ground team, when a concerned voice cut into the transmission. The voice quickly rose in tension, panic seeping in. Something was suddenly wrong aboard the *JunoVox*, but it wasn't clear just what. Colonel Mannx, the captain of the *Juno*, was heard ordering his communications officer to "hail the approaching ship—and fast!" A series of loud bangs was heard next.

Then the transmission went dead.

The *KongoVox* arrived over Doomsday 212 ten minutes later.

The small scout ship immediately vectored to the place were the *JunoVox* had made its last transmission, an area about twelve degrees above the planet's equator on its current day side. This is where they found the cargo ship. It was scattered in pieces across five miles of Doomsday 212's rough terrain, burning fiercely. There were no life signs from below. It had been blown out of the sky.

Off in the distance the *Kongo* could see two SG Starcrashers leaving the area, moving slowly, almost leisurely as they climbed to orbit. Oddly, their hulls were glowing with a reddish hue. A scan of the two SG ships indicated that their weapons had just been fired and, by studying the leftover subatomic signature, proved beyond all doubt these weapons had just caused the destruction of the *JunoVox*.

The CO of the scout ship took about five seconds to make his decision. He instructed the ship's historian to get his visual and audio recorders rolling. Then he ordered his crew to battle stations. What happened next would be a matter of debate for some time to come.

What everyone agreed on is that the two SG warships had their scanning equipment on, but to forward-scan only. This was done usually as preparation for moving up to orbit, to look for any aerial obstacles that might cause a problem as a vessel prepared to kick into Supertime. But this was not a procedure used during combat or shortly afterward.

Were the SG crews feeling pumped up after what they'd just done? Had an adrenaline rush clouded their actions? Or were they in shock? Too dazed to perform the rote duties of moving a two-mile-long warship away from a planet and prepare it for flight again in outer space?

There was no way to know.

Only one thing was clear: the SG crews in both ships had let their guard down.

They never saw the *KongoVox* coming.

• • •

The tiny SF scout ship had sixteen space cannons poking out of its nose and along the leading edge of its wedge-shaped body. One or two blasts from a space cannon—it was the equivalent in power to a land weapon known as a Faster Blaster—could have a devastating effect on an unprotected or unsuspecting target. An array of sixteen of the weapons could deliver a fusillade on the same destructive level as a small atomic bomb.

That's what hit the trailing edge of the second-in-line SG warship just as it was pointing its wedge nose up for the quick dash up to orbit. The *Kongo* let loose with a two-second barrage that sheared off one-third of the ship's aft section in a terrific, yellow blast. The SG vessel staggered for a moment and came to a halt in midair. Then, as if in slow motion, the huge ship turned over to starboard and went straight down on its back. It hit the ground with such an impact, it created a trio of mushroom clouds, each going off in succession, as the ship's prop core exploded and the debris fell into a singularity that opened and closed in the matter of microseconds.

Five hundred and seven people had been killed when the SG ships shot down the *JunoVox* just minutes before.

Now, more than eight thousand Solar Guards were dead, too.

The second SG ship had already jumped into Supertime; thirty seconds later, it was more than a light-year away.

But its CO, realizing what had just happened, quickly ordered the ship to turn about. Less than a minute after its sister ship had gone down, the second ship was streaking back through the atmosphere of Doomsday 212.

By this time, the *KongoVox* had kicked up to about 5,000 feet and had turned back toward the wreckage of the *JunoVox*. It had its scanners on 360 and thus saw the other SG ship coming. The tables were turned now. The scout ship was smaller but no faster than the huge SG warship. It was the essence of all vessels powered by the Supertime-capable prop cores that size and mass didn't matter. Everything moved the same, at the same top speed. The SG warship spotted the

Kongo just as the *Kongo*'s scanners lit up like a string of small suns. The scout ship turned one eighty, and its pilots booted into full crank, the highest speed a prop-core vessel could achieve within the atmosphere of a planet. The red SG warship turned six and went to full crank power as well.

The chase was on.

The only advantage the scout ship *Kongo* had was its physical size. It could go places the bigger SG ship could not.

Zipping up to orbit and spanking into Supertime was not an option for it, though. The dynamics said it would have to slow down ever so slightly to make the leap. When it did, the SG ship would have it at a disadvantage. Certain destruction would result.

No, the scout ship would have to use its diminutive size to get out of this one. And do so quickly.

The terrain of Doomsday 212 suddenly became its best ally, especially the craggy surface and the surfeit of valleys and mountain passes. The *Kongo*'s pilots brought their ship down to just 200 feet off the deck and kicked in the vessel's terrain-avoidance system. This would allow it to keep that 200-foot cushion between it and any object in its path. Or at least that's how it was supposed to work.

The pursuing SG warship, however, had enormous arrays of sensors and tracking equipment; it did not lose sight of the scout ship for very long. The SG ship was also bristling with weapons, most of monstrous proportions and designed to do battle over great distances in space with ships almost as large but nowhere near as quick as she was.

These were the dreaded master Z-beam weapons. They could destroy a two-mile-long warship at distances up to 50,000 miles. The crimson SG ship now trained these nightmarish giants on the fleeing scout ship and began blasting away with wild abandon. Overkill by any measure, but particularly hellish in this instance.

This torrent of destructo-rays made the fusillade that the scout ship had used to destroy the first SG ship look puny by comparison. The *Kongo* was twisting and turning through canyons, along valleys, up and over mountains, hitting hypersonic speeds, breaking the sound barrier with thunderous reports, the huge red behemoth not a half mile behind.

In this running barrage, mountains were disappearing, dry riverbeds were being blown to dust, buttes and mesas reduced to piles of subatomic glass crystals. And it went on like this for what seemed like a very long time, even though the chase became more desperate for the *Kongo* with each passing second. There was only so long the scout could keep zigzagging before the gunners on the big ship would find their mark or, more likely, collapse an entire mountain on top of them.

The heat of battle is a funny thing, a different mind-set takes over, whether the combatants are throwing stones at each other or trading blasts of vaporizing Z beams. The politics of the person shooting at you takes second preference over the desire of saving your own skin. Still, it was not lost on anyone aboard the tiny SF scout ship, as it careened its way through miles-deep river valleys and over titanic mountain ranges, that the people shooting at them—the same people who had just destroyed one of their capital ships—were not supposed to be their enemies. In fact, technically at least, they were supposed to be brothers. They all belonged to the same military, the Imperial Forces, and were sworn to the common goal of fighting against the enemies of the Empire and bringing the words and vision of the Emperor to every corner of the Galaxy.

But this, this was both alarming and unprecedented. The two services had been barking at each other for nearly three centuries—but there was no turning back from this. More than 8,000 were already dead in the internecine battle, and still it was less than a half hour old. So even as they were racing along at top speeds, knowing their lives could be lost at any moment, the crew of the SF scout ship knew that after this, no matter how it turned out, nothing in the Empire would ever be the same again.

Luck began running out for the *KongoVox* as the small scout ship approached an obscure mountain pass named, in the ancient language of the Galaxy, *Mons d'Sighs*.

It was essentially a natural stone bridge that connected two forbidding mountain peaks. The strange formation came up fast on the *Kongo*'s pilots. In a split second they had to decide whether to go over this thing—and risk providing a clear shot by the fast-pursuing SG warship—or turn sideways and go under it. Their flight computer told them their clearance from fuselage to either wall could be measured in inches. Still, going low was a risk they had to take.

The pilots punched in these desires, and the scout ship suddenly flipped over onto its side. At that same moment, the forward gunners on the SG ship let loose a barrage of Z beams from their nose-weapon array. These shots were fired too high. However, they hit the peak on one side of the stone bridge, instantly creating a rain of debris onto *Mons d'Sighs*. One huge boulder smashed into the ancient stone bridge, causing it to collapse onto the tail end of the fleeing *KongoVox*.

The impact of tons of burning rock was catastrophic. Suddenly the scout ship was missing about 100 feet off its left-side aft quarter. It streaked out from under the collapsing stone bridge trailing a long tail of black smoke and flaming debris. The control deck was in chaos: blinking lights, Klaxons blaring. The ship's prop core had been mortally wounded. Any disruption in power flowing through this mysterious drive device could only have disastrous consequences. As with the SG ship shot down just minutes before, whenever a prop core went dry, it tended to blow up with the force of several nuclear bombs and then collapse in on itself as it devolved into a self-made singularity. It was simply impossible for anyone on board to survive such a conflagration.

But the crews of Space Forces scout ships were traditionally tough and resourceful. Their flight bubble was telling them their vessel would be airborne for just twenty-two seconds more, and then it would crash, with the prop core blowing up just eleven seconds later. Not a lot of time to think about anything but survival.

So the crew began bailing out. At battle stations each person on board was strapped into a boost seat that would be ejected in times just like this. Panels on top of the ship began blowing off now, and these individual survival capsules commenced bursting through the openings. Each capsule was equipped with an escape rocket that could carry its occupant as far as five miles away. These rockets left a vivid yellow wake, so the display now coming from the crippled *KongoVox* was *mucho* spectacular when the huge flames pouring out of the back combined with the cascade of escape capsules firing off from the front and midsection.

None of this stopped the SG gunners, though. They continued firing away, and some of their shots were hitting the escape capsules, vaporizing them instantly. The scout ship was losing speed as the prop core began dying in earnest, and thus the SG ship was gaining on it by the second. The two ships passed out of the vast *Mons d'Sighs* region and onto a flat, open terrain that stretched almost all the way to the dark section of the planet.

As predicted, the scout ship began tumbling about seventeen seconds after being hit, and it crashed five seconds later. All but the captain and the two main pilots made it out alive; they had decided to go down with the ship, insuring that the rest of the crew at least had the chance to eject. The scout ship impacted on the long, straight, flat valley floor and went end over end for a mile before the prop core blew up. There was an enormous explosion accompanied by a nightmarish mushroom cloud, which then began falling in on itself, as if it were an explosion in reverse motion. It sucked everything within a few hundred feet into a black hole that was created and then disappeared again, all in less than a heartbeat.

The entire planet shook once; the impact of the crash was that terrific.

The scout ship's survivors were now scattered along the route of its death plunge, many separated by a mile or more. The SG warship had pulled up violently so as not to get caught in the small holocaust resulting from the *Kongo*'s crash.

The big ship did not boot into Supertime and leave the scene, though. In another devilish, seemingly inexplicable act, the ship turned around and slowed down to the lowest crank power, just a few knots of forward motion. Its gunners began searching the valley floor for survivors who had ejected from the dying SF scout ship. On spotting any member of the *Kongo* crew, the SG gunners opened up without mercy. Unprotected and many of them injured from their quick ejection and violent landing, these hapless soldiers made easy pickings for the SG trigger men. Within a minute, two dozen had been blasted to bits. Now scan lights were beamed out of the bottom of the slow-moving SG warship, further helping the gunners target the Space Forces soldiers who had no means of escape and few places to hide. A total massacre seemed to be inevitable.

That's when the SF Starcrasher *VogelVox* finally arrived on the scene.

The SF warship had been following the outlandish, confusing, disturbing battle via its long-range viz scanners.

The commanders of the two-mile-long aerial battleship didn't believe at first that those responsible for shooting down the *JunoVox* were in fact Solar Guards. It didn't make sense. Sure, the blistering conflict had flared up deep within the SG's unilateral forbidden zone, and indications were that the *JunoVox* had violated the SG's order and had dashed into the *verboten* area for reasons that seemed even stranger, the summary execution of an SF intell officer. But now, open conflict between the two services? It didn't seem real somehow.

The No-Fly Zone was the talk of the Empire's military, of course. For the most part, it was viewed by the Space Forces as an example of butt covering by the SG after they had been bested by the mysterious invaders on the planet Megiddo and then apparently lied about destroying the enemy fleet. Perhaps the murdered intell officer had uncovered just that, and for whatever reason, the SG decided he had to die, never thinking that word of the outrageous execution would get out so fast. (In many ways then, a robot, not a human, was responsible for the fratricide that had already taken so many lives and was about to turn the Empire on its head.)

What was clear was that SF troops were under attack, and the particularly vicious manner in which the SG warship had pursued the smaller scout ship and was gunning to death its helpless crew members on the ground only made the dangerous situation even worse.

So it was both emotions and duty that propelled the commanders of the *VogelVox* into action.

Again, it was a case of the people aboard the SG ship not considering themselves in a combat position. Its warship was still moving very slowly about 250 feet above the ground, picking off the survivors from the scout ship crash. It was not running its 360 scans—or if it was, no one was paying any attention to the scanning suite screens.

Moving slowly, close to the ground, looking down and concentrating on small targets—there was no better way to set yourself up as a big, fat target.

Had the *JunoVox* not been shot down so violently, there was a chance the commanders of the *Vogel* might have simply disabled the SG warship below them. But again, emotions were running high, and confusion was reigning now on several levels. In all this time, none of the SF ships had contacted SF headquarters on Earth to report what was going on; no one was quite sure what they would say. So the *VogelVox*'s commanders descended to a height about 1,000 feet above the unsuspecting SG ship and launched a broadside of Z beams at it.

The fusillade walked its way right down the huge SG ship. There was a series of explosions, four, five, six . . . seven. And finally, the prop core was hit. The frightening mushroom cloud instantly appeared, then disappeared just as quickly, taking about half of the hapless ship with it. What remained slammed into the ground seconds later, again sending a shudder around the planet. More explosions came, followed by great balls of fire rising from the barren, haunted surface. In seconds there was nothing but burning debris, scattered over a half-dozen miles, just like the *JunoVox*.

Then all was silent again.

After just a few minutes, the toll in this strange little war stood at two major warships, a cargo 'crasher, and a small scout ship.

More than 15,000 souls—good and bad—had been lost.

PART TWO

The Vanex Door

5

The first good thing Gym Bonz noticed about being dead was the warm, bright light.

It didn't appear right away. After the excruciating pain of being shot through the chest finally faded, he'd found himself floating above the forbidding terrain of Doomsday 212, looking down on his own bleeding body, crumpled among the rocks. Two of his executioners had kicked his limp form, then shot him again through the head, but Bonz never felt a thing.

The next series of events played out like a viz-screen movie. He knew—*just knew*—that word of his death had been flashed to SF ships riding outside the No-Fly Zone. He saw the first SF ship, the cargo vessel *JunoVox*, appear on the scene, saw its meager weaponry engage two of the remaining SG Starcrashers, only to get itself blasted out of the sky seconds later. He saw the scout ship *KongoVox* arrive and destroy one of the strangely crimson SG ships just minutes before it, too, was destroyed. The madness ended with the huge *VogelVox* blasting the second SG ship to atomic dust. Through it all, Bonz hovered above the grisly scene, feeling trapped and helpless, unable to do anything but watch. The fires, the destruction, the death. He couldn't believe that his demise had triggered the ferocious battle between the two Empire services.

But then Bonz found himself being drawn into a tunnel that had formed above him. Its sides were moving in a corkscrew motion, and some part of his consciousness told him this tunnel was made of swirling clouds. He began moving upward, growing cold, a strange feeling of loneliness overcoming him.

But then he saw the light . . .

And the light was warm, and it was revitalizing, and it felt good. *Damn good.* It filled the tunnel, and it filled him up as well. Bonz was floating, but at the same time he knew he was moving faster than any Starcrasher ever carried him. At the other end of the tunnel, a person, surrounded by this warm light, was beckoning him forward. And there was no doubt in Bonz's mind that's where he wanted to go.

So he let himself be swept up by the clouds and the warmth and the light and . . .

The next thing he knew, he was standing on a beach. A calm cobalt sea was in front of him. Jewel-like sand was beneath his feet. The sky was deep blue and streaked with rays of bright, golden light. This beach stretched beyond sight in both directions. It seemed to go on forever.

This was a *very* beautiful place. A friendly yellow sun was shining above; its rays felt warm and perfect. Behind him was a hill filled with rows of multicolored trees, swaying in the breeze. Bonz reached down and took a handful of sand; it was made up of trillions of tiny gemstones. He knelt to cup some water and brought it to his lips. It tasted of a nectar more divine than the best batch of slow-ship ever made. He took a deep breath, and felt as if life itself had reentered his lungs.

He'd never felt this good, ever.

"Where the hell am I?" he whispered.

He heard voices. He spun around and looked to the top of the hill behind him. Three figures were up there, waving and calling down to him.

A woman and two young girls.

My God . . .

He started running, off the beach, past a row of brightly colored flowers, up a path that led to the top of the hill. He'd never moved so fast, alive or otherwise. He felt like he was running on air, that his feet weren't really touching the ground. He reached the top of the hill in no time . . . and that's when he saw them up close.

They were smiling at him, arms raised, absolutely glowing. It was his wife and daughters.

"Is it really you?" he asked. *"Really?"*

His wife laughed sweetly. "Yes it is."

But Bonz just couldn't believe it.

She took a step closer to him. "Here, touch my face, see for yourself."

Trembling, he reached out and felt his wife's cheek. His fingers did not go through it as they had so many times with the holo-cube. Her skin felt warm and smooth, just like it did so many years ago.

"But . . . how?" he stammered. "How can this be?"

"You're in Heaven, Gym," she told him simply. "You've reached Paradise."

Suddenly his chest felt like it was about to burst. His eyes misted over. Tears of joy rolled down his cheeks. It was beginning to make sense.

"So I really must be . . ." He couldn't quite say the word.

His wife nodded gently. "Passed on? Yes, you are . . . and now you're here, with us. Forever."

In the next instant he was in their arms, hugging them as they hugged him, kissing them as they kissed him. Smothered with kisses—on the cheeks from his kids, long passionate ones on the mouth from his wife. They were all laughing and crying at the same time. They collapsed to the soft ground in a great heap of arms and legs and laughter and tears. His kids were yelling joyously. His wife was saying, over and over, *"I love you. . . . I love you so much. . . . We're together again!"*

Bonz's joy was indescribable. He was free. No more earthly worries, no more earthly pain. The nightmare that had haunted him for fifty years was gone. Suddenly washed away. He was in Paradise. He could feel it, inside and all around him. Total beauty. No hate. Just peace. Peace and harmony, forever.

They all lay back, arms around each other, neither wife nor daughters wanting to let him go. The warm sun fell on his face. The wind sounded like music. He breathed in deeply and again it felt like he would burst, there was so much happiness going through him.

"Thank you, God," he whispered. "Thank you."

They stayed like this for what seemed a very long while—hours even—it was hard to tell. He was kissing his wife, hugging his kids. He asked his wife what had happened in all the time they'd been apart. She told him that it didn't seem like any time had passed at all. That they had found themselves here, and that all their deceased family and friends were here, too, and that everything was perfect and good and eternal.

There were other individuals walking past them, some climbing up or down the hill, some suddenly appearing from nowhere. They were all wearing long white gowns and had a certain glow about them. They were all smiles and laughing, and they shared a bit of his joy as they passed by. The top of the hill was covered with emerald grass and many flowers, and below them were miles of fields and blossoming trees and trickling streams. It *looked* like Paradise, just as Bonz had always imagined it.

In between more hugs and kisses, Bonz noticed an elderly man climbing up the hill. He was not wearing a white gown; rather his was colored deep gold. He walked past their spot, nodding and smiling, but then stopped and turned around.

"Excuse me, isn't that a Space Forces uniform?" he asked Bonz.

Bonz looked down at his clothes and realized he was still wearing his SF one-piece, the inside liner for his combat suit. He suddenly felt foolish in it. Everyone but him was dressed in more heavenly clothes.

"Yes, I'm afraid it is," he replied.

"Interesting," the old man said.

Bonz shaded his eyes to see the old man better. He had long white hair, a long white beard, and a slightly bemused look to his wrinkled features. He seemed almost *too* old to be here in Heaven; for a split second, Bonz thought he was the Almighty Himself.

But then, incredibly, he recognized this man.

It wasn't God. It was Vanex, the Imperial Custodian, the

man who had disappeared without a trace along with Princess Xara about a month ago.

Bonz couldn't believe it. He scrambled to his feet.

"Captain Vanex? Is it really you?"

The old man looked him up and down and then nodded. "Yes, it is I," he said. "And you are?"

"Captain Gym Bonz, SF3—"

"Oh, so you're a spy, then?"

"I was," Bonz replied slowly. "And it is strange that I should meet you. Very strange . . ."

"How so, my son?"

Bonz just shook his head. "Because *you're* one of the people I was sent to look for on my last mission. In fact, the entire Galaxy is looking for you. You, and Princess Xara."

Vanex stared at him for a long moment. He didn't seem too surprised by this news.

"How is it you died?" he asked Bonz

"At the hands of the Solar Guards," Bonz replied simply.

Vanex's jaw dropped. It was as if he'd suddenly woke up from a stupor. "The Solar Guards . . . *killed you?*" he asked, astonished.

"Yes."

"But how? And *why?*"

Bonz told him the whole story, starting with his mission to the No-Fly Zone to look for the missing invading ships, and for Xara and Vanex himself, then his finding the forbidden area virtually empty, his landing on Doomsday 212, and his subsequent execution by the SG. He concluded with his account of the battle between the SF and SG that his murder had brought about.

By the end of it, Vanex was shaking his head in disbelief. "The Space Forces and the Solar Guards are actually *fighting* each other?"

"Yes, they are," Bonz replied, wanting more than anything else to get back to his family. "And I would guess that they will go on fighting each other. That's how bad the situation was before I . . . well, left the scene."

"This is very disturbing," Vanex was saying now, dithering as if he wasn't sure what to do next. "I just went out for a walk, that's all—and I suddenly find you here. And the fact that you arrived at this very spot, after all this time, carrying this news . . . it must mean something."

Bonz was a bit confused, but then he just shrugged. "Well, it doesn't mean anything to me," he said blithely. "Not anymore—"

Suddenly Vanex began pulling him back down the hill with him. "You must come with me. That's an order."

Bonz was dumbfounded; he resisted the old man.

"Come with you?" he said. "Why? For what?"

"Just do what I say," Vanex demanded. "It's important."

"More important than being reunited with my family?" Bonz demanded to know.

Vanex replied very sternly, "At the moment, yes. I have to say it is."

Bonz finally relented. With his family patiently in tow, he followed Vanex down the hill and up another, much higher one.

On the other side of this rise was a deep valley. It made for a magnificent view. Miles of emerald grass. Brightly colored flowers were in bloom everywhere. Rivers and streams and ponds. A soft wind was blowing above it all. And beyond this valley, over a line of gently rolling hills, was another valley just like it. And beyond that, still another valley—and another, and another. And then came a range of small mountains, and undoubtedly, over them, *more* beautiful places. The scene was so peaceful and serene, it reminded Bonz of the holographic religious cards priests sometimes distributed at space-church services.

Directly below, Bonz could see thousands of men and women, in groups big and small, stretched out in the warm sun, along the banks of a long, winding, gently flowing river. These people appeared totally at peace; they seemed to be radiating happiness.

There was just one thing odd about them. They were all wearing combat uniforms, specifically camouflaged tan with red and black blotches on them.

"*Those* are the people you were really looking for," Vanex told Bonz simply. "The people who invaded the Two Arm."

Bonz needed a moment for this to sink in. Then he just laughed.

"So the SG *was* telling the truth all along," he concluded. "Everyone in the invasion fleet *was* killed. . . ."

But Vanex was shaking his head. "No, my friend, just the opposite, in fact."

"Just the opposite?" Bonz asked. "What do you mean?"

"I must tell you a very deep secret," Vanex replied. "The SG's story *was* a lie. *No one* on the other side has any idea what happened to these people. The Solar Guards saw their ships on their sensor screens one moment, and in the next, they were gone. *That's* what happened. They weren't killed. They are just simply here, like you and me."

"In Heaven?"

"Yes."

"But how?" Bonz asked him. "How can they be here if they aren't dead? As dead as you and I?"

Vanex put his hand on Bonz's shoulder. "My friend, this will be the biggest shock of all," he said slowly. "And I don't expect you to believe it right away . . . but I'm not dead. Neither are the people you see below."

Bonz just stared back at him. "You're not dead? How can that be? If this really is Heaven, and you're here, then . . ."

Vanex replied carefully, "I guess you can say I came in through the back door. As did they."

Bonz just laughed again, even though the old guy was beginning to give him the creeps.

"Are you saying the Two Arm invaders are alive and *hiding out here*?"

Vanex nodded.

"Here . . . *in Heaven?*"

Vanex nodded again.

Bonz was speechless. If he was to believe the Imperial Janitor, then he was dead—and in Paradise. And the invaders were here also, but they and Vanex were still alive.

It didn't make any sense.

"I know it sounds strange," Vanex went on. "And it is a very long story, but everyone you were looking for is here. These people. Hawk Hunter. Princess Xara. Myself. We simply found a way to get to this place without losing our lives."

"But that's ridiculous!" Bonz erupted. "What you're saying goes against everything in nature. . . . It's impossible to believe you, and I *don't* believe you. *I'm* dead. *You're* dead. *They're* dead. Goodbye!"

He began walking back to his family; they were still all smiles, and lingering nearby.

But Vanex grabbed him by the arm again.

"Let me show you one more thing, then," he told Bonz.

Before waiting for a reply, he tugged Bonz around to the other side of the hill, leaving his family behind. Now they were looking into a different part of the valley. And that's when Bonz got the second shock of his afterlife: hanging about 250 feet above the ground were twelve enormous spaceships. Six antique, chrome-plated cruisers and six Empire cargo 'crashers floating next to a huge assembly of girders and wires. Bonz couldn't believe his eyes. It was the invasion fleet that had disappeared—the mysterious vessels he'd been sent out to the Two Arm to find!

He collapsed to the seat of his pants. Suddenly Heaven didn't make sense anymore. Souls that had passed on, he could see being here. But this . . .

"Those ships . . ." he began, stammering. *"What are they doing here?"*

Vanex just shook his head again. "Like I said before my friend, it's a long story."

6

At the moment Bonz arrived in Heaven, Hawk Hunter and Princess Xara were thousands of miles away, sitting beneath an apple tree, close by a gently flowing river, waiting for the stars to come out.

Fighter pilot, space hero, deserter, outlaw, and now a rebel against the Fourth Empire, Hunter had had many adventures in his strange lifetime. In fact, since finding himself stranded, without memories, on the desolate planet of Fools 6 nearly two years before, his life had been nothing but one long adventure—as well as a search for answers. Who was he? Where did he come from? How did he get to the Seventy-third century? Why was he here?

This quest had not been totally in vain: he'd found *some* answers. *Who was he?* He was an American. The red, white, and blue flag he carried in his pocket would never let him forget that. And he'd found other Americans lost among the stars, and in the process he'd discovered that they, along with the other peoples of the old Earth, had had their Mother Planet stolen from them by the rulers of the empires, both past and present. And, knowing this, he had come to believe that the reason he was here was for no less a purpose than overthrowing the present realm and winning Earth back for its rightful owners—or die trying.

He'd come close to fulfilling the last half of that bold pledge recently. So close, he'd managed to skip the dying part and fast-forward straight to the afterlife, along with the rest of the Two Arm invaders, also known as the United Planets Forces. Yes, they had given the Solar Guards the slip; they had found the perfect hiding place.

But since coming here, things had changed for him. Everything that had happened to him before paled by comparison. For now he was on the ultimate adventure.

He was in Paradise with the girl of his dreams.

How did they wind up here, in Heaven?

It was all Xara's doing. She was smart, shy, absolutely lovely, especially her gigantic blue eyes—and the only daughter of O'Nay, Supreme Ruler of the vast Fourth Galactic Empire, and the man that Hunter would seek to take down. Though just eighteen years old, she was brave beyond all measure, and unlike her deified relatives, had a sense of absolute right and wrong. It was because of her that the UPF fleet had been saved.

It all started a month before when a sympathetic Imperial spy told Xara that the leader of the mysterious Two Arm invaders was none other than Hunter himself. This came as a shock to her, as she believed, as did many in the Empire, that Hunter had been killed by the SG. But the spy also told her that the Solar Guards' REF was speeding to intercept Hunter's fleet, and that they were armed with special antistarship weapons, which would make short work of the invaders.

The spy then passed on to her a mysterious device known as the Echo 999.9. It was a very advanced holo-girl capsule—or so it seemed. Holo-girl capsules had been bouncing around the Galaxy for at least a couple thousand years. They came in all shapes and sizes. Some were programmed to present their users with a very real-looking holographic lady of the evening right on the spot, an experience that lasted about an hour before expiring. But the more sophisticated, more expensive models featured extremely elaborate scenarios in which the customer and holo-girl were transported to a paradise coastal setting. Here, they could romp nonstop and undisturbed for what seemed like weeks, before returning to the real world.

No one understood the technology behind the holo-girl capsules; their secrets had been lost, just like most of the history of the Galaxy, in the rise and fall of the empires. (One rumor said the holo-girls had originally been used as spies, only later morphing into near-flesh-and-blood sex objects.) In reality, though, even the most expensive holo-girl devices were very crude. Because the user assumed they were *inside* an illusion, no one ever explored any farther than their own little patch of sand; in many ways, the love beach was where an expensive holo-girl trip began and ended. But the truth was, the users were *not* inside an illusion. Although in every case except with the Echo 999.9, it appeared flat, almost two-dimensional, the place they were brought to was real. It was a different place. On a higher plane, no doubt of about that. But it *was* real. And it was *this* place, the same one that people down through the ages had thought of as Heaven.

After her meeting with the Imperial spy, Xara enlisted Vanex to help her, and together they used the advanced Echo to travel here to Paradise. Thus their sudden, unexplained disappearance a month before. After exploring their new environs, Vanex studied the Echo 999.9 capsule itself. There was another ages-old technology in the Galaxy called a Twenty 'n Six. It was a device that could move objects almost as large as a Starcrasher into the twenty-sixth dimension, where they could be stored indefinitely until being recalled again. During the liberation of the Home Planets, the concentration camp in the sky where the dispossessed peoples of Earth had been kept for more than four thousand years, Hunter and the United American Forces developed a Twenty 'n Six field by combining four of the devices to create a window of sorts through which they could elude the mercenary army who had been hired as the guards for the interstellar prison.

Vanex combined this Twenty 'n Six field idea with the powerful and mysterious Echo 999.9 technology and, in doing so, conjured up another sort of portal, one large enough for the UPF invasion fleet to pass through just seconds before the

Solar Guards were able to blast it with its special weaponry. So the truth was, the Solar Guards really didn't know what happened to the invasion force. And they still didn't.

It seemed impossible, though, combining something like a holo-girl device with a Twenty 'n Six and using it to get into Heaven. But it did work—and maybe the question is not how but why. And it might very well have had to do with this place itself. *Nothing ever went wrong in Heaven.* The impossible was possible, the most outlandish idea, a reality. All one had to do was think it, and it would happen. Vanex dreamed up this particular idea, and as a result, the twelve ships of the United Planets Forces and their combined 40,000-man crew had escaped certain death by coming through this back door to Heaven.

Hunter had come here a similar way. Captured just after the battle that never was, he'd been thrown into a cell at the bottom of the SG Starcrasher *ShadoVox*, the personal warship of Joxx the Younger. As it turned out, the famous SG commander, disillusioned about the Fourth Empire thanks to a mind ring trip Hunter had made him take shortly before he was captured, passed another Echo 999.9 to Hunter in the jail cell just hours before the pilot was due to be executed. Thanks to that last-minute act of heroism, Hunter had joined the others in the UPF fleet and was now, like them, hiding out in kingdom come.

But why did Xara help them? After all, her father was Emperor, and she was one of the most exalted persons in the Galaxy. Truth was, she did it for one reason only: she was in love with Hunter. They'd fallen for each other as soon as they'd met after his winning of the Earth Race. It was only after he'd arrived here and told her of all that had happened to him in the year he'd gone missing that she came to the same conclusion as he: that the Empire must be toppled and Earth returned to its rightful owners, even though it was her father who ruled the Galaxy with a muted iron fist, and her immediate family who served as the Empire's ruling class.

Very soon after coming here, Hunter had asked Xara a simple question: "What do we do now?" They had escaped certain death at the hands of the Solar Guards by finding their way to this bizarre hideout. But they were still holding the nasty little secret as to what made the Empires tick. So what *was* next?

Xara replied that they should immediately begin planning a return to the other side, to continue their fight against the Empire. But Hunter had another idea, one that stunned them both. He'd been fighting all his life, he had told her, and he was getting tired of it. Then he'd mused that maybe they could just stay here, in Eden, forever.

And why not? There *was* no better place to be. From the moment he'd popped in, Hunter had felt like he was walking on air. They all did. There was no pain here, no worries, no stress. No negative vibes. Everything was perfect. Nothing could go wrong, and everything always went right. Every time.

True, it was an odd place. There was no need to eat or drink here, because you never got hungry or thirsty. Yet you could do both if you wanted. The trees were filled with apples, very exotic apples, and the rivers ran cold with sweet-tasting nectars. You could eat and drink as much of them as you wanted, because you never got full and you never got fat. Such unpleasant things just didn't happen here.

It was only by sheer habit did they breathe. There was no need to bathe, as you were always clean, just as everything around you was always clean. The temperature was always pleasant, the atmospherics always fair. There was no real need for clothes, though most everyone still wore them. There was no sex here. Or, better put, no *need* for sex. In this place, the sensation one got from making love was the same feeling that was all around them, all the time. All you had to do was think it, and it would be there, at full strength, an experience that was even better if there was another person involved.

But where were they exactly? They weren't on a planet. There was no indication that they were rotating on an axis or that they were on a body that was orbiting a sun. There *was* a star nearby—or it seemed to be a star. It hung in place exactly eighty degrees in the northeastern sky. It was bright, radiant, and always pleasantly warm, which was good because it was mostly daytime here. But there was a kind of nondaytime as well. After some time went by—and not time as usually measured—this sun would set, and a kind of glowing twilight would come into being. Not darkness. And there were never any shadows. Just a kind of ebb of the radiance. An opportunity for the stars to come out.

And yes, there *were* stars overhead, great washes of them. Bright silver, yellow, and white, they spun out in spectacular arrangements that changed with every dusk. Mixed in were comets and meteor showers, and up to a dozen moons. Always of various sizes, the moons would suddenly appear in the sky, in different degrees of waxing and waning, a few so close, rivers and valleys and mountains could be seen on them. And after some time passed, the friendly sun would rise again and hang in place until twilight came once more. This odd interlude seemed to happen for one reason only: to benefit those who liked looking at the evening sky.

There was no time here. Or not time as one would normally experience it. Things happened, and memories were formed and so there was a past, and obviously a present. But there was no feeling that time was moving forward. Soon after arriving here, Hunter and Xara had walked to the edge of their home valley. It was a distance of at least thirty miles, and it seemed to take them many hours to make the journey. Yet upon returning to the others, from their friends' perspective, it was as if they'd been gone for only a short while. They soon noticed, too, that their fingernails, beards, and hair did not grow. The soles on their boots did not wear; their uniforms stayed perfect and clean. As the twilights did not come with any set regularity, it was hard to tell just how long the "days" were. Their only explanation was that there *was* no time here. Or, not time as they knew it.

However, they all still had their internal body clocks, and these seemed to be moving very fast. And this is where it really got strange: even though they had disappeared from the Milky Way less than a month ago, to their sensibilities it felt as if they'd been here, in Heaven, for ten years. Or even longer.

Of course, one question was bigger than the rest: Was this place *really* Heaven? Was this the place were all "good" souls came after living out their mortal lives? All the evidence seemed to indicate that it was: the constant euphoria, the worry-free existence, the miraculous surroundings. That this was the place that showed up in just about every myth and religion of Humankind seemed obvious. That Hunter and the UPF had found a way to come here without having to go through the nasty stage of actually losing their lives was definitely unnatural. But apparently not impossible.

As for the origins of this place, and who created it, and what its real purpose was—well, those were questions that were almost too deep, too disturbing for them to contemplate. Yet, luckily for them, they were saved by the very nature of this place from having to do so. Because it was impossible to be troubled by anything here, thoughts of such things as what this place *really* was, usually didn't last too long, if they even came up at all.

That was another bonus of Paradise: you never had to think too deeply about anything.

No surprise, then, that the UPF contingent had become enthralled with living in Paradise.

In the beginning they'd tried to plan a strategy on how and when to return to the other side, to continue their campaign against the Fourth Empire. But soon enough they realized that even *talking* about anything that had to do with combat or war or violence was very difficult here. Any time such a conversation would start, the participants would invariably find themselves getting sidetracked; one or two words in, they would suddenly begin talking about other, more pleasant things. Whenever this happened, the air would become extra thick with a sweet fragrance that was all around them anyway. When inhaled, it gave the most euphoric high. And Paradise became that much more alluring. And all thoughts of war would simply go away.

There was no doubt that some sort of manipulation was at work here. That something supernatural was watching over everything, pulling the strings, making sure that everything was as pleasant as possible. And after a while, all talk of conflict and hostility seemed silly, foolish, utterly human. They came to think of themselves as enlightened and above it all.

But were they really? Had they been spiritually elevated by the beauty of this place enough to see the futility of war? Or had they been lulled into it by some divine, unseen puppeteer, by that something in the air that made them all unintentional pacifists?

There was no way of knowing. But eventually, all talk of going back simply faded away.

There were many other souls here, of course. In Happy Valley, which they had come to call their piece of Paradise, Hunter estimated at least another 100,000 individuals inhabited the grassy plains nearby. And trillions of others were undoubtedly scattered throughout the infinite number of valleys beyond. Hunter and Xara had spoken to many of their neighbors inside Happy Valley. All had been friendly to a fault. No one ever questioned what they and the others in the UPF contingent were doing here, or why they seemed just a bit different, or even why there were twelve enormous spaceships hanging on the edge of the valley, just a couple hundred feet off the ground. The UPF had been accepted by the others in the valley simply because everything was good here, and there was never any basis for conflict.

At the same time, it was agreed among the United Planets troopers that they would not get into any details with the locals about how they'd arrived here or why they were all still wearing combat suits while everyone else wore little else than short white tunics or at most, the long white gowns.

Every authentically departed soul Hunter and Xara had spoken to here had another thing in common: not one of them had ever bothered to see what was over the next hill, never mind the next mountain. Just like the customers of the crude holo-girl trips, they were so happy where they were, they never had any reason to go anywhere else. The same was soon true for the 40,000 members of the United Planets vessels. This place was *so* beautiful, the desire to move beyond one's own sight line just wasn't there for them.

But not so Hunter and Xara. They were in love, but they were also very curious. Some things they just had to know.

So they had explored this place, setting off on journeys that took them hundreds of miles away from Happy Valley. They had seen many things in these walking trips, had met many souls, had discovered many things about this strange and wonderful place. And in doing so, they had become as close as two souls could be.

They'd begun this particular trek—their 113th—by going over the mountains northwest of Happy Valley.

It was a direction they'd not taken before. Most of their trips started out heading due west. As always, once on the other side of the small range, they'd come upon yet another row of valleys, all laid out, perfectly, in a series of rolling hills and vast, grassy plains. They cut across this row of valleys, then climbed over the next mountain range, then through the next series of valleys, and so on.

As with all their other journeys, the beautiful landscape never changed. Just like the beach and the ocean, they seemed to go on forever. They'd discovered that the number thirty-three was important just about anywhere they went. Each valley was exactly thirty-three miles around, had exactly thirty-three streams, thirty-three ponds, and thirty-three apple orchards. Always one long river wound through it; always exactly thirty-three miles long. They'd found no woods here, no forests, no cluttered glens. The largest group of trees they'd come across numbered, no surprise, thirty-three. The emerald grass grew everywhere, but not one blade reached more than three or thirty-three inches high. There were no weeds, no thistles, no thorns on any of the flowers. There were no rocks, at least not on the valley floors. No sinkholes, no ditches or exposed roots. The deepest part of any pond or stream either thirty-three inches or thirty-three feet exactly. The same with the river, which, at its widest point, was always thirty-three feet across.

However, this trip proved to be different, as they eventually came to a valley unlike any other they'd seen. It was located about fifty mountain ranges over from Happy Valley and featured the same gently meandering river, the same perfectly planted orchards, the same scattered concentrations of shiny, happy people. But this valley also contained a vast lake, right in the middle. Its water seemed as golden as the light from the sun. In fact, its surface reflected the sky so intensely, it was almost hard to look at. Smooth as glass, it was surrounded by hundreds of individual apple trees. Their blossoms scented the air with an almost orgasmic sweetness.

Hunter and Xara were both surprised by this change in the terrain. In all their other sojourns, the topographic pattern of this place had remained the same. But a bigger surprise was yet to come.

As they drew closer to the lake, they were able to see its far shore. On the other side was a city. It looked like an enormous palace, huge and bright; *so* bright, they could see it clearly even though it was still a great distance away. It had towers and spires and domed structures; some were spherical, triangular, some conical. The illumination seemed to be coming from the shimmering of the buildings themselves and everything contained within them. There was an almost visible vibration surrounding the city.

They stopped at the lake's edge; from here they could see people lounging on the far shore. They could also hear singing coming from the city, a call-and-response chorus between two choirs. The voices echoed across the mirrored lake, one choir singing from somewhere on high, the other from deep inside the dazzling metropolis. They soon realized there were many different songs being sung at once, by many different voices. Yet they were all in perfect harmony.

At one point, Hunter looked down at his feet and was surprised to see they were moving in rhythm to this music. Then he felt his fingers begin to snap, and his head begin to sway back and forth. Then it began happening to Xara, too. A moment later, they were both dancing! It was a crazy moment; Xara moved very gracefully and naturally, but Hunter had never danced a step in his life. He'd tried to stop himself, but at the same moment he knew he couldn't—and he didn't want to. He felt like he was being filled up inside. The joy was indescribable. There were no words for the sensation. *Ecstasy* didn't even come close. They danced like this for what seemed like a very long time, his feet moving, her body caught up in the ethereal orchestrations, both of them bathed in the reflected warmth of the water. Finally, their eyes teared up. And then the music stopped, fading out in one long echoing coda. They'd both collapsed to the ground, laughing and exhausted.

After a while, their wits returned and they got to their feet. They drank some of the sweet water and felt refreshed again. Then came a great temptation to jump into the lake and swim to the other side and visit the city. And they probably would have done this except for one thing: the city looked so magnificent, they were afraid if they'd entered the place, they might not want to leave.

So they'd moved on.

They went over the next mountain range and walked through the next series of valleys.

They met many congregations of people along the way; the scattered communities could usually be found near riverbanks or along the edges of ponds. They were always warm and friendly and, upon seeing them, would always exchange pleasantries. Sometimes Hunter and Xara would stop and chat and drink some water with them. They both knew they could stay a minute or a year; it didn't matter. They would be welcome whatever the case, and the interaction would always be rich and interesting. But never once did they mention where they'd come from, or how they got there, or why they were different from everyone else. Hunter wasn't sure if it would have made any difference. That's the way it was in this place. It was the ultimate in tranquillity. No need to worry, no reason not to be happy. There was only one difference between these souls and him and Xara. They had all died and passed over; Hunter and Xara had not. At least not yet.

They'd pressed on, walking nonstop for days, weeks, months, it was always so hard to tell. Even counting the twilight interludes didn't help because they didn't seem to appear on any regular basis. They just happened when they happened. But through it all, neither he nor Xara ever felt tired. They were never fatigued, never felt anything but vigor and energy and the desire to keep moving on.

They came to one valley—Number 399—where it was absolutely quiet. No breeze. No babbling of the streams. Stillness beyond explanation. Off to the right were mountains that seemed different, too. They were colored in the deep hue of sapphire and were uniformly round, with no peaks. On the near side of their slopes were thousands of lights, almost like there were thousands of tiny structures up there, and they had all become illuminated. And on the highest point was another city.

This one looked like something from a fairy tale. Towers connected to towers, connected to even more towers. It was covered with climbing foliage, and trees full of red and yellow blossoms, each one visible, even though Hunter and Xara were at least five miles away.

The city looked just as large as the one they'd discovered near the lake, yet it seemed to be teetering on the edge of this bright blue mountain. Rays of golden light were streaming up from someplace behind it. They rivaled in brightness and intensity those coming from the big friendly sun, hanging close overhead. That's why this city seemed to be made entirely of light.

Once again, they'd been tempted to draw closer and explore the place; Hunter was very curious about what lay within. But they decided not to, because once again, they felt they couldn't risk the temptation of entering the city and then not wanting to leave.

After another long trek, lasting maybe a month or so in their minds, in and out of another 134 more valleys, they came over a mountain to find yet another city. It was in the middle of a lush field about ten miles off in the distance.

Like the others, it was a collection of tremendously intricate structures, domes, towers: soaring, all of them. But they seemed to be made of crystal, a crystal that glowed with an extremely bright light from within. Over the long journey, they'd come to regret not visiting the first city—the City of Songs—and then the second place, The City of Light. Hunter couldn't resist it anymore. Neither could Xara. They decided to investigate this place up close.

They would come to call it the City of Smiles.

A long, winding road led to the front gates of the city. The closer Hunter and Xara got, the larger these gates seemed to become. Finally, they reached the outskirts, and they were standing before these gates. By this time they seemed to stretch so far up into the deep blue sky, they went out of sight. They were made of pearl—literally, pearly gates. Beyond were more structures and streets made of gold. The buildings sparkled with very intense light.

Hunter took one step forward and pushed on the gates with his finger. They opened, as if on some invisible command. Inside, very bright light was emanating from just about everywhere. He hesitated a moment. His chest was filled with electricity, an energy that was close to sexual, it was that intense. If this feeling could grow any further inside him, he knew it really *would* be hard to leave this place. He turned to look at Xara. He knew she felt exactly the same way.

They stepped inside. The city appeared to be made not just of crystal but also marble and gemstones. The buildings were just incredible in their sweeping designs, size, and majesty. They walked hand in hand down the main street. There were other individuals everywhere. They looked no different than those they'd encountered in the countryside, except they all seemed to have the most amazing, gleaming smiles. They were all friendly and gracious and peaceful. Hunter and Xara bowed and waved and smiled, but they didn't speak to anyone. Hunter still believed it was important not be loose-lipped about how they happened to wind up here, strangers in Paradise.

Most important, the city had a feeling of great sprit, and it had nothing to do with religion. The buildings were simply mind-blowing in their unearthly design and lavish, bright colors, but they saw nothing that even vaguely resembled a church. Nor had they run into any holy men here—or anywhere. No priests in Heaven? Hunter only knew one, his friend Pater Tomm, who was with the UPF contingent back in Happy Valley. And sometimes he wasn't too sure about him.

They reached a main square. It was gigantic, seemingly too big for the periphery of the city, but that's how things were here, too; the perspective always seemed to be a little deceiving. There was a crowd gathered at the far side of the square. They were listening to one person, clad in all white, who seemed to be elevated slightly above everyone else. Intrigued, Hunter and Xara moved toward the gathering, just to see what all the hubbub was about. But the crowd broke up before they got halfway across the square.

Small groups of people leaving the gathering walked past them, exchanging greetings and strobe-flash smiles, but the travelers were more interested in the being who had been doing the talking. They saw him, way up ahead, walking away from the square and down an avenue of particularly bright crystal, a group of followers in tow. Though his face was hidden from them, there was a glow around this individual that was unlike anything Hunter and Xara had seen since coming here. It certainly wasn't surrounding anyone else. As they drew closer, the glow around him became so intense, they could barely look at it. Now the excitement was beginning to surge inside them again. They both felt the overwhelming need to talk to this person. But the closer they got, the farther he moved away. After a while, they lost sight of him.

Finally reaching the end of the avenue of crystal, they found themselves in an enormous garden. It was filled with the bright emerald grass, and there were many trees, all of them full of flowers and apples. Xara reached up, pulled an apple off of one tree, and gave it to Hunter. He took a huge bite. Another apple immediately grew back.

There were many people in this garden. Some were sitting at easels, painting. Others were playing flutes that emitted only the sweetest of sounds. Dancers moving with incredible lightness and grace were all around them. The music grew, and more people were seen with instruments, and the voices rose, and suddenly a heavenly choir was on hand once again, making music that at once sounded different yet was playing in perfect harmony. Hunter looked down at his boots and saw they were beginning to move to the rhythm again.

He didn't want to embarrass himself a second time, so they left the garden and turned back toward the avenue. They looked in every direction, but by this time, the glowing being had disappeared for good.

Leaving the City of Smiles wasn't so hard after that.

They continued west, through more valleys, across more

shallow rivers, over more low mountains. They hiked on for what seemed like months.

They usually walked hand in hand, talking endlessly, stopping whenever they wanted to study more closely some little amazing thing, of which there was an endless supply here.

When they did stop, it was not to rest but just to lie next to each other and admire the sights. Sometimes they would watch the twilight from a mountaintop or hill and descend as soon as the sun appeared again. Sometimes they would lie naked in a shallow stream and allow the pure, crystalline water to run over them. They made love incessantly—in the heavenly way, that is. Hunter was always left panting at the sight of Xara's perfect and pert body. She, always in a perceptible glow, before, during, and after.

This was love in Paradise, perfect and beautiful. Who would not want to stay in this place forever?

What could ever make anyone want to leave?

They came to a particularly interesting river valley.

The sky seemed extremely blue above it. The colors of the meadow were extraordinarily bright, and the grass, as always, vividly emerald. They found flowers blooming in colors they'd never imagined before. The beauty was incredible. There seemed to be a soft white light glowing from everything within. It was almost as if they could see life itself inside the petals of the flowers.

They walked farther through these fields and were soon upon a river, near a grand apple tree, beyond which was a gently rolling hill.

This would be a good place to wait for the twilight—and this is where they found themselves now.

Strangely, Xara fell asleep soon after they'd arrived.

Hunter could not recall her doing this before, but the last thing he wanted was to disturb her. He caressed her as she lay, softly breathing. The dusk arrived, and the stars came out.

But this time they looked different. . . .

Instead of the ever-changing, swirling constellations, filled in with meteorites, comets, and swiftly moving moons, this twilight sky was static and nearly empty. There were only a few bright lights above him, and just one, solitary moon.

It took Hunter a while before he realized what he was looking at. This was a re-creation of the night sky above Earth! It was the view above Big Bright City, the capital of the Mother Planet and the place where Hunter and Xara first met.

Hunter took this as a romantic sign. He held Xara even closer. But then something else began happening, something else he'd never seen here before: the sky above had become cloudy.

These were not puffy white clouds that might produce an amazing colorscape at sunset. These were dark, ominous clouds, angry and so close, Hunter felt like he could reach up and touch them. They didn't last long, dissipating as the sun finally came up again.

But for the first time, Hunter thought things didn't seem so perfect here in Paradise.

He finally woke Xara. She was astonished to realize she'd actually gone to sleep. He explained to her what had happened and how the sky had changed, and how the dark clouds had made an appearance. She startled him by saying she'd dreamed nearly the same thing, only the clouds had been bloodred. Shaken by this experience, she suggested they head back to Happy Valley. Hunter agreed.

They started walking east. Over a river, and through a field, they found themselves moving much quicker than on the outbound trek. It was a very peculiar feeling. Then something told Hunter they could get there faster if they tried running. So they started running, and they were amazed at how fast they were able to run. Soon they were covering the distance across a valley in remarkable time.

Then the thought struck Hunter that if they started leaping—doing running jumps—they could cover more ground even quicker. So they began leaping together, and suddenly they were doing jumps that defied all manner of gravity, if in fact it was gravity that kept everyone's feet down here. Soon, with each leap, Hunter was putting his hands out in front of him and finding that whenever he did this, he would stay airborne for unnaturally long periods of time—ten to fifteen seconds at least. Xara started doing the same, both of them laughing madly.

The farther they leaped, and the more they were able to stretch themselves out, the more distance they could cover while airborne. Finally, they took one huge leap together, put their hands out in front of them, and stretched their legs out— and they stayed airborne like this, just a few feet off the ground, for what seemed like a very long time.

That's how Hunter and Xara discovered that, without needing an airplane or even a pair of wings, they were able to fly here in Heaven.

7

High Hill was deserted when Hunter and Xara returned.

This was odd. The hill looked out over Happy Valley and as it was the highest vantage point above the hovering ships, some of the principals of the UPF could always be found up here or at least nearby.

Happy Valley itself seemed strangely empty, too. A twilight had set in just as Hunter and Xara arrived back home. No one saw them land. And while a few figures were moving around in the dusk below, usually a large part of the 40,000-man UPF contingent could be found beneath the hovering ships, lolling about the emerald grass or congregating around the apple trees. But now the fields seemed virtually devoid of troopers.

This was not good. There was a standing order that should the status of their position here in Paradise ever change in any way, the principals of the UPF should head immediately for the fleet's flagship.

And that's where Hunter and Xara found them. Waiting in the combat center of the lead blue-and-chrome warship, *America*.

The entire inner circle was there. But no one was looking particularly happy or enlightened at the moment.

Erx and Berx, the normally jovial pilots who had found Hunter on *Fools 6* so long ago, now appeared very troubled and even pale. They barely looked up when Hunter and Xara walked in. Calandrx, the great warrior and pilot turned poet and Empire *bon vivant*, also looked uncharacteristically downcast. The Great Klaaz, star hero and the oldest of the group, looked *very* old under the low lights. Zarex, the explorer, and Pater Tomm, the space monk, were staring at their hands folded tightly on the table before them. Steve Gordon, the CIA man who had traveled out from Planet America with them, was going through the motions of writing something down.

The pilot just stared at them. Finally he asked a question almost never heard in Paradise: "What's wrong?"

Tomm was the first to reply. His voice was very solemn.

"Brother Hawk," he said. "You must hear this man's story."

He pointed to the person sitting at the far end of the table almost in the shadows. It was Gym Bonz.

Hunter fell into one of the hovering seats directly across from Bonz. Xara took a seat next to Vanex, the Imperial Custodian, who was sitting by himself off in a corner.

Bonz recited his tale. He began, as always, with his being assigned the spy mission inside the SG No-Fly Zone, how he found no SG activity within the forbidden area nor evidence of any battle. He told how SG troops riding in crimson ships wearing red uniforms executed him. His description of the battle between SF and SG ships that followed was particularly vivid.

When the SF3 agent was through, a dark silence fell upon the cabin. The lights grew a bit dimmer.

"You know how things work here, Hawk," Tomm spoke up finally. "Nothing ever goes wrong in this place. There just *aren't* any mistakes. And as you know more than anybody, this place is so vast, it really does seem to go on forever. And quite possibly it does. Yet of all the spots Mr. Bonz here could have crossed over to, he arrived here, right in our midst. It just can't be a coincidence that he has fallen into our laps."

Calandrx leaned over and lightly touched Hunter's arm. "We believe our new friend is here for a reason," he said.

Hunter felt his heart sink to his boots. He glanced over to the corner at Xara. She was about to cry.

It was Gordon, the CIA man who spoke next.

"We are battling the Empire, Hawk," he began. "And that means both the Solar Guards *and* the Space Forces. But now that we know they are fighting each other, we have to assume that they are distracted, at least for a while. If so, this is a chance that won't come again. If we don't take it, then we might just as well stay here. I, too, think this is a sign—a sign from the other side."

Hunter slumped farther into his seat. He knew what they were getting at. They had talked about this day many times since first arriving here. But after spending what seemed like more than a decade in Paradise, they'd almost forgotten that at some point, this day would actually come.

It was Zarex who finally spoke the words: "Brother Hawk, we believe that someone . . . or something . . . is telling us we have to go back."

Again, dead silence around the table.

Hunter looked at each of his friends. They all seemed particularly old at the moment, even though, in theory at least, they hadn't aged a day since coming here. His mind wandered back to the clouds he'd seen in the sky at the previous twilight—and Xara's dream that they were actually red. His spirits dropped even further.

Like the rest of them, he'd fallen in love with this place. And like him, the thought of returning to the other side with the intent of restarting their military campaign was repulsive, almost nauseating. But this place meant something even more to Hunter: while the others in the UPF fleet had met compatible souls here with which to share their time and desires—even the old-timers like Vanex and Klaaz had hooked up with significant others—Hunter already had Xara, his true love, when he arrived. And he had spent all of the past ten years with her, every moment of it, in total happiness with her. She was so beautiful, inside and out, that spending an eternity in Paradise was the ultimate in heavenly rewards.

Hunter didn't want that to change for anything. And he surely did not want to go back.

But the others had anticipated his reaction. It was up to Tomm to change his mind.

"Brother Hawk," the monk began. "Since I've known you and about your quest, you have made one point to me over and over again."

The priest looked around the room.

"We, your brothers, have joined you in your campaign to right the wrong done to the original peoples of Earth. We believed in you. We believed in your cause. It was honest. It was necessary. Something that had to be done for the betterment of all. But again, in all that time, I have heard you say to us that this is really *your* fight. You started it. You have vowed to finish it. True?"

Hunter nodded solemnly. Tomm was right. During both their struggle to free the Home Planets and while battling their way down the Two Arm, he'd always had an additional weight on his shoulders: that his friends really didn't own a piece of this fight simply because they weren't Americans, nor were they from any of the Home Planets. They really were like his brothers, and each in his own right, fierce warriors. But they weren't like him. They had simply joined his cause. The thought that one of them would get killed fighting his fight haunted him day and night as the campaigns progressed.

"While I owe you all a debt that I can never repay," Hunter finally said to them. "What you say is true; this *is* my fight, and my fight alone."

Tomm looked across the table at Hunter very sternly. Then he just shook his head.

"Brother Hawk, forgive me," he said. "But on that point you are dead wrong."

Tomm nodded to Gordon, who had repositioned himself at the room's immense porthole, at present covered by an atomic-silk curtain. With no little drama, Gordon yanked back the curtain and suddenly the room was filled with light. The twilight was gone, and the sun had returned to its place in the sky.

On the valley floor directly below them stood the entire 40,000-man contingent of the United Planets Forces, soldiers born and trained on the Home Planets after the prison colony was freed. The small army was assembled in thirty-five huge columns, each formation representing one of the planets contained inside the prison star system. Standing out front was the contingent from Planet America. Its flag was the UPF flag: the Stars and Stripes.

Hunter looked down at the assembled soldiers and felt a lump grow in his throat. They had obviously staged this for his benefit, and now he knew why the valley had looked so empty. But it was hard for him not to get the message. Tomm was right. This *wasn't* just his fight. This was their fight, too. All 40,000 of them, standing below, flags billowing in the soft breeze were the descendants of those who had Earth so cruelly taken away from them thousands of years before.

And from the looks of it, they were ready to leave Paradise today—and go to try and get it back.

Hunter glanced at the others around the table, then over at Xara in the corner. She was crying now, and they weren't tears of joy.

He looked back down on the army assembled below. His eyes locked onto the huge American flag out front and just would not let go. That flag meant something very deep and very real to him. Something that had not dulled over the trillions of miles or the thousands of years. In his eyes and in his heart, it represented just about everything that was good and just and right about humanity. Not perfect, but close enough. He just couldn't give up on it now.

"OK," he finally said, softly. "Let's go back. . . ."

No one knew why they found it slightly easier to talk about the nastiness of war when they were in the auxiliary engine room at the bottom of the flagship *America*.

Was it the proximity to the antique ship's revitalized ion-drive star engine? Or was it something about being in the gut of the hovering ship that put them out of sight from the big brother that seemed to be watching over them here in Paradise? Or was it just their imaginations all along?

There was no real answer to be had. But shortly after agreeing that it was time for them to finally return to the other side, Hunter and the rest of the UPF command staff huddled inside the small anteroom just off the main power system suite. Sitting on the floor, in near total darkness, heads down, they were trying very hard to concentrate on things other than peacefulness and light. They felt foolish, even childish. But this was the only place they knew where they could hide from God.

In the few brief discussions they'd had upon first coming here, it was agreed that there was only one way they could ever attempt a return to the other side: one ship would go first; the others would follow later. That first ship would carry a skeleton crew consisting of the original rebels: Erx and Berx, Calandrx, Zarex, Gordon, Pater Tomm, and Klaaz. Why them? And why just one ship? Because no one was sure if the Vanex Door worked in reverse. Could they leave the way they came in? There was actually a high probability they couldn't, and that those making the attempt to pass back over would be killed. If that happened, it stood to reason—if there could be any reason in these things—that the souls of the lost crew would return here and inform the others that passing back over was probably impossible. Then they really would have to stay in Nirvana.

But if all indications were that the ship and crew did make it back, then the others would follow exactly one week later. And while direct contact with the other side would be impossible—the Echo 999.9 capsules were good for onetime use only—those returning first would have to make sure that the reentry point was secure for the other eleven ships to pass through. Or at least that had been the original plan. Now, with news of the SF and SG fighting each other, the crew of the pathfinder ship would have its work cut out for them. The reentry spot—Zero Point—would be, Vanex had calculated, exactly where the UPF fleet disappeared in the first place: right in the middle of what was now the SG No-Fly Zone.

But that was only a small part of the enormous problem. Even if the entire fleet *was* able to make it across, the subterfuge and blitz methods they'd employed during the initial invasion of the Two Arm would no longer be possible. Once the shock of their reappearance wore off, the SG's Rapid Engagement Force—the *real* villains in this space opera—would be all over them. And no doubt, they would soon be joined by regular Solar Guards forces, and, not to forget, the ultraloyal Space Forces as well. In other words, the UPF would be facing the military might of the entire Fourth Empire. Just them, and twelve ships.

"If we make it back, the odds against us will be tremendous," Calandrx said now, his voice echoing in the dark little room. "But if we must go down, then we should go down fighting . . . and that means . . ."

He began stumbling for words. Everyone else tried hard to concentrate.

"And that means . . ." Calandrx began again. "That . . . the grass was especially brilliant earlier today. The wind was warm and soft and . . ."

He tried to bite his tongue to stop talking, but it was no use. He'd been sidetracked just like every time they tried to talk about anything that wasn't acceptable in this place of mandatory peace.

So Tomm tried to pick up where Calandrx left off.

"We will all have roles to play once we return to the other side," the monk started saying. "We know *how* we are going to attempt to go back. But there is no sense in talking about what happens after that now . . . because . . . as you know . . . the water down in the stream was especially tasty today, wasn't it? And . . ."

He stopped himself. It happened again. Heaven was intruding.

Klaaz gave it a try. "We will need more men, more weapons, more support," he began. "We will need to make sure that . . . that . . . we are all atop High Hill when the next twilight comes, because it will be extremely spectacular and . . ."

He, too, stopped talking. Three sentences were as far as he could get. The invisible euphoria gas was seeping into the closed compartment very quickly now.

Zarex jumped in. "Tomm is right; these are things we can only discuss once we get back," he said in rapid-fire fashion. "We can only plan it then. . . . We must be prepared to . . . eat the golden apples near the big bend in the river, as they are especially sweet."

"That they are," Gordon said. "I had one earlier and . . ."

He stopped himself, and everyone smiled. They could go no further. Happiness and peace had found them again. This was all that could be said.

But they all had the basic idea: get one ship across, try as best as possible to smooth the way for the other eleven to follow.

And then prepare for a massive, one-sided, and most likely suicidal last battle.

But leaving Heaven would be more difficult than getting in.

There were several technical problems to overcome, beginning with the so-called Vanex Door itself. It was an impressive structure, nearly a quarter of a mile wide and more than 750 feet high. Even more remarkable was that the elderly Imperial custodian had built it himself. Of course, he had the help of his electron torch, the do-it-all hand tool that could convert any kind of atom into any other kind of atom, and therefore allowed its owner to create just about anything out of practically nothing, so to speak.

Vanex and Xara had arrived in Heaven several days before the UPF fleet. To them though, their head start seemed the equivalent of several months, long enough for the engineer to conceive his genius invention and then actually construct it.

The structure was located near the south side of High Hill, about a quarter mile from the last bend in Happy Valley's river and a part of the UPF's little enclave where few of the local souls ever bothered to venture. It was a basic framework of thin, shiny girders, which essentially served as a 2,500-foot rectangular brace for the four Twenty 'n Six units. When connected, they created the crucial transdimensional field that made up the Vanex Door. The disassembled Echo 999.9, augmented by a ring of signal amplifiers, was positioned over the screen like a king's multijeweled crown. The Door was a magnificent achievement; gigantic and slightly asymmetrical, it was almost a work of art. It also looked as out of place as the twelve huge warships it helped bring here.

But it was its location that posed a significant problem. As each of the escaping UPF ships came through the Door, their power plants ground to a halt almost the instant they gained

the airspace over Paradise. There were nearly a couple cata-
clysmic collisions in the first few hair-raising seconds as the
ships had appeared so fast, their pilots barely had enough time
to move their stalled vessels out of the way before the ship
behind them popped through. This was why the UPF fleet was
hovering above the heavenly landscape in such a haphazard
fashion and not in any kind of a rigid formation.

The problem was rooted in the odd fact that once here, the
twelve ships lost all power, except what was needed to keep
them in their hover and to keep a few lamps illuminated. Many
took this as further proof that someone or something was pulling the strings here, and while that entity didn't mind the ships
invading its space, it was adamant about them not going anywhere once they arrived. Further proof of this: no electron
torches worked *after* the ships crossed over here, though they
had worked for Vanex before. Quadtrols didn't work here,
either. Subtle things. But the message seemed clear: strong
forces will become obstacles if you try to leave or even move
around.

The problem then was that the ships were out of position to
make the return trip back through the Door. The UPF engineers figured out that the tiny modicum of power that was
keeping the ships in the air could be used to push them forward
back out the portal, but not much farther than that. There
would not be nearly enough juice to maneuver the ships
around so they would be pointing back at the Door. The only
solution: the portal would have to be moved to accommodate
them.

The 40,000 members of the UPF fleet would provide the
muscle for this project. They would have to deconstruct the
Door's framework by hand and reassemble it, at a location
near one of the stolen cargo 'crasher ships, *Resonance 133*.

As it would be this vessel to attempt the first reverse crossover, the Vanex Door would have to be rebuilt just a few feet
off its nose.

There was yet another problem, bigger than the repositioning
of the Vanex Door.

This one had to do with Hunter himself. When the *Reso-*

nance 133 crew finally launched, there was no way he could go with them. Why? Because he'd not come here the same way they had.

They'd all come through the portal created by combining the Echo 999.9 and the Twenty 'n Six field. Hunter, on the other hand, had come here via an Echo capsule, as had Xara and Vanex. The more direct approach, certainly, but it raised a huge question: What would happen to him if he rode back to the other side in the UPF ship? If he had entered Heaven by one means and then left in a completely different way, would there be any cosmic repercussions?

They didn't know. The Echo 999.9 was such a mysterious device, it was a miracle—literally—that Vanex had been able to manipulate it as much as he had. There was even speculation among the UPF contingent that the device wasn't a holo-girl capsule at all, not a typical one, anyway. That it was something else, just dressed up in a clever disguise.

In any case, there was no shortage of theories of what would happen to Hunter if he went back as they did. Because he would be returning to a different place from where he started, and would be going through the extra step of passing through the twenty-sixth dimension, Erx thought he'd be reduced to a quivering mass of quarks and snarks long before he ever popped out on the other side. Zarex wondered if he might be caught forever inside the twenty-sixth dimension, unable to make the extra step to break through. Vanex, who was the authority on the matter, warned that while Hunter might make it to the other side in one piece, all of his atoms would be turned inside out.

None of these scenarios appealed to him, so Hunter had made up his mind early on: he'd come here via the mysterious holo-capsule, given to him by Joxx just hours before he was to be executed. He would have to go back the same way.

Actually, this was where the real problem lay. As far as they knew, there were only two Echo 999.9s in existence. One the Imperial spy had given to Xara and Vanex to get them here in the first place. That was the model Vanex had taken apart to make the escape window. The second one the same spy gave to Joxx to allow Hunter to escape. Usually, with lesser models, the romp on the beach lasted what seemed to be a month. Yet when the customer returned, it was as if no more than a few seconds of real time had gone by. It seemed like magic, but this was actually a customer-oriented feature of cheaper models, a reverse-time element allowing them to disappear for what seemed to be a month, but not be gone long enough for their spouse (or their boss) to be suspicious.

The Echo 999.9 was significantly different, only adding to the mystique of the strange device. As soon as Hunter arrived here, Vanex had taken apart his capsule, too, and had effectively frozen its built-in time clock. And then after noodling with it, he found a way to actually advance it.

When Hunter left the other side, he'd been just a few hours away from getting shot. He certainly didn't want to return in the same instant, still locked in a cell, waiting for the executioner's song. So Vanex pushed up his return time to parallel that of the fleet ships; they would all go back together and arrive in the same time frame. Or at least that's how Vanex hoped it would work.

However, there was nothing he could do about *where* Hunter would return. The pilot had left from the locked jail cell at the bottom of Joxx's starship, and that's where he'd reappear— one month later. No one could know what had happened in that month. Bonz had told him that at last report, Joxx had dropped out of sight, had been refusing orders, and was seen sporting a silver dagger in his belt—the weapon of choice for those wishing to kill the Emperor. Hunter knew that anything could happen once he returned, including the possibility that he'd find himself still behind bars.

So he had to be prepared for any uncertainty.

That's why when Bonz went looking for Hunter a few hours after the somber meetings in the *America*, he found the pilot atop High Hill, picking apples.

The valley below was alive with frenetic motion by now. The Vanex Door was about halfway reconstructed in its new place. It was quite an operation for the UPF troopers to try to align the huge framework with the gigantic cargo 'crasher. The rigging looked like a stiff breeze would blow it over in a second; luckily, there were no stiff breezes here in Heaven. The *Resonance 133* was almost ready to go, too. Crude ladders had been dropped from it, and technicians could be seen climbing up and down from them on a very regular basis.

Bonz meandered up to Hunter. His family was now living down on the valley floor.

"Not too long now," Bonz said to the pilot, looking down on all the activity.

"How can you tell?" Hunter asked him. Bonz grinned; he got the joke. There *was* no time here, so theoretically at least, nothing could take a long or short time.

Hunter resumed picking apples. He was looking for ones that were small enough to fit into the pockets of his flight suit, as self-contained survival kits, you might say. Bonz took down an apple himself and examined it. Clearly he had something on his mind.

"I just wanted to apologize to you," he finally said to Hunter, turning the apple over in his hands. "I'm really sorry—"

"Sorry? What do you mean?"

Bonz shrugged. "Well, I'm responsible for this mess," he said, spreading his hands out to indicate the whole operation of getting the *Resonance 133* lined up with the Vanex Door.

"What mess?" Hunter replied. "You're a hero. You got us back in gear again. If it wasn't for you, we would have stayed here forever."

"Like that would have been a bad thing?" Bonz asked, half-heartedly biting into the apple. "Being happy not just for the rest of your life, but for the rest of eternity: it's everyone's ultimate dream."

Hunter looked out on the valley below. It was even more magnificent than the first time he saw it.

"Well, it's yours to enjoy now," he told Bonz. "You're with your wife and kids again—as you should be. See how only good things work out here?"

"There's no doubt about that," Bonz replied. "But I have to wonder about something: Will I carry through eternity the knowledge you've imparted to me about the origin of the empires? There is no doubt in my mind that what was done to the original people of Earth is the greatest wrong of human history or certainly in the history of the Galaxy. They used to talk about the crime of the century in the ancient days? Well, this is the biggest crime of all humanity! It's mind-boggling. Billions of people, thrown off their planet after they fought to free it from one enemy, only to be betrayed by another? And these were the descendants who brought man into space in the first place, the descendants of the Ancient Engineers. Such an atrocity. And I'm now one of the comparatively few souls who know about it. Yet there's nothing I can do about it."

Hunter walked to another tree and began examining the apples on it. "Like I said," he told Bonz, "you did your part. You tipped us off on a great opportunity to go back. That's a big first step for us."

Bonz just shook his head. "I know. But look at it from my perspective. I spent more than a century serving a regime that is up to its neck in this treachery. Knowing what I know, I wonder just how peaceful my soul can really be."

Hunter stopped picking apples and looked at the SF3 agent.

"What are you suggesting?" he asked him. "Certainly not that you go back with us."

"It's crossed my mind," Bonz admitted.

Hunter stuffed another apple into his pocket. "Don't be crazy," he told the spy. "Like I said: You're the hero. It took you winding up here to light the fuse again, and that could have only come about by the horrible way you died. They used to give medals out for things like that. No matter what transpires now, it couldn't have happened unless you did what you did."

"Well, sure, that helps you," Bonz said. "It doesn't help me."

Hunter said to him: "Look, man, you lost a beautiful wife, two beautiful kids. Now they're not lost anymore. They are here. And so are you. And you're guaranteed an eternity with them."

"But that's just it," Bonz insisted. "They will always be here. I could go with the *R133* crew and maybe do some real good. Then, when I come back, it will be like I never left."

Hunter just shook his head. "Talk to Pater Tomm," he suggested. "He'll knock that thought right out of your head, either with a prayer or the blackjack he keeps in his back pocket. Bottom line is this: you are a soul who has passed over; the rest of us are not. When we go back, we hope we will be in the same shape and form as when we left. But what would happen if you went back? God, they think I'll turn myself inside out if I ride aboard the first ship. I can't imagine what they might think would happen to you."

Bonz paused for a moment and thought about this. Then he said suddenly: "You should marry her, you know. . . ."

Hunter stopped what he was doing. "Marry? Marry who?"

"Xara, of course."

Hunter tried to stay cool; he stuffed another small apple into his pocket. "Why would you say that?"

Bonz shrugged. "Hey—I'm a spook. It's my job—or it used to be, anyway—to be able to read people in a half a second."

"SF3 is turning out love connectors these days?"

"I don't have to be a wizard to know you're crazy about her, and she's crazy about you," Bonz said. "Whether I've been here ten years or ten minutes, it's rather obvious."

"So?"

"So, when all of this is over, back on the other side or wherever the hell the real world is, I suggest you marry her."

Hunter thought a moment. "But if I did that, that might make *me* Emperor someday."

Bonz suddenly shook Hunter's hand.

"Well, Major," he said, "I never thought I'd say this, but if there was one person I would choose to be top man in the Empire—in the entire Galaxy—that guy is you."

Hunter just laughed again, picked one last apple, and stuffed it into his pocket.

"Good luck, Gym," he said. "And enjoy your eternal reward."

8

It took what seemed like a very long while for the UPF troopers to complete the relocation of the Vanex Door.

Taking it apart, piece by piece, and carrying the sections to the other end of the small valley went smoothly enough. But when it came time to put the last half of the portal back together, strange things began to happen.

Soon after the main frame had been put up, a twilight came, one that lasted longer than anyone could remember. No moons appeared in the sky this time; nor were there any great washes of stars over ahead, at least not over Happy Valley.

The lack of starlight hampered the final phase of the repositioning. There was no artificial illumination in Happy Valley; there was never a need for any. When it became apparent that the dusk was going to last longer than usual, the UPF engineers tried to switch on the search and landing lights attached to the bottom of each ship, including *Resonance 133*. But none of these lamps would work. The power inside the ships was already very low; trying the lights only further drained the limited supply. Then someone suggested they try making a fire and then lighting torches. But no one could produce as much as a spark. There was no fire in Paradise, because there was never any need for it.

So the last part of the rebuilding project was done in the low light of the strange twilight, which made it all that much more difficult. But somehow the troopers prevailed. It was only as they were tightening up the last truss that the twilight finally ended. The sun rose; the dusk went away.

The Vanex Door, powered by the tiny cell included in the Echo 999.9, came to life a short while later.

There was never any doubt who would be going aboard the *Resonance 133* for this first attempt to break back through to the other side.

As the most seasoned pilots, Zarex and Calandrx would handle the flying. Tomm, Gordon, and Klaaz would lord over the primary controls. Erx and Berx would be back in the engine room, watching over the ship's dual-power system.

Why two power systems? It was the only solution to yet another complication. The *Resonance 133* was an Empire ship. It was powered by a prop core. But the juice it needed to draw from the Big Generator was nonexistent here; Supertime did not extend to Paradise. So taking a page from Bonz's experience on his ill-fated ship, the *ZeroVox*, the *Resonance 133* now had both an ion-ballast engine—actually a spare taken from one of the original UPF ships—as well as its own prop core. It was hoped if enough power could be diverted to the ion-ballast engine, it would give the ship the boost needed to penetrate the Vanex Door and to get through the twenty-sixth dimension.

Once on the other side, the prop core would be kicked in.

If the ship made it that far.

The bare-bones crew of the *Resonance 133* had prepared for their flight up on High Hill. A bridge connecting the peak and the access door to the ship had been constructed with materials left over from moving the Vanex Door. This way the crew could walk right across to the main hatchway to the waiting vessel.

The crew would have to wear their spacesuits, for they had no idea what was going to happen once they entered the Vanex Door. A short trip through the twenty-sixth dimension certainly, lasting just a microsecond in real time but seeming like an eternity for those going through it. This was how it had been on the trip that brought them here. But whether the *Resonance* could take the strain of all this transdimensional flip-flopping was a big unknown. There was a good chance the ship might break up upon reaching Zero Point on the other side. Spacesuits would give the crew about thirty seconds to say their last good-byes—and then, theoretically at least, head back to Heaven by more traditional means.

Another twilight came and went. The plan called for the *Resonance 133* to leave during a daylight period, so the final preparations hurriedly began. Helping to attend to some of the last details, Hunter was up on High Hill with the crew. That's when Tomm approached him and pulled him aside.

The two men knew each other very well. Hunter had met Tomm when the space monk was serving as a tagalong chaplain for the Freedom Brigade, the small band of American mercenaries who eventually led Hunter to find Planet America. Tomm had stuck by him in the worst days of the war to free the Home Planets and during the UPF invasion of the Two Arm. Next to Erx and Berx, the priest was probably Hunter's closest friend.

But Tomm was not a man without secrets. And one was known to very few people in the Galaxy; in fact, it was one of the deepest secrets in the history of all humankind.

Once they were a good distance away from the others, Tomm said to him, "We all realize that getting back to the other side will be an enormous undertaking and might not even happen at all. I also realize that as you will be going back a different way, we might not have a chance to speak again, ever."

He took something out of his pocket but kept it hidden tightly in his fist.

"I think I know where we can find an ally for our cause," Tomm went on, choosing his words carefully. "A very powerful ally. Someone who might not need much convincing to join . . . our fight. But I am reluctant to talk about him here, . . . for obvious reasons."

Hunter nodded. He fully understood.

"Finding him, though, is a mission that only you can see through," the priest went on. He finally passed the object in his hand to Hunter. It was a viz-screen capsule, a sort of compact image projection device used by soldiers in forward battle areas to receive orders from their superiors without jeopardizing string communications.

"I made this a very long time ago," Tomm told Hunter. "Right after we first met, in fact. I had hoped that I would never have to give it to you. I hoped things would never get so bad. But now, under the circumstances, I believe it is the right thing to do. The message it contains is in two parts. Open it when you get back. It will give you all the specifics you will need. We will all have a role to play when we reach the other side. I think this is the avenue you should pursue. And I think that is all we should say about it here."

At that moment, the *Resonance* technicians passed the word that it was time to go. Tomm shook Hunter's hand and turned to join the others walking across the bridge. But Hunter stopped him. He looked at the viz-screen capsule. "But Father, even if I do what it says in here, what are the chances of me actually succeeding?"

Tomm just shook his head.

"Truthfully, Brother Hawk," he said, "for *any* of this to work, we will need more than just one miracle."

The big moment finally came.

The ship techs pronounced the *Resonance 133* ready to go. The gigantic wedge-shaped cargo ship, dark gray against the bright emerald grass below and the shimmering blue sky above, looked very out of place, even more so now that the bubble top cockpit area was lit with a dim but eerie yellow light.

The crew walked across the bridge as the UPF troopers, back in formation on the valley floor below, stood at attention. The techs had hung a flag over the entrance to the *Resonance 133*. It was the Stars and Stripes. Watching from the top of the hill, Xara at his side, Hunter was not surprised to find himself choked up as the crew passed beneath the unfurled flag.

Once in, the crew turned on only the bare essentials. Their departure was only a short while away. Now came a crucial question involving time—or, more accurately, *keeping track* of time in this place that had none. Clocks didn't work here, no surprise in an environment that seemed designed to make one forget all about the concept of time. How then would they know when the week was up, and the rest of the fleet should cross over?

There was only one way to do it. Volunteers from the UPF army would be made "designated counters." As soon as the *Resonance 133* disappeared, these troopers would start counting, in rhythm. Sixty seconds to mark every minute, 3,600 seconds to mark every hour, 86,400 seconds to mark each day—for seven days.

Only then would the rest of the fleet follow.

The *Resonance's* departure also required a countdown.

It started at thirty. On a technician's cue, the entire UPF contingent assembled below began shouting out the descending numbers.

But strange things started happening again. The sky suddenly turned black, as clouds covered the sun. A darkness more acute than any twilight descended on Happy Valley. This was a frightening turn of events for the UPF contingent, not to mention the other residents of the area. Never had it grown so dark before in Happy Valley. Still, the countdown continued.

It reached fifteen seconds, and a sudden clap of thunder rolled through the valley. It was powerful enough to shake the Vanex Door, as well as everything and everybody nearby. Standing atop High Hill, Xara grabbed Hunter so tightly, her nails went right through his uniform sleeve. The countdown continued.

More thunder rumbled through the valley. The sky overhead became even darker, if that was possible. The countdown got down to ten seconds. Another clap of thunder, this one so powerful, High Hill itself actually began shaking.

"Someone does not want this to happen!" Xara yelled to Hunter, though he could barely hear her over the booming thunder.

The countdown reached five seconds . . . another tremendous clap of thunder.

Four . . . three . . . two . . . one . . . *zero!*

Now came two tremendous explosions. One was from the most powerful clap of thunder yet, the other from the *Resonance 133* as it instantly accelerated to top ion-ballast speed and disappeared through the Vanex Door. It was gone in a blink, leaving only a greenish mist in its wake.

The thunder continued, and the sky grew absolutely pitch black after the ship had departed. Those up on High Hill could hear the wails of the permanent souls throughout the valley. Xara was clutching Hunter so tightly now, her fingernails were digging into his skin. Several terrifying moments passed.

But then, gradually, the thunder abated, and the clouds drifted away. The sunlight returned, and wailing throughout the valley ceased. But it was obvious that the act of pushing the ship back through the Vanex Door had upset the very pristine order of things. They had angered the Creator Himself with their act of boldness, and it had been frightening to experience the reaction from on high.

But normalcy soon returned. Those watching over the controls for a subatomic Sweeper that had been attached to the *Resonance* reported that all indications were that the ship had at least made it into the twenty-sixth dimension.

Upon hearing this, everyone in the UPF contingent relaxed a little. Hunter and Xara sat down on the edge of High Hill and just held on to each other. Vanex walked down to the river and drank his fill of the sweet, intoxicating nectar. The formations dispersed, and many of the UPF troopers went for a swim.

It was only later that they discovered the soul of Gym Bonz was not among them.

Apples.

Hunter had picked thirteen of them, and now they were stuffed into the pockets of his combat suit, making him look a little too round in the rump.

He was down on the beach, at the exact spot where he'd faded in so long ago. He had his helmet on, and his boots were stitched up tight. He had a container of river nectar and a blaster rifle borrowed from one of the UPF troopers. These were the things he might need if things went wrong once he got back to the other side.

He knew there was a good chance he would wind up back inside the jail cell at the bottom of the *ShadoVox* on his return, and that the cell door would still be locked. There was also a chance no one aboard the ship would know he returned, so the apples would sustain him for a while, he hoped. If he was unable to blast the lock off the cell door with the borrowed ray gun, that is.

He'd had one last conversation with Vanex before leaving High Hill. It was mostly to thank the old guy for all that he'd done under the most unusual circumstances. The Imperial Janitor was still a bit of an enigma. Had he come around to their point of view, agreeing that the Empire had to be toppled? Or had he been helpful simply because he was very loyal to Xara? If Hunter had to bet on it, he would have guessed the old guy had done it for Xara alone.

Hunter took one long, last look at his surroundings. The sweet water, the hillside of bright flowers, the bejeweled sands. He knew the chances of him ever coming back here—at least by these means—were nil. The Echo 999.9 was a onetime device. The capsule Hunter had used to get here would be depleted as soon as he returned. The same was true for the first Echo, which had been disassembled to build the Vanex Door. Once the last UPF ship passed through it—if indeed the passing through was successful—it, too, would be depleted. So the ships could never return, either.

No, if he was ever to see Paradise again, Hunter knew he would have to get here the old-fashioned way.

That's what was going to make the next few moments on the beach so difficult. Because he knew there was a very good chance he would never see Xara again, either. She couldn't come with him, of course. And she couldn't have gone back on the *Resonance 133*, as the same thing that they feared would happen to him—that nasty atoms-turned-inside-out thing—would happen to her (and Vanex, too).

They were stranded here. In Paradise.

There was no way Hunter could leave with out saying good-bye to Xara—although he'd considered this. It would have avoided the painful moment they both knew had to come sooner or later. So he told her to give him a while to prepare, and then meet him down by the shore.

She arrived, cheeks still wet with tears, still looking beautiful but at the same time very sad. Her emotions had been running high since the departure of the *Resonance 133*.

Hunter took her hands and looked deep into those gigantic blue eyes. For the first time, he realized they were the same color as both the sky here and the cobalt blue ocean.

"So how long *has* it been?" he asked her. "One month . . . or ten years?"

She squeezed his hands in return. "Either way, it wasn't long enough, Hawk," she said, almost embarrassed. "That's the tragedy in all this. We could stay here for eternity. Instead, I'm losing you, probably forever. And if you succeed in your quest, then I lose my family."

She looked up, and Hunter could see the tears had started again. He tried to wipe them away.

"I'll come back," Hunter suddenly heard himself say, even as his heart was breaking inside. They both looked at each other, eyes misty. She knew better than to ask how. There was really only one other way to get to Heaven.

"I'll wait for you," she said, repeating a line from a poem she had written for him when he first left Earth on his quest to find the Lost Americans. "A million years, if I have to."

Hunter was trying his best to control his emotions, but it was a losing battle. His brain suddenly became saturated with the idea that he probably *would* never see her again, no matter what the cosmos had in store for him. One month or ten years? She was right; it hadn't nearly been long enough. And now, at this good-bye, he realized he didn't even have a holo-picture of her, nothing at all to remember her by.

She read his mind. She pointed to her heart. "In here, Hawk," she said. "No one leaves you if they live in your heart and mind. And no one dies; they move to the other side. I'll be here."

She leaned over and kissed him.

Then the Echo 999.9's time element finally ran out, and Hunter faded away.

PART THREE

The Messengers

9

Solar Guards Sublieutenant Walz Cronx had just gone off duty when the nightmare began.

He was a crew member of the SG Starcrasher *StratoVox II*. His position was second forward weapons officer, one of dozens aboard the ship. The *StratoVox* was a capital battle cruiser, and at 2.5 miles long, one of the largest space vessels in existence. It served as the flagship for Space Marshal Finn-Cool McLyx, a top Solar Guards commander, and a man known throughout the Empire for his heroism or his ruthlessness, depending on one's point of view

Lieutenant Cronx had not been to sleep in one hundred hours. He'd been pulling triple shifts without the benefit of a wake-up drop or any other kind of metabolic inducer while filling in for other lowly officers in such diverse parts of the ship as the auxiliary power room, the master bilge compartment, and even the communications bubbler. The *StratoVox* had been running at battle stations for more than three weeks now, ever since it left its patrol on the Six Arm. The nonstop high alert had been an intense, tiring process for the entire crew.

Finally one of the ship's doctors encountered Cronx staggering down a passageway and ordered him to take some time

off. Cronx was happy to comply. At the age of 201, he was
getting too old for these things. He dragged himself to his
quarters and was about to collapse on top his hovering bunk
when a duty captain appeared at his billet door.

"Get to your primary battle station immediately!" this officer
barked at him. "We are about to go into action. . . ."

As he was saying this, battle-imminent sirens started up all
over the immense ship. Cronx felt his stomach turn to stone.
It was the moment he had been dreading since the ship left
the Six Arm.

"Who is the enemy?" he half gasped,

The duty captain's face turned dark. "The Space Forces, of
course!" he screamed. Then he disappeared.

Cronx stayed frozen to his spot. Circumstances had been
building to this for three weeks, but it was no less distressing
now to finally hear the words. Just about everyone aboard the
StratoVox believed that their commanding officer, Finn-Cool
McLyx, had gone mad a long time ago. Now they feared he
was dragging them all down into his madness with him.

McLyx was a tall, heavy, blustery man with a scar that ran
from his right ear down to the center of his neck. His size
alone was intimidating to friend and foe alike, and he was
known to bully and even physically attack his superior officers.
Past commanders had been booted out of the SG for lesser
transgressions, but McLyx was a favorite of the Emperor. He
was also in line to take over one of the top positions in Solar
Guard Command someday. Not shy about anything, McLyx
bragged endlessly that his was the biggest ship in the SG's
fleet inventory.

He was also a master at invading unsuspecting backwater
planets out on the Fringe and bringing them back into the
Empire, whether they liked it or not. It was his *jonzz*, as the
saying went, and he took perverted pleasure in swooping down
upon these peaceful worlds, usually under the false pretense
that outlaws were hiding among the population, and blasting
anyone who stood in his way. In his long career, McLyx had
reclaimed thousands of wayward planets in this manner, brutally suppressing any resistance to his ship and soldiers and

reaping vast rewards of plunder that always accompanied the storm.

But McLyx reserved his special venom for the Space Forces. He absolutely detested the SF, from its top generals down to its lowliest privates. He hated everything the senior service stood for, especially the slower—some said more compassionate—way it went about reclaiming planets for the Empire. SG officers like McLyx had no time for the diplomacy-first methods used by the SF. Doing it his way was so much faster, not to mention more personally rewarding.

No surprise, McLyx was also a very wealthy man.

The *StratoVox* had been on patrol in the upper Six Arm when word of hostilities between the Space Forces and the Solar Guards reached the ship. Bits and pieces of news concerning the clash on Doomsday 212 trickled through first. But within hours, reports of all-out fighting between the two services were pouring into the *StratoVox*'s communications center. Though the SF and SG had started fighting each other in many locations around the Galaxy, the communiqués left no doubt that the heaviest combat was going on within the Two Arm's now-infamous No-Fly Zone.

The thought of the SF spilling SG blood made many hearts aboard the *StratoVox* race with both excitement and rage, especially among the battle staff. Adding fuel to the fire, the most outrageous reports—all unofficial—said the SF had somehow destroyed the SG's entire Rapid Engagement Fleet. This rumor had started only because no one knew where the REF was at the moment. Originally comprising thirty-six ships and nearly a quarter million men, they had all but vanished shortly after the supposed battle against the Two Arm invaders, only to reappear and then vanish again immediately after the first shots had been fired on Doomsday 212. The subatomic wreckage of two REF ships was strewn across that depressing planet. But everyone was now asking: Where were the other thirty-four?

This was all too much for the highly aggressive McLyx to take. Just hours after the first report came in, he'd ordered his ship and its fleet of six attending battle cruisers to turn about and head for the Two Arm. Ignoring pleas from the Imperial Court on Earth to stay on station, the *StratoVox* and its sister ships rocketed toward the combat zone at all-out full Supertime speed.

The trip of nearly 80,000 light-years had taken three and a half weeks. In that time McLyx's renegade fleet had grown. By the time it left the Six Arm, his seven-ship squadron had been joined by three dozen more SG warships. Like McLyx, their commanders had chosen to ignore orders from Earth and had sought to join the fighting.

They picked up more and more SG ships as they skirted the edge of the Ball and dashed along the outskirts of the inner Fringe.

By the time it reached the Two Arm, the impromptu battle group had swelled to more than seventy ships.

Several times over the past three weeks, Sublieutenant Cronx had stolen a precious few moments to make private-string contact with colleagues on Earth. This was how he'd received news—both confirmed and rumor—about what was happening both on the Mother Planet and throughout the rest of the Empire. None of these reports were good.

Fighting between the two services was spreading all over the Galaxy. Clashes on every arm had been confirmed. There had even been a skirmish inside the Ball, the ridiculously peaceful center of the Milky Way. Forces on both sides were ignoring all desist orders from Earth. Very hard-line SG individuals were even attacking isolated SF installations out on the Fringe. The SF was retaliating in kind.

Everyone knew fighting between the two services would not lead to anything positive. It further weakened an Empire that some believed was already reaching its breaking point. A too-hasty expansion policy, roughshod treatment of its newest citizens out on the Fringe areas, and an overall elitist attitude that was simply repulsive on many, many levels were bad enough. To have a war *within* its vast military was simply disastrous.

But why were the hostilities continuing? With all the command structures that lorded over both services, wasn't there any way to get the two rivals to stop? Cronx's friends on Earth said no—and the reason was simple: the only person whose words would be heeded by both sides, the Emperor O'Nay Himself, was unavailable. Where was he? In his tower, the soaring spiral that dominated the floating city of Special Number One, deep in his prayer mode. The perpetually detached O'Nay entered these meditative states quite often, or at least his Imperial Guards claimed he did. Once he was in such a trance, it could last for days or even weeks. And there were standing orders that he was not to be disturbed for anything.

His imperial bodyguards were obeying that order to the letter these days. So the internecine war was allowed to rage on.

Even worse, the SG had unilaterally declared a state of emergency within the Solar System. They'd flooded each of the original planets, from Mercury out to Pluto, with millions of regular SG troops. They'd stopped just about all flights around the Solar System and had sealed off the Pluto Cloud as well. They were even close to shutting down the entire One Arm. Cronx's friends described the situation as being no different than if the SG had declared martial law.

In the entire 600-plus-year history of the Fourth Empire, nothing like this had ever happened before.

Lieutenant Cronx reached the *StratoVox*'s flight deck to find the place in chaos: crewmen running everywhere, officers shouting orders above the wailing sirens, strobe lights flashing, bells ringing. Tension and anxiety were thick in the air.

The flight deck itself was supposed to be a monument to advanced Empire technology. It was contained within the ship's large, multitiered control bubble, which in turn was located near the forward point of the vessel's enormous wedge shape. The bubble was like a small city, large enough to hold 3,000 people. The bridge itself, it being on the highest level of this small metropolis, could hold more than 500 souls. It took all of these people, many serving in traditional if redundant capacities, to keep the ship running properly. Only this way could Starcrashers travel through space at speeds of one light-year every thirty seconds.

The situation up on the bridge was no better than the flight deck below. Cronx reached his station, an isolated seat located next to the lower echelon of pilots known as acolyte steering and directly behind the forward weapons array. A crew of sixteen was sitting in two semicircles around this array; their commanding officer was seated in an elaborate control chair hovering about eight feet above them. If anything happened to this primary weapons officer, it was Cronx's job to take his place.

Until then, Cronx would have a front-row seat for whatever was about to happen. His station was very close to the edge of the control room's immense bubble; it was barely an arm's length away. All Cronx had to do was turn to his right and look directly out into space.

The ship's enormous scanning screens were floating in front of him. These screens showed everyone what the "eyes" of the ship were seeing. And what they were seeing at the moment was very frightening.

The seventy-two SG ships, many of them two-mile-long battle cruisers, were running in their dark gray and black SG battle colors. The ships were spread out for as far as the long-range scanners could see. SG ships were so big, they rarely traveled in packs of more than a dozen or so. This, however, looked like a victory parade; they seemed to go on forever.

Trouble was, in their sights, dead ahead, was a fleet of SF ships that seemed to go on forever as well. They were mostly battle cruisers, but several pocket cruisers, also known as *culverins*, were in evidence, too. There were six dozen SF ships in all, or exactly the same size as the SG fleet. And they were just 15,000 miles away.

This battle group had not been dispatched by Space Forces command. Instead, just like the SG force, it had collected itself over the past few weeks from disparate squadrons, called here at first upon hearing of the intense battles in and around the mid–Two Arm and then rushing to the aid of comrades asking for help. It had grown steadily over the turbulent weeks into the enormous numbers it boasted now.

Cronx had seen combat before. But like just about everyone else on board the *StratoVox*, his experiences had been against space pirates, merc armies, or other interstellar outlaws. Fights where the SG always came in with an overwhelming advantage in the number of ships, weapons, and of course, the ability to move in Supertime, which none of their opponents had.

But now, this . . . this was terrifying. The huge SG fleet was about to collide with an SF force equal both in size and capability. Both forces were flying in Supertime, both forces were armed with the same awesome weapons, and both were crewed with men of equal training and élan.

Cronx swallowed hard. He was about to witness one of the worst military disasters in the history of the Fourth Empire. Imperial warships were never meant to fight each other. They were designed with only two missions in mind: to bombard enemy planets and to fight in space against much slower enemy vessels. Taking on ion-powered ships was relatively easy. When flying in Supertime, Empire vessels could see their slower adversaries while knowing the enemy could not see them. All the Empire ship had to do was drop out of Supertime and unleash its weapons. It could be more like target practice than a battle.

Fighting an enemy in Supertime was totally different. First of all, your opponent could see you just as soon as you could see him. Not only did both sides have the same weapons and crews, they both had the same capabilities for maneuvering and stealth. Both were also capable of flying just as fast—and in Supertime that was close to 67 million miles per hour. Two Empire ships closing on one another then were doing so at 134 million miles per hour. Almost incomprehensible speed.

Nor did Empire ships carry any kind of deflection equipment, again because they were never made to fight each other. They had no shields to protect themselves from incoming fire, no energy-dispersal arrays to sap the lethality from an adversary's fusillade. The only defense they had against an all-Supertime fight was a tactic known as *popping*.

When Empire ships traveled in Supertime, they were moving not so much in physical space as they were in time. The prop core found on every Empire warship was fed by the Big Generator, the mysterious, omnipotent power source located in the western desert back on Earth. This unknown power enabled the vessel to enter the seventh dimension and move very quickly in time.

Empire commanders were told that should an enemy ship ever enter Supertime—theoretically an impossibility, though it had happened on at least one occasion—then one way to avoid their incoming barrages was to slow down a bit, not in space but in time, just as the enemy fusillade was on its way. Essentially by putting on the brakes, just for a fraction of a second, the enemy barrage would reach its target just a little bit too early—and miss.

Popping was a spectacular thing to watch in action. All Empire ship commanders were required to practice it a few times early in their training, against fake blasts, of course. At high speeds, with leeway measured in microfractions of seconds, popping was an art form that no Empire ship CO ever thought he'd have to use.

Until now.

There were no hailing calls.

No challenges or ultimatums. No communications at all.

The scanning screens aboard the *StratoVox* were screaming that the SF fleet's weapons had powered up; all of the SG ships' weapons had just come on-line, too. Up until now, the fighting in and around the No-Fly Zone had consisted of brief clashes between individual vessels or small groups of ships, and only after much haranguing and posturing between opposing commanders. Now, these two grand fleets were ready to open up on each other without any prior taunts or threats— willing to let fate decide who would be left alive when it was over.

More blaring and beeping alarms distracted Cronx now. He looked up at the scanning screens again and saw the SF fleet was now just 10,000 miles away and still coming on very quickly.

He heard the booming voice of McLyx rising from behind him. "Train weapons!"

"Weapons trained, sir!" came the response from the weapons officers, all twelve of them.

"Prepare to fire."

"Preparing to fire, sir!"

Cronx felt his stomach turn over once again. Up until this moment he'd believed that despite the fighting and bad blood between the SF and SG, the damage that had been done already could be repaired somehow. But now, with these two gigantic fleets about to hit each other head-on . . . well, there'd really be no stepping back from this. Cronx checked the ship's position; ironically enough, they were just about in the middle of the No-Fly Zone, very near the place where the battle between the REF and the Two Arm invaders had supposedly taken place a month before. If there hadn't been a battle then, Cronx thought, there was certainly going to be one now.

The scans began screaming again. The column of SF ships was now just 5,000 miles away and still coming straight at the SG fleet. As the *StratoVox*'s weapons sections began tracking multiple targets, there came another bellowing order from McLyx.

"Ready all forward weapons."

"All forward weapons ready, sir."

Cronx gripped his seat tight. Was there any way to turn back from this? Any way both fleets would just veer off and go their separate ways, and preserve the integrity of the Empire for just a little while longer?

The answer was no, for just a moment later, McLyx screamed the fateful words: *"Open fire!"*

The *StratoVox* shuddered as every weapon on board fired at once. Space itself began shaking as the rest of the SG fleet followed suit. With tens of thousands of weapons blazing, the storm of SG destructo-rays tore into the SF ships. Thousands of gigantic explosions along thousands of miles of space. Then the *StratoVox*'s scans began blaring yet again: The SF ships were firing back.

The main weapons for both opponents were Z-beam guns. Their killing rays appeared in the form of thick blue bolts. Fired from a long distance, these bolts originated as pulses of incredibly bright light. Once a bolt got close to its target, the pulses coalesced into mile-long beams. Cronx now saw thousands of these beams flying right at him, even as the immense *StratoVox* began twisting and turning through space.

He was terrified—and he was sure many others on the bridge were terrified, too. This was already so unlike anything they'd ever faced, it *was* a waking nightmare, payback, for all those times they'd overwhelmed poorly armed, poorly trained adversaries in the past.

Ships were taking hits all around him. Some SG vessels were disappearing in puffs of sickly green fire. The *StratoVox* was gyrating itself through incredible, seemingly impossible maneuvers. In all his years riding them, Cronx had no idea Starcrashers could move like this.

At last, the two fleets collided. Cronx was suddenly looking out at a sky full of blue and white Starcrashers, all of them adorned with the star symbols of the Space Forces. This was another frighteningly new experience for him. He had never seen a Starcrasher in battle, not from this perspective. He was astonished by just how many weapons were firing off these gigantic ships: tens of thousands of bright blue and green streaks flying out in every direction, even as so many storms of multicolored beams were being fired at them.

It went on like this for what seemed like an eternity. Cronx was being thrown violently back and forth, even though he was pinned to his seat by his safety force field. The main weapons system officer was screaming at his forward array gunners, who were sending out megatons of destructo-rays, some finding their targets but many not. *Better him than me,* Cronx caught himself thinking. He could barely breathe, never mind move and actually operate a weapons system. The blaring of the defensive-systems communication array was earsplitting. Its mechanical voice was screaming at full pitch, but the control room was already filled with so many Klaxons and sirens wailing, it was very hard to think straight, never mind hear anything.

This cacophony made it almost impossible to decipher what the ghostly electronic voice was saying. But somehow one of the ship's twelve pilots heard the warning and displayed it up on the floating viz screens: An SF warship, the venerable *NovaVox*, was closing fast on one of the *StratoVox's* escort ships, the *VegasVox*, which had already sustained battle damage. Cronx could clearly see the wounded *VegasVox* off starboard side. A plume of jet-black smoke was streaming from its aft section; another was spewing out from behind its control-deck bubble. The *Vegas* had taken two random blasts from an SF *culverin*. Normally, two stray Z-gun blasts would cause little more than minor damage. But either by incredibly bad luck or the whim of the cosmos, these random blasts had hit two of the gigantic ship's most vulnerable spots. One had destroyed the *Vegas*'s main communications bubble; the other had exploded directly on top of its prop core. This meant the *Vegas* was without full prop-core operation and had no means to receive communications. It had no idea the SF warship *NovaVox* was coming right at it.

The SF ship opened up at just twenty miles out. The commanders aboard the *Vegas* only became aware that a massive fusillade was incoming when their forward scans suddenly lit up. The *Vegas*'s CO immediately ordered his ship to pop, but the *Vegas*'s prop core did not respond. It was still maintaining full speed but failing quickly. The SF barrage hit the *Vegas* full force an instant later. Its prop core blew up, and the gigantic ship split in two. All this happened not in seconds but in microseconds. The prop-core disintegration lit off a series of nuclear explosions, and 1/4000th of a second later, opened up a tiny black hole. The *StratoVox* peeled off just in time, but the SF *NovaVox*, coming on strong and not really expecting the SG ship to fail in its popping, was not so lucky. It slammed right into the *Vegas*, causing everything from its control bubble back to its cargo holds to simply disintegrate. The ship's rear magazines exploded, causing the *Nova's* prop core to blow, sending out another ripple of nuclear blasts and creating yet another black hole; this, just seconds after the first singularity came into being.

The resulting explosion was so powerful, many gunners in nearby ships were blinded permanently by the flash. The space-time fabric was torn for a thousand miles around. Just like that, the two enormous ships simply ceased to exist.

There were no survivors. There couldn't be.

More than 40,000 were dead.

• • •

Cronx had turned away from the apocalyptic scene at the last possible moment, thus preserving his sight. Still, one side of his face was severely burned. The heat had been so intense, it actually singed his hair.

The *StratoVox* veered right again, pressing Cronx against the side of the clear control bubble. He suppressed the urge to vomit as he saw hundreds of bodies go streaming by, all lifeless, some aflame. Some even seemed to be beckoning for him to join them. The nightmare continued.

Out beyond the massive debris field, Cronx could see dozens of ships on both sides still engaging each other, still firing madly. In the span of five quick heartbeats, three gigantic battle cruisers blew up, with two more smaller vessels being sucked into the resulting singularities. A few seconds later, the *StratoVox* flashed by a collision between two *culverins*. Another terrifying moment passed, then Cronx saw yet another SG battle cruiser explode under a broadside delivered pointblank from a SF warship riding alongside. This was madness, yet Cronx could not look away. His eyes felt like they, too, were on fire. He could hardly see, could hardly determine who was firing at who, or whose ships were being blown up, or whose ships were triumphant. All he could see on the outside were blue flashes and hot green fire.

Around the control bubble nearly everyone had their hands up to the eyes or were turned away from the effects of the blinding battle just outside their bubble. The control teams seemed petrified in stone. Faces white, drained of blood, none could believe what was happening, like small pieces of madness locked inside one grand madness.

Cronx looked ahead of him again. The main forward weapons officer was still hanging over his array, trying to pick out the shouted orders coming from McLyx above the din and transmit them to his gunners. Then this officer suddenly stopped what he was doing and looked back at Cronx, still pinned to his seat.

"Get ready!" he yelled at Cronx.

An instant later, a bolt of destructo-ray came through the side of the control bubble and blew the forward weapons officer to subatomic bits.

The direct hit continued on through the bridge, killing a dozen more of the steering crew before smashing into the auxiliary communications bubbler. The rush of air leaking out of the perforated enclosure was deafening, even as the control bubble began sealing itself. The deck was suddenly running with bubbler acids, blood, and gruesome body parts. The survivors were stunned. Death had come so fast to their colleagues, it hadn't even registered yet. McLyx was still screaming out firing orders, but no one was paying attention to him. The *StratoVox* had been in hundreds of battles in the last half century and had never lost a man. Now it seemed like everyone on the deck was soaked in blood.

Though he'd been cut on his head and face by pieces of broken superglass, Cronx was still somehow able to get his arms and legs moving. He staggered over to the weapons array. The blast hole had sealed completely by now, but it did nothing to clean away the gore that was spread everywhere. Cronx studied the battered weapons array. It was about 80 percent destroyed. Half of the gun crew had been killed as well. But that meant 20 percent of the weapons and six men were still able to operate. He started screaming firing orders, telling the surviving gunners to fire whatever weapons were available. No need to sight targets, he told them, and certainly no need to take aim. Following the orders McLyx was screaming to everybody, he was telling his men to simply fire every gun available, as quickly as possible.

All this made for a bizarre theater of sorts. The *StratoVox* was coursing its way through the storm of Z-beam fire and growing clouds of wreckage. The tradition of the ship called for the main steering crew—thirteen pilots in all—to reply to any command in unison, like some kind of dark choir. The same was true for the communications teams, the navigation teams, and so on. Each was made up of thirteen members. So whenever McLyx bellowed an order—a maneuver, a call to open fire, a check on his position—among the general chaos of the battle there came a chorus of responses, almost delivered in three-part harmony. When they were attacking poorly armed pirates or rogue merc armies with virtual impunity, these strange songs took on an almost mystical timbre. Now they were simply nonsensical and disturbing.

Added to this were the effects of popping the *StratoVox*. Whenever a ship slowed down a bit in time, everyone aboard slowed down, too. It was a very unsettling feeling: the human heart literally skipped several beats, leading to a moment of dizziness and disorientation, only to have these effects suddenly go in reverse once the body caught up with the right time frame.

In this moment, everyone on the bridge took on a ghostly glow, similar to the aura that appeared whenever a Starcrasher passed through a star. The *StratoVox* was now popping so often, the entire flight deck was bathed in the strange radiance. At the same time, the ship continued to maneuver wildly around the blizzard of SF Z-beam fire coming its way. After many long minutes of this, Cronx was not just worried about his stomach turning itself inside out, he found himself fighting to remain conscious.

Then came another blast; this one shot through the bubble top just a few feet above Cronx's head. It tore out what was left of the power tubes feeding his weapons array and kept on going, pinging around the bridge, killing another dozen random souls, including the rest of his gun crew. A few inches either way, and Cronx would have been minus his head.

Bleeding profusely, Cronx fell to the bloody deck and stayed there. He had the distinct feeling that the *StratoVox* was careening out of control, tumbling through the maze of warships bombarding each other. Blood began filling his eyes. Another blast came in and wiped out the entire communications team. Another took out the acolytes.

The screams of the wounded became horrifying. The ship twisted again, and Cronx slid right up against the superglass bubble, eyes looking out.

That was the only way he was able to see what happened next.

Throughout all this, McLyx was screaming out firing orders. His strategy was to fire all of his guns at once, as the SF ships were so thick around him that just by numbers alone he hoped he would hit something. That the other SG ships flying wildly alongside him had to avoid being a target apparently had little concern for him. This was war, and people died on both sides, and in the end it only mattered how many ships were left and who was controlling those ships.

It was in the midst of all this—the firing, the popping, the bizarre chorus, McLyx screaming, the dead and the dying—that a very bizarre event took place.

Cronx, his head practically stuck to the side of the bubble, was looking down as the swirling fight increased even further in intensity. Suddenly, there was a bright flash of light right below him, but it did not come from an explosion. This was pure white light, and it seemed to tear a piece of space right in two. Before this could register in Cronx's brain, a shape emerged from this flash of light. It was huge and black and full of lights. It was ship. A Starcrasher of sorts, but immediately Cronx knew it was not a combat ship. Not a typical one, anyway.

It was only by luck that he saw the ship emerge from the crackle of bright white light—and it did not come out smoothly. Rather it came out sideways, as if it were out of control, which meant it wasn't dropping out of Supertime. It also seemed at first that this strange ship was on fire, its quarter deck ablaze in a deep orange glow. And Cronx swore he detected a noise when this vessel so suddenly came into view, though this would have been impossible as there was no sound in space. But he was certain he heard a huge *crack* just a microsecond before the strange ship appeared.

How strange was this? A ship appearing out of nowhere, in the midst of this titanic battle, in the middle of the now-infamous No-Fly zone . . .

The mysterious vessel did not gain any sort of control after emerging from God knows where. It was careening all over the sky, just missing collisions with both SF and SG warships, but taking massive fusillades from both sides. Yet heavy electrical flashes could be seen going off inside as well, as if the vessel was undergoing a massive electrical storm within, even before it was hit and sent tumbling wildly all over space.

But then, everything got even stranger.

The *StratoVox* twisted this way, and the ghost ship twisted that, and suddenly they were heading right for each other. A call from the navigation team caused the *StratoVox* to veer out of the way at just the last moment. The mystery ship roared by them, not 1,000 yards off its starboard side, just seconds later.

It was so close, Cronx could read its serial numbers as it swept by.

And by this he was stunned.

"This is impossible!" he shouted.

The ship's serial number was X30499.

That number belonged to one of the six cargo 'crashers stolen by the Two Arm invaders, a ship the SG claimed it destroyed near this very spot in space, not a month ago. . . .

The ship named the *Resonance 133*.

10

The gigantic crevice was located a mile south of the ancient pyramid. It was hidden from view on one side by a set of craggy mountains. On the other was a huge impact crater that, at two billion years, was nearly as old as the pyramid itself.

The crevice was virtually bottomless. It was 2,000 feet at its widest and three miles long. Streams of putrid gases, rising from geostrophic activities near this tiny moon's inner core, further obscured the immediate area. Long shadows from two nearby suns only added to the permanent murk.

There was no atmosphere here. This dirty little rock had been bypassed by the Ancient Engineers when they puffed the Galaxy thousands of years before simply because of the presence of the pyramid. It was considered fatally bad luck—then and now—to set foot on any body that held a pyramid. Problem was, there were many of them throughout the Galaxy.

The name of this moon was Bad News 666. It orbited the dead world of Megiddo. It was located just inside the No-Fly Zone, was home to the pyramid and the huge hole in the ground. For all these reasons, it was the perfect place to hide a starship.

This had been the first goal, to get to this place, the same forgotten rock where Joxx the Younger had hidden his super-starship, the *ShadoVox*, during the battle against the Two Arm invaders for Megiddo below. They knew the Starcrasher would fit into the crevice and would be covered by the gas plumes, the shadows, the forbidding terrain, and the curse of the pyramid. If they successfully passed through the Vanex Door and crossed over from Paradise, they agreed this was the first place they would go.

And this was where the *Resonance 133* lay now.

That the ship appeared in the middle of one of the largest, most terrible battles ever fought in the history of the Empires—that was just an odd coincidence. That it had been hit many times with stray destructo-rays fired by both sides, mortally wounding it, well, that was a random event, too, part of the joke, so to speak. By all rights the ship should not have been able to fly after that, or even stay in one piece. But it did. That it reached here, the place it was supposed to go, without any of its power systems working, without any sort of flight controls intact, with a dead star engine *and* a blown prop core, *that* was near miraculous.

From the instant the ship had flown through the Vanex Door, Nature sought to rain nothing but chaos upon the *Resonance 133*.

An entire bus of control room string circuits burst the moment the ship left Paradise and entered the far side of the Twenty 'n Six field. A violent subatomic pulse went through the vessel $1/1,000,000,000$ of a second later, killing all internal illumination, tanking the gravity screens, and knocking out both the primary and the secondary environmental systems. Everyone aboard should have died at that point. But they didn't.

It took the ship exactly thirty-three seconds to pass through the twenty-sixth dimension. Because the place was filled with ghouls and undead and the trash of an entire civilization floating in a kind of starless void, all kinds of debris slammed up against the huge vessel in that horrible half minute.

Then the big cargo ship finally popped out the other side, only to find itself in the middle of the historic battle. There were a series of mind-blowing concussions caused by the shock waves from the fighting; they battered the cargo 'crasher the instant it emerged. The two-mile-long ship then plowed its way through the storm of Z-beam fire, taking hundreds if not thousands of direct hits. It forged on, however, powerless, and quickly left the battle area, with no one in pursuit. It reached Bad News 666 just moments later.

The interior of the ship was still dark. There were only seven souls aboard now; they had left with eight. One hundred percent of the ship's internal systems were glitched for good. The only light within was pouring through the lower part of the ship's superglass bubble. It was coming from the reflection of the devastated world of Megiddo nearby.

But even the light from the dead planet had turned strangely golden.

They remained still in silence for hours, not believing what they were seeing, not believing what had happened to them as soon as they'd crossed over. It shouldn't have been that much of a surprise to them, though. It even made sense, in a way.

It wasn't just that the *Resonance 133* flew here with no power, no controls, no good reason to do so. The seven souls within had changed, too—radically. They looked different. Their bodies were different. Their spirits were different. They didn't question it; they didn't have to. After a while, they knew the reason for their transformation. A child could have figured it out, though, could have told them it would happen. But the seven had been so caught up in everything else on the other side, the thought had never come to any of them that this might occur upon their return. And certainly not to Pater Tomm, who, of them all, should have been the expert on it.

Soon enough though, they'd begun to get used to it.

If that was possible.

"So, he was right," Tomm said finally, his voice cutting through the darkness of the ship's planning and control center.

"That the SF and SG were fighting each other?" Zarex said, his voice no longer booming. "Yes, he certainly was."

"Did anybody actually see him . . . ?"

Everyone indicated no. Except Calandrx.

"He may have been right beside me when we left. He may have been beside me when we passed through the twenty-six. But as soon as we passed back over, he was gone. And I think now, he will be gone forever."

Another silence. Their thoughts were bouncing all around the dark room. Off the tables and the chairs. Off the blackened, scorched walls. They did not need the light. Or the furniture. Nor did they have to speak. But at the moment, it seemed like the best thing to do.

"I suspect we will be able to talk about all things war now," Gordon said. He was perched on the edge of the room's huge planning table. Not sitting, but simply balancing perfectly on its tip.

"Talk about war again?" Tomm replied. He was hanging from the ceiling. "Aren't we the lucky ones."

"At least now we know how and where the REF managed to disappear to," Berx spoke up. He, too, was perched on the edge of the big table, a very comfortable position for him. "And why each time they come and go, things get that much more worse."

"I fear there will be a gathering of forces soon," Klaaz said, his voice strong. He, too, hung off the ceiling. "Them against us, and they will be overwhelming if we don't act. Our mission here is now different, but at the same time, it is exactly the same."

"Yes, we still must carry out the plan," Erx said, invisible in a darkened corner. "Just because this . . . this has happened to us, doesn't mean we don't have things to do. In fact, we'll have to do much, much more. There is still a cause to be won. Missions we must see through. Places we all have to go."

A murmur of agreement.

"All true," Tomm said, adding, "But at least now we won't have to take the ship."

11

No light. No sound either. The thick smell of iodine and seared cloth. A trace of burned apples . . .

Hunter's heart was in his boots, his soul was split in two. He was still on the beach in Paradise, touching Xara's face, his lips pressed up against hers. But at the same time, he found himself here, sitting in the stink and the dark.

He had never felt this low. He didn't want to be here. As the scenes of Paradise slowly faded, leaving only the murk, what he wanted was to go back immediately, to be in the warmth and light again. To kiss her again. And this time to stay there with her forever and not make the same mistake twice. But how? How could he pass back over? How could he return so quickly that he might find her still standing on the beach? Then it hit him. Yes, there *was* a way to do it and do it fast. All he had to do to was unstrap the blaster rifle from his shoulder, insert the muzzle into his mouth, and pull the trigger. With his head blown off, he would surely be on his way back to Heaven. True, there was no guarantee that he'd wind up in Happy Valley. But at the moment, he was willing to take the chance.

He didn't think about it for a second longer. He took the

weapon off his arm, put the barrel in his mouth . . . and pulled the trigger.

The gun didn't go off.

He tried again. Nothing.

A third time. Still nothing.

He reached down the weapon's barrel, his fingers fumbling for the gun's power knob. It was turned off.

Idiot . . .

He couldn't even do this right. His spirits plunged even further, if that was possible. But at the same moment, a more rational part of his psyche kicked in. There would be plenty of opportunities to dance with death in what he was about to do. And people were counting on him to stay alive, at least a little while longer. To take the pipe now would leave a lot of them hanging, and a lot of them in danger, too. He pushed the gun away from him. He owed it to everyone else in the UPF to see this thing through just a bit longer.

But where was he exactly? In the complete darkness, it was impossible to tell. He reached out and touched the nearest thing to him. It was a wall, cold and damp. He took some of the moisture onto his fingertips, then pressed it to his tongue. Bingo . . . It tasted of atomic hydro-gas, the lifeblood of any Starcrasher.

So, he *was* aboard a vessel belonging to the Empire; that much was established. He took out his quadtrol, the universal handheld device that could give a reading on just about anything. Luckily, it had survived the ride back intact. He asked the quadtrol to determine the speed of the vessel he was on. The response came back: "Point nine Supertime." This meant the ship was flying at about nine-tenths the speed of Supertime. He asked the quadtrol the name of the ship he was on. The reply: "The *ShadoVox*."

That sealed it. Just as advertised, the Echo 999.9 had returned him to the exact spot from which he'd departed. He was back in his prison cell. Before he left, though, there had been a bare light in his jail. But not now . . .

How much time had passed? Had he been gone a month? Had Vanex's time-advance solution worked? Or had he been transported back just a few moments after he'd left, just long enough for the cell light to burn out? If that was true, then he was still on his way to his execution, and his chance to see Xara again might come very soon after all.

All he had to do was rub his face, though—that's how he got his answer. He was sporting at least four weeks of stubble. And the hair on his head was much longer, too. Vanex's manipulation of the Echo 999.9's time element *had* worked. It was now about a month and a few days after the battle that never was.

He retrieved the blaster rifle and located its power knob again. He finally turned it on properly, but only to its lowest setting. He intended to use the glow that would result on the weapon's tip for illumination, so he could at least see his immediate surroundings. But he did not hear the customary hum of the weapon warming up, nor was its power tube crackling as it would if the weapon had held its full charge. This was not good. If the gun crapped out now, it would be a bad start to what was already sure to be a hazardous journey.

It took what seemed like forever, but finally the tip of the weapon began glowing, albeit very faintly. It was just enough light for him to check his environs. Yep, same old jail cell. Walls, floor, ceiling, locked door. He put the glowing muzzle down near his wrist, so he could see his ancient flight watch. People in the Galaxy weren't really into time; its measurement was relative to wherever you were standing at the moment, so trying to keep track of it galaxy-wide was nearly impossible. But Hunter was a time freak; it meant everything to him. And at the moment, knowing the correct time was crucial for what lay ahead.

He pushed a series of buttons along the watch dial and then set the countdown function. He was giving himself five minutes since arriving here, and exactly an hour between the time he left and when the *Resonance 133* had started its trip back across. That meant if the *R133* made it safely, then the rest of the UPF fleet would arrive exactly six days, twenty-two hours, and fifty-five minutes from now.

Much had to be done in that short amount of time.

His watch set, Hunter cranked up the power knob on the gun. His next intention was to blast the lock off the prison door. But not only was the weapon not warming up, the faint glow was growing even fainter. His heart sank further. There hadn't been enough pop in this thing to give his tongue a flesh wound, never mind blow his brains out. As for blasting his way out of the jail cell, that was now out of the question. It was as if all the gun's lethality had been drained out of it back in Heaven.

He made one desperate attempt to blow the lock, but it was hopeless. By pulling the trigger, he only managed to kill the weapon's meager power supply even quicker. A moment later, he was plunged back into complete darkness again.

Damn . . .

He slumped back against the wall, reached into his pocket, and came out with one of the apples. It was burning hot. He dropped it to the floor, but it bounced right back up and into his hand again. *Strange . . .*

Why was there no light in his cell? Maybe there was a power problem on the ship itself. He retrieved the quadtrol again and asked how many people were on board. In typical quadtrol language, the reply came back: "Less than three." Besides himself, that meant only one other person. Was that possible?

He asked the quadtrol to gauge the condition of the ship. The reply was unsettling: "Overall integrity soon to fail."

Not good . . .

He asked the quadtrol why. This reply was startling: the ship was on a collision course with a class-M planet.

Hunter was beginning to think the quadtrol had become skewed in the crossover, too, though the devices were almost never wrong. He asked it a summary question: Was it true that there was one other person on board the ship, and that person was allowing it to crash into a planet?

The answer came back as yes.

Hunter put his back up against the damp wall again, trying to figure out exactly what this meant. He was locked in the cell, in complete darkness, as the ship, apparently with a madman at the helm, was heading right for a planet at close to Supertime speed.

Could it get any worse than that?

Almost unconsciously, he brought the apple up to his mouth and took a huge bite.

Good thing he brought them along, he thought.

Wouldn't want to get hungry now.

Twenty-two Decks Above

The sixteen aluminum medals on the wall of the *ShadoVox*'s luxurious command cabin had become tarnished.

They were hanging next to twelve jewel-encrusted swords; like the medals, they'd been awarded for bravery and valor. But they, too, were looking dull. Between the two largest swords was a once-brilliant star-pearl combat helmet, oversized by one-third, as if the designer knew extra room would be needed to contain the owner's considerable ego. It was also showing the early signs of rust. Below the helmet, a pure white combat suit hung limply. The costume, once feared by many a foe, now looked curiously small and empty.

At one time, the trophies and the clothes were subjected to thrice-daily cleaning and repositioning, as their proud owner never wanted them to be a millimeter out of place. But now they were out of alignment, especially the medals. Any time the *ShadoVox* moved right or left, the medals would sway, but not in unison.

This was all that was left of the shrinking world of Joxx the Younger, son of the Supreme High Commander of the Solar Guards, nephew to the Great O'Nay, and at one time just three notches away from being Emperor of the Galaxy itself.

The musty control room was the brains of the most powerful, most advanced, most feared ship in all of the Solar Guards' space fleets. But now it was a mess. In the corners were piles of discarded transdermal injectors. On just about every flat surface, the tell tale leftover stains from a recently consumed pile of *jamma*, the highly addictive drug favored by the Empire's lower elements.

And sitting in the chair in the deck's observation bubble was Joxx himself, a pile of recent unwrapped *jamma* staring him in the face.

There was a time when Joxx had been considered the brightest star in the Empire's military. He bore chiseled good looks, a long mane of light-blond hair, and a natural swagger others would have died for. Just thirty years old, he was a youngster compared to his relatives, those lucky enough to have the Holy Blood in their veins. Despite his young age, he was the most highly decorated field officer in the SG, indeed, in all of the Empire's forces. He had won hundreds of battles against renegade mercenary armies and outer Fringe space pirates. He had conquered not just individual star systems but entire star clusters.

In fact, Joxx and his super starship had never lost a battle. Until recently, that is.

And while his close relatives would live to six or seven hundred years or even more if they played their cards right, at the moment, Joxx didn't look like he'd live to see another day.

Few knew what really happened to him after his failed attempt to stop the Two Arm invaders while defending the planet of Megiddo.

The official report, distributed to the masses, said Joxx had been kidnapped by the invaders, although briefly, and had somehow managed to escape from them. But three things were less well-known: that Joxx had been taken on a bizarre mind ring trip by Hawk Hunter during his short captivity, that Hunter was in fact the leader of the invaders, and that upon returning from the mind ring trip, Joxx was rescued by his own forces and Hunter was captured, imprisoned, and secretly sentenced to death.

But while all that was true, Joxx wasn't really sure he'd been rescued from anything. The mind ring trip Hunter had forced him to take had changed him in ways he'd never thought possible. Because of Hunter's manipulation of the rings' sequences, Joxx had been shown just how morally corrupt the Fourth Empire was and how deceitful and cruel the Second Empire had been as well. He'd also seen the direct line from that bloody, repressive second regime to the one presently in power, the seat from which he was but three heartbeats away. More chilling, he'd learned that the Emperor O'Nay was responsible for both the tyranny of the Second

Empire and the absolute authoritarianism of the present one. Or at least that's what the mind ring trip had led both Joxx and Hunter to believe.

If it was all true, then Joxx had been fooled, just as everyone in the ruling family had been fooled, as well as the citizens of the Empire itself. Fooled into thinking that the Empire had a divine right to claim everything and everybody in the Galaxy, no matter what the means were, simply because its leaders were so entitled, so enlightened, they could do no wrong.

But the dark truth, at least within the mind ring trip, told a different tale. It said the Empires had been set up and manipulated by forces way outside the normal realm of life. In fact, there was the possibility, this being the deepest, darkest secret, that those pulling the strings of the present galactic empire were not human at all.

Joxx had been on a vicious downward spiral since learning all this. First confronting his father and then refusing an audience with the Emperor, he'd gone on a *jamma* bender that began with a crawl though the more notorious drug dens in Big Bright City. After meeting a witch who seemed to know more about him than he did himself, Joxx decided to return to the *ShadoVox*, which at the time was transporting Hunter to his execution site, and do the right thing.

In disguise and trying to remain inconspicuous, he was leaving from the main spaceport just outside Big Bright City, four pounds of jamma stuffed in his boots, when he had another strange encounter, this one with an Imperial Court spy. The man approached him just as Joxx was about to climb aboard a single-seat Swiper, a small ultraspeedy vessel about the size of a scout ship. The spy somehow knew what Joxx was about to do and said he had a way of making it go that much easier. The spy then handed Joxx a small package and told him to deliver it to the person he was setting out to see. Joxx did just as the spy told him. Reaching his old ship again via a series of quick shortcuts, the first thing Joxx did was visit Hunter in his jail cell at the bottom of the enormous vessel. Very few words were spoken to the heroic space pilot that day. Instead, Joxx just handed him the spy's package and left. The package turned out to contain the top secret Echo 999.9 holo-girl capsule.

When the guards checked the prison cell a short time later, Hunter was gone.

Life had become a day-to-day, minute-to-minute proposition for Joxx ever since this incident. In the past month he'd done little else but wander the star lanes aimlessly, mostly up and down the Four Arm, snorting jamma and trying to dream up the perfect demise for a fallen angel such as him.

He'd jettisoned the temporary crew who'd helmed the *ShadoVox* after the disaster at Megiddo. (His original crew, elite and almost as well-known as he, had abandoned him at the height of the campaign, leaving him buried in the rubble of his command post and fleeing the embattled planet. Of everything that had happened to him in the past month, that might have been the cruelest cut of all.) As he had designed the *ShadoVox* himself, Joxx had no problem driving it alone in space. The flight bubblers handled all but the most important functions, and these he took care of himself. But he couldn't be everywhere at once. The ship was two miles long, and he'd yet to leave the observatory bubble adjacent to the control room for anything. Farther down the main passageway, just about out of earshot, the ship's comm room was echoing with messages from Earth ordering Joxx and the *ShadoVox* to return immediately. But there was no one on hand to reply, so the messages went unheeded. Joxx had not spoken to anyone back on Earth in nearly four weeks. Ironically, or perhaps fatefully, he had no idea then that the Empire was in as much turmoil as his own life.

Possibly even more.

One of the oldest traditions in the Galaxy had to do with the disposal of old space vessels. When a ship was used up, when it had passed its point of usefulness, or even when it had come to be considered unlucky, its owner would crash it into a graveyard planet, where salvagers could pick away at the carcass and retrieve anything that might be made workable again.

Joxx had wondered in these aimless days if the same thing could be done for a man's soul. By crashing it, by busting it up into a million pieces, could some of it then be found, rehabilitated, and maybe go on to be part of a more useful spirit?

Somewhere between his second and third pound of jamma, he decided to find out.

Which was why the *ShadoVox* was now heading straight for a world named Junky Munky 2.

A graveyard planet.

Hunter saw the faint light of his quadtrol blink once in the darkness.

The reading was disheartening. The *ShadoVox* was still on course to crash into the deserted class-M planet and would hit said planet very soon.

He leaned back and wondered what it would feel like, just moments before impact. The UPF would be on its own, after all, he thought. That is, if they made it to the other side at all. But would they be able to carry on the fight to Earth without him? He'd always felt strongly that he had been transported here to the seventy-third century for one reason only: to right the wrong that had been committed against the original peoples of Earth. His mission was to carry the American flag, as well as all of the others, back to the Mother Planet, returning them to where they belonged. How did his death at the bottom of a haunted ship serve that purpose? Had the cosmos been wrong all along? Was this the punch line of the long-awaited cosmic joke? Were the forces that brought him here, to this far-flung century, powerless to stop what was about to happen to him now? Or was he brought here simply to become a martyr for the cause?

There was no way he could know, of course, but then again, all was not lost. There was a silver lining to this very dark cloud. Because at the end of it all, he hoped, would be a way to return to that place from where he'd just come. And have another chance to walk the fields of Heaven with Xara.

And that wouldn't be so bad.

He would just have to endure these last few minutes of torture, and then crushing pain and death and—

Suddenly he heard a very strange sound. He looked to his left and saw the locked door of the cell slowly open. The creaking alone chilled him to the bone. No one was on the other side. No one had touched the clasp or disabled the electronic bolt. It was as if it had opened on its own.

Hunter was astonished. That door had been locked, sealed, practically ion-welded shut just seconds before. His quadtrol had confirmed it. Yet now it was wide open, and the bare light of the passageway was flooding in.

How could this have happened? How could a locked door suddenly spring open? How could his soul, so close to crossing over once again, be dragged back at this last moment?

He didn't have a clue.

Purely by instinct, he checked his quadtrol screen. The *ShadoVox* would hit the graveyard planet in less than five minutes.

He stayed frozen in place. He desperately wanted to see Xara again—but could the reunion wait just a little while longer?

He thought about this for a few moments, then jumped up and was out of the cell an instant later.

Up in the observatory bubble, the planet Junky Munkyz was quickly filling the field of view.

Joxx looked up from his pile of *jamma* and smiled weakly. It would all be over very soon.

Or would it?

He felt the ship begin to accelerate; then came the bright flash that indicated the vessel had just jumped into Supertime. An instant later, the *ShadoVox went right through* the graveyard planet, coming out, intact, on the other side.

Stunned that he was still in one piece, Joxx tried to understand what had just occurred. Starcrashers could go so fast in both space and time that they could pass through planets, too, but only if they were going at full Supertime speed. And he had not been, until a moment ago.

What happened?

He was suddenly aware that he was no longer alone inside the control bubble. He looked up to see a man's face and recognized it immediately. But there was no shock in Joxx's dead eyes.

"I guess I'm not so surprised to see you again," Joxx mumbled, badly slurring his words. "You'll be haunting me for the rest of my life—or what is left of it."

Hunter bowed slightly. He'd boosted the ship's speed at the very last moment, saving them both. But that had been ten long seconds ago. Now he was simply astonished at just how bad Joxx looked. Gone were the youthful, handsome features, the cold clear eyes, the great mane near-white hair. Joxx seemed to have sunken in on himself, as if he'd spent the last century slumped in his chair, doing *jamma* and staring into empty space.

"I had no choice but to return here," Hunter finally told him. "That's how the device you gave me works."

He looked up at the rearview viz screen; the graveyard planet was disappearing from view.

"And I thought I got here just in time," Hunter said. Then he eyed the pile of jamma. "But maybe not . . ."

Joxx seemed almost unaware that Hunter had just saved his life.

"And you accomplished your mission?" he asked Hunter instead. "Wherever the hell you went?"

"Let's just say it's still an ongoing process," Hunter replied.

There came an uncomfortable silence between them. By all rights they should have been bitter enemies: Fourth Empire golden boy and a time-displaced iconoclast. But events had changed that.

"You know I still have dreams about them," Joxx began, mumbling again. "Those two young girls . . . being dragged away like that. . . ."

His voice trailed off, but Hunter knew what he was talking about. At the climax of their shared mind ring trip, he and Joxx had been chained together and brought aboard one of the huge ships that were carrying the dispossessed people of Earth to their prison in the sky. In this sequence, a mother and her two young daughters had run to Joxx for protection against the enormous prison guards; men had made a habit of going through the swarm of deportees, picking out all the attractive girls and forcing them to provide pleasures for them and more. Two huge guards literally ripped the girls from Joxx's protective arms, leading the SG high officer to pummel a third guard nearly to death—a violent and telling epiphany for Joxx, even though it was all taking place within a mind ring trip.

If any incident during the whole experience changed Joxx forever, that was it.

"So . . . what now?" he asked Hunter. "You're here, but I am still in command of this ship."

And suddenly Joxx had a gun in his hand. It was a huge blaster pistol, and its power light was burning a hole in Hunter's retinas. Meanwhile, he'd left his own dead weapon behind in the cell.

"I could throw you back into jail," Joxx said, "and make sure that others carry out the Emperor's orders to execute you."

Hunter had anticipated this moment.

"If that's what you feel you have to do," he told the SG officer plainly, "then, do it."

Joxx looked back up at Hunter, conflict raging in his sad eyes.

"But if I don't lock you back up," he finally said. "What is it that you'd want me to do? Certainly not join you . . ."

"No," Hunter replied quickly. "All I want is for you to let me go. Let me get to where I need to be."

Joxx laughed. "To play hero again?"

"Heroism has nothing to do with it," Hunter shot back. "Whether you know it or not, the situation is desperate—all over. If there is something I can do to prevent needless bloodshed and find some justice somewhere, well, I have no choice but to do it."

Joxx slumped even farther into his seat. "I used to know that feeling," he said under his breath.

He turned the huge blaster barrel down; it was almost as if he was no longer strong enough to hold it steady.

"Go," he said finally, sounding like a man ten times his age. "Go and do what you feel you have to do. That way people will remember at least one of us was a hero to the end."

Hunter stepped forward and almost shook Joxx's hand—but he thought better of it,

"No matter what happens," he said instead, "you've just

played your part. If you hadn't opened my cell door, then—"

Joxx just shook his head again. "Cell door? What are you talking about? I can barely open my own eyes. . . ."

With that, he just waved Hunter away and put his face back down into the pile of jamma. Hunter started to say something but stopped. He checked his watch; precious time was ticking away here. He would have to figure out the jail cell mystery later.

He stepped into the control room, made a few more adjustments, and then was quickly out the door.

Hunter ran down the long passageway, wondering which power tube would bring him to the ship's launching rooms.

He finally selected one, climbed aboard, and hit the jackpot the first time. In seconds he was walking out into a cavernous compartment deep in the belly of the beast known as the *ShadoVox*.

Here was a huge maw that looked out into space. The opening was covered with an invisible membrane that allowed ships to move freely in or out, while keeping the airless void of space at bay.

Hunter stood there for a moment. He really didn't have a second to waste, but he just had to look at the stars. He hadn't seen the real things in how long? Since he captured Joxx in his own ship, since the mind ring trip they both shared. Everything up above had been not been real since then.

So they were still there. That great wash of real stars, real constellations. Real hydrogen, burning off real gas and spewing out real nuclear dust. This was strange. Hunter almost felt like he was being energized by these pinpricks of light. Where the hell was he? The Four Arm? Had he ever been to the Four Arm before?

It didn't matter. This was the real world. Not a mind ring trip. Not the fields of Heaven. It felt different being back here. Not better, just different.

There was something else he hadn't seen in a long time.

He moved to the center of the launching bay now, reached into his pocket, and took out something that wasn't there just a few moments before. It was a container, oval with a white pearl finish. It was a Twenty 'n Six, the same kind of device that Vanex had used in conjunction with the Echo 999.9 to create the portal in and out of Paradise.

But this Twenty 'n Six contained something very personal to Hunter, just about the only thing he could call his own in this very strange world he'd found himself in. He took a deep breath and let it out slowly. He'd been doing a lot of trans-dimensional jumping lately, time jumping from here to eternity and back. What effect did it have on him? On his psyche? On his physiology? His mental awareness? He didn't know. But here he was, and this was going to be a crossroads for him. If he activated this capsule and the thing inside fizzled—well, he'd really be out here, way out here, without a paddle. And he would have no choice but to ride the *ShadoVox* down with Joxx, whenever the fallen SG hero decided again it was time to go. Not the most pleasant end to the story.

So, with one more deep breath, Hunter hit the capsule's activation button. There was a flash of light and then a long stream of green mist began tumbling out of the capsule. It gathered on the deck about ten feet away from him. There came another flash, brighter than Hunter could remember. So bright, he had to cover his eyes.

When he took his hand down, before him stood his F-16XL spacefighter, his famous Flying Machine.

He felt like the weight of the Galaxy had been lifted off his shoulders—at least for a moment. He was happy. Happy that his magnificent machine was still intact. Even better, it looked to be in good shape. He finally let out that long, deep breath and felt relief run through his body. Suddenly things didn't seem so dim as before.

What was this Flying Machine? What made it so magnificent? No one was really sure, including him. In some ways it was a figment of his imagination. Something from a dream he'd had back on Fools 6 one night soon after finding himself stranded on that very desolate planet. He awoke from a long slumber and just started writing down calculations, design cues, formulas. Where it all came from, he didn't know. But when he visited the ancient crash site of a huge Time Shifter warship just over the hill from his location, he salvaged approximately two tons of material and with the help of an electron torch fashioned the machine that stood before him now. He'd been tearing around the Milky Way in it ever since.

The strange craft didn't look like anything flying in the Galaxy these days. All Empire warships, big and small, were shaped like a wedge; all ion-powered civilian craft were, too. But Hunter's vessel was long and tubular, with two stubby wings sticking out of its midsection and two smaller wings protruding from its tail. The nose was stiletto sharp and featured a cockpit with a tear-shaped canopy. It was painted white with red and blue stars emblazoned on the tail and fuselage. Strangest of all, it had wheels to hold it off the ground. The wheel was a technology lost in the Galaxy more than 2,000 years before.

It was also the fastest thing in the Galaxy. Faster than any Starcrasher. In fact, where a Starcrasher could tool along at two light-years a minute, the cruising speed for Hunter's machine was two light-years *a second*. And he had yet to open up the throttles all the way.

He jumped in now and felt like he was back in the womb. All the controls survived the transdimensional jumps, which was good. Everything seemed a bit bigger though, by a factor of 10 percent or so. But this was normal for something that had lingered in the twenty-sixth dimension for a long period of time. It was OK with him. Sometimes, bigger *was* better.

One other oddity: way back when Hunter entered the craft in the Earth Race, he was required to give it a name, something that could be entered on the race roster and the betting slips. He'd simply written in plain text on his cockpit panel: *Flying Machine*. For whatever reason, when the craft came back from the twenty-sixth dimension this time, his notation had been altered. Now it just simply read: *F-Machine*.

And for some reason, he liked the sound of that, too.

He hit the ignition switch and again was relieved when the unique star engine roared to life.

His control panels were telling him everything was good to go. Nav systems, gravity amplifiers, comm sets, flight bubbler. Weapons. Everything was reading green.

But where was he off to exactly?

It was time to find out.

He reached into his other pocket, dug down deep beneath the apples, and took out the viz-image capsule Tomm had given him on the sly back in Paradise. He looked it over quickly. It seemed to have survived the trip back from Heaven as well. He activated the device and suddenly a life-size image of Pater Tomm materialized in midair above his left wing. The diminutive monk looked younger, his hair was shorter, his cassock less ragged than in more recent times. In fact, he looked exactly the way he did when Hunter first met him about two years before.

"You are activating this for only one reason," the space monk began, getting right to the point as usual. "Things are so bad that desperate measures have to be undertaken. Are you still in one piece?"

"So far," Hunter replied.

The image smiled, then as a sort of inside joke, produced a flask of slow-ship wine and took a healthy slug. Hunter wished the holo-image—and the wine—were real. He needed a belt right now.

"I have only given this to you because I believe in your cause and fear that it might be close to being lost," Tomm's image said now. "Is this the case?"

Hunter nodded glumly. "I think that's an accurate assessment."

"And it is a question of getting help—ships, soldiers, fighters—for the cause?"

"At the very least, yes."

Tomm nodded beatifically—a strange look for him.

"Then I want you to go someplace," the monk said. "Someplace few people even know exists. It is there only by one of the deepest secrets of the Galaxy. It is called simply, Far Planet. It is out on the Seven Arm."

Hunter held his hand up, stopping the image for a moment.

"The Seven Arm?" he asked. "I thought there was nothing out there."

That was certainly the prevailing opinion in the Galaxy. Of the Milky Way's nine major swirls, the seventh was thought to be the least populated, the least inhabited, the least hospitable. And because the galaxy was actually asymmetrical, it was also one of the farthest points from Earth. It was little more than a very long, very thin string of scattered stars that petered out at one of the last points that could be called part of the Milky Way. There was hardly an Empire presence much beyond the opening reaches of the place, and simply none at all a few light-years in. It was a rare occasion to encounter anyone who called the Seven Arm home. It boasted no kinds of special starship designs, no kinds of exotic foods, no particularly potent strains of slow-ship wine. Nothing.

Bottom line: no one ever went the Seven Arm, simply because there was never ever any reason to. Or at least that was the impression Hunter had always got.

But now Tomm's image was smiling. "I guess you have to be around as long as I have to know what is real and what is not in this universe," he said. "Just get to the Seven and find Far Planet. Then activate this device again. I will instruct you further from there."

The image began to disappear, but Hunter had one last question to ask. It was an important one.

"How do I find one planet on an entire arm?" he asked. "I mean, I know there aren't many stars out there, but there are certainly still millions of them. I could be out there for years looking for this place."

Tomm smiled again, took another swig from his flask, and pretended to hand it to Hunter.

"How do you get to this place?" he asked with a wide, strange grin, pulling back the flask. "My boy, how do you get anywhere in this great big galaxy? You use a map."

And with that, the image faded for good, leaving Hunter alone once again.

Now this was a problem. His F-Machine had some maps stored in its memory, and his quadtrol did, too. But a quick check of both showed only the most rudimentary directions to the unlucky Seven, and these ended just an hour or two into the mysterious arm. What he needed was a star chart, one that was up to date. Or as up to date as something pertaining to the Seven Arm could be.

He sat still in the cockpit thinking for a moment. Then it

came to him. He was still aboard the most powerful ship in the Galaxy. Even though its creator had faltered, the *ShadoVox*'s inner workings were still vital.

Hunter leaped from his machine and ran to the nearest control bubbler; several were attached to the far wall of the hangar. He pulled out his quadtrol's extension probe and mated it with the bubbler's primary-system "blood" line. Essentially every piece of information stored aboard the mighty ship was flowing through this main line just as blood flowed through a body. Hunter tapped into the artery and commanded the quadtrol to locate and copy any star charts pertaining to the Seven Arm. It took only a few seconds for his device to literally suck the information out of the *ShadoVox*'s memory stream.

Then he checked the time. He'd spent thirty minutes escaping from jail, saving Joxx, and now learning where he had to go. Precious time, well spent. But there was no reason to dawdle.

He ran back to his ship, climbed aboard, and restarted his power pack. His star engine once again roared to life in response. Canopy down, he raised the wheels and put the F-Machine about two feet off the deck. Then he pointed it out toward open space.

"Don't worry, Xara," he whispered. "I'll be back as soon as I can. . . ."

He hit the throttles and was two light-years away a second later.

12

Venus was the second planet in the Galaxy to be puffed.

Only Mars had come first when the mysterious geniuses known as the Ancient Engineers set out to make first the Solar System and then the Milky Way habitable for the human race. No longer was Earth's sister planet enshrouded in thick cumulus, raining hydrochloric acid. Like Earth, its cloud cover was now just 30 percent at any given time. Also like Earth, it now had one ocean that spread around the entire planet, pole to pole. This one surrounded two massive continents and several smaller ones. One of these was the island continent of Zros.

Venus served as a very exclusive getaway for the extended Imperial Family, those known as The Specials, and for these fortunate souls, Zros was the only place to be. They owned tens of thousands of summer palaces, seaside resorts, vineyards, and spas on the island. One was called *La-Shangri*. Located atop the high cliffs on the west coast of Zros, it was a three-tiered palace that literally stretched for miles. Many of its structures hung way out over the greenish pacific sea, and the local atmosphere was treated with a combination of hyacinth scent and nitrous oxide. A happy experience was guaranteed for anyone lucky enough to visit here.

This place was usually devoid of military personnel. But shortly after dawn on this dark day, the air above the resort was suddenly filled with combat vessels. One of these was a cruiser belonging to the Imperial Guards, the army whose sole purpose was the protection of the Emperor's family. It popped into view just above the highest spire of *La-Shangri*. A cadre of soldiers was instantly beamed out of its hold. In seconds, the palace roof was crawling with these Imperial bodyguards.

Half the guards secured the roof; the other half ran down a passageway and into the chateau's enormous function room. A huge saturnalia of Specials was in full swing here; indeed, the party had been going nonstop for days. There were more than a thousand people on hand, most of them beautiful young women. As always, the atmosphere was both sexual and dangerous.

It might have seemed odd, with the turmoil plaguing the Empire, that its untouchables were partying the nights away. But not really. History was filled with examples of uppers who danced while their empires burned. There was nothing different going on here.

Heads turned when the Imperial Guards burst in, though. Some of the revelers simply looked them up and down, then went back to their drinking and merriment. But others stopped in mid-dance step, wondering why the heavily armed soldiers were here. The chief guard pushed his way through the crowd, looking this way and that. Finally he spotted the person he'd come here to protect.

She was dressed all in black. Jacket. Miniskirt. Stockings. Boots. Her low-cut top showed a generous hint of breasts. Her hair was blonde and flowing over her shoulders. Even with the heavy make up, her face was stunning.

She was the Empress of the Galaxy, the wife of O'Nay Himself.

The guard approached her slowly, then went into a deep bow.

"A million pardons, my lady," he said. "But we must evacuate you back to Earth immediately."

The Empress waved him off. "Go away," she said.

The officer repeated his request, this time more urgently.

She danced up close to him; he could smell a strong scent of slow-ship wine coming from her.

"I'm having some fun for a change," the Empress whispered in his ear. "Why would I want to leave now?"

"My lady . . ."

Suddenly she had a goblet of sparkling blue liquid in her hand. Draining it in one gulp, she tossed the cup away. Then her jacket came off. The music became louder; the mixture of pulsating bass and ethereal strings turned hypnotic. She floated away and was quickly swallowed up by the crowd. She could just barely be seen now, eyes closed, dancing slowly.

With no little trepidation, the chief bodyguard waded into the throng after her. Arms and legs and faces and breasts blocked his view, giving way very slowly and reluctantly. Suddenly the Empress was in front of him again. Her eyes were locked on to his. She began dancing even closer. The lights went down. The other partygoers were suddenly very intimate with each other. Many of the women were now topless. The chief bodyguard began to sweat.

The Empress was dancing so close to him now, she was rubbing up against his chest. She'd been known to use this tactic before.

"I'm sorry, my lady," the officer finally said. "But there is an emergency, and we have orders to get you back to Earth as soon as possible."

She laughed drunkenly and began dancing away from him yet again. But at that moment, another small army of bodyguards burst into the room. They were private hires and did not carry the burden of imperial protocol. They quickly found their lesser-class clients and with no little ceremony began hustling them out of the hall.

The music suddenly stopped. The laughter died down. Someone screamed. Panic began to rise. Obviously, something big was going on.

Concerned now, the Empress sought out the bodyguard.

"What is it then?" she asked him harshly. "Just tell me."

"There has been another incident, my lady," he whispered

gravely. "Between the Space Forces and the Solar Guards—
out on the Two Arm."

She stared back at him, her painted face twisted in confusion. "One more clash between our own soldiers? So what?
These skirmishes have been happening for the past month,
correct?"

The officer nodded soberly. "Yes, my lady," he said. "But
this was not a skirmish. This was a major battle. Forty SG
Starcrashers were destroyed, at least ten from the SF were also
lost. Nearly a million of our soldiers have been killed."

The number stunned her. *"A million?"*

"Yes, and a devastating defeat for the Solar Guards," he
whispered to her now. "So bad, they are going full speed ahead
with their new decree."

"What new decree?" she asked. "I've not heard about this."

The Imperial officer just shook his head. She was probably
the only person in the Empire who hadn't heard of the SG's
latest radical step.

"They are declaring it the Inner Planets Defense Order," the
guard said. "It calls for nearly half of their capital warships to
return home from the other arms. That's an incredibly large
number of ships and men, my lady. And they will soon be
occupying the entire One Arm with them. As it is, they are
not allowing any SF ships into the Solar System. And now,
they will probably not let any of us out. This is not a good
thing, my lady."

Even she understood this. As bad as the rivalry between the
two services was, it also served to keep each one in check.
This was especially true for the more ambitious Solar Guards.

"Can the SG really do such a thing lawfully?" she asked the
officer, as the big hall further emptied out.

"They are *writing* the laws, ma'am," he told her. "They have
free rein when it comes to protecting the Emperor. Though
this is taking their mission to its limit, no one can stop them.
Not now. And that leads us to the real problem."

"And that is?"

The officer was suddenly right up to her ear. "With so many
Solar Guards in the One Arm and inside the Pluto Cloud, there
is a real chance for . . ."

"Yes . . . for?"

The man could barely speak the word. "My superiors think that you and the rest of your family are in personal danger," he said instead.

Now she just stared back at him, speechless.

"What are you talking about?" she asked him sternly. "A revolt?"

He looked her straight in the eye and said: "No, my lady, not a revolt. A *coup.*"

The Empress was put on the heavily armed warship, which in turn was surrounded by a small fleet of scout ships and spacefighters. The flight back to Earth took just a few minutes. Her vessel passed through the cordon of sentry ships the Solar Guards had put up in orbit around Earth. There were so many SG vessels, it was almost difficult to find a pathway through them.

The Empress's ship went directly to Special Number One. Her bodyguards requested that she linger on the floating city only long enough for her to put a few personal items together. Once packed, they would whisk her to a safer location, this being another floating city, a secret one, called Special Number Two, which at that moment was cruising high above the North Pole. From there, plans would be made to spirit her out of the Solar System and off the One Arm itself.

But of course the Empress would hear none of this. She demanded to be brought directly to the Imperial Court, the large room located on the bottom floor of the enormous Imperial Palace. This was the seat of power for the Galaxy.

The court was usually crowded with small armies of courtesans, brokers, relatives, lobbyists, priests, diplomats, military types from all services, aides, guards, and spies. Many, *many* spies. The goings-on here were a daily scene of controlled chaos, with those few lucky enough to actually be in a position to petition the Emperor—or more likely his close imperial flunkies—trying everything they could from cajoling, to bribes, to threats of bodily harm, to get their voices heard. Some of the time, Emperor O'Nay Himself was actually on hand, sitting in a hovering throne exactly fifty feet above the fray, staring out at the nothingness, while the excitement and confusion played out below. At times, the noise in the court could reach deafening proportions.

But now, as the Empress burst into the enormous gold-leaf room, it was the silence that was overwhelming. She stopped in her tracks, as did the company of Imperial Guards traveling with her.

She couldn't believe her eyes.

The court was empty.

Her face fell; her pretty features seemed to disappear. For the first time in recent memory, she actually looked all of her 375 years.

"This . . . has never happened before," she whispered.

She turned to back to the bodyguards.

"Where is my husband?"

The chief bodyguard stepped forward again. "He was transferred to the secure location over the pole, my lady," the man told her nervously. "Which is why we want—"

"I could care less what you want," she snapped back at him. "Has *everyone* cleared out up here? Is there no one left in the city?"

The officer looked around at his men. One whispered something in his ear.

"The military staffs are still in their headquarters," the officer reported. "And some of the diplomats are still here. But they, too, seem to be intent on leaving quickly. Apparently no one knows how the Solar Guards are going to react, especially after what's happened out on the Two Arm."

"They'll react like everyone else," she spat back at him. "Like scared children."

The officer took a step closer to the Empress. "My lady, I feel I must remind you that some elements within the SG might be best described as *unpredictable* at a time like this. It is obvious that the situation is unstable. That's why I must insist that—"

She held up her hand and cut him off in midsentence. "You said some high military officers are still on hand up here?"

"True, my lady . . ."

"Who is the highest?"

The officer consulted with his men again. There was a burst of quadtrol activity. Then he came back with an answer. "The Secretary of SF Intelligence is still here. He is in his office at SF headquarters."

The Empress was surprised to hear this. The head of SF Intelligence was near the top of this privileged heap on Special Number One. He held advantages nearly as high as the imperial family itself. That he had stuck around after the others had obviously fled to safer, if not higher ground was fairly amazing. The Empress smiled. Her beautiful features made a brief reappearance.

"Fetch the Secretary, and bring him to my quarters," she ordered the bodyguards. "He'll know what's going on. . . ."

There were hundreds of SF special forces troops surrounding Blue Rock when the Imperial Guards arrived. The elite SF soldiers were armed with dozens of mobile sonic guns, their gigantic barrels pointed directly toward the opposite end of the floating city, where the Solar Guards headquarters lay.

Special troops were also stationed on every floor of the soaring SF headquarters. No less than a hundred of the elite soldiers were guarding the SF3 floor alone. They bristled when the Imperial Guards showed up, bearing their order from the Empress. They were neutrals here, both sides wary of the Solar Guards. But the SF troopers were very reluctant to let the SF Intelligence Secretary out of their sight. However, they could not refuse a direct order from a member of the Imperial Family and so had no choice but to let him go.

The Imperial Guards found the Secretary sitting in his suite on the ninety-ninth floor, calmly listening to star music. Unlike most of the people who lived and worked on the immense floating city, the Secretary's bags were not packed, nor was he was planning on leaving any time soon. Besides running the vast SF Intelligence networks, he was also brilliant in the areas of diplomacy, history, military matters and, most valuable, in the ways of intrigue around the Palace, and around the Empire itself. Thus, he felt he was most needed here.

He was somewhat surprised to see the Imperial Guards walk through his door, though, surprised to hear he was wanted in the Empress's private quarters. He made a rare joke: that maybe this wasn't the thing to do; being alone in the Empress's secret bedroom while her husband was far up north might start the tongues wagging. But not one of the Imperial Guards even cracked a smile.

So the Secretary donned his artificial-feather cap and simply told them to lead the way.

They reached the pair of enormous oak doors that led to the Empress's private quarters ten minutes later.

One guard pushed the doors open, but his expression made it clear that the Secretary was on his own from here.

He bowed to them, and the guards disappeared. The Secretary took one step in. The room was huge, and done in dark wood, a rare commodity on Earth or anywhere in the Galaxy these days. Yet there was a small conflagration in the fireplace, logs of both ash and pines were crackling away, and the place felt warm, if just a little too mysterious. Of course, this is exactly how the Empress liked it.

He took another giant step in, and finally he saw her. She was reclining on the couch in front of the fire, a goblet of golden wine in her hand. The Secretary had known her for years, but he never failed to marvel just how beautiful she was, even though she was approaching her fourth century. Or was it her fifth?

That Holy Blood really does the trick, he thought.

He bowed very deeply, removing his hat and sweeping it across his chest and under his left arm. As always, he was dressed in his long blue gown.

"My lady, I was told that you required my assistance," he said.

She indicated that he could rise from his bow.

"It is good to know that not everyone has abandoned me," she said. "Or has everyone just gone off on vacation at the same time?"

The Secretary regained his full height, put his boots together, and held his hat under his arm.

"If they be on vacation, my lady, they left at a most inopportune time," he said. "The Empire needs every heart and mind it owns to be here these troubled days, working for its preservation."

She smiled. "Please . . ." she said, indicating the extensive bar set up on the hovering table close by the fire.

The Secretary poured himself a modest goblet of gold slow-ship wine, then took a seat on a divan opposite from her. She was still dressed in her interplanetary party outfit: very short black dress, boots, plunging neckline. Stunning, still . . .

"You know what has happened, I assume?" she asked him. "Up in the Two Arm—between the Space Forces and the Solar Guards?"

He nodded once, deeply. "That huge battle? I certainly do. As a matter of fact, I have further reports, if it will not pain you too much to watch them."

"Pain is all too common today," she said.

He snapped his fingers. Suddenly, the room was filled with an enormous image of the Milky Way. It stretched for thirty feet. Every known star, every known planet, spinning, twirling, the Empire contained in a perfect holographic image before them.

It was jaw-dropping in its beauty—but all was not right here. Every few seconds, there would be a flash of light in among all the stars. First around the Three Arm. Then, over on the Four. Then, two more on the Five Arm, then on the Sixth. And the mid–Two Arm looked as if it was on fire.

"Those flashes?" the Empress asked. "What are they?"

"Those are battles between the Space Forces and the Solar Guards, my lady," he said.

The Empress just stared back at him. She had been expecting at the most a report of another incident between the two services somewhere inside the Two Arm. But not this . . .

"Quite simply, my lady," he began again, "heavy fighting has broken out between the Space Forces and the Solar Guards all over the Galaxy. Where these things have been isolated incidents over the past three weeks, we are now on the verge of an all-out war."

The Empress's alabaster face went even more pale, if that was possible. She began shaking her head violently.

"This can't be true!" she declared in a loud voice. "These reports you are getting must be wrong."

"If only that were the case, my lady," he replied calmly—he was too old for such extreme emotions. "But these reports cannot be disputed. They are showing up on the strings, the bubblers. Even the Big Generator is showing a seismic fluctuation whenever a prop core blinks out. And that only happens when one of our ships—either Space Forces or Solar Guards—is destroyed."

She fell silent for a long time, staring into the fire. It seemed as if life itself was draining out of her.

"Did you ever foresee a day such as this?" she finally asked him sadly. "When our own troops would be fighting each other—and apparently with no way to stop them?"

"It is disturbing," the Secretary replied. "I know for a fact that orders to desist are flying out of every military and diplomatic post we have—but sad to say, they are being universally ignored."

The Empress sipped her drink. "I know there has been disdain between the two forces for many years. But . . ."

She let her voice trail off.

"As in other cases of history, my lady," the Secretary told her. "It usually doesn't take much to strike the match. Rivalry and distrust can last below the surface for only so long. Then they become combustible, just waiting for something to ignite them."

"It all seemed to start with that invasion a month ago—short-lived as it was," she fumed. "The Solar Guards did not react well to it."

The Secretary lowered his glass a moment. He wondered if he should level with her, at the same time knowing he had no other choice, as it was widely rumored, and on good authority, that the Empress could read minds.

"I'm sure you've heard the same whispers as I," he said.

"That the Solar Guards lied about what happened at the end of that curious action?" she asked.

"They *did* lie, my lady," the Secretary told her. "One of my men had to die to prove it, but prove it he did. We retrieved his readings. Nothing happened out there. The invaders vanished, and the REF had no idea where they went.

"But even stranger—the REF's activities out in the area since the supposed battle have been very curious, to say the least. While earlier in the month their search for answers had been intense, lately it seems just the opposite is true. In fact, I've seen some reports that indicate they are not out there at all for long periods of time—and then suddenly, the No-Fly area will be filled up with them again."

"Are you saying the REF is flying in and out of its own forbidden zone?" she asked, puzzled.

He shrugged. "Appearing and then disappearing is the better term for it. And zipping at quite high speed to other points in the realm, only to return to the Two Arm—and disappear again. Very strange behavior. But whatever the case, they certainly didn't want anyone to see what they are doing out there. As I said, the man we sent out to investigate it all paid with his life. It is his murder that led to this fighting."

The Empress went silent again. The fire paled a bit. Then she looked the Secretary straight in the eye and asked, "Is Hawk Hunter involved in this?"

Again, the Secretary knew he had to be careful with what he said here. "There is a good chance he is. And if I can be so bold, there are reports that your daughter, the very beautiful Xara, may have had liaisons with this rogue."

He paused. "Have you heard any news about her? Where she disappeared to? Or Vanex for that matter?"

The Empress shook her head. Her emotions were rising slowly to the surface, a rare occasion for her. "They are still looking, or so they tell me," she said. "I'm hoping she is just off somewhere. In a snit. Furious for some reason. But safe . . ."

"I pray that is so, my lady," the Secretary said.

Another long silence.

"You can read tea leaves," she said to him. "Is it too much of a coincidence that all these things are happening to us? Missing people? This invasion out on the Two Arm. Now this war between our own forces—and even talk about a coup against the Imperial Court? Not that I think it wise to believe in coincidences, but . . ."

The Secretary bowed his head slightly. "My lady, a wise man once said, 'If coincidences don't mean anything, why do they happen so often?' I tend to agree with him."

"Then why didn't we see this coming?" she asked.

"Some people did," he replied. "It just wasn't anyone up here, on our lofty heights, who read the tea leaves, as you put it. Up here, we drank, we reveled, we swam in the riches that come as a result of this great empire that's been handed to us. Meanwhile, down there, in the back alleys of that great city below, out on the periphery of the periphery, where the thinkers, the prophets, and the poets reside, they saw this coming a long time ago."

He locked his eyes on to hers, trying to find something beyond the extra-long eyelashes and gobs of atomic mascara. It was a futile search.

"Is that a surprise to you, my lady?" he asked her. "That things are so different down there?"

The Empress laughed darkly. "Down there? I haven't been 'down there' in more than two hundred years.' "

The Secretary just shook his head. "Well, if I might be so bold," he said, "therein might lie part of the problem."

With that, he stood up, turned on his heel, and left.

The Empress retreated to her bedroom and conjured up another bottle of slow-ship wine.

She felt very uncomfortable now—and not just because the Secretary had taken such an ungracious leave of her. She was now alone; *that* was the problem. She didn't particularly like her own company. And all this uncertainty only made the isolation worse.

The Empire might be crumbling or it might not be, but one thing was for certain: it was changing, and she didn't like change, either. How would history see her role in all this? Certainly she would have no direct link to the Fourth Empire's fall—if indeed that's what was going to happen. That blame would be put on O'Nay's head alone. After all, what imperial wife has any impact on her husband's work? Not she. Yet on thinking that, the empty feeling in her stomach became that much deeper.

She sank into her floating bed and sipped her first goblet of the new wine. What would she do if the Secretary was right? Where would she go if all this nonsense eventually did reach Earth? She couldn't return to Venus; she was sure her relatives were leaving that place in droves by now. And if the SG fleets really did take over the One Arm, then the Solar System, and maybe even Earth itself—well, absolutely no one of any merit or grace would want to be within one hundred light-years of this place.

Perhaps it was wise then to take the Imperial Guards' advice. Maybe she *should* go to one of the other arms. It would be a new experience for her. Even though she was Empress of the Galaxy and had been for more than 300 years, she'd never even left the Pluto Cloud, never mind venturing out beyond the One Arm. But where would she go, exactly? Not into the Ball, of course. Though she was adored by billions in the peaceful center of the Galaxy, the place was so boring, she'd rather die here than flee there. No, it would have to be to one of the arms. But which one? She'd never heard anything good about the Two or the Three Arm and apparently the Five and Six arms were just dreadful, as were the Eight and the nearby Nine.

And the Seventh? No, there was nothing at all out there. Besides . . .

Suddenly, she felt a drop of water fall on her cheek. She reached up and touched it, only to find two more. Then another. And another. What was going on here? Water was spilling from her eyes. Her breath caught in her throat. She didn't realize it at first, only because it had been so long, but she was crying.

What kind of a mother are you? a voice whispered in her ear. It was a good question and one that she never wanted to face. Her daughter was missing. Had been for a month. Yet practically all she had done in those four weeks was party on Zros. Had it ever occurred to her that Xara might actually be in peril? Or even dead?

No . . .

Not until now.

Suddenly, every bad thing she'd done in the past 375 years

came back to her; it was a deluge, and the swiftness in which it arrived was startling by itself. There had been a lot of lying over those three-plus centuries, a lot of cheating, treachery, bigotry, and deceit. But no offense compared to the poor excuse of a mother she'd been to her daughter. In fact, she hadn't been a mother at all. A flood of tears came now; endless waves of repressed emotions exploded to the surface. Her entire life, she'd sought only to shine and not reflect, and now it was time to pay for that conceit. Her whole world was crumbling, within and without. The room seemed to spin black and become deathly cold, such was the turmoil she found herself in. She began looking for a knife, for if one was in her reach, she would plunge it into her heart and end all this right now.

But no dagger could be found; in fact, they were banned within the palace. So she simply buried her head in her pillow and let the tears flow unabated, ruining her makeup, soaking her covers, staining her sheets.

Suddenly, though, near the bottom of this seemingly bottomless pit, she felt an amazing warmth enter the room. Her dark emotions were being swept away by something even deeper. She stopped crying. She wiped her eyes and looked up.

Two figures were next to her bed.

They were men—but then again, they weren't, at least not in the first moment of their arrival. She had no idea how they had entered her room. The doors were all locked and laser-sealed. Her chambers were surrounded by security beams that prevented anyone from materializing from other locations unless she alone had authorized it. Nor had these two dropped in from the nearby sixth dimension, the place where the dour sentinels existed. Those phantom butlers always announced their arrival before intruding on imperial space.

No, these two were just *suddenly there*, not something that happened ever, despite this day and age of people popping in and out for all occasions.

And in that first split second of their arrival, she saw a strange glow around both of them. And both seemed not to be standing but floating a bit above the floor, this, even though it was virtually impossible for anyone to levitate in her presence.

The Empress of course blamed the hallucination on her breakdown just moments before—and the large quantity of slow-ship wine she'd ingested lately.

But then she realized that she recognized one of the two.

"Hero Petz? *Is that you?*"

Calandrx smiled warmly. Tomm was next to him. He smiled as well.

"You look so . . . different," she gasped. "Have you had your atoms recombined?"

Calandrx laughed a little. "Maybe," he replied.

She held her head in her hands. "I must have been drugged or spiked," she gasped. "Of all the souls I never expected to see again, you are among the top . . ."

She sat up and brushed the tears from her cheeks.

"But Petz, why are you here? You have become an enemy of the state. With one word this room will be swarming with guards, and you will be led away to the atomic gallows."

Calandrx told her directly, "Empress—just be still. We are here carrying messages, both good and bad. But our time is limited. Please listen closely to what we have to say."

But they were frightening her. She raised her hand and twisted it at an odd angle. This was her way of calling for her personal guards. Six of them were always no more than a few feet away from her bedroom door. But though she twisted and twisted, no one came. She tried to blink out, transport herself to another location nearby, a talent shared by most of the Specials. But this did not work either.

"How can this be?" she wailed. "Are my powers finally gone? What will happen to me if they are?"

"Just be still!" Tomm chastised her harshly. He was not adapting so well to his new role. "You are wasting time. . . ."

But the Empress twisted her hand again—and still no guards appeared. She tried to blink out again, too. Nothing happened. She was beginning to think this was all just a dream, which in a way, it was.

Finally she just gave in. She pulled the covers up to her chin. "Speak then . . ." she said. "Say what you will and then be gone."

Calandrx drew very close to her. It was as if he was floating right in front of her face.

"In the very near future you will be called upon to prevent a catastrophe," he told her. "This will save many millions, if not billions, of lives. When that time comes, you must be ready to heed the call."

She almost laughed. "Me? Save millions? And how am I to do that?"

"By helping in a small way the people to whom this Empire rightly belongs reclaim it for themselves," Tomm said. "It is theirs—and must be returned to them."

She almost laughed in their faces.

"Are you suggesting my family just *give away* the Empire?" she asked, astonished. "If that be, you are both mad, whatever the hell you are. . . ."

Tomm said: "Righteousness will prevail eventually, Empress. It is simply the manner in which it arrives that concerns us—and in the end, it will concern you, too."

She could hardly speak. "But why are you telling me these things?"

"Because something is coming," Calandrx replied. "Something that is bigger than us, bigger than you. Bigger than the entire Empire. Many lives will hang in the balance—innocent lives. When the time comes to save those souls, you must play your part and thereby make up for your own shallow life."

With that, Calandrx put his fingers on her forehead, leaving a bit of oil just above her brow.

She sensed they were about to leave. She suddenly sat up on the bed. "You also said you had good news to tell me. . . ." she pleaded with them.

The two hesitated. They were loath to do her any favors, considering the actions of her past. But they had no choice. They were messengers—and if it was news they were delivering, then it had to be both the good with the bad.

"Your daughter is safe," Calandrx told her simply. "And on that you can be sure, because it is impossible for us lie—"

"More or less," Tomm added hastily.

The Empress just stared back at them, stunned by the words. Her face betrayed tremendous relief. Her tears returned.

"But where is she?" she said instead. "You must tell me!"

"She is safe," Calandrx repeated. "And if you do your part, you might see her again."

"But when?" the Empress cried. "And how?"

The two never replied. They simply disappeared as quickly as they came. And at this point, the Empress really believed she was either asleep or going insane.

Because just before the pair blinked out, she could have sworn that both had sprouted wings.

13

The planet was well-named: *Sleepy Time 9.*

It was in a binary star system which also bore the fitting appellation of *Two Over Easy*. This system was located on the near side of the Ball, meaning it was a relatively short ride from Earth. There were two dozen planets here, all of them devoted to some kind of easy living. Retirement worlds, superspas and resorts, or simply pastoral settlements, many of the planets in *Two Over Easy* were so ordinary they didn't have names. Some were just referred to as *Second Out, Third Out*, or *Fourth One In*.

Sleepy Time 9 was a jewel of sorts in this somnolent part of space. Unlike the others, it was a retreat planet for the very well-heeled and -connected, including many retired Space Forces officers. The city of Pillows was its capital. It was built around a vast three-level artificial lake whose shorelines were crowded with palatial resort homes, some towering, some just one story high but sprawling over many acres. The three-tiered lake also featured several spectacular waterfalls, and it was by one of these that a grand six-level house stood. It was called Castillox Farms, and was a magnificent design of soaring angles, internal water springs, and miles of superglass windowing.

The resident of this house was not a retired military officer, at least not yet. He was once the most famous Starcrasher commanders in the entire Space Forces, indeed; he'd been in line to become supreme commander of the entire SF someday. His combat record was superb. Whether it was hunting down space pirates, chasing outlaw space mercs, or invading troublesome planets, in close to one hundred years of imperial service, he'd never lost a battle.

His name was Zapp Multx, and he was slowly dying—of boredom.

Multx was an impressive, charismatic character, with a big, muscular body, bald head, and a long, thin goatee. His home was filled with innumerable aluminum and gold-leaf medals, jeweled swords, battle helmets, and specialized dress uniforms—the typical clutter of a space hero. His ship, the *BonoVox*, was nearly as famous as he. In his heyday, Multx and his exceptional crew were frequently called on to get other SF battle groups out of trouble. On many occasions, Multx was able to move his ship over vast distances in impossibly short periods of time, always arriving, right on cue, to save the day.

The *BonoVox* was flying somewhere around the inner galaxy these days. Multx didn't even know where it was exactly. The Ball was so peaceful, he was sure his executive officers were simply out joyriding, killing time while the crew grew fat and lazy. The ship hadn't visited *Sleepy Time 9* in more than a year. In fact, six months had passed since he'd heard anything from the *Bono* at all. It was as if his heart had been ripped out and taken away from him. He missed being on her that much.

So why was someone of his stature out here, wasting away?

It had all started two years before. Multx and his men had just completed a successful attack on an enemy planet called *Vines 7* and were rushing back to Earth to accept the Emperor's blessings. Flying along in Supertime, a pirate ship suddenly materialized parallel to Multx's great vessel and started firing on it. Before anyone on the *BonoVox* could react, the pirate ship began dispensing troops. They were carrying heavy weapons and cutting tools, intent on slicing their way through the hull of the proud SF warship.

Such a thing had never happened before. First of all, the pirate vessel—it was a so-called *Blackship*, flown by the notorious Blackship pirates—should not have been in Supertime. Only Empire ships had such capability. Second, no pirate commander would be so foolish as to attack an Empire Starcrasher; the huge warships usually outgunned their pirate adversaries by a factor of one hundred-to-one or more. Yet that's exactly what occurred.

It was only that an incredibly courageous passenger being carried to Earth by Multx had the gumption to steal an armed shuttle, fly it outside the *BonoVox*, attack the Blackship, and wound it mortally that the attack stopped and the pirate vessel disappeared.

The name of that passenger: Hawk Hunter.

That Hunter went on to win the Earth Race and notoriety across the entire Galaxy was old news by now. Not so well-known was the SF Command's decision that someone had to take the blame for the bizarre incident. To this day no one could explain how the Blackship got into Supertime or how it had come so close to actually capturing the *BonoVox*. But the entire affair was an embarrassment to the SF, and a fall guy was needed. Multx fit the bill. The SF Command sent his ship on an open-ended patrol of the Ball, a place where no shot had been fired in anger in four centuries, in effect forcing him into preretirement. Giving him this grand house on *Sleepy Time 9* only added insult to injury. It was a magnificent structure, but its surroundings were peaceful to the point of nausea, at least to Multx. This was a place where old SF officers went to die—and he knew it.

All this was hell for a person like him. He was soldier, from a long line of soldiers. And he was loyal. He believed so strongly in the Empire that, as a younger man, he'd had O'Nay's face tattooed on his forearm. Being away from the battle, being denied the opportunity to defend the realm really *was* like death for him.

A very slow death.

Multx sat now in his grand room, the one that overlooked

the waterfall and offered a view of all three levels of the lake. It was still early morning, but he was already into his second bottle of slow-ship wine. Though he'd hardly been a teetotaler before his banishment to the Ball, he was a heavy drinker now. His cellars were filled with rare vintages of the popular star juice. But a year of chronic imbibing had done nothing to raise his spirits; actually, the opposite was true. In the past twelve months, he'd become a most melancholy man.

His work had always been his mistress. He was without a wife and already bored with the few eligible women of the dull little planet. He couldn't even dream properly anymore. During the previous night he'd imagined a bright light hovering above the skylight over his bedroom canopy. This light grew so bright, he'd been unable to open his eyes for several minutes. What he was able to see looked like a string of slowly developing explosions, brilliant in red, but also in white and blue. When it all finally went away, Multx was left to lie in his sweaty bed, fully awake, to wonder what had happened. A flashback from some long-ago victory of his? Another catastrophe in the making in outer space? Or maybe a host of goblins had arrived to finally take him away. In any case, he never did get back to sleep. When the planet's prime sun rose, he was up with it, drinking his breakfast of wine. By the time the second sun rose, he was close to finishing his second bottle.

He'd heard about the battles between the SG and SF, of course. Everyone in the Galaxy had by now. They did not surprise him much. Multx had had his own run-ins with the Solar Guards, and he knew their leadership to be both deceitful and deceptive. Like many in the SF, he believed the Empire would have been better off without the junior service. But all this just made his forced retirement even worse. Had the incident with the Blackship never happened, he would have been right in the thick of this internecine conflict. And at that moment he would have given just about anything, done just about anything, to be back in the fight again. Instead, he was here, looking out on an artificial lake with an artificial waterfall, early morning suns glistening off both, trying to pull the cork out of his third bottle of slow-ship wine.

It was strange then that just as the bottle's stopper finally came loose, he looked up to see two men standing right in front of him.

Instinct alone made Multx's hand go to his belt, as if there were a ray gun there. But then he stopped. He recognized these men.

In fact, they were two very old friends of his. Their names were Erx and Berx.

Multx was astonished to see them—and not just because they were both wanted men or that two years had passed since they'd last laid eyes on each other. It was also the manner by which they'd appeared. So quickly, so silently. They hadn't beamed in from another location. There was always a telltale flash and sizzling sound to presage such subatomic events. And it wasn't a transdimensional transfer; he would have noticed that, too. It seemed strange, but to Multx it was almost as if they'd been there all along, and he was now just seeing them.

"By the stars!" he finally managed to gasp. "Is it really you two?"

Neither man replied; both bowed deeply instead.

Multx studied them more closely now. They both looked so . . . *odd*. They had a strange glow around them. And they appeared to be much younger, much leaner, much more muscular than the last time he'd seen them.

Multx finally blurted out, "What has happened to you?"

"We've changed," Berx said solemnly, adding, "but perhaps for the better."

"But why are you here, brothers?" he asked them. "You have been fugitives for more than a year. By rights, I should have you arrested. Or I could be arrested just by being here with you."

"That won't happen, my brother," Erx told him. "No one will ever know of this conversation. As long as our friendship has been, you can count on that."

"We are here because we need you to do something for us," Berx said.

"You mean you need *my* help?"

"In a way, yes," Berx said.

Multx replied, "But I cannot help you. You are wanted men.

Plus, who knows what hijinks you've been up to since we last met."

"We bear only the truth, brother," Erx said. "We cannot bear anything else."

"Please," Berx said. "Just listen to us. . . ."

Multx hesitated a moment, but finally relented. "Only because our friendship is older than the stars," he said.

The two visitors proceeded to tell him everything that had happened to them since they last saw him. The story of the Home Planets. The invasion of the Two Arm. How Hawk Hunter learned about the deceit that had created the foundation of the Second and Fourth Empires. They also told how they had joined Hunter in his quest to topple O'Nay's Empire. Multx sat speechless as he listened to the fantastic tales.

At the end, he leaned forward in his hovering chair. He was obviously more confused than before.

"My brothers," he said, "in all my years, I have never heard of such things. I am certain that you believe them. But is it wise to align yourselves with Hawk Hunter in these uncertain times? I know you are close to him. You were the ones who plucked him off that backward planet *Fools 6* in the first place, after he saved your lives. And don't get me wrong. I have no problem with him, either. He saved my ship and my crew, too. But my brothers, the man is a cosmic oddity. How can we be certain that what he is advocating is anything more than what goes through that crafty mind of his? He probably has designs on the Empire himself!"

Erx told Multx sternly, "The greatest charlatan in the universe would not have endured what Hunter has, just to pull off some grand joke. He has put his own life on the line many times since we've known him. He has a passion than burns brighter than a nova. Look at the proof: he has more than half the Galaxy looking for him, yet he started an invasion of the Empire. So true he is to his cause—"

"See, my brothers? You admit he is a criminal," Multx cut in.

"He is a rebel," Berx corrected him. "And these days, there is a difference."

Multx drank more wine. His round face screwed up in disgust. "Those horrible beings of which you spoke? And Hunter's claim that the three brothers were raised from the dead? It goes against the greatest science of the Galaxy. Such things should not be happening."

"Believe us, brother," Erx said. "Much stranger things have been happening lately."

Multx sipped his wine again. "But *overthrowing* the Empire? I'm sorry, in all my years, never did I think I'd hear seditious trash from you two."

Erx and Berx shook their heads. It was hard to blame Multx for not believing them. They needed to play their trump card.

"If we could prove to you that our cause is righteous," Erx said. "Would you do as we asked?"

Before he could reply, Berx waved his hand in a circular motion a few feet from Multx's nose. Suddenly a small cumulus cloud appeared, billowing and growing larger by the second. A great wind then blew through the grand room, serving to part the small storm. Within it, Multx was astonished to see an entirely new existence. A place of emerald grass, gently rolling hills, and a cobalt sky. Rivers and fruit trees everywhere. More important, for the first time in a long time, Multx actually felt joy enter in his heart. It was overwhelming—at least until Berx waved his hand again and the vision faded.

Shaking, his fingers barely able to grip his wineglass, Multx now looked at his friends with new and growing trepidation—and it had nothing to do with their criminal status.

"Oh my God," he whispered. "You've become magicians. Conjurers. *Wizards . . .*"

"No," Erx said. "We have simply become enlightened. And through no design of our own. We've just showed you the place we've been to, and it is by returning from it that we've been changed."

"You expect me to believe that you've been to the place in that vision?" Multx asked them. "That place seemed like Paradise itself!"

"Think about it, brother," Berx said. "The entire Galaxy has been looking for us. Twelve ships—including six stolen Starcrashers—and 40,000 men. Where could we have hidden? In this day of being able to sniff out every last fiber of a human being, of being able look into the past and drag a stray radio signal into the present. In this day of tracking just about anything that is constructed of more than two atoms. Just where do you think we could have gone that no one—absolutely no one—could've found us?"

Multx was stumped for a moment. "You really went . . . *there?*"

Both nodded. Then they drew a bit closer to him. They were in a hurry.

"Brother Multx, we are messengers," Erx told him. "And part of the news we carry is grim. But with your help, certain disaster might be avoided. Or at least its effects lessened."

"But we are also here to present you with an opportunity," Berx went on. "An opportunity to be a hero of great caliber again. To once more prove your courage is beyond all measure. When the history of the man is finally written, your name will appear among the pantheon of heroes. All you have to do is one thing. . . ."

Multx was stunned by these strong words. "What nonsense is this?" he asked. "I am simply a flicker of light in a sea of stars these days. The Imperial Court doesn't even remember that I exist anymore!"

"They don't have to," Erx told him calmly. "We know you exist. Just do as we ask, and you will regain your stature and more. Much more."

Multx collapsed back into his floating chair. He wanted nothing more than to rehabilitate his image. But frankly, his two old friends were frightening him. Their appearance, their glow, the vision they'd just created and then taken away. They had changed in ways he wasn't sure he wanted to contemplate.

Still . . .

He looked out at the grand waterfall. At that moment, he hated every drop of water falling over its side and splashing onto the fake lake below. Every drop, every day, day after day, going nowhere but down. Just about anything would be better than this.

"Brothers," he finally said, "tell me what it is you want me to do."

Erx and Berx both smiled with relief. Then Erx touched Multx's forehead, leaving a drop of oil there.

"You will know soon enough, brother," he said.

Then they faded away.

14

Betaville, Planet America, Home Planets System

FBI agent Lisa Lee returned to her office after lunch to find her secretary looking a bit flustered.

At first Lisa thought Gloria was upset at her because she'd failed to bring her back a Coke as she'd promised. Their office was on the third floor of the tiny Betaville police station—Lisa was the FBI field agent for this part of Ohio—and even though they'd been here nearly eight months, a few kinks remained. Getting the soda machine on the first floor to work was just one of them.

While still a sleepy little town, Betaville was also a very famous place these days. It was here that the three visitors from outer space first arrived almost a year ago. It was they who passed on the knowledge that Planet America, as well as the other thirty-five worlds in the Home Planets system, was really part of a long-neglected prison camp in the sky set up thousands of years before by the very evil Second Empire. This celestial prison was trapped inside a time bubble that retarded technical advancement but allowed the unknowing inmates to live a civilized if antiquated way of life. Planet America had cars and factories and highways and railroads. It had cops and firefighters, priests and politicians. Post offices, sports teams, grammar schools, high schools, and colleges could all be found here. The tiny planet consisted of one large landmass that began in the east with cities like Boston, New York, Charleston, and Miami, and went right across to California, where the other West Coast states also lay. Across a very narrow sea was New York again. It was an artificial world, recreated in the image of the place that its first inhabitants had been forced from 4,000 years before. The people of Planet America were the descendants of those original deportees from Earth.

The three visitors changed everything. Not only did they bring the news of the origin of the Home Planets, they defeated the prison guard army who'd been watching over the three dozen imprisoned worlds, then raised a space army of their own and sailed off to win Earth back for its rightful owners. That army was called the United Planets Forces. The six ships they'd sailed on were known, on Planet America at least, as the First Fleet.

Those half dozen vessels had left nearly eight months before; nothing had been heard from them since. Forty thousand soldiers representing each of the thirty-six planets, flying under the Stars and Stripes of Planet America's flag, were out in the cosmos somewhere, fighting a great battle for all of them back here. They were gone but not forgotten. Indeed, American flags had been strung from every light pole, every front porch, every overpass, from the top of every high city building in the entire system when the fleet sailed. Those flags were still flying today.

That these young soldiers were so far away, fighting and dying for the people back home had not been forgotten here.

Lisa was out of the Chicago FBI office, and as Betaville had become a place of notoriety, the Bureau thought it wise to open a field office here. Lisa had played such a significant part in the space visitors' first appearance—she had been the original investigating agent after they arrived—so it was only natural she be put in charge of the small office.

It had been a success so far, but there were these little glitches that had to be worked out, and one of them was the chronic malfunctioning of the first-floor soda machine. It worked only sporadically; today it was shut down for good.

And had Lisa been a gambler, she would have bet that no Coke was the reason for Gloria's obvious discomfit now.

But it was a bet Lisa would have lost.

She began to apologize to Gloria, but the middle-aged woman gently stopped her.

"There's someone waiting for you in your office," Gloria told her in a whisper.

Lisa didn't understand. She had eaten her lunch, as always, out on the bench next to the only working door leading into the police station. She had seen no one come into the building except the usual gang of cops. How could someone be waiting for her in her office then?

"Who is it?" Lisa whispered back.

"He asked me not to tell," was the secretary's reply, still a little breathy. That's when Lisa noticed Gloria had a drop of oil on her forehead.

"Are you using a new moisturizer?" Lisa asked her.

Gloria just shook her head no, then motioned for Lisa to get inside her office immediately.

Lisa just shrugged. She was a pretty redhead and always tried to look her best. So she flattened out her skirt, fluffed her collar, ran a hand through her hair, and walked into her office.

Her visitor was standing behind the door. She was completely in the room and turned around before she saw him.

"Oh my God . . ." she breathed.

He was enormous. Much bigger than she remembered him. And he looked so *different*. There was a white haze surrounding him, and he seemed just a bit out of focus, or better put, seemed to be existing in a kind of soft focus. But still, even in this state, his muscles looked huge.

She knew who he was immediately. He was another visitor from outer space. Not one of the original three. This man had come to Planet America right after the victory against the Bad Moon Knights' prison guard army. At the time, he was the oldest man Lisa had ever met. But now, he looked about a thousand years younger.

His name was Klaaz.

"Do you remember me?" he asked her sweetly, his voice different, too.

"Of course I do," she told him, nearly collapsing in her chair. "How could I forget? Your friends freed our planet. Then you helped build the UPF First Fleet."

Klaaz just smiled. "I tried to help where I could," he said.

Lisa was still staring at him, amazed at his transformation. When she'd last seen him, he was bent over, had wrinkles on top of wrinkles, and could barely walk. Now he was standing straight up, with large, broad shoulders, enormously powerful hands, and an extremely handsome face. It was like looking at a photograph from the very distant past and realizing for the first time that the person you knew as ancient had once been a very handsome man. A hunk, even.

Yet here he was, standing before her. That hunk, in real life.

"Why are you here?" she asked him, a little breathless herself now. "Everyone thinks you're with the fleet, off fighting in the Galaxy somewhere."

"And they would not be wrong," Klaaz told her. "But something rather important has come up, something that must be taken care of. I came here because I know I can trust you. Please, can you tell me the status of the Second Fleet?"

The Second Fleet was another UPF squadron of ships that had been under construction since the first one left. It was being manufactured, in bits and pieces, on just about every planet in the system, this, as another army of UPF troopers was being trained. The new force was meant to be purely defensive in nature, however. Both ships and men were intended to serve as protection for the very out-of-the-way Home Planets system.

"The last I heard, the Second Fleet was about a month away from trials in space," Lisa told him. She was finally over the initial shock of his sudden appearance and the slightly ethereal look about him.

"And the state of the army being raised?" he asked.

"About the same. A month away from activation."

Klaaz thought a moment. "This will all have to be moved up," he said finally. "The ships and the soldiers must be ready to leave within twenty-four hours."

Lisa was confused. "Leave? Why?"

"They are needed elsewhere," Klaaz replied. "Urgently needed . . ."

Lisa shook her head. "I'm no expert in these things," she said. "But I'd have to think that would be almost impossible."

Klaaz smiled again, a little sadly though. "My dear girl," he said. "I've just recently learned that *nothing* is impossible. And I know this is suddenly out of the blue. But I will need your help to get these things done."

"But why?" she asked him. "Why are these ships and men needed?"

"Because a great battle is coming," he told her simply. "Perhaps one of the greatest since the Creation."

"Since Creation? Are you serious?"

He nodded solemnly. "Yes, I am. The opposing sides will be like the elements of Nature itself, battling each other for the right to exist. In the very old days, this might have been called Armageddon. And, at this point, the outcome is still very uncertain. But I will tell you this: no matter what happens, things will never be the same again. Here or anywhere else in the Galaxy. The universe, even. Such is the message I have brought today."

Lisa was shocked by his words. And she had no doubt that he believed they were the truth.

"But where?" she asked him. "Where will this great battle take place?"

Klazz simply gestured over his shoulder to indicate a place far, far away.

"Closer to Earth than I ever thought I'd be," he told her.

Word soon flashed around the tiny planet that Klaaz had returned.

Within hours, authorities on each of the Home Planets had been apprised of the situation and the message he had brought.

The ships of the Second Fleet were being assembled on Planet America and Planet France, using components from all the other home worlds. Troops were training on Planets Pacifica, Africanus and Britannica. Of the twenty-eight ships under construction, two dozen were deemed spaceworthy. Each

ship was built in the spitting image of the six original UPF
vessels, which in turn were more than 1,000 years old. These
new classics were blue and chrome like their predecessors but
were carrying more modern star engines and room for nearly
twice as many soldiers, many of whom doubled as members
of the crew. Fully manned, the ships could put nearly a quarter
of a million men on the field of battle.

But there was a problem.

The ships were powered by updated ion-ballast motors, fast
but not Supertime fast. As the Home Planets were actually
thousands of light-years *outside* the Galaxy, the trip by the
first UPF fleet inward had taken six months—and that was just
to the tip of the Two Arm. The voyage had strained the limits
of those antique ships and just about expended their bingo fuel
in the process. If the great battle was shaping up deep within
the Milky Way, what good would the Second Fleet be if it
arrived on the scene many months too late?

During the flurry of meetings Klaaz had with the leaders of
the Home Planets, as well as the engineers and the crews of
the new fleet themselves, this question came up time and time
again. On each occasion, Klaaz replied, "Don't worry." Getting the ships where they had to go was his concern.

There was little fanfare when the new ships departed from their
launch pads on Planets America and France.

Little time was available to plan anything more than a quick
good-bye to the soldiers from their families and a universal,
system-wide wish of Godspeed and good luck. The twenty-
four ships made rendezvous in orbit around Planet America;
here, they were checked out for spaceflight integrity. That they
would be traveling much greater distances than had previously
been thought had little bearing now. As Klaaz had told the
system's leaders, this was not something they had to worry
about.

While the soldiers inside the ships acclimated themselves to
life in space, a first for many of them, their commanders reviewed the information Klaaz had passed to them. The situation was simple enough. In its battles within the Galaxy, the
UPF had made an archenemy in the Empire's military, most

especially the Solar Guards, and even more especially the almost ghostly Rapid Engagement Fleet. This was the force the Second Fleet was expecting to fight way down in the middle of the Two Arm.

And they would be a formidable foe. The enemy force awaiting the fresh UPF troops might number anywhere from a half million to several billion men. The number of ships they might face could run into the millions as well. But Klaaz was also always quick to remind the new UPF commanders that their mission would be "blessed." And though he did not go into any details, Klaaz did say on many occasions that he was not using the word lightly and that it should not just be taken in a context of simply boosting morale. The Second Fleet would literally be blessed. Their mission was for pure good, and its intentions were even grander than the recovery of Earth, though both goals, were still absolutely linked.

The UPF commanders didn't pretend to fully understand what Klaaz was telling them. They knew only that he was a great hero and that he was someone who would never steer them wrong.

In other words, they trusted him completely, a trait that was in drastically low supply among the stars these days.

The twenty-four ships all checked out within a few hours of reaching orbit around Planet America. One good thing about the ships' design was their brilliant simplicity. They were essentially quarter-mile-long hulls with engines attached and soldiers inside. Fewer systems meant fewer things to go wrong. In no time at all, the fleet's commanders reported that they were ready to go.

Exactly what happened next would be spoken about for many years to come.

Klaaz was very well-known to the people of the mid–Five Arm. Over the centuries, he'd saved entire star clusters within the middle Five from marauding space mercs and pirate groups. He was a marshal in many armies in that part of space; his face adorned the currency of more than a dozen star systems there. No surprise then that hundreds of stories about his adventures had been written, sung, and memorized. Heroic legends about the Great Klaaz had been passed down through generations on the Fifth Arm for several hundred years.

But the legend of Klaaz and the Second Fleet—true or not— would soon become the most famous of all.

It was witnessed by tens of thousands of people, yet the exact details of what occurred that day would never be very clear.

Shortly after the twenty-four UPF ships took to orbit, Klaaz suddenly disappeared. Though he was still in communication with the fleet commanders via string comm, even this was in question, as some claimed Klaaz wasn't actually talking through the ship communicators but that his voice was just appearing to be heard in this manner somehow.

Whatever the case, just minutes after the ships reported they were ready for deployment, a small object was sighted on the fleet's joint scanners coming up behind the UPF starship *Missouri*. Many people who saw it both on the viz scanners and with their own eyes said this was actually Klaaz, flying in space, without a spacesuit or oxygen or other extravehicular needs. It was said Klaaz came up on the tail of the huge warship, put his mighty hands beneath its center tail fins, and pushed it. The vessel rocketed away at an incredible speed, traveling much faster than in Supertime. Once the *Missouri* was gone, Klaaz flew up to the starship *New Jersey* and did the same thing. Then he went to the *Arizona*, then the *Wisconsin*, then the *Oklahoma*.

Within minutes, Klaaz had hurled all of the two dozen ships away at incomprehensible speed.

And just like that, the Second Fleet was gone.

No one would dispute that something very strange happened that day. Indeed, the UPF ships were gone from orbit, gone from the Home Planets system itself. But how? There was no way of telling that, because even though they tried for days, those back on the Home Planets were never able to establish string comm contact with the two dozen new ships.

As for Klaaz?

Shortly after the Second Fleet disappeared, they said, he vanished as well.

15

Upper Five Arm

The castle was filled with hundreds of beautiful women.

Blondes, brunettes, redheads. All of them were scantily clad; many were topless. Some were even real.

The castle was known as Ruby Ridge. It was located on a high cliff near the equator of a planet called *Rocks 32*. The mountainous, tropical world was a well-known gambling mecca in the upper Five Arm, a wild part of the Galaxy if there ever was one.

Rocks 32 was a sunny place for shady people. More than gambling went on here. Much more. The planet was a hotbed of drug dealing (*jamma* mostly), moving illegal slow-ship wine, and most of all, black market weapons trading, both buying and selling. The planet's police were all paid off; its politicians were, too. And while most of the people on *Rocks 32* knew about the Fourth Empire, no imperial ship, whether it be SF, SG, or X-Forces, had been in the system in almost twenty years.

There was only one way to buy or sell weapons on this hot little world: hit town with a big splash, rent the most audacious resort possible, throw a huge party with plenty of beauties, good food, and drink—and then wait for the money to come to you.

Which was exactly what was happening inside the magic castle this day. On the top floor of the tallest tower sat the man who had organized the weeklong bash. His name was Rexx VonRexx. Just eighty years old, he was small and thin, with a long, wispy beard, a head full of braided hair, and a fetish about always wearing black. Suave, charming and, thanks to a reconstituted face, very handsome, he was also extremely rich. In fact, he was among the richest men in this part of the Galaxy.

Moving stolen weapons was VonRexx's specialty. He'd been buying war toys in bulk for the past twenty years, mostly from the enormous black markets farther down the Five Arm. These parties were the means by which VonRexx moved his merchandise, selling them to midlevel customers who could afford his high prices. He'd been laying groundwork for this gathering for weeks. Calling old friends, setting up meetings, replicating the food, the booze, the jamma, and the girls— spending money like water, which sent ripples around the mid-Five like a volcano orgy. That was the intention, of course. This bash was practically guaranteed to produce results.

It would also attract many guests, invited and otherwise.

Ruby Ridge Castle was forty-four stories high. There were nearly 600 holo-girls, 300 or so real females, several hundred potential customers and their entourages on hand with a small army of hired guards watching over everyone. Security throughout the fortress was tight, especially on the ground floor. This was the hottest party in the mid-Five at the moment, but still, no one got through the front gate without a thorough scanning. Those not meeting a strict set of criteria were turned away and told not to return. If they refused, they were beaten to a pulp.

While most of the raucous partying took place on the lower floors, VonRexx only did business in the top suite during these events. He would stay up for days, schmoozing potential clients, getting them fed and oiled—and in the mood to do some buying. When things got slow or whenever the mood would strike him, he would let word filter down to the lower floors that he was in a selling mood again. And that prices were being reduced. This would bring an influx of moneymen up to the top suites, ready to do business. They had to stop at the forty-third floor first, though, where they would be checked over once again, this time by VonRexx's personal bodyguards. They would be scanned for weapons—ironically, none were allowed on the top floor—and their purses searched to make sure they were carrying real money.

Anyone passing this gauntlet would still have to wait until VonRexx himself approved a face check on them.

Only then would they be allowed into the forty-fourth floor.

The party in the castle had just begun its third day when word went through the building that VonRexx was discounting again.

As predicted, this brought a fresh wave of buyers to the huge penthouse, leaving behind the sinful pleasures of the lower floors. Those cleared by security began drifting into the spacious top suite. The lights here were always low, the conversations hushed. With star-jazz music tinkling from everywhere, it was more sophisticated, more mysterious. As always, VonRexx could be found reclining on a large divan in the far corner of the room, a location from which he could see just about everybody and everything. He was surrounded not by security men but by a battalion of absolutely gorgeous women. It was understood that anyone entering the room had to acknowledge VonRexx with a slight bow or a tip of the hat. Like tribute to a king, it was important to remember just who was paying the bill for all this. Plus, VonRexx loved being the center of attention.

He'd been tipped by his security men that three arms buyers from the nearby system of *Slingerlands 7* were on their way up. This was good news. Though the Slingers were usually violent and volatile individuals, they always bought the most expensive stuff, such as e-mines, sonic torpedoes, and thermo-grenades. And they always carried real money. No chits; no credit sales for them. They were VonRexx's kind of customer.

He saw them coming. Deep purple uniforms, high black

boots, lots of tattoos. The three Slingers pushed through the crowd by the door and started making their way across the dark, congested room. Once the trio was within twenty feet of him, VonRexx waved half of his·girls away, clearing a path for the three men to approach. But oddly, they did not go to him. Instead, they veered off for the opposite corner of the room, where a very tight circle of partygoers had formed without VonRexx realizing it.

Mystified, he climbed off the couch and wandered over. Music was playing, guests were imbibing, and sexual antics were quietly going on throughout the room—yet an entirely different thing was happening over here. True, the penthouse was dark and crowded, and VonRexx couldn't keep his eyes everywhere at once. But he was surprised he'd missed this.

About a dozen well-known arms dealers were standing around a huge individual under a bare light in the corner. VonRexx himself had OK'd everyone who'd been allowed into the castle's top suite. He could not recall clearing someone this large to pass through. The man had his back to him; VonRexx could only see the faces of those gathered around. They all looked fascinated. Whatever this man was saying to them, he seemed to have put them in a trance.

Two of the arms dealers were having a particularly hushed conversation with the mystery man. Then came a round of handshakes and hugs, and the two men departed. They walked by VonRexx without giving him so much as a nod and hurried out the door. Strangely, each man had a dab of oil on his forehead.

Finally, VonRexx moved close enough to see the big man's face. He was shocked.

He knew him. He was one of his old competitors.

His name was Zarex Red.

Zarex had once been very famous in this part of the Galaxy. A rare combination of gunrunner and explorer, he had specialized in getting weapons to people who were in desperate need of firepower and willing to pay his premium prices. In turn, he used his profits to explore places so deep in the Five Arm, few people ever dared to venture to them. Of late, though, the rumors had it that Zarex was either dead, lost among the stars, or had taken up with a band of rogues who were trying the impossible: the overthrow of the Fourth Empire.

Which was why VonRexx was so surprised to see him here now, a very large, uninvited guest. How had he made it past security? How was it that he could so cavalierly draw the attention of the unsavory weapons dealers and rivet them so? VonRexx studied him from afar, fascinated that so many of his potential customers were hanging on Zarex's every word. The huge ex-explorer *was* charismatic, he supposed. But he'd never seen him draw a crowd quite like this.

He looked different, too. To VonRexx's eyes, Zarex seemed bigger, if that was possible. More muscles, more height, but there was also a strange glow about him, a halo of sorts around his head. This aura was not the greenish haze that could be seen trailing someone who'd spent a lot of time crashing stars. This was something else entirely.

VonRexx made sure Zarex did not see him, hiding himself in the dark crowd of holo-girls and guests. The man's presence here was a mystery but also an opportunity. His former dual-occupation had made Zarex wealthy by saving some of the Five Arm's most famous freedom fighters. But it had also made him some big-time enemies as well. Gunrunner and explorer, Zarex was also a wanted man—and not just by the Empire.

And his robot was nowhere to be seen.

Interesting, VonRexx thought.

Day turned to night and back to day again, a matter of just a few hours on *Rocks 32*.

With the dawn, two men arrived at the castle's front gate. They were wearing long, black cloaks with their hoods pulled up. The ground-level security team ran them through the rigid scanning procedure, but they passed quickly. They had done business with VonRexx before, and they'd just been in touch with the weapons king before they arrived. That was enough for them to proceed directly to the forty-fourth floor.

Here they were scanned again. They were also checked for that most important thing of all: cash. The pair did not disappoint. They were carrying thirty solid aluminum pieces, a huge amount of money in this part of the Milky Way. The security troops let them in and sent word to VonRexx that they were in the house.

The two men still had to fight their way across the very expansive room; it was like hiking through a forest of dazzling women and very drunk men. Finally, the cloaked pair reached VonRexx's location. No one saw them hand VonRexx their money pouch. Thirty pieces of true aluminum, VonRexx took it without a blink.

The men then made their way across the crowded room to the far corner where Zarex was still holding court. They saw the fascinated faces of the hard-core weapons men, many now with dabs of oil on their foreheads. Just a few minutes of eavesdropping confirmed what the two men had expected to hear. Zarex was not buying or selling weapons; he was asking for volunteers to help him fight some great battle that was about to take place on the Two Arm.

The two men had heard that the explorer had been visiting many planets in the region in the past few days; in fact, there had been several reports of him showing up on two different planets simultaneously. And he was doing then what he was doing now: addressing some of the most noxious arms dealers, the sleaziest and the chronically dishonest, and trying to convert them—that was the only term applicable—to join him on this mysterious crusade to the Two Arm.

What was truly amazing was that many of the weapons dealers were agreeing to go. As a group, most gunrunners were patently dishonest and habitually greedy, the hazards of the trade. While they had easy access to fully stocked weapons ships and men to run them, they never did anything that would be considered idealistic. And they never did anything for free.

Yet this seemed to be exactly what Zarex was getting them to do. At least two dozen ships stocked with weapons and technicians had been reported leaving the Five Arm for the Two over the past few days. And several more were in orbit around *Rocks 32*, apparently ready to embark for the same location. One of these was even a ship from *Slingerlands 7*.

But all this was really of little concern to the two men. Why a group of slimy arms dealers had so suddenly found religion did not interest them.

They were here for a different reason.

One of the two men finally approached Zarex and shook his hand.

"I understand there is a big fight brewing somewhere?" the man asked Zarex.

Zarex looked him directly in the eye. "Yes, and I am here to recruit souls turned good to help in the cause. Are you interested?"

"Maybe," the man told Zarex. "We've both felt the need for redemption lately."

"For what crimes, my brother?" Zarex asked him, bending slightly to hear the man.

The man just shrugged. "Take your pick," he said.

Still locked onto his eyes, Zarex thought a moment, then breathed four words: "My guess is betrayal. . . ."

At that moment, a small ship suddenly appeared over the castle. It could be seen clearly through the glass roof of the penthouse. Zarex looked up at it for a moment. When he looked back down, the two men were holding blaster guns on him.

Zarex laughed out loud. "What is this?" he asked. "A holdup?"

The men did not reply. They just simply pulled their capes off to reveal combat uniforms beneath. They were not arms dealers. They were Bad Moon Knights. Hands down the worst, most ruthless merc army on the Five Arm. They'd been after Zarex for nearly a century.

The partygoers scattered at first sight of them. A few women screamed. Somewhere, a blaster gun went off. Wine goblets crashed to the floor. The ship above the castle drew closer. A pulse beam appeared from its bottom, smashing through the glass roof and engulfing Zarex in an ice-blue ray. He was instantly frozen in place.

"Getting very sloppy in your old age," one of the two men told him.

"Or maybe this is the way it's supposed to be," Zarex managed to gasp.

Suddenly, a second red beam came down from the bottom of the hovering spaceship. It hit Zarex with the force of a sonic blast. He crumpled helplessly to the floor, unable to move, barely able to breathe.

Slowly, painfully, he faded away.

The next few hours went by in a dull, red haze for Zarex.

He was bundled aboard the small ship that had appeared above the castle and brought up to orbit, where he was transferred to a larger ion-powered vessel. Still encased in the crimson force field, he was placed in the control room of this second spaceship and put on display for the crew. A sign grafted onto the field read simply: *Zarex Red—Criminal Condemned to Die.* Many of the crew spat at him or tried to punch him through the force field. Some succeeded, some didn't. He was completely frozen and couldn't retaliate though, not that he would have anyway.

That his captors were hard-core Bad Moon Knights was without dispute now. He'd had many close calls with the bloodthirsty mercs over the years and escaped a number of assassination attempts by them. If anything, he knew them *too* well. Their black uniforms and perpetual scowls were hard to mistake. And he was sure this particular crew was in for a huge reward, now that it appeared they had him for good.

But then all this changed, for somewhere along the way, the BMK ship was attacked by the Solar Guards. Not ordinary SG, either. These raiders were outfitted in bright red uniforms and armed with bizarre weaponry. Zarex watched from the relative safety of his force field as the SG troopers—enormous every one of them—flooded aboard the BMK ship and ruthlessly mowed down the black-suited mercs. It wasn't a battle as much as a slaughter, strange because the SG and the BMK had shared many shady alliances in the past. Zarex actually felt sorry for the helpless BMK soldiers as the SG's strange weapons carved them into two or three pieces before each slice slowly dissolved away. Their screams were so loud, Zarex could hear them clearly, even through the force field.

The Solar Guards were here for him, of course, and no sooner had the firing died down when they moved Zarex to yet another ship. He knew by its interior that this was an SG Starcrasher; odd, too, as everywhere he looked, he saw the color red. Walls, floors, ceilings, men, weapons, wires, bubblers, tubes—all red. Back in Paradise, the SF3 man, Bonz, had described his executioners as strange SG troops dressed in crimson battle suits. That description matched these characters exactly.

They were acting strangely too. Zarex was again placed right up in the control room of the ship, but this time his captors all but ignored him. The SG crewmen running the ship seemed particularly robotic, with little interaction and zero conversation. It was almost as if they were under a spell or maybe a very strong hypnotic suggestion. How they'd known that the BMK had captured him, this after VonRexx had tipped off the BMK, Zarex had no idea. His proselytizing for help in the battle to come had carried him to many of his old haunts on the Five Arm, and he knew going to VonRexx's fire party was like walking into the belly of the beast. But that's exactly what he was supposed to be doing in these days since his return, transformed, from Paradise.

Now, all he could do was wait and see what his new tormentors had in store for him.

After a wild ride at Supertime speed to a destination impossible for him to determine, the SG ship made rendezvous with another vessel, the shape of which Zarex could not see. He could tell there was a meeting only because the SG ship came to a dead stop in space, and dark figures began beaming aboard just out of the corner of his eye.

Then he was moved again. This time under a blackout, meaning the force field was increased to the point where he could not see anything. He relied on his memories of friends and good times to get him through this very dark period. When he was able to see again, he realized he'd been released from the force field and was being dragged down a passageway by two huge SG soldiers. He'd been stripped of everything, including the Twenty 'n Six containing his faithful robot, 33418.

The guards remained mute as they pulled him along the corridor. This was definitely not a Starcrasher he was on now; the passageway was curved, a design element not found on any Empire starship. They eventually arrived at a doorway that was covered with strange hieroglyphics. Suddenly the door opened, and Zarex found himself staring into a dark and very strange control room. It was cramped, oval-shaped, and stuffed with odd, almost unrecognizable metallic gizmos, some of which appeared to be alive. They were full of tubes and glands and pumping and spurting weird liquids. Sections of the control room floor were covered with vomit. The smell was overwhelming. Zarex felt his stomach do a flip. He couldn't imagine a place as disturbing as this.

One of the guards pushed him through the open door. The moment he crossed the threshold, he was hit by a bright yellow beam. It struck him with the force of a Z-gun blast. He dropped to the deck—hard. His body began trembling uncontrollably. He went blind. The screeching in his ears became deafening. It felt like he was being ripped in two.

He was dragged to his feet and thrown into a hovering chair. It was covered with a sticky red substance Zarex could only guess was blood. He heard a crack and felt something tear across his face. The pain was unbearable. Another crack, this one ripping through the skin on his shoulder. Incredible pain, blood spurting everywhere. A third crack; this time it felt as if a slice had been taken out of his torso. Excruciating pain—but then he was able to open his eyes.

He was looking at about a dozen individuals. Crowded around his chair, under a single bright light, they were looking right back at him. Half were wearing red SG uniforms. They were huge, with strange weapons hanging from their belts, and skin that was also the color of blood. One of them was holding an atomic whip. A well-known favorite of torturers across the Galaxy, Zarex had already tasted the weapon three times—and was about to have a fourth. The other six figures were standing back in the murk. Zarex could barely see them. They were very short, half the size of the huge SG soldiers, and appeared to be wearing gray uniforms. It was impossible to see their faces, impossible to see anything more than shadows. But Zarex was sure at least a few of them were standing in the pools of vomit.

He was hit again with the atomic whip. This time across his

throat. Then it came again. And again. And again. Blood flowed into his eyes; he was half-blinded once more. His chair suddenly went horizontal. Now he was on his back, facing straight up. The light was shining directly above. A gaggle of probes dropped from the ceiling and began violating him in every orifice. Even while this was happening, he was hit by the atomic whip again. And again. And again.

He finally passed out; the pain was that intense. But even then, there was no relief. In his unconscious state he saw horrible little beings with large heads, huge eyes, and no mouths poking him, pinching him, sticking awful things into him. He tried to scream but couldn't. He tried to fight, but his arms would not move. The little beings were swarming all over him. The horror seemed like it would go on forever.

He woke from this nightmare somehow, only to find he'd been beaten with the whip even while unconscious. Judging by the burns and welts on his body, the flogging had gone on for several hours, even though in his experience lately, seconds seemed like eternities and an eternity could pass by in a second.

He was back sitting upright in the blood-sticky chair. He could not move now; he could barely see. The room was darker but at the same time seemed to be glowing an even deeper bloodred. And twice as many figures were standing around him, most of them Solar Guards, again all dressed in red, with sickly crimson skin. They looked as demonic as he did angelic. The probes were gone, but now he seemed to be held in place not by bonds but by the force of will of his tormentors. In a strange way, Zarex understood this.

One of these characters drew close to him now. This man stank; his body odor was overwhelming, his breath like a bilge trap. He was dirty and sweating and had an aura of disgust surrounding him.

"What do you want of me?" Zarex finally wailed, not out of pain but out of frustration.

"We want nothing from you except the pleasure of torture," the man hissed back at him. "There is no need to beat any information out of you. We already know what your cohorts are up to. We know their plans."

Zarex laughed in his smelly face. "That's a lie. . . ."

"Is it?" the man asked back. "How so?"

Zarex didn't mince words. "Because only a handful of people within your reach know what is to take place, and they are all beyond reproach."

The man let out a horrible laugh. "You assume we have a spy in your midst? We are above such things. Look at us. Don't you think we can just look in on your friends anytime we want?"

"We are as powerful as you," Zarex shot back. "What protects us from you is that we are the exact opposite of you."

The smelly man laughed again; Zarex heard some gurgling noises coming from behind him.

"You are new at this game, as we once were," the man hissed at him again. "Too bad for you."

Another crack of the atomic whip lashed Zarex across his face; it hurt tremendously. He decided to play their game.

"If you know what our plans are, then tell them to me," he said to the smelly one. "Prove you're not lying."

"You really doubt that we know?" his torturer asked.

"You *cannot* know," Zarex taunted him, "because you cannot read my mind. And you have not successfully captured any of my friends and made them talk. If you had, you wouldn't be bothering so much with me. So I dare you, then; tell me of our plans."

The smelly one laughed again, but this time it sounded like a shriek. He came up very close to Zarex's face.

"There is a point in space," he began in an ominous whisper. "It is inside the Two Arm, inside the Moraz Star Cloud, inside the No-Fly Zone. You simpletons have termed it *Zero Point*. You are very familiar with this place because it is where you so cleverly disappeared just before we were to drive the stake into you the first time. It is also where you reemerged when you foolishly decided to return to this side of things."

The smelly man got even closer.

"Your plan is this: you sent ahead one ship of the twelve you were using to hide in . . . in . . ." It was clear he could not speak the word, but it didn't matter. "This one ship comes out—lays the land, so to speak—for the others to follow ex-

actly seven days later. How do you know on the other side
that seven days have passed? Because you have people back
there counting, wasting their time and energy, but ticking off
the seconds one by one. Then they, too, will break through to
the other side. And when they do, we will be waiting for
them—and we will destroy them. And then the clash of pure
good against pure evil that must take place every million years
or so will happen again—and our side will win. And we will
rule until the next battle in another million years."

Zarex was stunned. He was sure that it showed on his battered face. The man hadn't been bluffing. He knew their plans
exactly.

"But how?" was all he could say.

The man laughed again; others in the background did, too.

"How?" he asked. "Take a look around you. Does this appear to be an Empire ship to you? Do we appear to be simple
Solar Guards?"

Zarex was hit by the whip again.

"Foolish questions asked by a fool!" the smelly man said.
"But at least now you know our purposes for keeping you here.
It is simply to make you feel more pain, more distress. And
to know that all history aside, we will finish the job on your
friends that we should have done the first time. When they
emerge at Zero Point, we will destroy them so completely,
they will not be able to go to either place, up or down. They
will be fated to stay in the middle, the worst place of all."

Zarex was speechless. Evil wanting nothing more than more
evil? There was so much sickness in that it was hard to fathom.
Whatever happened to these SG soldiers, whatever turned
them red, it was clear that depravity only made them stronger.
And Zarex had no doubts that they would follow through on
their boast to destroy the UPF fleet.

Worst of all, there was no way anyone could warn his
friends in Paradise that disaster would be waiting for them as
soon as they emerged from the other side of the Vanex Door.

Unless . . .

Zarex suddenly conjured up the strength to break through
his invisible bonds. He reached out and grabbed the smelly
SG man by the neck and crushed his throat. The man went

down to the deck, bleeding tremendously. Zarex then lashed out with his mighty left hand and hit another SG soldier so hard, he fractured the man's skull. He, too, dropped to the floor. Zarex was quickly off the chair, grabbing a third soldier and throwing him across the room—he hit with a *splat!*—but not before Zarex was able to take his blaster pistol from his belt.

The rest of the torture squad drew their weapons now, and a massive firefight broke out. Zarex was blasting away at anything that moved, though it seemed as if there were three times as many individuals in the dark room as before. He was hitting targets; he could hear bones breaking and skin sizzling, typical results of being pummeled by full-power blaster beams.

He, too, was being hit. In fact, it looked like a storm of green and red bolts coming his way. Instinct alone had him ducking this way and that, but many of the discharges found their marks and even the glancing blows were very painful.

This isn't working, he thought.

So he stopped firing, stood straight up, ready to take the barrage of full-power blasts head-on. But his tormentors stopped firing, too. Suddenly everything in the room was quiet again. Then something *very* disturbing happened.

The first man he had attacked, the smelly man with the horribly crushed throat, slowly got to his feet. He was still bleeding profusely, and his larynx was now just a knot of bones and gristle, but he was still very much alive. No sooner had he risen, when the man who'd suffered the fractured skull from Zarex's fist also got up off the floor. His wound was much more grisly; in fact, he should have been killed instantly. But he was grinning madly at Zarex, even as the gore slid down his cracked skull. Now the blasted and bloody bodies began rising all over the dark control room. Laughs and shrieks suddenly filled Zarex's ears.

He was horrified. The madness was more overwhelming now than the smell of this place. The message was clear, though: these characters couldn't be killed, and they certainly didn't want to kill him. They really did want nothing more than to torture him endlessly

What to do . . .

Zarex suddenly began speaking. About Paradise. About all the beautiful things he'd seen there. About the people and the emerald grass and the blue sky and the golden sun and the spectacular twilights. About how everything was good and pure and clean there.

Yes, he was new at this game, but that didn't mean he couldn't learn, and learn quickly.

His strategy had the desired effect. The smelly men could not stand it. They began whipping him harder and harder, but he did not stop talking about Heaven. They began striking him with electric swords, horribly painful, but he continued on about the mountains and the sea and the rivers than ran with nectar. It went on for a very long time, but eventually, the smelly ones began wailing. They couldn't take it anymore.

Suddenly, one of the smaller figures was in front of him. Still nothing more than a shadow, it drew out a long, shiny needle and plunged it right into Zarex's chest. He felt it go through his heart. Pain beyond description, but it was exactly what Zarex wanted his tormentors to do.

He died a moment later.

16

How *fast* was fast?

When flying in Supertime, Starcrashers could travel two light-years a minute. Small scout ships called Swipers could reach 2.5 light-years a minute for short periods of time.

Hunter's F-Machine cruised at two light-years *a second* at a setting he'd dubbed "Ultra Overdrive." But the name was misleading. It wasn't really "ultra" anything. It was just the throttle position he'd selected when he first started zipping around the Galaxy; the speed at which the few controls he had on his panel seemed to work best, the speed it took him to complete the Earth Race in almost no time at all.

But how fast *was* fast? His Ultra Overdrive setting was barely one-third of what he believed was his total available power. He'd never opened his aircraft to full speed; he knew serious consequences could result. He had gone up to 50 percent power a few times, and he'd traveled so fast on those occasions that he was literally able to get ahead of himself in time and thus become invisible. Great for spying on the bad guys, but the side effect was a real whammy on his mind and body. A sort of psychic hangover. Not a pleasant experience.

Now he was faced with a very long distance to travel in a very short amount of time. The clock was ticking down to when the rest of the UPF fleet would emerge from the Vanex Door. He really had no way to contact those who came over in the *Resonance 133* and was operating on the assumption that they made it and that the other eleven ships would, too. But in any case, time was running out, and he had no idea what would be waiting for him once he reached his goal. So getting there had to be done as quickly as humanly possible.

He'd crossed over from Paradise to find himself on the Four Arm, that piece of space where Joxx had taken to wandering. Now he knew he had to get to the Seven Arm. The problem was, it couldn't have been farther away. Because of the way the Milky Way was shaped, the Four Arm was at the exact opposite end of the Galaxy as the Seven Arm. This was a trip of nearly 95,000 light-years. The Galaxy itself was about 100,000 light-years across. A typical Starcrasher, traveling in Supertime, would take more than a month to complete such a trip. For this not to be a complete fool's errand, Hunter had to make it there much quicker.

So it was a question of him finding out just how fast fast was.

Once he'd left the *ShadoVox*, he pushed his throttle up to normal cruising speed, two ly a second. As soon as he was certain that all of his vital systems had survived the transdimensional jump from the Twenty 'n Six (and they sometimes didn't), he began pushing the throttle ahead even further, though bit by bit. He had to get to the other side of the Milky Way, so navigating wasn't a concern. He simply plugged his quadtrol directly into his flight bubbler and told it to lead the way. The route spat out by the quadtrol actually had him skirting the top of the Ball, the terminally pacific center of both the Galaxy and the Empire. So far in his travels in the seventy-third century, Hunter had come nowhere near this place.

Once his flight plan was set, he inched the throttles up a bit more. At 50 percent power, he watched the controls on his panel slowly begin to go backward. As before at this setting, he was getting ahead of himself in time. He nudged the throttle ahead a bit further, to about 60 percent power, unknown territory for him now. His panel indicators began flying backward now; meanwhile, the stars outside were beginning to blur. Another push forward; his eyes began to water. He touched his face and felt his beard—several weeks old now—start to retreat back into his skin. The hair on his head began getting shorter, too.

I hope nothing else starts to shrink, he thought.

Another push forward. Seventy percent power. The atomic paint on his nose cone began getting wet and ripping off. Why? Because it was getting younger very quickly. And as a drying process was always ongoing, it was reversing itself. Or at least that's the only theory he could think up at the moment.

A push up to 80 percent. Now he was really into a bizarro situation. He was going so fast in space and time that his speed indicators actually showed him in the negative. He had no idea just how fast his velocity was, or even if *velocity* was the right word at this point. Whenever he would hit the quadtrol to ask this question, it would reply so strangely, he had to assume it was answering questions he had yet to ask it but would do so in the near future. At one point it read: "*Saturn 5.*" At another, "*F-4 Phantoms*" popped up. These things were vaguely familiar to him but disturbingly so. And what if he saw a readout that said: "*Catastrophic flight termination,*" quadtrolese for "*Blown to bits*?" At this point, with all that was going on, he really preferred the cause of his demise to come as a surprise.

So he stopped asking the quadtrol any more questions.

He pushed the throttle to 90 percent and suddenly found the control panel just a few millimeters from his nose. He wasn't leaning forward; actually, he was moving so fast, the atoms in his cockpit were stretching out, distorting themselves, trying to catch up with themselves. His cockpit glass became a mirror; he caught his reflection in it. It was frightening; he, too, was distorted: huge head, his helmet looking gigantic, while the rest of his frame was shrinking down to infinity. Whenever he moved his hands, it looked like he was stretching out for a mile or more, even though the real distance was just a couple feet at the most.

One final nudge—up to 95 percent. A glimpse at his reflection now showed a fantastic distortion; he didn't even seem real anymore. He was no longer flesh and blood; he looked more like an animated character, a drawing, in vivid reds, yellows, and blues, and absolutely two-dimensional, as if he were suddenly existing flat on a page. Even the strange voice in his ear was speechless on this new development. Three words somehow popped into his head though; he thought they might have come from somewhere way back in his childhood: *comic book character.*

That's what he looked like. At close to total power, that's what he'd become.

The Ball went by him in a blur.

Again, he'd never been anywhere near the center of the Galaxy before. And even though he was just skirting it, not going any closer than 200 light-years to what was considered its outer border, what he saw on his long-range scanners was fascinating in a strangely sad way. There were billions of star systems in there, but many of them were remarkably alike. Either one or two stars, all of approximately the same size, all with six to eight planets revolving in perfect orbits. He saw none of the celestial exotica one could find very readily out on the Fringe. No wild nebulas, no titanic multicolored gas clouds, no really weird things like triple-ringed planets or ocean worlds, or planets that were entirely sand or snow or jungle or metal. It was odd, because even though the vast majority of the Empire's citizens lived on the planets within the Ball, the place lacked any kind of character or personality. There was no sense of discovery here. No sense of wanting to see other things, other places, other people.

As he tore by, moving faster than fast, his mind, working on a strange kind of time delay, started musing about this center of the Empire. Did the people here even know about the UPF's invasion of the Two Arm? Had they ever heard of the mythical Home Planets? Or the lost race called the Americans? Did the thought ever come to mind that all was not so perfect with the Imperial Court on Earth? What would be the reaction of the people who lived here if they ever found out that the Fourth Empire, like the Second, had been built and based on lies and deceit of, well, *galactic* proportions? Would it have an effect on them? Would it drive them to protest the Empire? To take up arms against it?

Looking at all those perfect little planets in their perfect little star systems as he flew by at about a billion miles an hour, the answer that came back to him was a distinct *No*.

He never thought he'd ever admit it, but for once he actually craved being out on the Fringe.

That's when he heard a voice in his ear say, *"Remember Hawk, Earth is part of the Fringe, too. . . ."*

Something strange—or strange in a different way—happened about halfway across the Galaxy.

Hunter had his string comm set on wide scan, meaning it would pick up anything within fifty light-years of his location at any given time. As he was flying so fast that location was changing with every microsecond, so he was essentially sweeping a large part of the Milky Way with this long-range communications device. The first few minutes into his dash across the Empire, he heard little more than star songs in his headset—the natural sounds of the stars as they revolved around the center of the Galaxy.

But suddenly, his string comm unit began screaming with trouble calls coming from both near and far. There was so much of this panicked chatter on his headset, Hunter had a hard time determining who was doing the calling and what was happening to them. He was able to pick up some coherent words here and there. They spoke of horrific things: planets being attacked, ships being blown out of the skies, innocents being slaughtered, both in space and on planets. Some of these calls were coming from the Six and Five Arms; others were coming in from as far away as the Three and Nine Arms. It seemed as if the outer Galaxy was suddenly in the throes of something very wicked and evil. And the perpetrators weren't the usual gang of suspects like space pirates and outlaw mercs. Nor were any of these calls linked to the fighting between the SG and SF. That war was still going nonstop, but those hostilities were not related to this. This horror was coming from somewhere else.

He listened to it all for about a minute, the only one link being that those doing the attacking were mysterious, unknown, and in many cases unseen.

Then suddenly it all went away. His headset returned to

nothing more than the gentle sounds of the star music and the warm and fuzzy static coming from the Ball.

Weird . . .

Finally, up ahead, Hunter saw the Seven Arm come into view.

He yanked back on the throttles, returning to his slower cruising speed of two light-years a second. Everything seemed to turn back in on itself again. He caught his reflection in the canopy a second time, and it appeared that he'd returned to his old self. He was three-dimensional again, and all the colors around him had toned back down. He checked all his vital parts, first on his body and then on his spacecraft. All were normal. He'd survived the mad dash, and his machine had survived, too. With the brief burst of horrible Mayday calls still ringing in his head, he finally asked the quadtrol a serious question: How long had it taken him to go from one side of the Galaxy to the other? At his normal cruising speed, it would have taken fourteen precious hours.

Now the answer came back: *14 minutes.*

And his F-Machine wasn't even breathing hard.

Approaching the Seven Arm was not like coming up to the border of the Galaxy's other swirls. In most cases, there was a definable frontier that separated the beginning of an arm from the outer layers of the Ball.

The Seven Arm was different. There was no border, no immediate one, anyway. Here the stars simply petered out into a kind of no-man's-land, a twilight zone that stretched for more than a thousand light-years. No stars, no planets, nothing—just a total void. If one were flying in an ion-ballast ship, it would take a long, very lonely time to pass through here. Even in a Starcrasher, it would make for an uncomfortable nine-hour trip. Hunter pushed his throttle to 45 percent; he was hoping he could get through this in a matter of seconds.

Still, it was very odd. Whenever he had his ship going at faster than cruising speed, the sensation was one of the stars becoming streaks of light that passed all around in a fantastic light show, not unlike the visual while riding aboard a Starcrasher but much more intense. He'd just seen fourteen minutes of this in his sprint across the Milky Way.`

Crossing the void, though, there was nothing really to hold on to. Any stars to be seen were very very faint, and the feeling he got was not of traveling through a piece of starless space but of falling into a deep pit of nothingness. With few frames of reference—combined with the effects of nearly double ultra–high speed—it suddenly became difficult to judge up from down, left from right, even though these things did not really exist in space.

The quadtrol had told him previously that there were standing orders for both SF and SG ships to avoid this place, simply because it was unsafe for normal passage. Hunter was beginning to think that maybe this wasn't the only reason the Empire never ventured here. The quadtrol had also told him that many spaceships had been lost in this void at the beginning of the Fourth Empire, and that the place had been considered unlucky or cursed since. As the people of the Galaxy were known to be very superstitious, one hint of any place bearing bad karma would be enough for it to be avoided *en masse*.

Difficult to transit *and* unlucky? No wonder no one ever came here.

He finally started to see the mass of the arm ahead of him, his equilibrium returning as the pinpricks of light turned into star clusters and then individual systems. He was now approaching the "crowded" part of the Seven Arm.

But immediately he knew something was wrong.

He called up several star maps from his flight bubbler showing this part of the Seven. The maps had come from the star charts he'd filched from the *ShadoVox*, and it would make sense that they would be extremely accurate, flawless even.

But this wasn't the case.

Hunter conjured up a floating screen that would serve to match up what was on the map with what he was seeing up ahead. That was the problem; there *was* no match. None of the star systems or their alignments looked like anything what he was viewing on the float screen. This didn't make sense. The charts were just a few years old, put together not from on-hand observation but through long-range scans from Earth, scans that were supposed to be accurate to the millimeter. Yet the stars in front of him weren't just out of alignment, their overall dispersal was different.

Everything moved inside the Galaxy. Stars, planets, moons—people. But nothing moved this fast. Entire star systems didn't just change positions overnight. True, while the Galaxy had been settled for nearly 5,000 years, some parts had been lost as the empires fell and rose. But the Fourth Empire was on the verge of reclaiming nearly 90 percent of the inhabited planets these days, and it certainly had the technology to have the entire realm mapped.

The only logical conclusion: the official imperial star charts were not only wrong, they'd been intentionally drawn that way.

He reached the first star system. It wasn't on the map. It was just the first place he came to. And here was another surprise.

He'd been led to believe that not only was the Seven Arm practically empty, it had never been settled by anyone in the first place. Yet this first system held a medium-size sun with seven planets going around it, and it was these worlds that told the strange tale. The F-Machine's ultrapower scanners showed the planets all to be empty. But just about every square inch of their surfaces appeared battle-scarred, horribly cratered, and torn apart. Ancient cities on every planet, bombed into dust. Man-made debris was everywhere. So much that rings of it were not only orbiting each planet, but massive clouds of the stuff were drifting throughout the system as well.

Hunter knew at least partly what had happened here; the devastation on the planets was the result of a titanic battle, fought a very long time ago. But what about the free-floating space junk? The stuff between the planets? He plugged his quadtrol into his long-range scanner and was soon reading information on sampled pieces of the debris. The initial indications showed they'd been floating around for a thousand years, maybe more.

A large chunk of junk came up on him. Hunter slowed his machine to a crawl. The piece of debris was about a half mile long and half again as wide. Metal in character. At least a thousand years old, so the quadtrol told him. The question was, what was it? Or, what had it been?

Hunter asked the quadtrol again. On his scanner screen, it presented three dozen holographic images, seemingly random pieces of space junk, coming together to re-form their previously original state. What he saw was an enormous metal ball, 250 miles across, with several thousand mile-high spikes sticking out of it all over.

What the hell was this? It wasn't an artificial moon; it had never had an atmosphere. It wasn't any kind of battle station, for the same reason.

Then it came to him.

It was a space mine. A massive weapon built to explode should anything or anyone come near it. And there were millions of similar gigantic pieces for as far as his eyes could see. That's when the cold reality of the situation hit home. Millions of pieces of this kind of debris could only mean one thing: He was in a minefield.

A very large, very old one. One in which all the mines had exploded a long time ago, and no one had bothered to pick up the debris.

Or didn't want to.

He continued winding his way through the massive, jumbled cloud, going very, very slowly. He knew it would take him much longer to make it through the debris field than it did to fly the starless void preceding it. All the while, he was passing the system's outer planets, and each was like the one before it: battered, torn up, ancient cities reduced to sand.

Once out of the system, he was tempted to boot his throttle ahead a bit. But the ocean of wreckage went on unabated, and he had no choice but to continue weaving his way through it. Even as he saw the next star system come into view—it, too, was uncharted, or more accurately out of place on the star map—everywhere he looked were waves of space junk. Twisting and turning the flying machine around it was difficult, even for a skilled flier like himself. But one thing was clear: there was no way a typical Empire ship, military or civilian, could make it through, first because of the ancient minefield and now these bands of floating obstacles.

Obviously that was the intention all along.

He passed through a dozen star systems. All of them were deserted, abandoned, uncharted. All of them thick with long bands of metallic space junk. Not just pieces of exploded space mines now but also gigantic chunks of ancient spaceships, artificial moons, natural satellites. All of it very, very old—but still making for a very effective barrier.

Like barbed wire . . . he thought.

By the time he entered the thirteenth system, his brain was fighting hard to put everything together. First, a minefield. Then the celestial equivalent of barbed wire. What did this tell him?

Or better yet, what could he expect next?

The answer came a moment later when his spacecraft's defensive warning systems began blaring. It was so loud, Hunter thought his crash helmet would split in two.

He pushed his quadtrol and asked it what the hell was going on. The answer from the know-it-all device was both chilling and brief: "Antispaceship missiles closing in. . . ."

Pull up, Hawk!

Hunter didn't even think about it. He yanked on the F-Machine's control stick and put the superfighter on its tail. An enormous missile roared beneath him not two seconds later.

He leveled off with a reverse loop, but no sooner were his wings straight when the defensive warning alarm went off again. He didn't have to ask the quadtrol what was going on this time. He could see the flare of another huge missile coming his way. He veered right purely on instinct and saw the giant missile pass by an instant later.

His defensive warning system never shut down; it kept right on blaring as more missiles were headed for him. The quadtrol said the weapons were not being fired from any hard surface, so there weren't people down there on those devastated planets trying to knock him down. Rather the missiles seemed to have been left dormant in space, programmed to come alive whenever an intruder came near.

Another flare showed up straight ahead. Hunter played it

smart this time. Just as he was going into his third evasive maneuver, he hit his quadtrol's universal event inquiry switch. Essentially, this was asking the device to scan anything unusual within its vicinity. It quickly assessed the missile as it roared by. The weapon was a true monster, at least fifty times bigger than the F-Machine and too big to have been built as a simple antispacecraft weapon.

That was enough for him. He hit his throttles hard and rocketed away from the area with an incredible burst of speed. It took some fancy maneuvering to get around the waves of space junk in his path. But he counted to three and then pulled back on the juice again. He found himself twenty-five light-years away from the missile barrage—and this time he was breathing hard.

Once stable again, Hunter asked the quadtrol exactly what kind of a missile had been being shot at him back there.

The answer came back: *Saturn 5*.

Hunter stared at the readout for a moment. It was the reply he'd received while tearing across the Galaxy; now it was appearing in the right time context. But why did the name itself sound so familiar? It wasn't any kind of rocket he'd heard about since coming to this century. But how about in his last?

He asked the quadtrol what the missile's original function was. The reply that came back only pricked his memory: *"Original lunar exploration vehicle booster."*

Hunter finally asked the quadtrol when and where the missile had been originally designed. This reply took a while to churn out. When it did, it was both startling and mystifying.

It read: *"Earth, 1961 A.D."*

Hunter had learned by now that few things in this time and place made sense, especially out here in the wilds of outer space.

But all this was especially absurd. He was supposed to be in an empty part of the Galaxy, yet already he'd encountered an ancient minefield, light-years of obstructions and ancient debris. Now a barrage of gigantic missiles, designed more than 6,000 years ago, on Earth, of all places, weapons that would turn him into subatomic dander if one ever hit him.

What was the explanation for this?

Before he could come up with a suitable answer, the comm set inside his helmet suddenly came to life again.

"This is your one and only warning. . . . Leave this sector immediately. . . ."

The voice was gravelly and distorted. It sounded like it was coming from a million miles and a few thousand years away. Which was not that far from the truth.

"We have orders to shoot you down," the voice said again. "Leave at once. . . ."

Hunter turned around in his cockpit and was astonished to see three spacecraft had crept up on his tail. *Always watch your six.* Those four words came back to him loud and clear now. His failure to do so had suddenly put him into a very grave predicament. Another band of space junk was lying dead ahead. It stretched for light-years in every direction, up, down, left, and right, and was much denser than those before it. Pushing himself into ultra-ultradrive now could prove fatal or, at the very least, slightly suicidal.

In other words, he'd fallen into a trap.

At that moment, one of the strange craft pulled up alongside him. It was about the same size as the F-Machine, and the similarity did not stop there. It also had a wing under midfuselage, though its tips were cranked upward at both ends. It had a tail supporting two small wings in the back, but these were pointing downward. Its nose was conical and blunt, and it was carrying four ancient yet extremely lethal-looking missiles underneath its body.

There were two men in the glass bubble cockpit staring back at him. Helmets on, oxygen masks in place, he could only see their eyes. Hunter's psyche was flashing like crazy now. Memories were washing up inside him. This craft was the closest thing he'd seen to his machine since coming to this century. And he'd seen its type before. Way, *way* back, in that other life he had led, before all the insanity began.

He asked the quadtrol: What is it? But he already knew the answer. He'd seen it during his quick galactic crossing.

"F-4 Phantom," was what the quadtrol screen said.

Somehow Hunter knew this might take him ages to understand, but at the same time, he realized the quadtrol was right.

This plane was a Phantom—or better yet, a re-creation of one that had the ability to fly in space. He knew this type of flight machine. He had fought alongside these aircraft in his previous life; he was sure of it.

But what could they possibly be doing here?

There were more of them coming up to meet him. But he didn't want to fight them. The Seven Arm was supposed to be deserted—though all this had given lie to that notion. But whatever the case, he was the intruder here. And he had already passed through a number of defensive barriers and still he had not stopped.

In other words, these guys had every right to shoot him down.

Still, he had to get away from them. He had to find Far Planet, or this whole exercise would become a huge, senseless joke. But the debris was still pretty thick up ahead. He still couldn't boot his craft up to any kind of ultrapower as he wasn't sure if he would pass right through the debris or simply crash into it.

Maybe a warning shot will scare them away.

Hunter pushed his weapons bar, and a mighty multiblast shot out of the front of his craft. Six beams of blinding X-beam power. But then something strange happened: the flight of ancient aircraft suddenly started shooting—not at him, but at the barrage of X beams he'd just fired.

Their weapons seemed extremely elderly, but they twisted and turned and intersected his barrage perfectly, causing an enormous explosion, which resulted in a gigantic ball of flame and debris.

Hunter let go another barrage. Again the Phantoms fired at it. Again they hit it on the nose. Another ball of flame was produced; this one quickly joined with the first.

Counterweaponry? The word just popped into Hunter's head.

Before he could ponder it any further though, more bells and whistles went off in his cockpit.

One was from the quadtrol, and it was bearing surprisingly good news. He'd asked it way back at the beginning of the journey to look for any world that would qualify as Far Planet. At least according to the star charts. The strange thing now was, the device had found it.

How? By checking the map. Just like Tomm said.

Hunter was astonished. Every point and star on the chart was wrong and intentionally put out of place, except the small dot of a world called Far Planet. It was right where it was supposed to be. And that was no more than a few hundred miles below his present position.

He immediately put the nose of the craft down and boosted his throttles, hoping to shake the Phantoms and make for the planet as well. But then came the second warning, this one from right inside his head.

Hawk, check your six!

Damn . . .

Hunter turned around and saw not the flight of Phantoms coming at him, but the ball of flame and debris that had resulted from their counterblasting his warning shots. Before he could hit his throttles, the orb of high-speed shrapnel slammed into the back of his spacecraft. He nearly went through the canopy, the impact was so great. His spacecraft immediately began spinning out of control. There were so many warning buzzers going off now, he couldn't tell which one was warning him about what.

He went hard right and pointed the nose straight down—this took him out of the spin and punched him through the top of the planet's atmosphere. He yanked the throttles back to 1/10,000 percent power—this to avoid a very nasty collision with the ground below—only to look behind him again and see that the tail of his Flying Machine was on fire. He turned forward and started pulling on his joystick. A steep ascent back into space might put the fire out. But it was no good. His controls were not responding.

There was another explosion, and the curve of the planet below became more acute. Smoke began filling the cockpit. The fire was crawling up his wings. He began pushing control panels, hoping something would work. But it was no use. All of the lights on his flight board had blinked out for good.

Came one final explosion—and everything started to go black.

Hunter couldn't believe it.

He'd just shot himself down.

17

Hunter awoke, facedown, in the middle of a shallow stream.

The water was cold. It was running up his nose and into his mouth and even into his ears. He could not move. Every bone in his body was broken, or at least that's how it felt. He couldn't see, either. Something warm and sticky was keeping his eyelids shut. Most of all, his head hurt. A lot.

I guess this isn't Heaven, he thought.

He managed to roll onto his back, allowing the water to pour over his chest. It felt like ice, but it seemed to revive him. He cupped a handful of water and brought it up to his eyes. It was so cold it stung, but it helped clear away whatever was blocking his vision. Another splash of water, then another. Finally he was able to see.

He was in the middle of a forest. His uniform was burned and ripped; his helmet was floating in a pool nearby. The F-Machine was caught in an enormous tree off to his right. Hanging about twenty feet off the ground, its wings and tail section were still on fire. Hunter felt a sharp pain in his chest; the aircraft looked irreparably damaged. The canopy had fallen off, his ejector seat had activated, and his ancient parachute had billowed open. But it was hanging off another tree nearby.

This didn't make sense. How had he wound up here, dumped not on the jagged rocks that surrounded the bottom of the huge tree but in the freezing-cold stream? It had not been a soft landing for him. But it had not been a fatal one, either.

He managed to lift himself to his knees and then finally got to his feet. Though he was in a deep woods, it was very warm. There was a large yellow sun almost directly overhead; it felt strangely soothing on his battered face. The air here was dry and sweet. Wherever he was, the puff was holding up well. The trees were numerous in all directions, with only the stream running through them, and a small grassy bank on each side.

He took a step and was amazed that his legs weren't shattered for good. Two more steps, and he was out of the water. He half expected the Phantoms to swoop down on him at any second, so he made for the cover of the nearest tree. But the only things overhead were fair weather clouds and the deep blue sky. Nor was there any sound, except the wind in the leaves.

He retrieved his helmet, then made his way over to the tree holding his Flying Machine. He took one long look, then fell to the seat of his pants. The fuselage bent and scored. The cockpit insides were still burning, and the tail section was in dozens of pieces. The crash had been catastrophic. His aircraft was destroyed. Dead . . .

But how could he still be alive?

He began walking.

The trees ran very thick past the tiny grassy bank, so he followed the stream, trying to retrace the path the Flying Machine took on its way down. He finally reached an outcrop of rock, which after climbing, he was able to look back toward the crash site. What he saw astonished him. There was a wide swath cut through the dense forest, clearly made as his machine had burned its way in. The damage to the tops of the trees was extensive—big limbs cracked and torn asunder, small pockets of flame still burning fiercely.

He had no memory of this; no memory of ejecting or separating from the aircraft at the last moment. Had he passed out? Had he been knocked unconscious? He didn't know.

Only one thing was for sure: there was no way he should have survived that kind of crash.

He sat down on a flat rock and activated the image capsule Tomm had given him; it had somehow survived as well. Suddenly the spitting image of the space monk was floating in front of him.

"You are activating this for only one reason," the diminutive priest began. "You made it to Far Planet. Are you still in one piece?"

Hunter reviewed the various bumps, bruises, and contusions covering his battered body. "We'll have to see about that," he said.

The image smiled. "Is this place what you expected?"

Hunter shook his head no. "I was expecting someplace much wilder . . ."

"Wilder?"

He scanned the pastoral setting. "It looks like any other scrub planet in the Galaxy. Lots of grass. Lots of trees. After what I had to do to get here, I thought it would be much different. I thought there'd be big cities and lots of people."

The image of Tomm laughed. "Brother Hawk, I know at some time in the past I must have counseled you on this, but allow me to do so again: Few things in this universe are as they first seem. Keep an open mind out here, my friend. You are going to need it."

"So what's your crucial advice?" Hunter asked the image. He was anxious to get going, keenly aware that the clock was still ticking and that if he didn't at least try to complete this part of the mission—whatever the hell it was—then there was a good chance there would be a disaster at Zero Point when the rest of the UPF fleet emerged.

"The most important thing to know is this," the image said. "Do not tell anyone why you are here until you get to the person you have to talk to. They are extremely clever out here, and very protective. They will do just about anything to make you break your confidence—and the strange thing is, they can absolutely follow through on whatever they might use to tempt you. And they *will* tempt you."

Hunter would have laughed if he wasn't hurting so much. "How can I be tempted any more than a chance to stay in Heaven with the girl I love, instead of coming back here to fight a war that will be almost impossible to win?"

The image smiled again but didn't completely understand.

"I think you'll be surprised by this place, Hawk," Tomm said. "Just go with the flow, as they used to say, and see what happens. Be strong, though. I'm sure everyone is counting on you."

With that, the image disappeared.

Hunter just stared at the empty piece of space where Tomm had just been.

"Wait! That's it?" he yelled.

He tried to activate the image again but got nothing more than a crackle of static. He tried again and again. Still nothing. The capsule was depleted. He couldn't even conjure up the first two images. In frustration, he threw the capsule away. It seemed to travel more than a mile before finally disappearing into the woods.

This was just great. Here he was, literally at the end of the Galaxy, with no way home, no way to contact anybody, nobody to contact if he did—and no idea what he was supposed to be doing here. He reached into his side pocket and felt one of his last apples had turned to mush.

And nothing to eat, either, he thought.

He got up and began walking again.

After an hour of trudging through the forest, he reached a long narrow field that led to another outcrop of rocks. He climbed these rocks cautiously and looked out on the other side.

He found himself atop a tall hill. Directly below him was a closely cut field of grass with a water fountain in the middle and park benches surrounding it. Beyond that was a main street that led into a small town. He counted two dozen buildings at most, both homes and businesses, on either side of the street. He also saw lots of trees and flower boxes and streetlights and even fire hydrants.

Looking down on the sleepy little settlement, he just shook his head. "I came across the Galaxy—*for this?*"

• • •

He made his way down the hill and past the village green. His blaster rifle had been lost in the crash, but his ray gun had survived, tucked away in his holster.

He walked to the edge of the small town now, gun in hand. The village didn't look any different than a trillion other settlements scattered throughout the Galaxy's billions of planets. If anything, it looked like something more readily found in the Ball. Peaceful. Bucolic. *Uninteresting*.

It also appeared deserted. Hunter saw no signs of life. He studied the main street. It was well-paved and ran for two blocks where it widened out into the town square. There was a small bandstand here and a flagpole, but no banner was flying from it.

He moved down the street, sticking to one side, always checking around him, in back of him, and methodically scanning every door front. The names on some of the stores were vaguely familiar to him. Howard Johnson's. Sears Roebuck. Woolworth's. Rexall. These were obviously places to eat, to buy clothes and appliances, to buy medicines. Though they were way down deep in his psyche, it was always a small triumph when he remembered something from his past life. But what were these ancient things from a long-ago Earth doing way out here, at a point just about as far away from Earth as one could get?

What about the Phantoms and the Saturn 5s?

He hoped he would find out.

"Hey mister, want a ride?'

Hunter turned around toward the voice; instinct alone had his gun up and ready.

What he saw was a very, very long ground vehicle, painted white, with many windows and four wheels. Hunter was familiar with this type of machine. It was called a limousine.

There was a teenage boy behind the steering wheel. He was wearing a black suit coat, a bow tie, and a black cap.

"What did you say?" Hunter asked him.

"I asked you if you needed a ride," the kid yelled back. "There ain't no buses running today, and you look like you've got someplace you want to go."

Hunter just shrugged. He couldn't search the entire planet on foot, looking for somebody he didn't even know. On the other hand, whoever was running Far Planet obviously knew he was here. It would have been hard for anyone to miss his grand entrance. So, he supposed, the best way to find out where he was going was to let them take him there. Or something like that. Like Tomm said: Just go with the flow and see what happens.

He climbed into the back of the limo.

They roared out of town and a minute later were speeding along a deserted country road.

The limo was so long Hunter could hardly see the driver. The backseat was incredibly comfortable. His frame sank a good six inches into it. There was a fully stocked bar within reach. He even liked the twinkling lights that ran the length of the limo's interior.

He put his weary head back to rest. He couldn't remember the last time he'd gone to sleep. It sometimes seemed like he hadn't caught any Zs since he arrived in the seventy-third century more than two years ago. If he could just close his eyes, just for a few seconds and . . .

Wake up, Hawk. . . .

He was suddenly awake, gun up and ready. How long had he been asleep? A minute? An hour? He couldn't tell. They were still tooling along the country road, but the landscape outside had changed. They were now driving past sand dunes, some covered with beach grass, some bare. Hunter thought he could smell ocean air, even though the limo's windows were all shut tight and the air-conditioning was going full blast.

They topped a hill, and the limo began to slow down. They turned left and were now on a gravel road, driving between the sand dunes. Hunter was tempted to yell up to the kid and ask where they were going, but he saved his breath. He knew he would find out soon enough.

They made another turn, and now straight ahead Hunter could see a single building standing out among the dunes. It was like a big box, with a huge rolling door on its front and a smaller door on the side. There was a long apron of black asphalt in front of it. Beach grass and sand covered the other three sides.

The limo driver pulled up to the front door, then looked into his rearview mirror for the first time.

"Want to stretch your legs?" he yelled back to Hunter.

But Hunter was already climbing out of the big car. He stood in front of the stark building; it was made of very thin materials, plastic and tin. As unremarkable as it was, it was familiar to him.

It was an airplane hangar.

He turned to ask the driver why they had stopped here and was startled to see the car had departed. He just caught a last glimpse of it as it retreated back down the dusty road.

When Hunter turned back to the hangar, he found an elderly man standing in front of him. He was small, bent over, with a huge mustache and a nonatomic cigar jammed in his mouth. He was wearing mechanic's overalls and was rubbing his greasy hands on a very greasy rag. A name tag over his left side pocket read D. Jones. He looked vaguely familiar.

"You here to pick up the buggy?" he asked Hunter with a rasp.

"Buggy?"

The old guy looked at him like he had two heads. "Yeah, the buggy? Your wings? Your airplane?"

"*My* airplane?"

The old guy just rolled his eyes, put the rag in his back pocket, and opened the hangar door.

Inside was Hunter's spacecraft.

He nearly passed out. It didn't seem possible. But here it was, not only fixed but looking better than ever. The paint job alone was superb. The ship was now bright white, with bright red and blue stripes and a scattering of white stars here and there. It was dazzling.

Hunter staggered forward, numbly climbing the access ladder that had been placed up against the open canopy. The interior of the cockpit was completely repaired; even his seat was refurbished. Everything looked the same as before, only newer and better.

He reached in and pushed his flight control panel to life. He was soon looking at a diagnostics holograph of his power pack, the mysterious combination of Time Shifter components that he'd had put together so long ago on Fools 6—it was the reason the F-Machine could go as fast as it did. The power system looked as new as everything else on the craft.

He turned back to the mechanic, who was waiting at the bottom of the ladder.

"How?" was all Hunter could think to ask him.

The old guy just shrugged and chomped down on his cigar again.

"Do you have any idea how long I've been working on these things?" he asked Hunter. "Believe me, I've seen some wrecks in my day. But this one was a peach."

Hunter slid back down the ladder and shook the man's dirty hand. He was so ecstatic, he was missing the big picture—at least for the moment.

But then it dawned on him. "What's the catch?" he asked the mechanic.

The old guy just shuffled his feet. "No catch," he said. "Consider it a favor."

"For a favor in return, you mean?" Hunter asked.

The old guy walked him back outside. "Let's just say I'm a curious guy," he said.

"About what exactly?"

"Who are you here to see?" the old guy asked him, suddenly dropping the aw-shucks act.

Hunter just shrugged. "I don't know," he replied truthfully.

The old guy nodded. "OK, that was a tough one," he said. "Why not just tell me why you came here?"

Hunter hesitated, but only for a second. "I was told not to talk about that," he said finally.

The old guy just shrugged again. "OK by me," he said. "After all, I just work here."

With that, he closed the hangar door and began to walk away.

Hunter stopped him.

"Wait a minute," he said. "What about my airplane?"

The old guy just looked at him and shrugged.

"What airplane?" he asked.

He disappeared around the corner of the building. Hunter walked over to the big door and slid it open.

The hangar was empty.

The old guy had vanished as well.

Though Hunter searched all around the barn for him, he was nowhere to be found. He searched inside the hangar, too. But there was absolutely no evidence to indicate his aircraft was ever there.

With little else to do, he walked back down the dusty path to the main road. Here, he found another vehicle waiting for him.

It was a sports car. It was painted deep blue and had flame decals plastered all over it. Hunter had seen a similar vehicle back on Planet America—and probably many times in his previous lives.

It was called a Corvette.

Another young kid was behind the wheel. He was about the same age as the limo driver, but he was not so dressed up. And his hair was as greasy as the mechanic's rag.

"Need a ride, mister?" he asked Hunter.

Hunter looked in all directions. There was nothing out here by the dunes and the road.

"I guess I do," he finally replied.

Seconds later, they were screaming down the winding, hilly road. Hunter was holding on for his life as the young kid wordlessly went through all five gears in about as many seconds. Hunter hadn't experienced these kind of *g*-forces when he was dashing across the Galaxy. And he wasn't sure, but he didn't think these Corvettes came equipped with ejection seats. He was glad he was still wearing his crash helmet.

It turned out to be a short but very fast ride. They soon found themselves driving through a more wooded area, leaving the dunes and sand behind. The temperature changed rapidly; suddenly it was cool and raw, with some mist in the air. They began climbing a hill. Hunter would have thought a downshift was in order, but his tight-lipped driver did not concur. They went right over the top of the hill, all four wheels leaving the pavement before slamming back down again.

Around one more bend, and then the kid stood on the brakes. The car came to a screaming halt.

When the dust and rubber vapor cleared, Hunter found himself looking up a steep hill. At the top was a ramshackle house with a distinct lean to the left.

Hunter looked over at the driver, who just looked back at him. It was obvious this was the end of the line.

"Keep in touch," Hunter said, climbing out of the car.

He walked up the hill toward the house. It looked more familiar to him with every step. He reached the porch to find an elderly woman coming out the front door. Hunter stopped in his tracks. She not only looked familiar, she looked like him—that is, there seemed to be a strong family resemblance.

"We've been waiting for you, Hawk!" she exclaimed, throwing her arms around him. There was a familiar scent of chocolate and flour on her hands.

Before he could say a word, an elderly gentleman came out onto the porch as well. The man had tears in his eyes. He could have passed as Hunter himself, if Hunter was about three times his present age.

He embraced Hunter in a bear hug.

"Great to see you again, Hawk," he said.

Hunter pulled away from him.

"Who are you people?" he asked, not really sure he wanted to know.

They both laughed sweetly, but they completely avoided the question.

"Come with me," the man said instead. "I want to show you something."

Hunter followed him into the house, walked across the ancient-looking living room and into the kitchen. The man moved a false panel on the other side of the kitchen cupboard. Behind it was an elevator. It looked very cramped, and there was no light inside. Just a dull red glow from the elevator controls. The man indicated Hunter should climb in, and he did.

They rode the lift down together, not talking, Hunter barely breathing. The elevator moved very slowly and took a long time to reach its stopping point. When the door finally opened, they stepped out into an underground chamber. There was a guard post outside a huge door, but it was unmanned at the moment.

The man opened this huge door by hand, and they walked down a long corridor. Hunter imagined that they must be at least a mile underground. They reached another thick steel door. The man punched in some kind of code, and the door opened with a great *whoosh*.

· Beyond was a blue-hued chamber that looked like something from a viz-screen movie set. All crackling pipes and wires and machines and test tubes, it was a madman's vision of a laboratory. The man directed Hunter inside, and they walked past many electrical devices, gizmos, and doodads. They reached another massive door. Another code, another twist of the lock, and now they were inside a very small vestibule and facing yet another door. They both stepped inside, and the man locked them in.

Hunter looked around the small metal chamber and saw some strange things. There were straps fastened securely to the sides of the walls. *Why would they be here?* he thought. *What could their purpose be?* There was also an ordinary bucket filled to the brim with rocks.

Rocks? Why?

But even odder, in one corner of the vault was a box of parachutes.

Parachutes?

The man strapped Hunter into one of the harnesses and then did the same to himself. Then he punched another code into the lock of this fourth door. The lock spun and clicked and then sprang open.

The next thing Hunter knew, he was looking out at the clear blue sky.

This made no sense, of course; they were several thousand feet underground. Yet it all seemed familiar to him somehow.

"What is this?" Hunter asked the man. "How can this be?"

"It's called a key way," the man told him, dropping a few of the rocks through and watching them fall. "It's a passage to other times, other dimensions. Other places."

Bits and pieces of all this were coming back to Hunter, but

try as he might, he could not put it all together as a whole. He began to say something, but the man held up his hand.

"Wait for it," he said.

A moment later, there came a tremendous roar, and suddenly three aircraft zoomed through the sky not a hundred feet below him, trailing long exhaust plumes.

These weren't spacecraft, Hunter knew. They were jets. *Jet fighters*. That's what his craft was—or, more accurately, used to be.

The three planes turned and passed by again. They were long and thin, very short wings, high tails.

"T-38s," Hunter whispered. Again, something from his past had gurgled up.

"That's right, Hawk," the man said to him. "Now be careful, but lean out there and get a bit of a better look."

Hunter did so, grasping the restraints tightly. About a mile or so below them was an ocean. By leaning out a little farther, Hunter could also see a large rocket-launching facility along its coast. He could clearly pick out gantries, huge control buildings, support vehicles. And people everywhere.

"Cape Canaveral," he whispered.

"Exactly," the man said.

He pulled Hunter back from the precipice.

"Let me fill you in," the man said. "Below is the Kennedy Space Center. The year is 1987. Down there, you are about to lift off as part of a crew of something called the space shuttle. In one of your lives, you will not be able to make this trip because something called World War Three is about to break out. But, if you should pass through this portal now, I can arrange for you to be in one of those jets and for it to have engine trouble and you can simply step through with a parachute, land, and be rescued. There will be no World War Three. You will be the youngest person to fly in the shuttle. You will lead an adventurous, exciting life. The life you should have led before all this craziness entered into it."

Now it was Hunter who was almost in tears.

This part of his life came flooding back to him. He was the youngest kid ever to attend MIT, the youngest ever to fly for the U.S. Air Force, the youngest ever to be accepted for a shuttle flight by NASA. World War Three, between the U.S. and the Soviet Union, threw all that into turmoil and then— well, like the man said, the craziness began.

"It can be yours again, Hawk," the man told him. "Just say the word."

Hunter turned back to him. He didn't want to ask the next question, but he knew he had to.

"What's the catch?" he asked the man.

The man just smiled. He seemed like a good guy. Someone Hunter almost felt close to.

"I think you know the catch," he said. "Tell me why you are here."

Hunter shook his head. "I can't."

"Tell me who you came here to see then," the man pressed him.

Hunter looked back through the hole in the sky. The T-38s were still flying around, and the ocean below looked very inviting. There was even a parachute within his reach. It wouldn't take much for him to slip it on. Jump through. *Go back to where it all began . . .*

He turned back to the man.

"Sorry," he said.

The woman was crying as Hunter walked back down the hill, leaving the old house and the strange things beneath it.

He knew what was going on here. He was being tempted with the most important things in his life. This life. His previous life. And just as Tomm had told him through his image projection, the people doing the offering could absolutely follow through on their promises. There was no doubt in his mind about that. All Hunter had to do was break his confidence about why he came here and what was behind him seeking out the one he had to talk to—and, by inference, the end of his trip would be at hand, his mission would end, and he would go on to a much better place.

It was brilliant. Like the colossal minefields and the light-years of "barbed wire" debris and the Saturn 5s and the Phantoms, now that he was on the ground, so to speak, these temptations were just another part of a very sophisticated security system. One designed to keep whoever Hunter had to see here insulated from the rest of the Galaxy. These people didn't *really* want to know why he had come or who he was here to see. They *already* knew these things. All this was just a way of testing whether he could keep a secret or not. And that secret could only be the identity of the person he'd come here to see.

But who could this special person be?

He sat at the side of the road for a few minutes before he saw another vehicle approaching.

It was an automobile but was not anywhere near as glamorous as the limo or as racy as the Corvette. It was big and green and ugly, with wood paneling, four doors, and a pull-up hatch on the back. A station wagon.

It arrived with a screech and a cloud of dust right in front of him. Another kid of about eighteen or so was behind the wheel. He seemed as bored as Hunter's first two drivers.

"Hey mister," he said wearily. "Need a ride?"

Hunter silently climbed in.

They continued down the paved road, the landscape changing from the cold and dampness of the house on the hill back to fair weather and a more rural setting.

Hunter didn't speak, and neither did his driver. The surroundings changed again, to a terrain more woodsy, and the road straightened out. They passed a sign that read *Montana Route 264*, and another spark of familiarity went off in Hunter's head. He'd seen that sign before somewhere.

They continued on, passing under an overpass, and now there were trees on either side of the roadway. A mountain loomed ahead. His driver wordlessly slowed down and turned onto an unpaved dirt road, and soon they were traveling deeper into the forest. Hunter sniffed the air and detected not just the scent of sweet pines but also that of burned rubber and combusted fuel.

The woods thinned out considerably. The stink the air was almost to overwhelming now. Around one more corner, and the driver stopped. Straight ahead, in the clearing next to the mountain, lay the remains of a large aircraft. It had fallen out of the sky, time indeterminate, but obviously quite a while ago. Hunter looked at his driver, who simply nodded, indicating Hunter should get out.

He did, and approached the crash slowly. This was an ancient airplane. Long, swept-back wings, a long silver fuselage. Very primitive thrust-producing engines on its wings, four in all. On its tail were three letters that had been painted over; but the paint had melted away in the crash. The three letters were TWA.

Hunter reached the edge of the crumpled fuselage. He knew this plane was a Boeing 707. An airliner—that's what they used to call them, way back, wherever it was he'd come from.

Though it still seemed as if the crash had happened some time ago, there was still a lot of heat around the site. The ground was steamy, and some bare patches of snow at the base of the mountain had melted into warm mud. Everything around the site was very, very quiet.

After a short climb, Hunter reached the back of the airplane. One of the rear doors had been torn off in the crash, and this provided a means of entry. He stepped inside.

The interior of the plane was empty. No seats; the plane had been a cargo carrier. He started making his way forward, naturally drawn to the cockpit. It was slow going at first: the plane's fuselage was badly crumpled. Strangely, the floor was covered with long strands of weeds—*hay* was the archaic word for it. He saw scatterings of an ancient grain called *oats*.

He eventually reached the cockpit door. It, too, was smashed and twisted, but he was able to squeeze his way through to what was left of the flight deck.

There was a body strapped in the pilot's seat, wearing a tattered green flight suit and helmet. Hunter froze. Did he really want to do this? Only compulsion pushed him on. He made his way up next to the body to find it was a skeleton.

Its hands were still locked in a death grip on the plane's control yoke. Its mouth was open, almost as if it was caught forever in a devilish laugh. Hunter felt he had to find out who this person was—or used to be. Very gingerly he reached into the skeleton's breast pocket and found a piece of heavy paper inside. He removed it and unfolded it.

It was a photograph of a woman.

Hunter felt like a lightning bolt had hit him in the chest. A sizable portion of his past lives had come back to him during this bizarre journey, but at that moment he was suddenly aware of another, much deeper truth. He'd lived lives that a million other souls combined could never hold a flame to. He'd flown faster than humanly possible, he'd invaded a titanic empire, he'd led huge armies and fought gigantic battles. He'd been to Heaven and back, for God's sake. And through all these things, the excitement, the absolute tidal waves of adrenaline, and whatever the hell else was running through him, had peaked and peaked again, to the point that it seemed he was *always* in the middle of some kind of body rush.

But nothing was like the body rush he was getting now. Because the picture he was holding in his hand was the same as the photo he'd found in his pocket when he woke up on *Fools 6* that day so long ago. The photo of the mysterious woman that had made the transition along with the tattered American flag.

But this photo was not faded and worn like his. In this photo he could see the woman's face clearly.

And for the first time since coming here, he knew who she was.

Her name was Dominique. . . .

The absolute love of his former life.

"Hey mister," he heard a voice from below the cockpit yell. "Wanna go see her?"

They were quickly back on the road, he and his driver and the station wagon.

They had driven out of the forest, had returned to the highway, had passed around the mountain, and were heading back into the beach terrain again.

And this time Hunter was being very vocal.

"Go faster!" he was screaming at the kid. "C'mon, boot it!"

And now it was the kid who was looking concerned.

"This thing wasn't built to go that fast, mister!" he yelled back at Hunter.

The driver had simply told him he would bring him to see

the woman in the picture, and at that moment Hunter wanted to do nothing more in his entire life. He was caught up in some preposterous game here, some kind of incredibly elaborate charade just to see if he could keep a secret. Well, yes, he could keep a secret. But that didn't even matter anymore. He knew every time he had looked at that faded photograph that the woman behind it would hold more to the key of who he was and why he was here and more important, where he had come from than anything he could find or be tempted with here, be it his airplane again, or even an alternate, better life.

He had to see her.

"If you people are so scary smart," Hunter was badgering his young driver, "why didn't you send the Corvette to take me to this point? This piece of crap can barely do fifty miles an hour!"

The kid was always too busy driving to reply. He just kept telling Hunter over and over, "Just calm down, mister. We'll get there soon. Just calm down!"

They finally did get there. They climbed a beach road that led up a hill and eventually broke out into a small cliff. Now Hunter could see the water—finally it was an ocean. A real ocean. He could hear the waves breaking; he could smell the salty air.

They drove up to a small house—smaller even than the other house on the hill. Hunter knew immediately where he was. This was *his* house, way back then, way back in that other time and place. It was his farm. His hay farm. He'd lived here with Dominique.

It was called Skyfire.

He jumped out of the station wagon even before it stopped moving. He hopped the gate and ran up to the front door. He went inside. Everything looked just as he remembered it.

He walked through the living room and into the kitchen. Everything still familiar. He walked to the screen door that led out to the backyard.

And that's when he saw her. She was outside in the garden, picking herbs.

He stood at the back door for an eternity of moments just watching her.

She was beautiful. The photograph did not do her justice. She was wearing a long white gown and a wide-brimmed hat. Even working in the garden, faced smudged a bit, she was gorgeous. The gown was low cut, and he could see her unencumbered breasts. She had long blond hair, delicate hands, delicate bare feet. She was smiling, singing to herself. She did not see him.

He felt his chest become filled with pure emotion. The circle had been completed. Here she was, and here he was. End of chapter. End of book. End of series. He wanted nothing more than to swing that door open, walk out onto the porch, and call her name.

Screw the battle against the Fourth Empire.

He wanted to stay *here* with *her* forever.

His thumb was on the latch of the door. His boot was up against its bottom; he knew he would have to give it a little kick, because it stuck every once in a while.

Her name was on his lips. . . .

But then he stopped. Stopped moving. Stopped breathing. Stopped thinking—except about one thing.

He couldn't do it.

He believed this was real and that he could stay here and live with her and never have to fight in a war again.

But a buzz in his brain told him no. He started walking backward, out of the kitchen, turning only when he reached the living room, and then quietly leaving by the front door. He did not want her to see or hear him.

He staggered back down the front path and went through the gate this time. It was loose on the hinge, and he remembered that he was always meaning to fix it.

Too late now, he thought.

The station wagon was gone. He made his way back down the road, walking quietly until he was out of sight of the house. Then he slumped to his knees and put his head in his hands.

What kind of life is this?

No matter what he did, he could never be happy, never be free of worry. Never just be.

Why him? Why had this mantle been handed to him? He had one talent: he could fly machines that went very fast. So what? Why was he involved in all this other cosmic crap? He had bare memories of him having to save the world back in one of his former lives. Now, it was up to him to save the whole freaking Galaxy? And in order to do so, he had to first go through all this heart-wrenching past-life regression. Why? *Why was he doing this again?*

He found his hand go to his left breast pocket, digging for the other thing he always kept there. Not the faded photograph but the tattered American flag.

He took it out, unfolded it, and ran his fingers along its stars and stripes. He felt a surge of electricity go through him—and then he had his answer. After more than five thousand years, this flag still meant something. Not just on Earth but in the vast Milky Way as well. It stood for basic freedoms and basic truths. It stood for heroes past. It stood for the kind of life where every person has a right to be themselves, to do what they want, just as long as they didn't infringe on anyone else's right to do the same thing. To be a good American was nothing more than that. And the simple understanding of this basic belief was worth defending, worth dying for, so that others could be free, too. That *was* America. Way back then on Earth, and now, all across the Galaxy.

Why was he doing all this again?

He held the flag up to his face.

"Oh yeah," he thought aloud. "*This* is why. . . ."

18

He walked about a mile down the road before he heard another vehicle coming up behind him,

It was not any kind of car; it was a truck. Old, battered, cracked windshield, with yet another kid behind the wheel. He stopped a few feet from Hunter and stuck his head out the window.

But Hunter already knew the drill.

"Yeah, I want a ride," he told the kid.

He walked around to the other side of the cab but found the door was locked. The kid just looked at him and then gave him the thumb, indicating Hunter had to sit in the back. He hesitated only a moment, then walked to the rear of the truck and climbed aboard.

The rear was filled with boxes made of very thin wood. Hunter took a seat among them, then looked inside one of the boxes.

They were packed with turnips.

They rode for a very long time.

The road never changed, but the terrain did. From the beach, to the mountains, to the long, straight fields again. It was a bumpy, uncomfortable ride, but Hunter could have cared less.

He was beyond worrying about his own personal comfort now. He just wanted to get to the next stop, because he was convinced it would be the last in this long charade.

The kid driving the truck acted more like he was driving the Corvette. He was moving at high speed and never met a bump he didn't like. They were approaching a mildly steep hill when the truck hit a pothole so violently, Hunter went airborne. The truck and its contents went one way, and Hunter went the other. He was thrown from the back, landing hard in the roadway, a broken box of turnips smacking him on the head.

The truck driver never even looked in his rearview mirror. No brake lights. No downshifting. Nothing.

He just kept on going.

Hunter picked himself up, dusted himself off, and started walking up the hill.

He reached inside his back pocket and found the remains of another apple. It was crushed and mostly mush, but he ate as much of it as he could. It tasted awful but, he supposed, it was better than eating a turnip.

He reached the top of the hill, only to find the road dipped and then led up to another hill, this one even steeper. Hunter stopped, scratched his head, and wondered if he was going in the right direction.

He turned around and was astonished to see an enormous blue screen had appeared right behind him.

Now this froze him to the spot. When he took part in the Earth Race, part of the competition was to pass through huge blue screens—huge as in infinite. The screens were part of an elaborate mind-blowing obstacle course. Passing through one screen meant that the next obstacle was coming up, each one matched to the personalities or the fears of the individual contestant. For Hunter this included everything from saving a girl from being assaulted to trying to get his craft through the teeth of a gigantic set of jaws. On the other side of each screen was something that was always crazier than before, until that is, he broke through the final one. The strange thing was, they'd been popping up every once in a while ever since.

Now he was looking at this one, and it really did go in all

directions. He didn't want to pass through it, especially since it was behind him; only something unpredictable could result. If in fact this thing was real.

But Hunter worked off instinct, and his instinct was telling him that he should at least try to understand what this thing was and why it was here. So he stuck his hand, then his shoulder, and then finally his head through the screen. What he saw was astonishing. He was looking at the barren landscape of *Fools 6*, the planet where he'd been found by Erx and Berx two years ago, the planet where he'd suddenly woke to find himself in the far-flung future.

But there was something strange here. He was about a mile away from the very familiar mountain where he'd found himself in a house he didn't build. But the house wasn't there. This could only mean he was looking at *Fools 6* not only before he arrived but before the house had been built as well.

What the hell does that mean?

Suddenly, he found himself falling through the screen to the dusty road below. The screen had disappeared so quickly, he wound up hitting the road hard, with a mouthful of dirt to boot. He lay there for a moment as the vision of *Fools 6*, still burned on his retinas, slowly faded as well.

Then he picked himself up, wiped his clothes off, and found himself wondering if the screen had ever been there at all.

He walked down into the dip and up the next hill.

It was getting hot again, and he was perspiring by the time he reached the top of the hill. Up here, off to the left, was a country road, little more than a path.

Hunter turned on to it. Impulse, instinct, whatever it was, he knew this was the road to take.

It passed through a group of trees and then to a wide clearing. Here was a bright green field. A small rise.

At the top of the rise was a small cottage. Nondistinct. Except there was a flagpole outside.

Flying from it was an American flag.

He walked up the bare pathway leading to the cottage. As the small house was built on a hill, the higher he climbed, the larger he realized the grassy fields beyond it were. They seemed to go on for miles now.

He reached the front door and stopped. He could hear some movement inside. And the sounds of something mechanical, pumping, running. Breathing. *Wheezing*.

He knocked once, but in doing so, the door slowly opened. He stepped inside. He still had his gun, but he did not take it out. It had stayed in his holster since he'd climbed into the limo. He knew he wouldn't need it here.

He walked into the hallway. Again it looked more like something from his emerging previous lives than anything in the seventy-third century. *Quaint* was the first word that came to mind. The place was a bit dark, a bit subdued, but smelled of fresh flowers and some kind of spice. There were paintings of children on the wall, and an ancient time-keeping device called a grandfather clock in one corner. In his modern battle suit and his oversized crash helmet, Hunter felt very out of place.

What was awaiting him here? Another test of his will to conceal? He didn't think so.

He followed the wheezing sound to the first room on his left. The door was open. Hunter peered inside. It was a bedroom. An ancient four-poster bed was set against one wall. There was still a label on it that read, Sears Roebuck. On its mattress another label read, Sealy. There was a small table next to the bed and on it a tiny radio with the letters RCA emblazoned across its dial. Next to the radio was a small white machine, with a black liquid dripping into a pot underneath. A coffeemaker. *It* was making the wheezing sound.

There was a person lying on the bed. It was a man, presumably, dressed in a spacesuit, one that looked thousands of years old. A thick helmet was covering his head; on his hands were Velcro-lined gloves. His feet were shod with bulky, self-heating magnetic boots. On his left shoulder was a patch bearing the letters *NASA*. On the right, an American flag.

The man was an astronaut.

Literally, an ancient astronaut.

How did Hunter know? Because on a shelf above the bed there was a small digital clock—made by Timex. Its readout had been modified to count in hours, days, years. At that moment, it read 5,248 years, 14 days, 13 hours.

Now, this is strange, Hunter thought—and not just because of the dichotomy before him. Back on Earth, he'd been told the legend of a man living somewhere out in the Galaxy who could not die. Someone who was hanging on to life without the benefit of Holy Blood, the fuel that kept the Fourth Empire going. But the story of the eternal man was just that: one of millions of tall tales that floated around the Milky Way like so much stardust. Or so he had assumed. Could this be the man in that legend?

More important, was this the person Hunter was here to see?

He stepped into the room and realized there were two women sitting near the end of the bed, hidden behind the door. They were both wearing short white dresses and strange white caps on their heads. They both had large, outrageous hairdos but were very pretty in other ways. They were both reading magazines and chewing gum.

Nurses, Hunter thought.

They barely looked up at him as he walked in.

The astronaut, on the other hand, acknowledged Hunter right away. He let out a long breath and moved up a bit on his pillows.

"Well, I see you made it through all of our security rings," he said, his voice sounding very mechanical coming from behind his helmet's front visor. Hunter could not see his eyes or face.

"Are you the one I'm supposed to talk to?" he asked him.

"I am," the astronaut replied confidently.

"How do I know for sure?" Hunter asked.

"Because we have a mutual friend," the astronaut replied. "Pater Tomm sent you—and he and I have been *amigos* for longer than I can tell you. We haven't seen each other in centuries, though. Is he well, I hope?"

"Last time I saw him, he was," Hunter replied.

The astronaut indicated that Hunter should sit in the chair next to the bed.

"It must be something very important for you to come here," he said. "And to go through what you did."

"I can't disagree with you there . . ."

"OK, then," the astronaut said. "Tell me everything. Start at the beginning."

But Hunter hesitated. This was probably the guy Tomm wanted him to see. Either that, or he was a hell of an actor. And God only knew how he'd wound up here, in the old spacesuit, in a house right out of ancient America, ticking off the years like other people ticked off seconds. It must be a hell of a story, Hunter was sure. But there was a huge battle looming on the horizon. And the campaign to restore Earth and the Empire to its rightful owners was at stake, as were hundreds of thousands of lives. Weird planet or not, how could this man do him any good? And why should he tell him anything at all?

Then again, what other choice did he have? Here he was, stranded at the end of the Galaxy, with no way to get back to where he had to be. There was actually a good chance he'd be stuck out here forever. So why be coy now? Why not let it all out? And even if this was another test to gauge his ability to keep a secret, if he flunked it, at least *something* would happen. And something was always better than nothing.

So he told the ancient man his story. Waking up on *Fools 6*, being rescued and brought to Earth, winning the Earth Race, the search for Planet America, the invasion of the Two Arm. While he was speaking, one of the nurses retrieved an ancient martini shaker, mixed a huge potion of gin with a bright orange powder from a jar labeled Tang, and gave it to the astronaut, running a straw from the shaker under his helmet to his mouth.

Hunter concluded his tale with the most recent chapter, how he and the others had escaped to Paradise and then felt compelled to return to the other side again.

At the end of this part, the astronaut laughed.

"So you and your friends really think you were in Heaven?" he asked.

Hunter nodded, but with uncertainty. "You mean, we weren't?"

The astronaut sipped his Tang martini but did not reply. He changed the subject instead.

"I can see why Tomm sent you above others, Major Hunter," he said. "You've certainly lived an interesting life so far. After all these adventures, do you have any idea why you are here, in the seventy-third century? Have you figured it out yet?"

Hunter just shrugged. "Not completely."

"And why not?"

Hunter shrugged again. "I guess I've been busy with other things."

The astronaut laughed. So did the nurses.

"But don't you see?" the astronaut asked him. "Those 'other things' are *exactly* the reason you are here. I think it's fair enough for me to tell you that."

Hunter was puzzled, and it showed. "Please explain," he said.

The astronaut sat up a little. The other nurse adjusted his pillows.

"Well, let me guess: you've been too busy to think about yourself because you've been doing these 'other things,' like saving all the unfortunates of the Milky Way?"

"Well, trying to," Hunter replied. "I mean, it's been a full-time job."

The astronaut laughed again. "I'm sure it is, and that's *precisely* why you are here. You weren't just dropped out of the sky, out of time, for no reason, or as a fluke, my friend. This was no small thing, your coming to the seventy-third century. It took very powerful forces on many astral planes to pull off such a feat. It might have seemed like a random event, and it *was* intended that way. But don't disparage it as such. Nothing is random in this universe, and certainly not in this little speck of a Galaxy."

The astronaut raised his primary visor and, for the first time, Hunter could see his eyes. They looked old but they were twinkling. And Hunter could tell he was smiling.

"Simply put, you are a savior, Major Hunter," he said. "One of several chosen over the ages. You are here to save us. Save us all—from them. From evil. From tyranny. From the Fourth Empire. Hell, when they write the book on this, it might be titled *Hawk Hunter Saves the Universe*!

Hunter just stared back at him. Was he kidding? On one hand, the ancient man seemed so cool, so calm. And *so* American. And he really gave the impression that he knew what he was talking about—and that in a strange way, he couldn't be wrong. About anything. But on the other hand, there was no getting around it. He was an old guy in an old astronaut suit. He could be a *maccus*, a clown, for all Hunter knew.

"But how do you know this?" Hunter finally asked him. "How would *you* know that I was brought here to do these things?"

The smile left the astronaut's eyes. He was quiet for a long time.

"Because," he said finally, "Five thousand years ago, I was brought here for the same reason."

A long silence. The nurses were paying close attention to the conversation now.

The astronaut sipped his drink.

"And I will let you in on *my* whole story some other time," he said. "But at the moment, the reason you came here is more important. So, tell me again about this REF. There's something that really frightens me about them."

Hunter did as asked. He explained how at the height of the battle that never was, the United Planets fleet managed to disappear, only to find out that shortly afterward, the REF had disappeared as well. Later on, the REF ships began showing up again, now painted red and apparently operating with little regard for SG headquarters or the Imperial Court back on Earth. Judging by their actions, their desire to create havoc and commit the utmost in cruelty seemed apparent.

The astronaut listened intently, becoming visibly upset when he heard further details about the REF's actions on *Doomsday 212* following Bonz's murder. He slumped farther into his pillows, pushing the drink away from him. The nurses were becoming uneasy, too. They didn't like seeing him this way.

"Tell me something," he finally said to Hunter. "Have you seen the madness yet?"

"Madness?" Hunter replied. "I think I've seen it everywhere since I was dropped into this place."

The astronaut shook his head. "No, I used the wrong term;

of course you've seen madness here. It *is* everywhere. What I mean is, have you seen or heard of other acts of unspeakable cruelty, above and beyond the pale? Something like what the REF did to the helpless SF troopers on *Doomsday 212* after shooting down their ships?"

Hunter had to think. He'd been out of the loop so to speak for a month or so, so he wasn't privy to everything that had happened in the Galaxy while he was away. But there *was* that burst of panicky Maydays he'd heard during his dash across the Milky Way. From what he could determine, it seemed like innocent people both on planets and in ships were being killed, horribly, for no good reason. He told all this to the astronaut, and the old man became even more upset.

"This is the worst of all possible scenarios, I'm afraid," the man said gravely. "Can't you see what's happened?"

Hunter just shook his head. The nurses did, too.

"As you and your friends were so clever to find an escape door to Paradise," the astronaut began. "The REF did the same thing—except they went in the *other* direction. You opened up a portal, a split in the fabric of space, and they were somehow able to take advantage of it, too. Or maybe they just fell into it and never told anybody in power after it happened."

Hunter needed a moment to connect the dots.

"Are you saying," he asked the astronaut. "That as we went to Heaven, they went . . . *to Hell?*"

"And found a way to come back," the astronaut nodded. "Just as you did."

Hunter's brain started doing a slow spin.

"Is . . . is that really possible?" he asked the astronaut.

"Why would you think it is *im*possible?" the man replied tersely. "Why do you think one place could exist, and not its opposite? You were in Paradise, correct? Where everything seemed good. Where there was no conflict, no need for anything negative. And I have the feeling that upon returning, some of that would travel back with you. In varying degrees, I suspect.

"But what you have to realize is that for a place so wonderful to exist, an opposite place would have to exist as well. And if a door opens to one place, then a door must open to the other. That's the dilemma, you see. Where a traveler to your place might see nothing but beauty and light and knowledge and passion, a traveler to the other place would see only the power that comes from evil. Pure evil. A very tempting thing, especially if you are predisposed to it, which I suspect these people in the REF were. Ages ago, back on Earth, before we ever went to the stars, the yogis used to say that good and bad are actually two sides of the same thing. These two places—where you went and where they went—are the same idea, but exact opposites."

"Like matter and antimatter," one of the nurses said.

"Precisely, my dear," the astronaut replied. "And we—those of us who live here, within humanity, in the Galaxy, in the universe—are simply caught in the middle. It's been like that through the ages. And be advised: this has nothing to do with religion. The good place exists, the bad place exists, but their religious significance amounts to little more than a drop in an ocean. Religion is just the simplest way to explain something very complex, something that even the most advanced physics in the Galaxy today cannot begin to understand. But they are there. In the infinite number of planes that exist above and below this universe, these two are the ones right next door."

The astronaut shifted on his bed again.

"This is not good," he went on. "Something has been opened up here that cannot be so easily closed. The madness—the *real evil madness*—is out. Again."

"So this sort of thing has happened before?" Hunter asked, not really sure he wanted to know the answer.

"Only all throughout history," was the astronaut's reply. "And I don't mean that dopey history back on Earth that barely went back ten thousand years. The history of the universe is as old as the universe itself. Take a good look at one of those pyramids someday. Not the ones on Earth. I mean the ones they've found near the Ball, or on some of the real isolated moons on the Fringe. Some of those things are *billions* of years old. And someone had to build them back then, right?"

He let his voice trail off.

"So what can be done?" Hunter asked. "If what you say is true, this just got a lot bigger than merely my friends trying to get back across. And I'm only one person. It sounds like impossible odds."

"All very true," the astronaut replied. "But that doesn't mean you still can't beat them. The real problem is that I suspect the REF knows what you and your friends are up to. Don't ask me how, but I bet they do. So you'll have to be careful, too. Remember, when it comes to these sorts of things, there is nothing new under the stars. The evil ones may be devious, but it's only when things start turning against them that they become especially cruel. And they fear you and your friends because they must know you've been to the good place, and there is power in that alone. So, I predict, their first trick will be to put innocent souls in harm's way to counter anything you might try to do. They will be willing to kill millions, hell, billions to get what they want. And what will you do then, Mr. Superhero, if the choice is between billions losing their lives or you just backing away? Is it better for innocents to live in tyranny and evil than not at all?"

Another long silence. Hunter had no reply. The coffee machine started wheezing again.

"It would not shock me to learn that they are going back into their bag of dirty tricks right now," the astronaut went on. "Dreaming up something that everyone will fear is new but will also be something they've done, successfully, in the past. They are inscrutable, and they are probably getting help from somewhere else in the underworld. There are many kinds of devils down there. Trust me, I know about these things. Just because I've lived five thousand years doesn't mean I've spent all of that time lying here in bed. Yes . . . they will try to make you defeat yourself. They will try to use your good conscience against you. You must be ready for that."

He leaned back on his pillows, suddenly exhausted. "A big one is coming," he said. "A terrible battle that could have terrible consequences. Whether it was your doing or not—opening the way to the other sides—that was a huge mistake. And if you ever have the chance, I would look into exactly who the person was who provided you the means to get to Paradise, because, whether they knew it or not, they also allowed the REF to get to the other place. By doing so, they put in motion the terrible events that are approaching us now.

"If my guess is right, the REF will come back again and again to wreak havoc on everyone and everything, and they will continue to do so until they are stopped. And they *must* be stopped, or they will hold sway over everything for the next million years or so. They will spread so much evil that all of civilization will end—again. And it will have to start from scratch—again."

The astronaut fell quiet once more. The nurses were beside themselves now, fretting and sobbing. They'd been through this before. That was obvious.

"How long did you say before the rest of your fleet crosses over?" the astronaut finally asked Hunter.

"We gave it one week," Hunter replied. He checked his watch. It was still counting down. "But now we are talking about less than five days."

The astronaut rolled his eyes. "You could have given yourself a little more time. You know, built in some margin for error."

Hunter just shrugged. "Who knew?"

The astronaut thought for another long while.

"Well, all this means that I will have to help you," he said finally. "And that it was a good and brave and a *lucky* thing that you managed to make it here, and that you proved yourself to be trustworthy. Tomm was wise to send you. Though he must have known that only the most precipitous and dire situation could make me get involved. But now that I am, we will have to move very quickly. . . ."

Hunter looked around the very spare room. Again the question came back to him. This was a very old guy in the care of two nurses. What could he possibly do?

"I appreciate your advice and counsel," Hunter said. "But seriously, how can *you* help me?"

The astronaut brightened a little, then waved his hand in an unusual fashion. "I will conjure up all the powers of the Third Empire, of course. . . ."

Hunter just shook his head. *The Third Empire?* What did that have to do with this? Of all the mysteries in the Galaxy, the Third Empire was one of the deepest. Almost no one knew anything about it, only that it disappeared into the void of time between the end of the Second Empire and the beginning of the Fourth, a span of at least two thousand years that had a number of smaller empires and several Dark Ages mixed in with it. That's why Hunter was surprised to even hear it brought up.

"You actually *know* about the Third Empire?" he asked the astronaut.

Everyone in the room laughed—the astronaut, the nurses. Everyone but Hunter.

The astronaut nodded to one of the nurses. She led Hunter over to the nearest window, the one that looked out on the vast valley of fields and grass.

Hunter couldn't believe his eyes. Where just moments before the sky had been empty, it was now filled with hundreds of ancient but powerful-looking starships. And the grassy fields that seemed to go for miles were now covered with formations of enormous soldiers; they also stretched for as far as the eye could see. All of this had suddenly appeared, with the wave of the ancient man's hand.

"Behold the mythical Star Legion," the astronaut declared from his bed with no little delight. "But they are not so mythical, as you can see. They are the bravest soldiers in the history of creation. And they will help you in your fight."

Hunter could barely speak.

"So you *do* know the secret of the Third Empire?" he asked numbly.

"The secret of the Third Empire?" the astronaut roared back. "My friend, we *are* the Third Empire!"

PART FOUR

War of the Angels

19

The three *culverins* breezed past the gauntlet of Solar Guards ships patrolling Earth orbit and fell easily through the atmosphere. Their destination was the floating city of Special Number One.

The entire Solar System was under *de facto* martial law. The Solar Guards were stopping, searching, and arresting the crews of any unauthorized vessel found moving inside the Pluto Cloud. Yet this trio of ships flew on through all the warnings, defying orders to stop or be shot down, and landed in the middle of the vast Imperial Plaza, practically on the steps of the Imperial Palace itself.

The three ships were immediately surrounded by SG shock troops—they had forcibly relieved the Imperial Guards of all their duties earlier that day. The Solar Guards blinked a number of heavy weapons to the scene, ready to blast to dust anyone who stepped off the ships. But there was an air of hesitation in their actions, too.

The hatchways on all three ships opened, and eventually people came tumbling out. The SG troops raised their weapons but did not fire. The intruders were not soldiers intent on attacking them. These were Specials, the very close relatives of the Imperial Family. This particular gang of three hundred or so had been flying around the Solar System ever since Venus cleared out, and they'd quickly become bored. Absolutely nothing was happening on any of the other original planets. With nowhere else to go, they'd flown back to Earth, hoping to resume their revelry.

Their timing couldn't have been worse. Confusion had reigned atop the imperial aeropolis for days. Taking their emergency security edict to the extreme, the SG controlled all of Special Number One now, except for the northern tip, where a small army of Space Forces troops was still protecting the SF headquarters of Blue Rock. The two sides had been exchanging blaster fire off and on since that morning, and whispers of an SG *coup* were still thick in the air. Out among the stars, the war between the two military services was still going on, with rumors of atrocities happening all across the Galaxy. And with O'Nay reportedly riding around in a secret floating city up near the North Pole, there was a large power vacuum here, at the center of the Galaxy. It seemed inevitable that the Solar Guards would soon attempt to fill it.

But none of these things had any effect on the Specials. Intoxicated and jammed-up, most of them, they spilled out onto the concourse to the amazement of the grizzled Solar Guards. The SG had orders to shoot anyone deemed a security threat, but even the most hardened SG trooper would never fire on a Special. Not only was it against every imperial law imaginable, it was also considered extremely unlucky, as there was a belief that Specials couldn't really die, not completely anyway, and thus had the power to haunt a person forever.

So the SG soldiers simply let them run wild.

A few of this drunken, privileged group had a mission in mind, though. They had to find the Empress, their soul leader. They hadn't seen her since the evacuation of *La-Shangri*, and they knew starting a good rave would be impossible without her.

So while the majority of new arrivals commenced frivolity in the imperial square, taunting and teasing the grim-faced SG troops surrounding them, a smaller contingent—three men, three women, all reeking of Holy Blood—headed for the Imperial bedrooms.

They didn't encounter the usual battalion of House Guards at the palace's front door. In fact, the doors weren't even locked. The hallways within were dark, empty, cold. No body-guards, no servants, no spies. There was even some debris strewn about the imperial corridors. Signs of a hasty departure by many people were everywhere.

The half-dozen Specials moved unchallenged through the long passageways until they reached the Empress's private quarters. They pushed in the door, expecting to find their shining light inside, surrounded by tankards of the best slow-ship wine—and maybe some *jamma*, too.

But while they *did* find her, she was not bathing in a sea of intoxicants. Nor was she in any kind of racy party uniform. Instead, she was in her dreary sitting room, packing a trans-dimensional bag. What's more, she was wearing a *kafka*, a long, black ceremonial dress usually worn only in the unlikely event that someone in her immediate family was about to pass away.

Her relatives were shocked to see her dressed like this.

"Who is dying, my lady?" was the first question they asked her.

She looked up at them for the first time. Her hair was tied back. She was not wearing makeup. She looked horribly plain. And for some reason, she had a drop of oil on her forehead.

" 'Who is dying?' " she asked in reply. "Take a look around you, you fools. The Empire is dying. . . ."

Then she looked each of them up and down and added, "And you're all dying along with it."

The revelers were stunned. This wasn't like her; she just wasn't herself. They tried to tell her so, even offering her some *jamma*. But the Empress wasn't listening. She was simply get-ting annoyed.

"I have somewhere I have to go," she told them. "So, if you don't mind . . ."

With the arch of her eyebrow, she indicated that they should all leave. But they were much too thick to get the hint.

Instead, one relative begged her, "Please tell us where you are going. . . ."

"We will go with you," another pleaded. "We need to celebrate . . . *something!*"

"I am going to the desert," the Empress told them harshly. "Alone."

They were shocked. *Going to the desert . . . alone?* This seemed not only foolhardy but dangerous as well. There was no water out in the desert. And without water, the Empress could actually die—and this they could not allow. She was the center of their universe. If she disappeared, they all would.

"But my lady," one asked her, "why would you want to go to such a horrible place?"

"That's not of your concern."

"But how? How will you be going?"

"By air car," was her surprising answer.

Now her relatives were simply baffled. Did the Empress even know how to drive an air car?

"But my lady, by air car, a trip to the desert will take days."

"I know," the Empress said.

With that, she pushed past them and was gone.

20

Two miles away, on the ninety-ninth floor of the Space Forces headquarters building, the Secretary of SF Intelligence was also packing a bag.

It was just a precaution, though. He'd told the SF troopers guarding the building that if the SG attempted to take over Blue Rock, then they would have to carry him out in a box. But this was a rare case of bluster from the Secretary. He was much too valuable to the SF to be skinned alive by the Solar Guards—and he knew it. There was an evacuation plan in place, and a space cruiser docked on the roof. Should the Huns make a grab for the rest of the aerial city, the Secretary would be the first one on that ship out.

Until then, though, he vowed to pray over every piece of intelligence that came into the soaring building and, to the best of his ability, try to figure out what the hell was going on out there, among the stars.

He'd just finished packing when the secure bubbler in the corner of his office came to life. It began spitting out the morning's SF3 intelligence summary, a compilation of field reports from across the Empire. The Secretary retrieved the viz doc, floated over to his desk, poured himself a shot of slow-ship, and then sat down to read. Usually the summary was dry and

routine. But one look at the opening passage of this report told
him it was a shocker.

It detailed a number of horrifying incidents that had happened across the Galaxy in the last twenty-four hours—events
of sheer madness that had been widely rumored across the
Empire. An X-Forces ship in the Eight Arm came upon a
convoy of transport vessels lying dead in space, covered with
blaster burns and with huge holes torn in their fuselages. The
convoy had been carrying more than 12,000 passengers, including many members of the SF Youth, future officers in the
Space Forces. Everyone on board had been killed.

An interstellar hospital at the bottom of the Three Arm had
been evaporated by a gigantic blast from an X beam. More
than 250,000 patients and nearly 20,000 doctors were inside
the facility at the time. Now their bodies were floating in loose
orbits around the point in space where the hospital had once
been. There were no survivors.

A huge agri-planet called *Kansi One* in the Nine Arm had
been attacked by two warships using X-beam arrays. Each bolt
had the force of one million thermonuclear strikes. The two
ships vaporized all of the planet's farming complexes, destroying billions of tons of grain and foodstuffs. Not only would
millions across the Galaxy face starvation because of this act
of terror, the subatomic residue from the X-beam strike had
poisoned the soil of *Kansi One* forever.

The report went on and on and on. Attacks on isolated civilian ships, massacres in schools and orphanages, unprovoked
bombardments of innocent worlds, some of which were unaware that the Empire even existed. There was little doubt who
was behind these barbarities. So many people had reported
seeing the REF's mysterious Red Ships before and after the
attacks, they were too numerous to discount. And these
weren't military strikes, the report concluded. Nor were they
part of the interstellar war still going on between the SF and
SG. Each incident seemed to have just one goal in mind: to
be especially cruel to the especially helpless, to cause only
misery and pain.

The Secretary was both furious and baffled. Why was the
breakaway SG unit doing these horrible things? How could

the elite special operations group so suddenly turn into an army of bloodthirsty thugs? No one knew, certainly not the Imperial Court, nor the SF—not even the Solar Guards themselves. Of this last point the Secretary was sure. How? Because SF3 had been eavesdropping on SG string communications for decades. The Secretary frequently knew their high-priority orders before some of the people inside SG headquarters did. And he knew that not only had the REF stopped responding to orders from Black Rock weeks ago, Black Rock had no idea where the REF was at any given moment. Nor did SG Command have an explanation for the REF's ability to appear and then suddenly disappear apparently at whim, or for their unexplained thirst for innocent blood, or even why they murdered SF3 agent Gym Bonz on *Doomsday 212* in the first place.

The most recent SF3 snooping had picked up a conversation inside Black Rock among the top SG officers on Earth. While it was clear by their nervous chatter that the Solar Guards were becoming overwhelmed by both their war against the SF and maintaining their *quasi*–martial law over the One Arm, one question that haunted the SG staff was especially telling: Where and when would their renegade REF strike next?

There were twelve SG officers in the top-level meeting. Not one of them had a clue.

The Secretary poured himself another drink. This time a strong one.

In his centuries of working for SF Intelligence, he'd never faced a situation quite like this before. Strangeness was rarely in short supply in the Galaxy, but there seemed to be a surplus of it these days. Case in point: forty-eight hours before, he'd received a report from several SF ship commanders who had just fought in the huge battle against the Solar Guards up in the Two Arm. These men swore that at the height of that battle, they'd seen a ship suddenly appear amid the chaos. It hadn't come from Supertime, because they were all *in* Supertime when it materialized. Nor had it come from any of the other single-digit dimensions because it had left absolutely no sub-atomic wake. But the strangest thing was, the SF commanders insisted this ghostly vessel was actually the *Resonance 133*, one of the cargo 'crashers stolen by the Two Arm invaders in the same area just a month before, only to disappear with the rest of the invaders' fleet shortly afterward.

The Secretary now reread this report as well as the long list of recent atrocities. *What is really going on here?* As if the Empire tearing itself apart wasn't bad enough, he now had dozens of inhuman brutalities taking place, plus a ghost ship suddenly appearing as if from nowhere.

He sipped his drink, and suddenly his mind kicked into overdrive: Could there be a connection between all these things?

He quickly called up every viz doc he'd received in the past five weeks, ever since the short-lived invasion of the Two Arm, and assembled them chronologically. The time line read like a bad novel. First, the rebel fleet invaded the Two Arm, defeated Joxx at Megiddo, and incurred the wrath of the REF. Then the invaders disappeared somewhere in the middle of the Moraz Cloud, after which the REF lied about destroying them. Soon after, the area was declared a No-Fly Zone, the REF disappeared as well, only to reappear, at least some of them, with their hulls painted red, to wreak havoc across the Milky Way. A war soon erupted between the SF and the SG, and in the middle of a battle between the two services came this report that one of the rebel ships had suddenly reappeared out of nothingness.

A question popped into the Secretary's head: *Are the REF Red Ships appearing out of nothingness, too? From the same spot as this stolen rebel ship? Is that the reason the REF declared the No-Fly Zone in the first place?*

He snapped his fingers and called up a device known as the Fourth Analytic Bubbler, or more simply, the FAB4. This highly secret *el tuti* of bubblers could take in trillions and trillions of bits of information from all over the Empire and, in a microsecond, coalesce them into an information globule that was both concise and sensible. This gave it a kind of prescient quality.

He asked the device a question: "Is there a connection between the No-Fly Zone and the REF's recent activities? In effect, is the REF using the No-Fly Zone as a safe haven from which to appear and disappear?"

The answer took a long time to come back, but when it did, it read, "*Possibly*."

The Secretary asked the FAB4 a second question: "Does the REF's recent atrocities have a goal in mind, or are they meant to simply inflict pain on innocents?"

The answer that came back was surprising: "*Both*."

A third question: "With the recent spate of atrocities in mind, would the REF strike again?"

Definitely "*Yes*."

"Is it possible to determine where in the Galaxy the REF would strike?"

This time, a definitive "*No*." Just like the SG officers who had no idea they were being bugged, when it came to divining the REF's next victims, the FAB4 didn't have a clue, either.

The Secretary hesitated a moment before he asked his last question. The FAB4 could be accessed from all over the Empire, and its use could be traced back to him. For this reason, he didn't want to leave the impression that he was beginning to panic or even becoming disloyal. But there was no way to put the words nicely, no way to finesse them or obscure their meaning. So he just took the direct approach. "*Is the Empire in danger of collapse?*"

The FAB4 didn't take more than a second to spit out its reply: a definite "*Yes*."

The Secretary drained his drink and thought about this for a long moment.

Then he floated over to where his emergency trans-bag was packed and opened its electric clasps. True, he'd had centuries of intelligence work to rely on, and he still possessed a very sharp mind, especially for someone his age. But he knew that when in doubt, it was best to seek out some unorthodox help. And while the SF Intelligence network had thousands of analytical bubblers, as well as billions of string comms at its disposal, sometimes simpler *was* better. And more discreet.

So he reached into his bag and came out with his trusty quadtrol.

Making sure no one was watching him, he did a quick link from the FAB4 to the small handheld device, technically a violation of SF Intelligence rules, but at this point, the breach was of little concern to him. Once it was filled with all the latest information, the Secretary punched in the ultimate question, something he would never have asked the FAB4, as such a politically dangerous inquiry would undoubtedly come back to haunt him.

He asked the quadtrol: "How can the SF save the Empire?"

The quadtrol beeped and burped and took a long time before it came up with an answer, but when it did, its conclusion was very unexpected. Strangely, its reply had little to do with the REF or the war between the services. Instead, it had to do with the case of the *Resonance 133* suddenly showing up in the midst of the battle between the SF and SG. Though it was still highly secret that the stolen 'crasher had reappeared, the quadtrol determined that not only was the ship still out there somewhere, there was a good chance that the rest of the rebel fleet might reappear, too.

Why? Because when all the bits of information were considered, it really came down to one thing: regardless of how they were able to do it, ever since the nonbattle against the rebels, the REF had been appearing and disappearing at will. And now at least one of the rebel ships had done the same thing. Therefore, there was a high probability that all of the rebel ships would return shortly as well. That's why the device suggested the Two Arm be thoroughly searched, not for the REF, but for the rest of the rebel fleet. In fact, the quadtrol said, doing so should be the SF's number one priority.

It was a strange response, because at the moment, it might have seemed the number one priority for the SF would be the dual crises at hand: the war between the services and the REF's nonstop rampage. In fact, events and recent history had relegated the short-lived invasion of the Two Arm to the back bubbler, so to speak. But there was a subtle beauty in the quadtrol's conclusion. By the strictest interpretation, protecting the Emperor and the Empire *was* the number one priority of the Space Forces, and at the moment, only the rebels had the stated purpose of disposing of O'Nay. The interservice war and the REF's activities, while extremely troubling, were actually sideshows. It was detecting the return of the rebel fleet first that would give the largest political advantage to the SF.

It would show that while the SG was in effect running wild, it was the SF that had to be called on to deal with the enigmatic invaders.

In other words, for the ultimate big bang, if and when the rebel fleet reappeared, the SF should be there to meet it, attack it, and utterly destroy it.

And if they did this, when everything else settled out, the SF would be credited with nothing less than saving the Empire.

21

There was an empty piece of space located halfway between the bottom of the Two Arm and the entrance to the One. It was called the *Andromeda Zee*.

The Zee was astride the main star road leading to the original Solar System. Traditionally, this was a place where civilian cargo vessels parked while awaiting authorization to enter the One Arm. Most of these ships could be found floating around a string of artificial moons. These big satellites had concessions for necessities such as water, food, power spikes, and of course, slow-ship wine.

Usually no more than several hundred ships would be lingering in the Zee at any given time. But now there were more than 50,000 ships here. Many were crowded inside the Zee's ill-defined border, but many more were hanging on the outskirts, hoping to get in, both for the proximity to provisions and the relative safety in numbers. Small pirate gangs had been nipping at the edges of this outer mob for weeks.

The 50,000 ships were part of the same makeshift fleet that had recently carried millions of civilians away from the Two Arm. Starting about a month before, those who hadn't fled in the panic surrounding the Two Arm invasion were forced from their homes after the SG declared a large part of the Moraz

Star Cloud a No-Fly Zone. Once they'd been herded from the *verboten* area, the SG had left all these civilians high and dry, with no protection, only orders not to return to their home systems in the Two Arm under penalty of death. Hundreds of thousands had reached the Zee, exhausted and out of money. Many had no choice now but to remain there.

Exactly how many people were crowded into the Zee? No one knew for sure. The best guess could be determined by estimating 10,000 bodies per ship, multiplied by 50,000 ships. That was at least a half billion souls with nowhere to go.

In other words, the Zee was no longer just a truck stop among the stars.

It had turned into an enormous refugee camp.

The conditions inside the forgotten ships had been deteriorating steadily since the first week. These were not top-flight Empire vessels, in which just about every desire of comfort or nourishment could be had by a mere wish. These were civilian carriers, hardscrabble star buses and hastily converted cargo humpers that contained a few inches of space for each individual and accommodations that equaled the worst of steerage. Many people had already died from this overcrowding. Many more lay sick, especially in those vessels just outside the Zee.

That the SG so suddenly left them in this interstellar lurch was considered typical of the Empire's second service. As the Solar Guards were essentially the police force of the Galaxy, the Empire's citizens on the whole both distrusted and feared them. The SG was known throughout the Milky Way for being heavy-handed, corrupt, and ultra-authoritarian. While they were famous for going after some outlaws with a vengeance— such as tax dictators and space pirates—they were also known to be heavily involved with people of the same ilk. Rumors of shady alliances with space mercs and freebooters for black-market wine, aluminum, and even *jamma* were rampant.

The SG's fascistic antics lately only added to this grim perception.

It would always be hard then to determine exactly how the startling news first reached the Zee. Few of the stranded ships still had workable scanners on board, and none of them had other kinds of deep-space detection equipment. What was clear, though, was that on the morning of their thirty-third day in limbo, a fleet of Solar Guards warships suddenly showed up close to the enormous floating refugee camp.

Absolute terror swept through the dour collection of ships, especially after it was determined, again somehow, some way, that the ships belonged to the SG's REF. Even isolated out here in the celestial wilderness, the refugees had heard whispers about the REF's atrocities across the Galaxy. How their intent these days was to inflict as much pain as possible upon the most innocent and vulnerable souls in the Milky Way.

And at that moment, there was no group of people more innocent or vulnerable than the unfortunates caught in the *Andromeda Zee*.

But then a string comm message arrived on all of the ships—this whether their communications systems were working or not. The message was from the REF, and it was very surprising.

They weren't here to harm anyone, the SG commanders said.

In fact, they told the refugees, the REF was here to take them home.

When word of this spread around the Zee, the SG were suddenly hailed not only as heroes but as saviors.

Their plan seemed simple, too. The trip back to the Two Arm would take just two days at ion-power speed, and it would be done under the protection of the SG warships the entire way.

It seemed too good to be true. The dispossessed had just one question: Once back in the Two Arm, what would be the procedure for returning them to their individual home systems, their home planets, their homes?

That's when the faceless SG officers running the operation informed the refugees that this was not part of the plan.

CIA Agent Steve Gordon knew something was wrong.

He'd first felt it two days before. The universe had shifted a bit. A little cosmic energy had been lost. Then, an overwhelming sadness had come over him, and even now, forty-eight hours later, he'd yet to shake it.

Gordon was the one who stayed behind. To watch over the ship. To watch over the handful of Twenty 'n Six capsules the messengers now considered sacred. To be as close as possible to Zero Point without being detected.

He'd spent all of his time here alone, perched on the highest peak of the moon, very close to where the *Resonance 133* still lay, hidden and battered, not far from the moon's immense pyramid.

He'd learned many strange things in this time here. That things like breathing and eating were no longer necessary, but a deep understanding of nature and the cosmos was. He'd watched the sky intently, these long days alone, studying the stars and thinking about them in a way he'd never been able to before. He also looked beyond those stars that were part of the Milky Way to the other pinpoints of light, up there in the heavens. Those stars weren't stars at all. They were other galaxies—billions of them. And they made up the universe of which the Milky Way was only a very small part.

Thinking beyond the realm. It was just not done these days—and hadn't been for thousands of years.

Until now.

It was while he was looking up at the skies, thinking about them in this new and different way, when another very distressing feeling came over him. Something was coming. In fact, it was heading right for him, traveling very fast, from somewhere very deep in space.

It arrived just a few moments later, screaming in like a small missile and crashing not a hundred yards from the *Resonance 133*. It caused a huge explosion on impact.

But it was not a missile. It was something else.

Gordon flew to the crash site in an instant. Here, he found the remains of 33418, Zarex's robot. Its knees were broken, its fingers were smashed, and it had two massive holes in the back of its head.

It was dead.

This is not good, Gordon thought. *Not good at all.*

He looked up at the stars and whispered a few words, and suddenly the others were around him. Summoned through the ethers by this turn of events, Tomm, Erx, Berx, Klaaz, and Calandrx were not there one moment, but simply there the next.

They all hovered above the robot's mechanical corpse now. Profound sadness times six. They had all been fond of the mighty clanker, almost as much as Zarex had.

"Not a random act, its landing here," Tomm said, lightly touching the bent and twisted remains. "Nor is Zarex's absence among us."

"Someone is trying to tell us something," Calandrx said. "And I fear it will not be the best of news."

They laid their hands on the tin man's remains, and after a while, a dark crimson mist began rising out of its chest. The red fog slowly coalesced into a viz screen. A recounting of actual events had been implanted in the robot's indestructible memory banks, events someone wanted them to see.

The images were like those in a bad dream. They were inside a dark place, misty and damp and the color of blood. Disturbing just to look at. Shadowy figures were moving back and forth through the scene; some were almost floating, but in a most unnatural way. Bizarre equipment that looked alive was jammed in everywhere. In the middle of this place was Brother Zarex. He was bound to a hovering chair. The shadows became clearer. They were REF troopers—or at least some of them were. Unmistakable in their red uniforms. They were taunting Zarex even as he was struggling with them. They were telling him they knew exactly what was going to happen at Zero Point. They knew when the UPF fleet would be passing over, and thus, they would be in a position to destroy it when it did—and there was nothing he could do about it.

Zarex fought them bravely, tossing them about like dolls. But suddenly, he just stopped. And that's when one shadow ran him through again and again with a long shiny needle. A very painful way to die.

This vision faded to be replaced by another. It showed REF troopers rampaging through ships, slaying innocents, bombarding defenseless planets, vaporizing orphans and children. In one last hazy vision, so distorted the six knew it probably hadn't happened yet, they saw thousands of ships unloading millions of people on a very bleak planet. In the background hovered the Red Ships, weapons ready. This vision disappeared as quickly as the first, but the message was clear.

"The devils implanted this memory," Erx said somberly. "They want us to know that they have our plans. And that if we interfere, they will kill millions on that planet in the near future, just as they have already killed thousands in the recent past. And if they succeed, the bad side of things will hold sway here for many ages to come."

"That planet can only be one place," Calandrx said. "An appropriate piece of Hell . . ."

"And the world closest to where it all started," Berx agreed. "So they're being ironic as well."

"Or not," Tomm added.

Klaaz said, "It was wise that we fulfilled our missions as messengers; these things will help us. I just wonder if it will be enough. There are many more of them than there are of us."

"For the moment anyway," Erx murmured.

"But at least we have one bright spot in this," Tomm said. "One chance that could help swing things our way."

They all knew what he meant.

"Brother Zarex was actually a very clever man to do what he did in the end," Calandrx said. "As well as a very brave one."

They were silent for a while. Finally Gordon said, "And so it begins."

"And there is still much we have to do," Tomm added.

They knew, then and there, it was finally time to leave *Bad News 666* for good.

They were needed elsewhere.

23

The enormous transport ship lowered itself through
the planet's thin atmosphere and set down on the forbidding,
rocky plain.

Its massive cargo doors swung open, and it began hastily
unloading its cargo, more than 5,000 people, mostly women
and children, all late of the floating refugee camp at the *Andromeda Zee*. Those reluctant to step off the ship were prodded
by faceless SG soldiers in bright red combat gear and holding
blaster rifles. Any further resistance, and the offending refugee
was painfully reduced to a pile of subatomic dust.

Once empty, the ship quickly lifted off and disappeared into
the barren, predawn sky. It was one of several waves of refugee ships to land on this stark, radiation-soaked planet.
Thousands of vessels from the Zee had been dumping their
ill-fated passengers all over this dreadful place, under the eye
of ominous low-orbiting SG ships that, for whatever reason,
had hulls painted like blood.

The conditions for the hapless refugees did not improve
once they were landed here. If anything, they became worse.
The REF did not provide food or water or medical supplies
throughout the trip from the Zee, nor were any forthcoming
now. There was no shelter anywhere on the planet. No pro-

tection from the harsh cosmic elements. The planet's sun was weak and far away, but because the atmosphere was almost nonexistent, its rays could burn clear through the skin in a matter of days or even hours. At the same time, the nights were so cold, frostbite was probably the most humane way to die here.

Such were the conditions on the aptly named planet of *Doomsday 212*.

Why would the REF move millions of refugees from a horrendous situation to one that was even worse? And why pick this notoriously unhealthy planet, ground zero for the schism that was now tearing the Galaxy apart? For those unfortunates so suddenly plunked down here, on this not-so-little piece of Hell, these questions were in the fore. None so much as for a man named Alfx Sheez.

It had been a long strange trip for Sheez. He was 251 years old, overweight, bald, short, and perpetually sweaty. He was also the ex-president of a planet, the infamous Megiddo, where SG wonder boy Joxx the Younger had made his stand against the Two Arm invaders a month ago—and lost miserably. Sheez got out just before his planet was destroyed, but it had been an inglorious departure. Previously wealthy from the largesse that came with being a top man, his escape from Megiddo left him with little more than the hat on his head and the boots on his stubby feet.

Sheez had been caught up in the massive tidal wave of refugees fleeing the Two Arm, first in a panic to escape the invading forces, and then by order of the SG when they established their No-Fly Zone. Sheez bribed his way aboard the last space bus leaving Megiddo, thinking he'd be on it for three days at the most. He wound up spending the next five weeks on the flying bucket of bolts instead, stuck in the Zee with the half million other star-crossed souls who'd once called the mid–Two Arm their home.

He'd seen so much misery since, it had almost changed him as a person. Conditions on his transport grew steadily worse as food and medicine ran out and no more was to be had. Rations got down to one food cube a day, and then none at all. Sheez had even tried bartering food from the dying—a futile enterprise if there ever was one. He'd cursed the SG many times for creating these intolerable conditions, and cursed the fools on Earth for doing nothing about so many of its citizens suffering so close to the Mother Planet.

So he, too, was surprised when word first arrived that SG ships would be escorting the refugees back to the Two Arm. But that appreciation quickly turned sour once they learned that those ships belonged to the REF and that they were planning on unloading everyone on this barely habitable planet, a place that Sheez was all too familiar with, as it was in even worse shape than his own decimated world, just a few light-years farther up the Arm.

Sheez never thought he'd miss Megiddo. But compared to this place, his old home seemed like paradise to him now.

His group of 5,000 was marched off the high plain where they'd been deposited and into a narrow, three-cornered canyon. It was hard on the edge of a mountain range that stretched north for as far as the eye could see. Sheez knew that he was somewhere way up in the upper half of the planet. He'd caught a glimpse of a snowcap as they were entering the rarefied atmosphere. He guessed he was now about twenty miles south of the frost line.

The three-sided canyon was only a few acres in area; once his group had been jammed in, it became as crowded as the putrid cargo hold they'd just left. They were being guarded by a hundred or so enormous red-suited SG troopers who had stationed themselves on the high rocks bordering the canyon. There had been more than 15,000 people on his ship, but just where the SG had dropped off the rest of them, Sheez didn't know or care. Their erstwhile protectors seemed intent on leaving large groups of refugees piecemeal around the planet. Spreading them out, for reasons unknown.

At first, many of those in the crowd thought that they had been brought here because the SG was going to distribute food and water soon. Sheez was not so naive. Like every tin-pot leader in the Two Arm, he'd had many dealings with the Solar Guards in the past, and the REF in particular. Most of these encounters had been unpleasant. And these red-suited SG troopers especially frightened him. No, the refugees had not been brought here for any kind of nourishment or rehabilitation. It was more likely that they were here as pawns in some cruel, unknowable game.

Either that, or they'd simply been dumped here to die. Or to be killed. Whatever the reason, Sheez wanted no part of it.

No sooner had he been shoved into his sitting space when he began looking for a way out.

While the narrow canyon was bordered on three sides by the high peaks, the fourth side held the remains of an ancient hillside city.

It was one of many built on *Doomsday 212* ages ago, when the planet's puff was still vital. Although the SG soldiers were strung along the peaks, the old city was not being guarded at all. Behind the ruins was the mountain, and what was beyond Sheez had little idea. He'd barely caught a glimpse of that area on their descent, and as it was still several hours before dawn, all he knew was that it was flat and vast. But it had to be better than where he was.

That this was not a food and water stop was beginning to sink in to the crowd by now. Some of the women started wailing. Many of the elderly were already having trouble breathing. Sheez's own substantial stomach was aching badly. Worst of all, he was getting thirsty. And the sun would be up in a few hours. And that's when it would begin to get hot.

Very hot . . .

The unfortunates would have to face that heat without any kind of overhead protection. Again, a weak puff meant all kinds of cosmic rays were able to get to the ground. Some acted quickly, others very slowly. In any case, they were all deadly, and combined with the oppressive temperature, Sheez guessed a third of this group might be dead by noon. Maybe him included.

He checked the soldiers on the peaks again. A bolt from a blaster gun could be fatal at 300 yards. Trouble was, there was nothing but open space for at least 400 yards or more before the cover of the small, ancient city. There was no way he could get away under these conditions. He was so big and slow, if he tried to make a break for it, he'd be shot down like a target in a shooting gallery.

He pulled his shirt over his head for cover and sank his head into his knees. Sheez was hardly a religious man. He had never prayed before in his life.

But he was praying now.

The question was, could anybody up there hear him?

Twenty Light-Years Away

The all-black Space Forces Starcrasher was named the *XenoVox*.

Officially it was an LRC, a long-range communications ship of the type that frequently accompanied SF fleets on long patrols. Unofficially, though, the *Xeno* belonged to a top secret SF unit called the Omega Force. And it was hardly just a radio ship.

The Omega Force was the SF's own version of a rapid deployment fleet. It was made up of the best soldiers and warships from the SF's five sectors, they being the Space Navy, the Air Service, Planet Forces Infantry, Space Marines, and the Orbital Bombardment Group. Unlike the Solar Guards Rapid Engagement Fleet, which consisted of thirty-six Starcrashers crammed with corps of Star Rangers, the Omega Force had 100 ships and three times as many soldiers, and those soldiers were good at doing many things. The unit was so secret, few people inside the Empire hierarchy knew it existed, including many inside the SF itself. On the other hand, everybody knew about the REF. There was another difference between the two outfits: once on the scene, Omega still took all its orders from SF headquarters. The REF always acted on its own.

The *XenoVox* was the forward eyes of Omega. It carried a crew of just fifty people and flew without weapons. Its role was to go into a trouble zone first and do vital recon, which was then flashed back to the fleet. But how could a ship that was nearly two miles long be able to fly near a flashpoint without being detected? Simple. The *Xeno* could become invisible. By engaging vast energy deflector screens, string comm dispersers, and a highly reflective opaque paint scheme, the vessel could not be seen on long-range scanning arrays, either coming from other space vessels nearby or from planets below.

In other words, it was a stealth ship.

The Omega Force had been deployed to this section of space near the edge of the Two Arm forty-eight hours before. The deployment had been done by the order of just one man, the Secretary of SF Intelligence himself. Without a doubt it was to be Omega's most classified mission.

Only Omega's half-dozen squadron commanders had been briefed on the very secret operation, and even they only knew what was going on up to a point. Essentially, the squadron commanders had been told two things: that no one knew how and when the fighting between the SF and SG would end, and that no one knew what the rampaging REF would do next. However, despite these two things, there was a good possibility that the fleet that invaded the Two Arm about five weeks earlier—the one that started all this trouble in the first place— still existed. That it hadn't been destroyed by the REF as the SG had originally claimed.

Omega's orders were to look for this rebel fleet, as it was thought it would soon turn up somewhere inside the Two Arm, near the place where it first disappeared. And what would happen if the mystery fleet was spotted? That's where the Secretary's order took an unusual twist: if the Omega Force *did* detect the rebel ships, they were to intercept and destroy them immediately, without waiting for any further instructions from SF Command. In fact, while the entire secret mission was going on, Omega was ordered not to have any contact at all with Earth or anyone else. They were to operate under a complete communications blackout. That's how sensitive this operation had to be.

To this end, the stealth ship *XenoVox* had been operating deep inside the No-Fly Zone for the past forty-eight hours. And it had seen at least a couple strange things so far.

Because the ship was, in effect, the ears and eyes of the Omega Force, most of its ultralong string devices scanned space at 360 degrees. Just two hours after arriving on station, the *Xeno* picked up a strange group of vessels, not inside the No-Fly Zone but apparently heading for it. This was not an organized fleet of any kind. They were all ion-ballast driven and seemed to be of all different types and sizes. But as they drew closer, it was obvious they did have one more thing in common: they were interstellar gunships, vessels that carried one or two big weapons and just enough people inside to operate them. In many cases, arms dealers themselves drove these kinds of ships. These ships were rare in the Galaxy though, and it was odd to see more than two of them flying together. Yet here were more than a dozen.

But the strangest thing of all was the direction from which these ships were coming. Their combined subatomic wake traced them back to their point of origin: way, way over in the Five Arm. And it was a rare ship indeed that came to the Two Arm from that far away.

The *Xeno* had also been watching the strange events unfold on *Doomsday 212*. Sometimes flying no more than a half light-year away, they'd detected SG ships dumping millions of people onto the desolate, hazardous planet. People, it would soon be determined, that had come from the floating refugee camp at *Andromeda Zee*. More important, the SG ships doing the relocation appeared to belong to none other than the infamous REF. But why they were doing this was a mystery.

Even stranger, there were faint indications that something else was going on either on the planet's surface or in low orbit just above it, something besides this mysterious delivery of innocents. Subatomic debris. Indications of huge blaster discharges. Excited but distorted comm messages. Was a small battle taking place somewhere on the dead planet as well? Or even a series of small battles? It was hard to tell, because the planet's weak puff actually hindered the *Xeno's* eavesdropping capabilities; there was not much air for the signals to bounce around in, so they could be quickly lost in space. And the stealth ship's commanders didn't want to get too close to the graveyard planet. But clearly something very unusual was going on down there, and it involved the infamous REF.

All this put Omega Force in a difficult position. With one

call, the 100-ship fleet could have swooped down and engaged the murderous REF and at least put a dent in its activities.

But that wasn't Omega's mission.

They were out here for one reason, and one reason only.

That was to find and destroy the rebel fleet.

Doomsday 212

Alfx Sheez lay on his back, at the edge of the crowd, staring up at the stars, terrified by the dawn that was soon to come.

He'd been like this for about an hour now. Alternately cursing and praying, fighting off waves of bitterness, not quite believing his life was going to end here, cooked alive on this bastard planet, with a bunch of wretched people he didn't even know. If only he'd been a better person in the past. Would it have done him any good now?

In between battling these emotions, he could clearly see pinpricks of light moving high overhead. Were these the last of the refugee ships leaving orbit, heading for destinations unknown? Or were they something else? Oddly, he thought he could see bright flashes of light coming from somewhere near orbit, too, almost as if a space battle was going on up there. And at one point, he swore he saw first one, then two spaceships plummeting through the thin atmosphere, on fire and trailing debris, presumably crashing hundreds of miles away.

Then he began to see all sorts of things flying overhead, way out, moving very, very fast. Different shapes, different colors. In the distance he thought he heard heavy weapons fire, and at first he wondered who the hell would be shooting at the SG. It wasn't like anyone lived on *Doomsday 212* and had suddenly decided to protect their planet. It was more likely that the REF had finally turned its weapons on the refugees.

That was the only scenario that made sense.

Another hour went by, and the dawn drew closer. The conditions in the small canyon were getting worse. It was growing very hot. Kids were crying. Some of the adults were, too. Fear was rising among the refugees.

Sheez sat up again and resumed whispering the only prayer

he knew over and over again, this while continuously watching the SG troopers up in the peaks. They seemed fanatical about guarding their captives, scanning the mob with high-intensity star lamps and viz-screen rays. They had melted several huge weapons into the rock, with muzzles pointed to the heart of the crowd below. Sheez put it all together and came to one sad conclusion: unless something extraordinary happened, the chances of his getting away now were nil.

He began praying even harder, though it didn't seem to be doing any good.

He'd been resting his eyes, head on his knees, mouthing the words of the petition, when something streaked very low over the small canyon.

It was going so fast and was emitting a noise so loud, it literally shook the dust from the hard ground around them. Sheez immediately looked up but only caught the tail end of the object as it disappeared over the horizon. It appeared as if it was totally engulfed in flame. Was this another starship crashing? Or some kind of natural phenomena? Or something else entirely?

There was no way to tell.

But at that exact moment, the still-darkened sky suddenly became alight with something else. It looked like rain at first, coming down from high up in the very thin sky. Red rain. As everyone had been stirred by whatever had just rocketed over them, everyone in the mob saw this coming, too. Flames, smoke, and now an ear-piercing, hellish scream the likes of which Sheez had never heard before.

Then, just as they were about a thousand feet above them, Sheez realized what these things were. *Fire rocks*. The deadly rain of loose particles left over from *Doomsday 212*'s deteriorating ring, one of the many things that made the planet a particularly hellish place to be. Though these things fell nonstop at the equator, they were much less prevalent up here in the northern hemisphere. Yet a swarm of the deadly boulders was coming down right on top of them, right now.

Or so it seemed.

Just as the fiery volley was about 500 feet over them, there was another sonic blast, and the formation of fire rocks suddenly began to break up. Instead of coming straight down, they began veering off in all directions; even sideways, some of them.

Then, in a vision that seemed like a dream, the fire rocks began slamming not into the mob of helpless people but into the red-suited SG troopers stationed on the peaks around them!

One by one, the soldiers were picked off, almost as if an invisible hand were directing the fiery chunks at the enormous troopers. Sheez watched in astonishment as the string of kinetic explosions went right around the top of the canyon wall. The noise was tremendous. Each fireball strike was blinding. It was so exhilarating and confusing at the same time, some people in the mob started screaming. What was going on here? How could this be? Sheez wondered. Then it hit him: somehow, some way, his prayer *had* been answered. This was just what he needed.

Without another second of hesitation, he got up and started running.

As he had estimated before, it was at least a 400-yard dash from the edge of the mob to the foot of the ancient ruins. As soon as he took off, Sheez heard some shooting behind him, but he didn't dare turn back to see where it was coming from. He stumbled several times in the waning darkness, badly cutting himself on the hard, rocky ground. But each time he managed to get up, right himself, and start running again.

Somehow he reached the edge of the ruins without having a massive coronary. He was out of breath and his knees were horribly scraped, but he was still in one piece. The ruins turned out to be those of a small settlement. A few dozen structures, made of ancient ion concrete, worn away long ago. But Sheez was hardly an *aficionado* of the past; he never even broke stride. He kept running through the ruins, up what was left of the main avenue, intent on reaching the summit of the small mountain and hopefully some cover beyond.

It took another few minutes of hard climbing and heavy breathing, but reach the top he did. And on the other side of the mountain, he saw the vast rocky plain that stretched from one horizon to another. But there were hundreds of thousands of refugees down on this plain, strung out in large clusters along the valley floor, with thousands—of REF troops watching over them. Even worse, there were dozens of REF armed shuttlecrafts flying overhead and even a handful of red Starcrashers hovering just a couple hundred feet off the ground. Sheez was crushed. Any thoughts that the other side of the mountain might provide some refuge were dashed, just like that.

Then Sheez heard a disturbing noise coming from behind him. It was loud and pounding, like a stampede. He turned, certain that he would see a small army of REF troopers running up the hill after him.

But he was in for another surprise. There *were* people running up the old avenue behind him, but they weren't SG. It was the rest of the crowd, the mob of refugees from which he'd just escaped. They'd seen him make a break for it and had followed right behind him. This was not good. He could see a certain look in the eyes of the first dozen people climbing up to him, and as a politician, he knew that look well. These people had misinterpreted his act of cowardice for one of courage, and now they wanted him to lead them to safety. And that was the last thing Alfx Sheez wanted to do.

The first group of refugees reached the summit and begged him for help, begged him to save them all. Sheez looked back into the valley before him; there had to be at least 50,000 REF soldiers within sight alone. There was no way he could go down there, alone or with the mob. But he couldn't stay up here, either.

Off to his left, to the north, about a quarter of a mile away, the ridge they were on split in two. Between the two high grounds was another canyon, this one holding a patch of overhead vegetation, extremely rare on the planet. It was brown and it was dying, but it was also cover from the REF and maybe even the coming heat of day. Sheez thought about simply making a break for this sanctuary alone, but then something stopped him—*physically* stopped him—as if an invisible hand had taken hold of his chest and was preventing him from moving another step in any direction. The crowd was now bunching up on the hilltop and on the trail below. They were presenting themselves as a huge target. He had no doubt that if the REF saw them, they would simply blast them all away.

Sometimes life forces you to be a hero, he heard a voice whisper in his ear. He spun around, yet no one was there. A shudder went through him. He had heard those words so clearly. He turned back to the growing crowd of people reaching the top of the ridge. And that's when it dawned on him: the only way he was going to save himself was to save all of the other refugees along with him. And that's when the invisible hand let him go.

"OK!" he finally yelled. "Everyone follow me!"

The crowd stole along the narrow ridge and began climbing down into the gorge without being detected by the REF.

Sheez did his best to pick out the safest path for them to travel. There were so many women and kids in his troupe, he found himself helping just about all of them over the roughest spots. All the while he was keeping an eye on valley to the east. The REF troopers were still coming in by the shipload; the thousands of refugees below looked puny in comparison. Sheez was also on the lookout for any REF troopers that might have survived the incredibly fortuitous fall of fire rocks back in the three-sided canyon. He even went so far as to run back to the rear of the escape column to make sure no one was following them. Or, if they were, he'd be the first one they'd try to shoot.

It took them more than an hour, but somehow, all of the refugees made it down into the hidden canyon and under the cover of dead vegetation. Sheez carried the last kid down into the gorge himself.

There, he thought, *my heroic duty is done.*

But as soon as he reached the bottom of the gorge, he was in for a surprise: there were about four thousand refugees already hiding under the vegetation. Again, mostly women and kids, they were from other groups dumped by the REF nearby. Remarkably, they, too, had escaped their captors by way of a near-miraculous event. One group had been freed when a landslide, caused by some kind of sonic boom, crushed the contingent of REF troopers guarding them but not harming any of the refugees. Another group had been penned up inside a force field when a bolt of lightning hit the generating unit maintaining the invisible jail, once again killing their captors but not harming any of them. Others swore that men with wings appeared to them, telling them to make it to this gorge, where they would find a man who would lead them out of this wilderness.

Men with wings? Sheez thought wildly. *Were they talking about me?*

He was immediately barraged with questions from these new refugees as to what they should all do now. Problem was, Sheez had no idea. He'd been fully intending to take off on his own from here, having done his good deed. But then that same invisible hand returned and began pounding him fiercely on his chest.

It's up to you, he heard a voice say, again as if someone was whispering in his ear.

Sheez spun around and, just like before, there was no one standing behind him. But again, he found it impossible to move. If anything, the hand pushing on his chest felt heavier.

This time he got the message quick enough.

He had to lead these lost people across the expanse for at least a little while longer.

The morning finally came, and the weak sun appeared. But the coverage of the dead vegetation kept the mob of refugees safe and relatively cool, especially in the initial heat of the day. Sheez wasn't sure how long this sanctuary would hold up, though, especially with so many people now crowded inside. At some point the REF would realize that a lot of their hostages were missing, and they would come looking for them. Then what?

As the others tried to stay hidden, Sheez slithered to top of the ridge and studied the REF in the vast valley below. The number of refugees down there had swelled again, as had the red-uniformed troops watching over them. Some of these soldiers were right at the bottom of the mountain now, no more than a 500 feet below.

If the REF ever found them up here, it would be a massacre—a short and quick one. But where else could they go?

Water was their most critical need. The ridgeline ran all the way to the northern horizon, and Sheez reasoned the farther north they went, the better the chances they would reach a snowline, and then maybe even a frozen lake or stream. The trouble was, in many places the ridgeline veered extremely close to the valley full of REF, and all it would take was for one kid to cry out or one old person to stumble, and the game would be up.

So it was a choice to either wait here and die or try their luck by moving hopefully toward water. And it was up to him to decide. Sheez's heart was pounding, he was scared shitless, but the voice in his ear was getting louder all the time.

Just keep moving, it said. *These people are counting on you.*

So move they did. Sheez got everyone on their feet, and they all climbed out of the gorge and up to the ridgeline again.

Staying low and walking as quickly as possible, they headed north. The sun grew higher, but a weak wind kicked up, and it seemed to lessen the effects of the heat. Sheez stationed the strongest men he could find at crucial points along the route; they would help those who were too weak or feeble to walk along the roughest parts of the ridge, and then turn them over to the man at the next station and so on. This way they were able to keep the line moving while making sure no one would be left behind.

The ridgeline provided a natural path, and sometimes it was wide enough for several people to walk abreast. Sheez always took the lead, though. It was very unlike him to be courageous, but something very odd was happening here. Damned if Sheez knew what it was, with voices in his head and the hand pounding on his chest, but somehow, some way, he had become *responsible*. And it was just too strong for him to fight. So, if there was any trouble up ahead, he wanted to be the first one to see it. And if anyone was going to fire on them, it was only right that he take the first blast.

The biggest surprise, though, was what he saw off to his west. Other streams of refugees were off in the distance, heading north as well. It was almost as if they were under the influence of a siren call. And then he spotted other groups of refugees much closer to him. Some were moving right below the ridgeline and, seeing his group, fell in line with them. By the time Sheez had even walked a mile, his troop had swelled to nearly 10,000 people.

They kept moving, and the farther north they went, the stranger things became. Huge flashes of fire and light were going off way up in the sky, some even as high as orbit. They heard enormous explosions, some so powerful the mountain itself shook beneath their feet. REF ships of all sizes rocketed over their heads. Some were Starcrashers, some were smaller shuttlecraft, all had hulls painted red. And while Sheez always had his people take cover whenever he heard something coming, there were several times the aircraft flew right over them and didn't do a thing. Almost as if they had other things on their minds.

Very strange.

About three hours into their trek, there came such a tremendous explosion, Sheez yelled for his people to hit the dirt. A moment later, a huge SG Starcrasher went right over them, not more than 200 feet above their heads. It was in flames and falling apart, trailing pieces of debris behind it. It came down about three miles west of them, exploding on impact. The refugees leaped up and let out a great cheer, but Sheez screamed for them all to stay down. The ship's prop core blew up a few seconds later, creating a huge mushroom cloud before it all fell back in on itself. Once the smoke cleared, all that remained was a mile of smoking wreckage, or so it seemed. Incredibly, Sheez could see tiny figures moving around inside the skeleton of the burning ship. Were these REF troopers who had somehow survived the crash? How could that be? Were they *that* hard to kill?

Keep moving, the voice told him. *Just keep moving. . . .*

They walked for another hour, making good progress, considering just about everyone was in need of food, water, and rest.

But the farther north they moved, the more violent the rumbling under their feet became—and more frequent. And soon enough smoke began appearing on the far horizon. Then they could see the glow of flames as well.

It soon became obvious something big was happening up over the next peak. Sheez picked out two young guys and sent them ahead to check it out. Meanwhile, he had the rest of the group lay low.

It took the two runners about a half hour to move up, see what was happening, and then run back to the group's position. When they reached Sheez again, they were both so excited and out breath, it was hard to get anything out of them at first.

Finally all one of them could say was, "Boss, you won't believe what's happening up there. . . ."

It took Sheez just fifteen minutes to get up and over the line of hills, his suddenly energetic body moving quicker than ever before.

With each step, he heard more tremendous explosions and felt the ground literally quake beneath his feet. The sky ahead was incredibly bright with flame and flashes of light. There was so much smoke and dust in the air, he couldn't see anything else across the entire northern horizon.

Finally he reached the top of the peak and peered over the other side. And his young scout had been right. He *didn't* believe what he saw.

Sheez had never been a soldier. He'd never carried a weapon in combat, he'd never been on a real battlefield. Surely, he'd seen the results of battle. He'd witnessed the beginnings of the destruction of his planet Megiddo. But he was long gone before the hammer really came down.

That's why what he saw before him now was so astonishing.

It was a battle—at least that much was clear. The crisscross of blaster fire was blinding, the smoke and flying debris tremendous. There were ships of all shapes and sizes coming and going, explosions all around them in the air. But there were other ships firing at them, too, or sometimes firing at each other. It was confusion times ten. Times a hundred. Times a thousand.

Sheez had to clear the dust from his eyes. He tried to figure out who was fighting who and who was caught in the middle. It was very hard to do at first, but gradually things started coming together.

He was looking down on another immense valley. This one was long and rectangular, typical topography for *Doomsday 212*. In the middle of the valley was a huge circular trench— yes, a trench dug into the concrete surface of the dead, rocky planet. So what he was looking down at was a defense perimeter. But Sheez couldn't believe what else he saw. Inside the trenches were thousands of robots, huge mechanical men with huge blasters, seemingly firing in every direction. And these weren't ordinary clankers. Sheez recognized them. They were the robots of Myx.

He knew these tin men all too well. When the Two Arm invaders attacked Megiddo, they'd sent streams of the almost-invincible robots raining down on Joxx's defensive positions. The defending troops did their best to blast the flying robots out of the sky, but that proved impossible, as the robots would simply pull themselves back together again and fly away. As it turned out, their attack was actually a very successful effort to distract Joxx from the invaders' real objective: the artificial planetoid of TW800, where they managed to steal six cargo 'crashers. Nevertheless, Sheez knew what these monsters could do. But what the hell were they doing here? Certainly the Two Arm invaders weren't involved in this.

Or were they?

There was no way Sheez could tell how the robots had gotten to *Doomsday*, or who was controlling them or why. He could see that they were lined up shoulder to shoulder in the trenches and firing wildly out of the circle. And who were they firing at? Thousands—no, *tens* of thousands—of REF soldiers. Entire armies of the enormous red-suited troops were trying breach the trench line. And the robots were doing everything they could to keep them out.

In the middle of this perimeter—the circle was probably a half mile in diameter at the most—Sheez saw a dozen or so strange starships, some on the ground, others hovering just above it. These ships appeared to be from another part of the Galaxy entirely. Even so, refugees were be being led into them. That much Sheez could tell because at certain points around this huge battlefield, he could see streams of refugees pouring into the perimeter, somehow dodging all the blaster fire, the smoke and dust, and running right up to the waiting ships under the protection of the huge robots.

It was only then that it dawned on Sheez exactly what was going on here. This wasn't just a battle; it was an evacuation, a rescue effort. Just as the REF had dumped thousands of refugees onto *Doomsday 212*, and may have been dumping them still, probably to die, someone else was trying to lift them off and save their lives.

And even in the middle of all this—in his very dangerous position as it was all happening a relatively short distance from him—Sheez, former hustler, former crooked politician, former tin pot dictator, was struck by something.

He heard it come from his own lips; there was no voice whispering in his ear this time.

"Noble . . ." he said, uttering the word for the first time in his life. "What a Goddamn *noble* thing to do."

Five Hundred Miles Away

It was on its next pass through the No-Fly Zone that the SF stealth ship *XenoVox* finally got a close-up look at what was happening on *Doomsday 212*.

Flying within a hair's breadth of the planet, its crew discovered a ground battle had erupted in its northern hemisphere. It was so immense, the smoke and flame obscured even the *Xeno's* most powerful scanners, and they could usually see through just about anything.

Above the battlefield, there were ships going in and coming out; some were the same sorry vessels that had dropped the refugees onto the planet in the first place. But now they appeared to be under someone else's control. Even stranger, there were other ships involved here: the mysterious fleet of arms dealers and gunships the *Xeno* had detected flying in from the Five Arm earlier. Among them were the REF Red Ships, trying to fire on these disparate vessels. But somehow the arms dealers were also using their huge guns to protect the refugee ships leaving the planet's orbit.

None of this made sense to those aboard the spy ship. Was

this small force of arms dealers from the faraway Five Arm actually taking on the renegade REF? As unlikely as it seemed, that appeared to be at least partly the case.

The *Xeno* dashed away from the area and was about to report these bizarre developments back to the Omega Force, when suddenly its ultra–long-range scanners started going crazy—again.

They had picked up something else very strange, not down on the planet or even inside the No-Fly Zone. This was coming from somewhere very, very far out.

The *Xeno* crew began triangulating, and soon their bubblers were telling them they had detected a number of starships heading *down* the Two Arm, moving toward the trouble zone at incredible speed. Even more fantastic, the *Xeno*'s subatomic scramblers could not pick up a contrail from any of these ships, which suggested, foolishly, that they were somehow moving without the aid of star engines. But then again, they weren't traveling in Supertime, either. They were actually flying *even faster* than Supertime.

However, the most startling piece of information was the point of origin of these ships. The *Xeno*'s superbubbler was insisting that they had flown into the Galaxy from a location someplace *outside* of it.

This made no sense. It was the stated policy of the Empire— and the almost universally held belief among the citizens of the Galaxy—that all life in the universe was contained within the Milky Way. Therefore, it was impossible that any life could exist outside of it.

But now, here were indications that at least twenty bizarre starships of some type were moving down the second swirl at inconceivable speeds. What did it mean? The *Xeno* crew asked their superbubbler. The answer that came back startled them: From all appearances, the bubbler said, this was an invasion from somewhere outside the Galaxy, by beings unknown, who possessed technology that seemed to dwarf even Supertime.

It wasn't the invaders the Omega Force were supposed to be looking for.

But it was an invasion, nevertheless.

● ● ●

The flagship of the Omega Force was an enormous M-class Starcrasher called *TempusVox*.

This colossus was two and a half miles long, carried a crew of nearly 10,000, plus thousands of weapons and an entire of corps of Space Marines, numbering more than 25,000.

As it was the lead ship of Omega, all orders for the special fleet were generated from here. Since the fleet was on a highly secret mission and there were to be no communications at all back to SF Command, the *TempusVox* had the final say for the entire operation.

The commander of the *Tempus* was a 150-year-old veteran of the Space Navy named Haxx Grinx. Handsome, bright, and energetic, Grinx was also a highly capable 'crasher driver who had helmed Omega's flagship for the past twenty-three years. He was well-connected within SF Command and respected by his contemporaries throughout the Empire. He was also very loyal to the Emperor.

Grinx was on his bridge when the startling message came in from the *XenoVox*. He read over the communiqué several times before it actually sank in. The *Xeno*'s report seemed so outlandish, he doubted its credibility at first. But still, in these days of high uncertainty, he knew everything had to be taken as truth unless proven otherwise—even the most outlandish. So Grinx put out a call to the rest of the Omega fleet, telling them to move into a close battle formation at a point just outside the Two Arm. He then ordered his squadron commanders to beam aboard his ship immediately.

The six SCOs were standing in Grinx's war room a few moments after that. Grinx explained what the *Xeno* had found. Twenty-four ships were confirmed to be heading toward the mid–Two Arm at incomprehensible speed, and these ships appeared to have an origin point *outside* the Galaxy.

To a man, the squadron commanders were shocked upon hearing the news.

"An *alien* invasion?" one of them blurted out. "Is that even possible?"

The other SCOs were visibly uncomfortable with their colleague's choice of words. The phobia about life in other parts of the universe was so prevalent in the Galaxy that the word *alien* was not allowed to be spoken in public nor did it appear anywhere in the Empire's string documents or charters. Nor was it taught to schoolchildren. It was, in effect, a nonword.

"Anything is possible these days," Grinx replied somberly. "And I just don't know what else it could be."

"They must be some kind of ultra-advanced craft if they can move quicker than Starcrashers," another squadron CO said. "Who knows what kind of weapons they possess? What powers they have?"

"And if they get by us," Grinx said, "they could be on Earth in a matter of hours, minutes even."

"But what can we do?" another officer asked. "We are probably the only souls in the Empire who have this information already."

"We must fight them, of course," one commander said defiantly.

Grinx bit his lip. Fighting them might prove suicidal. Though Omega outnumbered the incoming force, their technology seemed so highly advanced there was a chance that Empire weaponry might not have any effect on them. Plus, these ships would be in their area in just minutes. There certainly was no time to bring any other SF ships in to do battle with them.

"But what about our orders?" another SCO worried. "They are as strict as any I've ever heard. . . ."

Grinx thought about this, too. But he knew sometimes orders had to be broken.

Especially when it meant trying to save the Empire.

The Omega Force turned about in a matter of seconds and realigned into ten arrowhead formations.

Their orders set, the squadron commanders were preparing to beam back to their ships when another report from the *XenoVox* came in. The mysterious alien force was close enough now to get a fuzzy visual on them. The *Xeno* commander uplinked his viz to the *Tempus*, along with a warning that what the fleet commanders were about to see was rather startling.

The viz appeared on the *Tempus*'s huge battle management

screen. It showed twenty-four ships, and indeed they were heading right for them at inconceivable speed. But the startling thing was this: the ships were of an almost ancient design, right down to their blue and chrome color scheme.

This made no sense, but the time to question anything was over. Grinx was the person solely responsible for the Empire's very survival now, and he ordered his ships to prepare for battle. They would try to stop these mystery ships here; if not, then they would break all the orders and inform Earth what was coming their way.

The squadron commanders agreed. But as they prepared to jump back to their ships, three images suddenly materialized on the bridge of the *Tempus*.

Grinx and the squadron commanders were astonished. These three people had not transported in by usual means; they would have been detected by the ship's security auras. Nor had they dropped in from another dimension. This, too, would have been caught by the security systems.

They had literally come from nowhere.

Even more astounding, the trio was well-known to Grinx and his SCOs. One of them was none other than Skol Fyxx, a ten-star general emitrus for the Space Forces. Loy Staxx, a very well-known starship SF commander, was the second man.

Most astounding of all, the third man was Zapp Multx, quite possibly the most famous SF ship captain of the past 400 years.

Grinx somehow got up the gumption to have the three men scanned. Remarkably, they all passed. They were the authentic items. In this trio was more than 1,000 years of high-caliber service to the Empire and the Space Forces. Oddly, though, each one was wearing a drop of oil on his forehead.

"We must talk," was all Multx said upon their sudden arrival. "Alone . . ."

Grinx immediately cleared the bridge. In seconds, only he and his squadron commanders remained.

"You've detected an incoming fleet," Multx went on. "You cannot interfere with it. It is here to do good, and it will not harm anyone who doesn't deserve it. You have to let it reach its destination unimpeded."

Grinx was still getting over the shock of the sudden appearance of the three spiritual leaders of the SF.

"With all respect to you, sir," he began, "we have indications that this is some kind of an alien force that seeks to—"

Multx cut him off at the quick. "These things are very complex, Commander Grinx," he said. "And not so easily explained. I wouldn't dare pretend to understand them myself. All I can tell you is that what will happen here seeks only to right a wrong committed ages ago. And in a way, it has very little to do with what is happening inside the Galaxy these days. In fact, it involves something even bigger. I know it is hard to believe, but what the people in this fleet—as well as others—must do is for the benefit of us all. Of everyone in the Galaxy. And that's why you must let them do it."

Grinx turned to Staxx and Fyxx. They were nodding in agreement.

"But what you are advocating is seditious and disloyal," Grinx told them. "I cannot just sit back an allow an alien attack on the Empire!"

"It is not an attack on the Empire," Multx said, cutting him off again. "Do you know three people who are more loyal to the Empire than us?"

Grinx thought a moment, but then just shook his head. "No," he murmured.

"Do you think we would be here advocating anything that was not in the best interest of the citizens of the Empire? Either now or in the future?"

Again, after some thought, Grinx had to shake his head no.

"Then, please," Multx said, in his very persuasive way, "just trust us—and do as we ask."

Grinx just shook his head. "And if I don't?" he asked.

The three men just looked at each other. Then Multx clapped his hands. If this didn't get him back in the history books, nothing would.

Outside the *TempusVox* control room bubble a gigantic starship suddenly appeared, again as if from nowhere.

It was the very famous *BonoVox*, Multx's old ship. Sensors said all of its weapons were powered up and ready to fire.

Before anyone could say a word, another SF ship appeared behind it. This was Staxx's old ship. Then another materialized: Skol Fyxx's former vessel. Then came another . . . and another.

In seconds, there were more than a hundred SF ships surrounding the tightly boxed Omega Force. These ships all belonged to elderly, retired, or SF commanders who had fallen from favor and, like Multx, had been relegated to the Ball.

"If you don't do as we ask," Multx now said in a very even tone, "then I'm afraid we will have little choice but to blast you all out of the sky."

A moment of immense tension went through the room. The SF and SG fighting each other was bad enough. But SF ships against *other* SF ships? At that moment it really *did* seem like the entire Empire was about to collapse.

But then, suddenly, a million bells went off all over the bridge. The ship's comm string sector was instantly ablaze with warning lights. The midrange scanners began going absolutely crazy.

Grinx hastily called up a mini–scanning screen. He took one look at it and nearly fell over. He was sure that the scanner was malfunctioning. The reading he was getting was almost impossible, even more so than an alien force coming down the Two Arm.

But Grinx made some quick instrument adjustments and determined that what the small scanner was telling him was not a mistake. With trembling fingers, he hit the panel that would bring the information up to the main screen itself and give everyone on the bridge a visual of this latest turn of events.

The screen came alive, and every squadron commander let out a gasp. This didn't make any sense. The screen was showing *another* huge fleet of strange, incredible vessels. These ships went beyond the word *alien*. They seemed impossible. In design. In shape. In size. And in speed, for they were traveling even faster than the smaller fleet coming from outside the Galaxy. They, too, were heading into the No-Fly Zone. And they were all shining in the brightest gold.

"My God," Grinx said, staring at the visual, seeing it but hardly believing it. "How can this be?"

Multx touched the drop of oil on his forehead.

"As I said before . . ." He smiled. "Some things are just not easily explained."

Doomsday 212

Down the mountain, across the hills, to the field below, Alfx Sheez was running as fast as he could.

He'd watched the battle from the top of the mountain for so long, he'd almost become mesmerized by it. In that time, the blaster fire around him grew more intense, and the robots of Myx were fighting more fiercely, sometimes even hand to hand. But the number of red-uniformed SG troops entering the fray seemed to be growing with every second as well. So many red-hulled Starcrashers were unloading troops nearby, they were nearly colliding with the rescue ships taking off full of refugees. And all the while, more innocents were streaming into the defense perimeter.

The entire scene was so intense, so confusing, Sheez finally had to snap himself out of it. He couldn't waste any more time. He had to get his people to the evacuation point and at least give them a chance to get off this hellhole.

That's why he was moving so fast now.

He returned to his troop and quickly explained as best he could what was going on up ahead. Between his story and the breathless report of the two runners before him, the mob of refugees soon got the picture. It wouldn't be easy, but Sheez was going to try to get them off *Doomsday 212*.

There was a pass between the two mountains nearest to them. On the other side of this pass was the edge of the evacuation zone. If his people were able to climb over the shallow hills in between and then down through the pass, they might be able to fall in with the other streams of refugees, get into the defense perimeter, and hopefully get on a ship that would lift them out.

How could they all make it that last half mile, though? Many of the elderly refugees could barely breathe at this point; others couldn't walk. The worst heat of the day had passed; still it was brutally hot. But Sheez had a plan. He would put the

strongest individuals in his group at the rear of the column
and the most feeble, along with the women and kids, up front.
He would then lead the group over the hills and toward the
evacuation ring, and those who fell behind would be helped
by the stronger ones at the back. They would physically carry
them to the rescue site if they had to.

Word passed down the line of refugees that they would be
moving forward. The sky all around them seemed on fire now.
The smoke was swirling like a hurricane, the sounds of explosions, blaster fire, and rocket engines was deafening.

But Sheez was feeling good. There was a chance that he
just might pull this off.

He got his people positioned, women and kids and the elderly up front, stronger males at the back. Then he stood up,
raised his hand as the signal to move forward . . . But suddenly
there was a tremendous blast.

Sheez looked down to find a huge hole burning its way
through his through his chest.

He started to fall over, but then everything began moving
in slow motion. He saw a huge vessel landing in front of him.
A second ship was setting down close by. Both were Starcrashers, both painted red. REF troops began pouring out of
these ships, even before they touched the ground. Weapons
raised, it was one of these soldiers who had shot Sheez.

Still falling over, with one last breath, he screamed, *"Everyone get down!"*

No one in his troop hesitated. Just on the sound of his voice
alone they hit the dirt. A storm of blaster fire went over their
heads an instant later. There was another tremendous blast of
light, and Sheez was hit again . . . and again . . . and again. . . .

The next thing he knew, he was on his back, his clothes on
fire, a half dozen blaster holes burning through him.

A tremendous glow was suddenly all around him. On his
hands, his body, in the very air itself. In saving his group one
last time, he'd taken a fatal barrage himself. He tried to move
but couldn't. He tried to speak, but no words would come out.
His people were down, but he could also hear the sounds of
the SG troops coming up to them, weapons crackling with
power. His people would all be dead in a matter of seconds.

Damn! We came so far, only for it to end like this!

Sheez felt life itself slipping out of him. Tears rolling off his face, body going numb, he was looking straight up—and above him, saw a very strange sight.

It was a ship. A starship. But it was unlike any he'd ever seen.

It was not shaped like a wedge, as were all starships in the Fourth Empire. This vessel looked like an ancient sailing ship, bare images of which had survived over the ages. Things made of wood with great cloth sails that pushed them across the waves. It was strange the things one recalls before dying, but back then, Sheez knew they'd called these ships *galleonis*.

But this ship was in the air, and it was made of gold. And where once might have been sails of cloth were now sails of subatomic strings meshed together. And it was armed. Heavily armed. To his fading eyes, it seemed to carry more weapons than a Starcrasher, yet it was barely one-half the size.

For a moment he thought he was already dead and what he was seeing above him was a hallucination—a vision—before the darkness filled in.

But then a bright gold beam shot out of the bottom of the strange ship, and an instant later, an enormous soldier was standing over him. This soldier was encased in armor from head to foot. Gold armor. And he was carrying a huge gold weapon and wearing a huge gold helmet with flared-back wings.

Sheez was sure this was just another REF soldier, for some reason painted gold instead of red and riding in a strange old ship, and that with more strange gold soldiers and those soldiers already on the ground, they would brutally murder all his people.

But in the end, Sheez had it all wrong.

The next thing he knew, the gold soldier raised his enormous gold weapon and started firing at the REF troopers. Suddenly blaster bolts were going off all around him. Sheez heard more screams, but he couldn't tell if they were coming from his people or from someone else. He saw more soldiers dressed in gold armor materializing as if from nowhere. Hundreds of them. *Thousands of them.* Then more gold ships suddenly appeared overhead. More explosions. The ground beneath him lifted him up, it was moving so violently. All the while, the pain in his chest was getting worse and worse, until it stopped hurting altogether. It went on like this for what seemed like an eternity.

Then, just as quickly as it started, all the firing stopped. The explosions ended, and the smoke blew away. With his last ounce of strength, Sheez managed to look up. He saw before him an unbelievable sight: the field and the hills were littered with piles of dead REF soldiers. The two red Starcrashers were burning fiercely in the background. And he could see his column of people, all moving together, the soldiers in gold leading them off to the rescue site. Some of the refugees were waving good-bye to him; many were in tears.

Then the huge soldier in gold, the one who had first appeared nearby, knelt down beside him. He took off his helmet, and Sheez saw his face. And that was the one last shock of his life. Sheez recognized him.

Rugged, handsome, steely eyes, but still with a friendly face, he was the one person, more than any other, responsible for destroying Sheez's old planet of Megiddo. Yet he'd just saved his people. And Sheez even knew his name.

It was Hawk Hunter, leader of the rebel forces.

What the hell is he doing here?

Sheez grabbed his arm and spat out his last words.

"My people," he gasped, his voice fading. "Please . . ."

"Don't worry," Hunter told him. "They're safe now, every last one of them. Thanks to you . . ."

Sheez was fading fast. "And what about me?" he asked Hunter softly. "What will happen to me now?"

Hunter checked his wounds and knew it was amazing that Sheez had lasted this long.

"You're off to a better place," he said. "Believe me, I know."

Sheez looked up at him and suddenly realized he *did* believe him. A smile finally spread across his battered face. He closed his eyes.

And then he died.

24

Earth

The Empress landed her air car in the middle of the desert.

Or at least it looked like a desert. It was flat, for the most part, though there were some mountains directly to the west. It was dry and hot, too. But the sand beneath her feet was actually a mixture of tiny glass globules and not authentic silica.

She had never been here before. Still, she knew she was in the right place because way off on the horizon she could see a group of plain white structures built astride a huge dry lake bed. Even at this distance she could tell the buildings were absolutely ancient.

She would not need the air car from here.

Flash!

Suddenly she was standing at the front entrance of the largest building. A faded sign next to the door read: *Domain 51*.

Flash!

Now she was inside the building itself, looking down at the entrance to a huge amphitheater. There were dozens of soldiers in stark black uniforms standing at rigid attention around this sizable portal. The only means of illumination that she could see was by candles; there were hundreds of them everywhere.

Their flickering cast odd shadows on the Z-gun turrets built into the walls of this place.

Flash!

She was now inside the chamber itself. It, too, was lit only by candlelight. In the middle of the chamber was a huge black monolith. It was a hundred feet high and about half that measurement square. It stood alone. A huge, seamless, impenetrable presence.

It was the Big Generator.

It, too, was guarded by an army of black-uniformed soldiers; these were the Sacred Guards. They were standing at attention in small groups scattered around the inner chamber. They did not seem to notice that the Empress was there. Not yet, anyway.

She had never seen it before. This big, ugly, holy thing. No sound was coming from it, as she had expected there to be. Nor was there any means of access, or dials or switches or panel lights on the thing. There were no controls—at least none anywhere nearby.

This was strange because the Big Generator made everything possible in the Galaxy. The power it generated went everywhere and encompassed everything. It ran all of the Empire's spaceships. It ran the planets. It ran everything *on* the planets. From the dimmest panel bulb on the most distant world to the prop core of the largest Starcrasher, all energy in the Empire came from here.

The Empress moved down the aisle and finally caught the attention of the guards. They were startled to see her, to say the least. They were not aware of the particulars of what was happening back east or out in the Galaxy. They were mind-eunuchs. Their only role was to protect the Big Generator with their lives and not let anyone unauthorized near it.

But did this include members of the Imperial Family?

None of the guards was sure.

The captain of the guard gingerly approached the Empress just as she arrived at the electric railing that surrounded the Big Generator.

"My lady?" the man asked her. "Can I be of assistance?"

"Yes," she replied. "You can leave me alone."

She started to cross the barrier to the stage where the Big Generator sat.

The officer reached out and held his hand in front of her.

"I'm sorry, my lady," he said, very nervous, "but you are not allowed in there."

She turned on him. "Not allowed?" she hissed. "Do you know who I am?"

The officer began stammering. "Of . . . of course, I do. But, still, my lady. This is a restricted area."

At that moment, the officer felt something pushing against his chest. He looked down to see that it was a blaster pistol. The Empress had it pointing directly at his heart.

"Do you know the difference between Heaven and Hell?" she asked him crossly.

He numbly shook his head no.

"People like us don't go to Heaven automatically," she told him. "We've got to work to get there."

25

Doomsday 212

Hunter threw the last bit of dirt on Sheez's grave, then wiped the dust from his hands.

Tremendous chaos was still going on around him. The sky was filled with enormous warships. The battle at the evacuation site had grown more fierce. Large quakes were running through the planet itself. There was smoke and fire and wind and soot. But still, Hunter felt this man deserved a decent burial. It didn't take much to determine that he'd led the huge group of refugees to the rescue site and that he gave his life so that they might keep theirs. He had done the simplest thing in human existence then. He had done the right thing.

Hunter patted the last of the dirt down with his hand and paused a moment.

Another hero, he thought.

One of many to be made this day.

It would have taken volumes to explain how Hunter had arrived at this spot, at this exact time, wearing the armor of a Third Empire soldier. It all started with a great secret—and some simple mathematics. The Galaxy held billions of stars, those stars held hundreds of billions of planets, and those planets held trillions of people. The people who ruled it all, the

Fourth Empire, were very secretive—and for good reason. Among those staggering numbers, they knew of things so volatile, so potentially disruptive on a galactic scale, that they were forbidden to even write them down, this under penalty of death, no matter how high the offender was in the imperial hierarchy. These things were called the Cardinal Secrets, and there were at least five of them, though many believed there were at least several more.

One Cardinal Secret was the name of the person who invented the Echo 999.9. Another was the origin of the Big Generator. Another was the secret behind the life-extending properties of Holy Blood. Still another, the reason why Starcrasher prop cores worked as they did.

The fifth Cardinal Secret was that there were actually two empires in the Milky Way. One was the vast Fourth Empire, which ruled from Earth to the Ball, out to the end of each of the nine major arms, except one: the tip of the Seven Arm. This area was known collectively as Far Out, with its capital, Far Planet.

It was here that the Third Empire, thought long lost and clearly forgotten by many, still existed.

It was small as empires go.

Just the equivalent of four star systems, clustered together, containing just twenty-seven planets, fifty moons, two minor asteroid belts, and several dozen free-floating battle stations and docking ports. And how the Third Empire came to exist—and survive—was a long story worth telling, but not today. Suffice to say, at one time, nearly two thousand years before, it, too, had occupied just about the entire Milky Way, and it, too, had embarked on a mission to reclaim all the planets and people lost after the catastrophic fall of the Second Empire and the long period of Dark Ages that followed. That the Third Empire still existed was the result of a titanic struggle against an enemy of whom only a handful of people knew the identity, and they certainly weren't talking. The result of that struggle, though, that aftermath, it being the topic of many a lost war poem and heroic saga, was an agreement and a compromise: that the Third Empire, actually the last ember of the once pangalactic realm, would be allowed to remain, but only at one of the farthest points away from Earth, and only in the deepest, darkest secrecy. And that never, ever would there be contact between the two. Thus the great obstacles, both physical and in the mind, encountered by anyone trying to get from one place to the other.

Hunter had been given a tour of the Third Empire, a trip that lasted just an hour or so. But in that short time, he discovered many remarkable things about the place.

The people who lived there were very similar to the people he'd found on the Home Planets. That is to say, they were like the Last Americans, and the people from the other thirty-five planets in that concentration camp in the sky. They were people who were more like him than the strangely different, looking-, and acting people who made up the Fourth Empire, a place where it seemed that everyone's name either began or ended with an *X*.

This, of course, all had to do with the Ancient Astronaut, for the Third Empire was his doing, and it was his story that would fill another book. But the people around Far Planet worshiped him, not in a religious sense—though it bordered on that—but mostly because he was a hero, a great hero. A man who saved billions and when faced with a cruel choice, chose to stop fighting, and thus saved many billions more.

The burial complete, Hunter looked up at the gold warship over his head. The Legionnaires called these vessels Sky Chiefs and it was an appropriately cool name. Hunter was suddenly talking to the ship's two pilots—no comm set needed here—just another trick of the Third Empire that he'd been made privy to.

They could leave, he told them. He was finished down here. The field of dead REF troopers had all turned to ash by now; there'd be no burial for them. And the people Sheez had saved had made it into the evacuation circle and would soon be lifted off this hellhole. So, that was one mission was accomplished. The problem was, they had about a million more to go.

The Sky Chief departed, flashing over to the evacuation site to help the ongoing rescue effort. Hunter pulled an oblong box from his pocket. It was gold, of course; both the color and the precious metal were revered by the Third Empire. There was a tiny spindle on top of the box; Hunter gave it a twist. There came a huge puff of smoke—not a flash of light—and it lingered longer than it should have in the wind. But eventually it began forming into a familiar shape. It was a machine, long and slender, with a sharp snout, two wings, and a glass bubble on top. It was a contraption that was a stranger in both empires. But not to Hunter. It was his F-Machine, rebuilt, repaired, and revitalized, all in the blink of an eye, shortly before he and the Star Legion left Far Planet to fight this faraway war.

His heart jumped on seeing it again. He was always glad when his buggy reappeared from transdimensional storage. This time it did not come not from the twenty-sixth dimension; the oblong box was not a Twenty 'n Six. It came from a much more orderly place, rediscovered by the Third Empire a long long time ago: the sixty-sixth dimension. And the machine looked fine, there being only one difference. No surprise, his aircraft was now the color of gold.

He felt a bit of wind on his face, and from this, he knew it was time to get going. He moved his left hand in a circular motion, and an access ladder appeared at the side of his jet. Another hand movement, and the canopy opened. He ran over to the ladder and was up and into the cockpit in a shot.

He pushed the flight control button, and the aircraft's power plant came to life. Another great feeling. He did a quick check of all his vitals; everything was green. He checked his watch. It was ticking down to the moment the UPF fleet would attempt its crossover from the other side—the main reason for all this. He couldn't believe it. The time of return was now just sixty minutes away.

He felt a jolt of anxiety go through him; it was an emotion he'd rarely felt before. But everything the Ancient Astronaut had predicted would happen here was coming true. That the REF dumped the Zee refugees on *Doomsday 212* and put so many innocent lives at stake gave the forces of good the hard choice of either defending the lost souls or battling the REF until the UPF fleet crossed over. Even now, the Third Empire gold ships were lifting off as many refugees as possible, helping in the already ongoing effort.

But would it be enough? Would they be able to save everyone before the UPF made its long-awaited appearance? And would there be enough ships left over to battle the REF itself before it could destroy the heavenly fleet?

No one knew, and Hunter realized that he and his flying machine might well be the determining factor. That's why he had much to do in the little time that remained.

He pushed his power bar forward, but the craft did not move. It was getting juice, but something was preventing it from lifting off.

This is strange, he thought.

He checked his flight panel; everything was still functioning. He hit the power bar again. Still nothing.

This was not good. There was a huge war going on all around him, and he did not want to be struck here, immobile and flightless, in the middle of it. Once again he studied his control panel, trying to ascertain the problem. He hit his diagnostic viz screen, a device that would scan the aircraft and tell him what was wrong. When he saw the resulting holo-read-out, he was stunned. According to the image, the reason the ship wasn't taking off was because six people were sitting on its wings and nose. Pure nonsense—or so it would seem.

But when Hunter looked up, he discovered it was true.

Crouched on the nose of the craft was Pater Tomm. Balancing on the canopy tip was Calandrx. Sitting on his left wing were Erx and Berx. On his right, were Klaaz and Gordon.

Hunter just stared out at them. Was this a dream? Or a stress-induced hallucination? A huge battle was going on nearby. Vessels of all shapes and sizes were going over his head. The planet itself seemed ready to come apart. Yet here were his old friends, sitting all around him just staring back at him, calmly, coolly. Smiling widely.

He hadn't seen them since Paradise.

And they looked so . . . *different*.

They were all bigger, stronger, with Zarex-sized muscles, and most bizarre, behind each one, barely visible, as if not really in this dimension, was a pair of enormous wings.

Hunter popped his canopy and was able to utter just one word: *"How?"*

Tomm just shrugged. "This is what happens when you go there—and then come back," he said. "At least the way we did it."

Now they all studied him, but he looked the same.

"Obviously, ours has been the more dramatic transformation," Calandrx added dryly.

"Do you understand what's going on here, brothers?" Hunter finally asked them. "I mean the big picture. Did your minds become enlightened as your bodies did?"

Pater Tomm shrugged, and it made his nearly transparent wings move up and down for a moment.

"The ultimate battle between good and evil?" he replied.

"Is that all?" Hunter replied sardonically.

Tomm shrugged again. "Sounds strange, but might be as simple as that."

"It happens every billion years," Calandrx chimed in. "Or so they say. Usually when there is a simultaneous tear in the fabric of space and time, which is what happened, I guess, when we went one way to Paradise, and the REF went the other way to . . . well, you know where."

Hunter could only nod in agreement. This was exactly what the Ancient Astronaut had told him. He quickly explained to the six what had happened to him at Far Planet. The extraordinary security measures. His three temptations. Meeting the Astronaut himself, and the Third Empire agreeing to break their ages-old isolation to come and fight this important battle. Tomm was especially interested in hearing Hunter's brief recounting of his latest adventure, especially his tale of first meeting the Astronaut.

"Nothing would make me happier than to go there myself and reminisce with him," Tomm said, not without a trace of sadness. "I've been to Heaven, but I believe I could be just as happy on Far Planet. Such a wonderful place. But—"

"But the clock is ticking," Calandrx interjected. "And while we can do many things, stopping cosmic time isn't one of them. We've done our part, Hawk. We turned around the refugee ships, and we've got the robots of Myx involved. And obviously you've done your part, too."

"And more help is on the way," Klaaz added. "The question is, will it be enough?"

"I think you would know better than I," Hunter said.

"That's the problem," Tomm said. "Unlike just about everything else in the universe, the outcome here is not predetermined. No one knows which way this one will go—and I mean *no one.*"

He raised his eyes upward, indicating to Hunter some kind of Higher Power.

"We've really gotten ourselves into the thick of it," Tomm went on. "We can only pray that it goes well. The enemy has tricks. They are deceitful. They will try everything to stop the rest of our fleet coming over, because that means there will be forty thousand more of *us* floating around in this existence, and that is simply too much good for them to take and be able to survive for very long."

Hunter was astonished to hear it put this way. "Who knew?" he asked. "Who knew when we all left Planet America that it would turn out this way?"

The six archangels laughed. It echoed across the barren, forbidding, smoldering landscape.

"Yes, eternity is funny like that," Calandrx said. "You never know what's going to happen next."

The six laughed again, but Hunter could only shake his head at the inside seraphic joke.

Suddenly Gordon was at his left hand. "But whatever transpires in the next hour, Hawk," he said, "the people back in the Home Planets will always owe you a debt of gratitude. You gave them something they would never have had without you: their freedom. The most precious thing in all of life."

Klaaz—old, bent-over ancient Klaaz—now huge and muscular, floated up nearby, too. "Many people have called me a hero over the years," he said, his voice incredibly vibrant. "But you, sir—*you* are *my* hero."

Erx and Berx were beside him now as well. His oldest friends in this lifetime.

"This is a great battle we face," Erx said. "It has to be

fought, and it has to be won for you to finish why you were brought here, to this time and place."

"Which means you must keep fighting, Hawk," Berx said. "As we will . . . no matter what happens."

"Good luck, Hawk," Calandrx told him. "It is our honor to have known you. And perhaps, on a higher place, we will all see each other again."

Hunter could barely speak. "This is sounding a little too much like a last good-bye," he told them.

A tremendous explosion overhead shook everything around them. Hunter's flight screen began going nuts again. He had to push a few panels to get it back under control.

When he looked up again, the six were all floating around his jet. They waved—sadly—and then shot straight up into the sky. He tried to see where they were going, but they were gone in a flash.

They had disappeared before he could ask them why Zarex wasn't there.

Hunter finally got his craft to take off and was soon zooming up through the thin atmosphere of *Doomsday 212.*

The fighting around the evacuation site below was still raging out of control. Ships carrying refugees off the planet were struggling to get up to orbit, having to run a gauntlet of blaster fire coming from what seemed to be swarms of REF warships as well as huge weapons the red-uniformed soldiers had set up on the ground.

But the situation here was no worse than the six other evacuation sites Hunter discovered had been set up around the burning planet. Thanks to the intercession of Tomm, Calandrx, and the others, and their use of the mythical robots of Myx as their infantry, thousands of innocents *were* being rescued.

The sudden appearance of the Third Empire ships could only help. Even now, as Hunter attained low orbit over the embattled planet, he could see the bright gold Sky Chiefs rushing to trouble spots around the planet, to assist in repelling the rampaging REF ships, all of which seemed intent on shooting down every rescue ship and killing every last innocent soul possible.

And again, this is exactly what the Ancient Astronaut said they would do: put many helpless souls in harm's way and give their rescuers the option of saving them or allowing the REF to attack the original UPF fleet when it crossed over.

But would their efforts carry the day here? How could they possibly do two things at once? With less than an hour to go before the clock ticked down, Hunter still wasn't too sure, especially with one important question still unanswered: How many REF ships were there exactly?

This had been a mystery since the renegade SG troops started their campaign of terror across the Galaxy. Many of their ships had been spotted over *Doomsday 212* before SF3 agent Gym Bonz was murdered. Up to five had been seen during the attack on the agri-planet of *Kansi One* over on the Eight Arm just a few days before. Another half dozen were seen in the area of the hospital destruction in the Three Arm. At least five were thought to be involved in the massacre of the SF Youth convoy.

There had been thirty-six ships in the original REF, before the special ops fleet found its way to Hell and back. Hunter's concern now was that not all of them had been in on the galactic terror campaign, that some were still on the other side, waiting for that moment when the other UPF ships would cross over and fly right into the weapons sights of the red-suited devils.

But again, how many REF ships were we talking about?

With just fifty-five minutes to go the UPF fleet was due to cross over, Hunter felt he had to find out.

He booted up to full power and did one circuit around the planet.

He keyed his scanners to look only for the elusive REF ships. The numbers on his viz screen started whizzing by. But to his dismay, they wouldn't stay constant. They kept changing. One moment, his readout said there were fifteen REF ships in the immediate area of *Doomsday 212*. Then suddenly that number dropped to twelve, then to nine. Then it zoomed back up to fifteen, then seventeen.

This made no sense, of course, but it almost seemed as if the huge ships had the ability to appear and then disappear off his screen at will. If they would only stand and fight, he and the Star Legion could give them a stiff battle. But just as they'd been doing since appearing on the scene, the REF was being very sneaky. They were almost refusing to duke it out, head to head, toe to toe. It was just another part of their insidious strategy.

Hunter had to do some math then. There were thirty-six ships in the original REF. Two were shot down, right here, on this woeful planet, in the opening moments of the war between the SF and the SG. At least four had been shot down and destroyed in the opening stages of this current battle. That left thirty.

The highest reading Hunter got on the REF number was seventeen. Did that mean thirteen others were still waiting on their side of the crossover point? Still lurking in Hell?

There was no way of knowing. And without an accurate reading of how many ships they were dealing with, it would be almost impossible to defend the area around Zero Point when the heavenly fleet crossed over.

Not good, he thought. Knowing the strength of your enemy was rule number one in any battle.

He checked his timepiece.

The time of crossover was now less than fifty minutes away.

Hunter climbed to midorbit, still looking for REF Starcrashers. With so little time left, this was the only thing he could think to do: find as many of the enemy ships as possible, and shoot them down.

He found one lurking over an evacuation site close to the planet's equator. He didn't hesitate. Coming out of the weak sun, he sent a stream of Z beams right into its control bubble. The devils within never knew what hit them. The huge ship turned over and began going down on its back.

Hunter followed it all the way to the ground, firing blast after blast into its midsection, and the vital compartments in its enormous caboose. It exploded just a few hundred feet above the surface, breaking up in an incredible ball of fire and light that quickly transformed into a horrific-looking mushroom cloud. It actually made Hunter nauseous to look at it; he'd seen such a thing only a few times before and really never

wanted to see one again. But because this had been his hand-
iwork, he was compelled to watch. The mushroom cloud attained an altitude of about two miles, when it started falling
back on itself, finally shrinking into a self-made singularity,
which exploded again, on cue, taking three-quarters of the
massive ship's wreckage along with it. And slamming the rest
to the ground. But incredibly, among those pieces of flaming
debris left behind Hunter could see tiny black figures moving
amid the smoke and flames. How could anyone—or anything—
survive a crash like that?

He didn't know. But very quickly, he was down on the deck,
his six-gun Z-beam package firing at full power, strafing the
shadowy images as they staggered about the smoldering,
wreck. He hit targets; he could tell by the flare of green flame
on the ground whenever his blasters found something with a
pulse, but even though he made more than a dozen strafing
runs, there was no way he was sure that he had eliminated
every living devil inside the kill zone.

He checked his timepiece. Five minutes gone. Less than
forty-five minutes to go. He couldn't waste any more time.

He and his machine would be of more use elsewhere.

He screamed back up to orbit.

Approaching the planet's southern pole, his comm set suddenly exploded with excited chatter. He could tell by the pitch
that the noise was coming from one of the Sky Chiefs.

He turned over, amazed that even large portions of the
planet's subarctic region below him seemed to be engulfed in
flames. He hit the power bar and told his flight computer to
get him to where the radio buzz was coming from.

He soon came upon an astonishing sight. It was happening
about 120 miles directly above *Doomsday 212*'s south pole.
One of the Sky Chiefs had cornered an REF Starcrasher coming off the planet before it could kick into Supertime.

The two ships were riding side by side, not more than a
mile separating them, firing massive fusillades at each other.
This was crazy. Starcrashers were designed to fight at very
long distances in space, not this close in. The Sky Chiefs,
grand and flowing, and about half the size, had been originally
built to do the same thing. For both ships to use their incred-

ibly powerful weapons at such short range was almost incomprehensible.

But something else was going on here. In the chaos of the battle, hundreds of beams were being shot out of both ships, but they were not of the same type. The REF ship was firing X beams—green and deadly. The Sky Chief was firing something else—thick and deep, deep blue. These two different beams were meeting each other, perfectly, about halfway between the Starcrasher and the Sky Chief. In the collision that followed, space was being lit up with an incredibly bright light, like that a thousand suns.

Counterpower was the word that came to Hunter's mind, though it might have been whispered in his ear by the invisible voice that seemed to be following everywhere during this incredible adventure. In the confusion of the moment, it was hard to tell. The Sky Chiefs did not carry offensive weapons. They couldn't; it was against the very foundations of the Third Empire. But the Sky Chiefs did have the ability to hit incoming beams with something strong enough to neutralize them. They were called negative-energy weapons—a very Third Empire concept. When used properly, they were the perfect defense against just about any other weapon in the Galaxy.

But this was war, and the counterweapons could do more than just negate what was being thrown at them. As Hunter streaked toward the scene, he saw something else take place. It happened in less than the blink of an eye, and he didn't know whether it was caused by an imbalance in the two competing bursts of energy or an anomaly in the flight path of the Starcrasher. But when the REF ship let go with an enormous fusillade, it was hit by the Sky Chief counterpunch and turned back on itself. The REF's own X beams crashed back on it like a wave, smashing against its midsection and instantly splitting it in two. The rear half of the Starcrasher made a vain attempt to accelerate, but it was much too late. The entire ship disappeared in a huge nuclear cloud, which went back down into itself almost instantaneously.

The big starship, in effect, had shot itself down. As a witness to it, Hunter had to laugh grimly.

He knew the feeling. . . .

Forty minutes now to the crossover time.

Another burst of chatter from Hunter's comm set. Someone else was in trouble. This time not near the planet's surface or in orbit. This time there was trouble out among the planet's rings.

The last ring surrounding *Doomsday 212* was its largest. It orbited the dismal planet some 40,000 miles out. Unlike the inner rings, which contained smaller pieces of space debris that eventually turned into fire rocks, the fragments making up the outer ring were huge, some of them twenty to thirty miles across. They were all irregular in shape, and many of them tumbled endlessly. They made for a very dangerous piece of space to navigate.

They also provided the perfect place to hide a warship or two. Or even six.

The pilots of those ships carrying refugees lucky enough to escape the horror of *Doomsday 212* had only one kind of flight plan in mind. They wanted to put as many light-years behind them as quickly as possible. While many of the rescue ships were the same vessels that dropped the refugees onto the planet in the first place, their commanders were intent on delivering their battered passengers to worlds farther down the Arm, where they could at least be safe from the madness of the No-Fly Zone. How they would eventually return to their home worlds would have to be determined later.

Ten of these rescue ships had found each other rising up from the smoldering planet at about the same time. Their holds filled with the confused, former REF prisoners, it took just a few bounces between the string comms for the ship commanders to agree to form up in a column and leave the area together. They did this not so much for safety, but in case any ship suffered mechanical failure, the others could help it out.

But what the ship commanders didn't count on was one distressing constant: evil did not rest. It couldn't. It had to exploit itself anywhere and everywhere it could, at any opportunity, whenever, wherever it was found.

So while the battle back on *Doomsday 212* was still raging, its outcome still teetering and undetermined, six ships belonging to the insidious REF had drawn away from the fray and had hidden themselves here, among the tumbling rocks, looking for unsuspecting vessels, whose occupants believed that they were finally safe from harm.

The convoy's pilots successfully navigated the largest of the outer ring's fragment clouds and saw only clear sailing ahead. But then their forward scanners lit up. Their comm sets erupted in static. That's when the half-dozen REF ships suddenly swooped down on them and positioned themselves directly over the center of the convoy.

At first, the convoy's commanders thought their viz scanners were wrong. After escaping from hell, how could they possibly run into this? But then their true visuals—their own eyes—confirmed the awful truth. The REF Starcrashers had them trapped. There was no way they could outrun them, no way they could fight back. They were doomed.

Or so it seemed.

From the point of view of those aboard the convoy, what happened next happened in less than a split second.

One moment two of the Starcrashers were just a mile above the lead ships, their weapons about to fire, when suddenly there was a great rush of flame and light and then two huge explosions. Hunter's machine went flashing by an instant later. Two blasts from his Z-guns, and just like that, two REF ships were reduced to subatomic dust.

But there were four left. And they quickly scattered.

Hunter keyed in on the nearest enemy ship. But again, he was faced with a Hobson's choice. If he took on this singular ship, the remaining three REF vessels would be free to attack the defenseless convoy. But if he protected the convoy, all four ships might get away. Actually, it was no choice at all. Killing the REF was what he was doing out here. He bore down on the REF ship closest to him and opened fire. Again, he hit the control bridge first and then went after the vulnerable underbelly. He was moving much too fast for any of the REF's weapons to hit him. That was the ironic thing. Once he had them in his sights, he could dispatch the devils in an instant. It was getting enough of them in his sights that was the hard part.

This one went down under a ten-second barrage of his Z

guns. Explosion, nuclear cloud, violent singularity, and then a cloud of subatomic dust. But in those precious ten seconds, the convoy and its three remaining antagonists were nearly a light-year away.

It took just an eyeblink for Hunter to catch up with them, but that's when he came upon a truly incredible sight on this long day of incredible sights.

As he came up on the convoy again, the REF ships were repositioning themselves for their one-sided attack. Suddenly, twenty-four distinct Z-beam bolts went right by the convoy and impacted squarely on the trio of REF ships. Three more explosions, three inverted mushroom clouds, three singularities. Three more clouds of dust. The convoy just kept on going; they'd had enough of this sick game.

An instant later, twenty-four streaks of light, traveling at incredible speed, went by Hunter like some kind of titanic solar storm.

But then they slowed down, and Hunter met them seconds later. He clenched his fist in a small triumph. The forces of good needed all the help they could get. And here was more help.

The second wave of United Planets ships, those "aliens" from outside the Galaxy, given a great push by the Great Klaaz, had flown right by the Omega Force and had arrived to join the battle.

Hunter escorted the two dozen gleaming spaceships down through the atmosphere of *Doomsday 212*.

He spoke to the fleet's commanders on the way and tried his best to explain the confusing situation below. There were still hundreds of thousands of innocents on the planet unaware that they had a chance to be rescued. At the moment, their safety had to be a top priority. With this knowledge, the Home Planets ships plunged right into the fray. They quickly added their substantial weaponry to protecting the six evacuation zones, helping the Sky Chiefs ward off the slippery REF ships, as well as attacking those REF troops on the ground trying to overrun the rescue sites.

Once the blue and chrome ships were in position, Hunter

began climbing back toward orbit. He checked his timepiece. Thirty minutes to go.

Where was Zero Point?

It wasn't a coordinate exactly, so it couldn't be found on any star map. It had no aura. No identifying nebula to mark its location. It was simply a point, floating in space, with absolutely nothing special around it. The only reason the sad world of *Doomsday 212* was even connected to it was that it happened to be the closest planet of any size near the place.

But where was that place now?

The REF knew where it was, of course; not only had they been using it regularly since the start of their galactic wave of terror, they had had a hand in creating it a month before, during the battle that never was. But Hunter and his friends were never too sure of its location. Why? Because everything in space moved. The stars moved around the center of the Galaxy. The Galaxy was speeding through space. The question was, had the location of this portal moved as well?

It was an important thing to know. If the UPF fleet's crossover was to be successful, the anti-REF forces would have to defend this invisible yet magical place. That meant that Hunter had to do some detective work and find it.

Quickly . . .

Once in orbit, he activated his wide-screen scanner again. It told him that at the moment there were nine REF ships somewhere within a light-year of *Doomsday 212*. Of course, he blinked, and the number bumped up to a dozen, and then just as quickly, it fell back to nine.

That was the trouble with the wide-screen scan. It was good technology, but it was not perfect. While it was able read a wide area and locate subatomic wakes, the telltale sign of Star-crashing space vessels, these ships moved so fast, as soon as a blip was found, its owner could be a light-year or more away, in any direction, thirty seconds later. In other words, the wide-screen scan couldn't tell you where an enemy ship was exactly, only where it had been.

But Hunter believed the device could still help him determine where Zero Point was.

He did a smaller scan and saw that two REF ships had been at a location above the planet's north pole just a few minutes before. Their wakes were somewhat stagnant, indicating they were lingering there, possibly coming up with an attack strategy. Hunter plunged through the atmosphere once more, leveling off 1,000 feet directly above the pole. He did another narrow scan and was just able to pick up two subatomic wakes heading in the direction of the original evacuation site several hundred miles away. These were the same two REF ships he'd detected from orbit. He began following them.

One of the scanner's other talents was its ability to pick up sonic vibrations. Hunter pushed his flight panel to call up this function, and seconds later he heard the noise. It was earsplitting, gut wrenching, and he recognized it immediately. It was the racket made by a Starcrasher at crank, the speed a prop-core ship could fly within the gravitational pull of a planet. It was quick but nowhere near Supertime quick. And these two were making a lot of noise, meaning they were going very, very slow.

Hunter caught up to the Starcrashers just as they reached the edge of the original evacuation site. They were flying just 500 feet off the ground and moving disturbingly slow, not even 100 miles per hour. Hunter kept his cool, fighting off the temptation to put a couple Z-beam blasts into them and be done with it. At the moment, though, he was concerned about something other than greasing two more flying devils. Besides, he was hoping his friends on the ground were on their toes.

The first Starcrasher went over the chaotic rescue site and opened up with a fusillade of X-beam fire aimed at the soldiers and robots defending the site perimeter. A pang of horror caught in Hunter's throat. Again, Starcrashers were designed to fight at very long distances in space, thus their incredibly powerful weapons. To fly so low over a target and use those same weapons on ground targets, at such close range, was almost incomprehensible.

But then something else happened. Not a split second after the Starcrasher had started its incredible gunship run, a storm of blue beams rose to meet it. There was a series of huge explosions, and in the next instant, the Starcrasher was gone.

But those on the ground beneath it were not immolated as they should have been.

Hunter breathed a sigh of relief. The Third Empire soldiers at the rescue site had set up a negative-energy weapon and, like the battle he'd just witnessed in space, they had countered what would have been a devastating pass by the first Starcrasher. By their actions, the Star Legionnaires had saved of thousands of lives on the ground—at least temporarily.

The second Starcrasher roared in, its weapons also blasting away. Again they were countered by the negative-energy weapons on the ground. The second REF streaked off, as unsuccessful as its dastardly comrade. But then the first Starcrasher showed up again, cranking in from another direction, its weapons in full roar. The first attack had been a feint. But somehow the counterweapons crews on the ground were able to wheel around in time to meet this new fusillade head-on. Again, whether it was an adjustment in power or a vagary of the wind, the red Starcrasher's broadside was hit by the counterpunch and turned back on itself, crashing into the nose of the attacking ship. The Starcrasher made a vain attempt to gain altitude, but it was too late. It came down, hard and violently, five miles away, disappearing in a huge nuclear cloud.

The remaining REF ship came back around but obviously, after seeing all this, wanted no further part of the attack. It turned first north, then west, avoiding the evacuation site altogether. Hunter twisted and turned and in seconds was just ten miles behind it. This was just what he wanted. He finally pushed his weapons panel and sent a very long stream of Z beams right into the REF ship's aft section—just nicking it, but on purpose.

Predictably, the REF ship went nose up and began climbing out of the atmosphere.

Hunter stayed right on its tail.

He followed the ship right up through orbit and beyond. The Starcrasher was damaged but not terribly, which had been his intention all along. Where would a damaged REF ship go if not back to its point of origin? He was hoping the wounded vessel would lead him to the spot in space where Zero Point existed.

He'd expected to trail the ship for at least a dozen light-years after leaving *Doomsday 212*, but then came his first surprise. The Starcrasher started slowing down not more than 10,000 miles out from the planet. Sure enough, his wide-screen scanner indicated a lot of subatomic activity in this area of space just in the past hour. Some of these telltale wakes even stopped right in midspace, and now the damaged Starcrasher was moving forward but at a crawl.

What more proof did he need?

He'd found Zero Point.

He checked his timepiece. It was now twenty-two minutes before the UPF crossover. He had to make contact with all his allies back on *Doomsday 212*. His guess was that many REF ships would start congregating in this area very soon. He and his friends had to be ready to do battle with these ships and defeat them before the unsuspecting fleet from Heaven tried to break through. Many refugees had been lifted off the planet below. Many more would eventually be rescued. But as horrible as it was, *Doomsday 212* was just a sideshow now. The *real* battle would have to be fought here.

He closed in on the wounded REF ship. His plan was to shoot it up before it was actually able to escape. That would bring the number of REF ships down to just two dozen or so, manageable as his forces were now almost three times that number. He let go with a Z-beam barrage and . . .

Flash!

Suddenly Hunter was blinded. His craft was thrown backward at an incredible rate of speed, spinning wildly out of control. He tried reaching out for his control panel, but the *g*-forces were too intense. He couldn't move his hands. He couldn't move his feet. He could barely breathe. He began punching his side panels, those controls closest to him. Auxiliary levers, power boosters, inertia dampeners—but nothing was responding. His craft sounded like it was about to come apart at the seams.

Somehow, he summoned up enough strength to lunge for the power bar. He found it and was just barely able to wrap two fingers around it. He was spinning even faster now and was close to blacking out—for good. He pushed the accelerator forward and clamped his foot on the right rudder, an old pilot's trick. He felt massive resistance, which meant he was nearing a point of gravity. He was finally able to jerk his helmet's visor down, and slowly his vision began to return. The first thing he saw was the scarred hulk of *Doomsday 212* rushing up to meet him.

This was not good. He yanked back on his controller, boosted power even further, and slammed the right rudder down. Three eternally long seconds later, he somehow recovered flight. His ship skipped off the top of the planet's thin atmosphere and soared back into space. He caught his breath and checked his position. The controls said he'd been thrown nearly 10,000 miles in a matter of seconds. That seemed impossible. With shaking hands, he turned back toward Zero Point.

He pushed his accelerator up to ultraoverdrive, but no sooner did the power kick in when . . .

Flash!

Another massive explosion sent his craft reeling again. This time he began tumbling ass over end. With his visor down, he'd avoided the blindness from the first blast, but it also allowed him to see every light on his control panel blink off—and stay off. Extremely not good. He punched the flight board with his fist, and everything suddenly blinked back on. He pulled back on his power and managed to stop tumbling. Everything started working again a second later.

He breathed a sigh of relief and checked his boards. This time he'd been bounced 5,000 miles backward, again in a matter of seconds. Again, seemingly impossible. It was almost as if something was trying to keep him away from this piece of space—and maybe for good reason.

He turned back toward Zero Point once more, and that's when he saw the most disturbing sight of his life. The fabric of space and time was tearing itself in two, creating a huge, almost bloody gash, exactly where he had determined Zero Point to be. Though it was thousands of miles away, it seemed to be happening not 500 feet off the nose of his craft. Within the schism he saw the deepest red fire imaginable. Deeper than the color of blood. This was a gush of flames, almost liquid fire, spewing out into space all around it. It was disturbing beyond words. He could feel the heat on his face. It felt as if it was burning right through to his bones. Even worse, he could smell it, impossible as that might have been. It was in his oxygen system, in his hose, in his mask. The odor was sickening: dead flesh, vomit, putrid smoke, all mixed together. He suddenly felt like he was sucking all these things into his lungs. He began choking, losing his breath. Losing control of his spacecraft again.

He pulled back on his power, but his ship did not respond. He tried to will the illusion of suffocating away, but he couldn't. He was heading right for the schism at very high speed; it was sucking him in. The stench was becoming worse. He nearly ripped the mask from his face—sheer foolishness. But it felt as if Evil itself was entering his body through his lungs.

He closed his eyes, gripped the flight controller, and tried to go first left, then right. But again, the controls would not respond. He started to breathe deeply. *Fight it.* It was too painful. *Don't be fooled by it.* Several long seconds went by. He pushed the controls again, but once more, nothing happened. *Fight it.* But how? Then it hit him. He thought of Paradise. He thought of the rivers and the lakes and the City of Smiles. He thought of the stars, and the beach, and the clear blue sky. He thought of Xara. It seemed to work. He pushed all the images of what he had just seen out of his head, and he began breathing again, deeply. The stink faded away. His heart settled down. His stomach stopped turning. He pushed his controls to starboard, and this time they went the way he wanted to go.

Then he took another deep breath and opened his eyes . . . but only to see something even more horrifying than before.

A deluge of warships was pouring out of the schism. Red Starcrashers bearing the unmistakable markings of the REF. Two of them, three, four, six, *ten!* Traveling incredibly fast. But behind them came a stream of other vessels. Huge blunderbuss ships, as large as Starcrashers but bulbous, bullet-shaped, with a blunt nose and ridiculously small fins in the back. And each one had an impossibly huge blaster on its back, running the length of the ship and attached by a series of concentric atomic rings. Like the REF vessels, these ships, too, were the color of blood.

Hunter couldn't believe it. He'd seen these types of starships before! A long time ago, when he took a mind ring trip that put him back when the evil Second Empire was in power, these monsters were the ships of the line. Crude and gigantic. And now they were spewing out of the huge tear, surrounded by flames that turned Hunter's stomach to salt just looking at them.

What was going on here? These ships were more than 4,000 years old. Were they missing ships? Ships lost over the ages? Ships destroyed while doing battle with nefarious reasons in mind? Or had they simply fallen into the same hellish pit the REF had—several millennia ago?

Or was this all just a sick, distorted dream?

Whatever the case, Hunter hastily put out an SOS to *Doomsday 212* below. Three dozen ships came off the planet, rushing to answer his call. They were beside him in an instant, almost *too* quickly, just impossibly fast. He didn't have to deliver the bad news to them; they could see it for themselves. No longer did they have just a couple dozen enemy ships to deal with. Now there were hundreds.

And those ships were still streaming out of the schism nonstop. In a way, they didn't look real. There were so many of them, it almost seemed like Hunter was looking at a viz-image loop playing over and over again. But once more, the words of the Ancient Astronaut came back to him. The bad side was trying to overwhelm them with madness—and at the moment, doing a very good job of it.

For one very revealing moment, Hunter wished, truly and deeply wished, that he had gone through that screen door of the house back on Far Planet. That he made his presence known to Dominique and that he could have washed his hands of all of this. It would have been the cop-out of the ages, and so much of what he wanted would have been lost. But still he was only one person, only one soul. There was only so much he could do. Sure, sometimes life forces you to be a hero. But that didn't mean you had to like it.

The moment of uncertainty passed as quickly as it came. There were other voices urging him on here; they had been since this whole crazy adventure started. In fact, there were so many of them now, he couldn't begin to separate one from the other. If he was back where he belonged—back in that world the man with the hole in his basement gave him the opportunity to return to—they would have surely put him in the booby hatch. *That's* how many voices he was hearing in his head these days.

So there was no sense in fighting it. Too many spirits were counting on him, both here and in other places. He *had* to do the right thing, whether he wanted to or not.

Or die trying.

And even that prospect wasn't so bad.

The first problem, though, was stopping the flow of ships coming from the schism. How does one go about binding a tear in the fabric of space/time? Did anyone know? The Creator included?

As this uncertain notion was going through his head, Hunter's comm set exploded in a great burst of static. Suddenly he was hearing not just one voice, but many. *Real* voices. Some were talking rapidly, some were screaming. Some were even laughing. Then through this storm of voices, he clearly heard someone shout, *"Dear God—look at that!"*

Instinct turned Hunter away from the schism to a point in space that was almost devoid of stars. That's when he saw it. It was a huge starship. It was traveling very fast and heading right for the opening.

It was a Starcrasher—there was no doubt about that. What's more, Hunter's scans told him that the ship's prop core was overheating manually and was about to blow. In other words, the ship was going to explode on purpose. What was happening here? Was the person driving the Starcrasher going to blow it up at the entrance to Hell? Was this an attempt to seal the schism with a prop-core implosion? What madman would do such a thing?

Hunter got his answer a moment later. His scans told the tale: The Starcrasher was an M-class, the biggest ever made. But unlike all other Starcrashers, this one was pure white, and was all smooth edges, and was more swept back than any other. By these things alone Hunter recognized it. There was only one like it in existence.

It was the *ShadoVox*.

And Joxx was at the controls.

How the fallen SG prince knew what was going on out here, Hunter would probably never know. He started to yell into his comm set; maybe there was a better way to do this. But it was too late.

The grand ship went right by him, its outer skin already turned deep blue, the sure sign that the prop core was going to blow. Joxx turned the ship just slightly, twisting through the stream of ships escaping the schism. A few tried to stop him by firing at him. A few even attempted to ram him. But Joxx got by them all.

He hit the schism at full Supertime speed but with a prop core that was 1/1000 of a second away from destabilization. The outcome was nothing less than apocalyptic. The ship blew up, or rather it disappeared into an enormous explosion an instant later. And an instant after that, the explosion turned in on itself. And with another blinding flash, the schism sealed up, and everything around it was gone. Just like that.

Then came a dreadful silence.

It was as if everything just stopped. The stars. The planets. His comm set. Life itself. A collective state of shock, silently exploded and moved like a nova, rushing by everybody and everything. Joxx was gone, and so was the entrance to Hell. At least temporarily.

Somehow Hunter thought to check his timepiece.

Nine minutes to go.

Then, just as suddenly, everything started moving again. The light returned. Ships were moving again. *Space* was moving again.

The shock of what had just happened wore off, too. It was clear that by his action, Joxx has stemmed the tide, but there were so many devil ships now, even the combined force of Hunter, the Home Planets ships, the arms dealers' gunships, and the Sky Chiefs couldn't possibly engage them all. There were just too many of them. And now there was just eight minutes to go.

But then, instead of lining up to do battle with the friendly forces, the great swarm of huge ships suddenly accelerated and began zooming off in all directions.

Hunter felt like someone had punched him in the stomach. This couldn't be happening. Those ships had to be filled with the inhabitants of the underworld, a great swarm that was now roaring off in every possible direction. Off to infect the entire Galaxy!

He just couldn't let that happen.

Hunter didn't even think about it. He began shouting orders into his comm set, and the crews of the friendly ships started reacting immediately. The combined fleet dispersed in seconds and took off, chasing the huge ships that had just escaped from Hell.

Hunter took off after the largest group of huge blunderbuss ships. There was three dozen of them, and they'd turned as one away from Zero Point and appeared to be heading down the Two Arm—and maybe toward Earth itself.

As he booted up to full power, his wide-screen scan began spitting out information on these strange vessels. They were capable of carrying more than 20,000 passengers; but at the moment the scan could not confirm that anyone human was aboard. In fact he could not detect any life signs on board at all. *Do devils have a pulse?* Hunter thought as he sped after them. Did he really want to know?

The scans were also telling him that despite what was inside, the weapons carried on the backs of these giants were very real. They were a huge version of an X-beam blaster gun, a combat weapon still used by some Fringe armies. A single bolt from one of these giants could destroy a good-size asteroid or even a small moon. A dozen direct hits could vaporize an entire planet.

But most disturbing of all, the scanner told him that these ships were powered by prop cores. This made no sense. As far as anyone knew, prop-core propulsion didn't come along until the beginning of the Fourth Empire. These ships were designed thousands of years before that. Was there a spaceship factory in Hell?

It was weird because as soon as Hunter received this startling information, the thirty-six ships suddenly accelerated up to almost Supertime speed. It was almost as if his thoughts had caused them to move even faster.

Hunter pushed his acceleration bar ahead, too. The chase was on.

It took only a few seconds for him to catch up with the three dozen ships. Their tight formation broke up immediately, and two fired their huge blasters at him as he streaked by. A twin storm of green bolts came right at him. They were gigantic and momentarily filled his entire field of vision. Hunter pushed his nose down and banked right, thus avoiding both titanic blasts. Still, they rocked his ship violently as they went by. Meanwhile, the huge fleet regrouped and just kept plowing forward.

Hunter pulled ahead, looped over, and came back at them head-on. He had to find a weak spot in these giants, and he had to do it quickly. He pushed his weapons power switch forward and ordered a blast at full power. Six streaks of Z beams exploded from his nose. He directed them at the ship in the vanguard of the fleet, aiming the barrage at its huge control bubble up front. The ship fired a gigantic blast at him; it went by him in a huge flash. At the same moment, his Z beams tore into the ship's bridge. Secondary explosions appeared an instant later, and then a massive blast went all the way down to its stern. The ship blew apart a moment later. Hunter had guessed right. The ship's power magazine was located right behind the bridge and just below the gun. He pushed his ship into ultraoverdrive. Now he knew how to destroy these behemoths.

Suddenly he was flying so fast, he was leaving a trail of red, white, and blue particles in his wake. He was spinning, twisting, looping, diving, climbing, and firing all at once. His hands and feet were moving like lightning. Right hand on the throttle, left hand on the joystick, he was lining up targets two or three ships ahead of the ones he was attacking. The storm of gigantic green destructo-beams were going past him in one long blur. He was avoiding all of them, but some residue bolts were exploding dangerously close to him. No matter. One well-placed blast, and he'd be washing up on the beach back in Heaven again. Or so he hoped.

He plunged on, defying every hurdle, avoiding every X-beam blast headed his way. With every ship blown up, he felt two sensations inside: simultaneous exhilaration with another victory accompanied by a slight pang of guilt that he might be killing up to 20,000 souls a pop. But were they souls really? Were they really human beings—just ones that had somehow come back from Hell? He'd seen what happened to his friends when they crossed over from Heaven. They'd become what, through the ages, people had called angels. Didn't it make sense then that any people occupying these ships would then be devils?

No matter. He sure wasn't going to stop one and find out.

It went on like this for what seemed like forever. Hunter kept weaving his way through the loose formation and kept destroying targets. They weren't avoiding him exactly, but at times it seemed like the number of enemy ships was endless. He'd grease one, and it was as if two would take its place. He'd splash another one, and two more would pop up behind it. It was madness! And he'd become part of it. But he had to keep going. He couldn't let any of them get by him. He kept firing and firing and firing.

But then, suddenly, he just stopped.

He literally put on the brakes and stopped his ship in mid-space—and thought a moment. Something was wrong here. This was almost too easy. The words of the Ancient Astronaut came back to him. The devils will use everything to get what they want: deception, distraction, deceit.

They will try to make the heroes fool themselves.

Hunter checked his timepiece.

Damn; the countdown had less than thirty seconds to go!

And that's when it hit him. These ships probably weren't carrying anybody. They were able to fire. They were able to present themselves as targets. But they were a distraction.

And it had almost worked. The heroes *had* almost fooled themselves.

But not Hunter. He turned his ship 180 degrees and venge-fully hit his power bar again.

An instant later, he was screaming back to Zero Point.

There were twenty-four REF ships waiting there.

Some had flown through the schism just before it had closed; the rest had come up from *Doomsday 212*. All of them had their weapons systems cranked up to full power. All of them had their crews at battle stations. With the ships of the good forces off chasing the empty decoys from Hell, the REF ships were able to align themselves in four attack formations of six ships each. Their noses were pointing to a piece of space not far from where their portal to Hell had been sealed. This was the exact spot where the UPF fleet had disappeared just a little over a month ago.

This was where that same fleet was due to emerge.

The REF ships never saw Hunter coming.

Too intent on ambushing the UPF ships once they crossed over, their crews were distracted. They weren't paying atten-tion to anything but the matter at hand. The gold F-Machine came upon them so suddenly, they didn't even move. One ship went up, hit by a massive Z-beam barrage on its control bub-ble. Another went up, hit by a murderous fusillade on its prop core. A third exploded, its aft section blown away from the rest of its gigantic body.

In five seconds, three ships were destroyed.

Trouble was, there were only twenty seconds to go.

Hunter twisted over and lined up another huge Red Ship. Another barrage from his Z beams; the ship was instantly a flaming hulk. He turned over again. The REF crews were re-luctant to change their positions; they wanted to stay ready to pounce on the UPF ships as soon as they appeared. This made it easier for Hunter to pick them off. But it was more a matter of time now than numbers. He put the next ship in his sights and pushed his weapons bar. It went up in a flash.

Fifteen seconds to go—still nineteen REF ships lying in wait.

Hunter screamed through them again. Some were firing at him now, but he easily twisted through the scattered X beams.

He went after the ship closest to where the UPF would pop out. He drilled it stem to stern with his Z guns. It split right down the middle and exploded.

Twelve seconds to go. . . .

It was like target practice now, but Hunter could not stop time—at least not in this circumstance. It took him several precious seconds to nail a ship, and those seconds were running out. He couldn't possibly get them all.

Ten seconds to go. . . .

He hit two ships at once, leaving his Z-beam guns engaged and slicing through a pair of monsters that had chosen to ride too close to one another.

Seven seconds to go. . . .

Another quick blast, and Hunter took out what looked to be the REF command ship.

Five seconds . . .

Hunter hit his wide scan. There were still fifteen REF ships in wait.

Three seconds . . .

He'd done all he could.

Two seconds . . .

One . . .

Nothing happened.

There was no bright flash. There was no huge explosion.

No glorious parting of space and time. No tear at all.

The time had come and gone, and absolutely nothing at all had happened at Zero Point.

Thirty seconds went by.

Hunter was loitering just a few hundred miles away, watching it all on his wide-screen scan. A full minute passed. Still nothing. The REF ships stayed frozen in place, waiting for something, anything.

But nothing happened.

Hunter couldn't believe it. He checked his timepiece. Had it been set wrong? Obviously not, because the REF had lined up at the spot at the same time he determined the fleet would break through. Had Joxx's brave action sealed the portal from Heaven as well? Hunter's gut told him no. But now nearly three minutes had passed, and still there was no sign of the UPF ships.

Something must have gone wrong, he thought.

There was no other explanation.

This eventually dawned on the REF ships, too. Stunned into inaction for a few moments, they were beginning to stir again.

Had he thought longer about it, Hunter knew he could have predicted their actions. But now he watched in horror as they formed up into a single attack line, turned around, and headed right back down toward *Doomsday 212.*

Damn!

It was the other side of the coin again. The planet lay practically unprotected now, and these fifteen ships were loaded with weaponry. By using either orbital bombardment or firing their weapons down on the surface at full crank, they could complete the massacre of the millions of innocents still on the planet, along with the soldiers on the ground who were trying to help them.

Hunter desperately tore after them again. But they were no longer sitting still for him. He was moving fast, but they began moving fast, too. And even he couldn't shoot down fifteen Starcrashers at once. It became a numbers game again. While he was greasing half of them, the other half would be able to vaporize the planet in seconds, especially now that they no longer had any use for the people below as hostages. Hell, two Starcrashers could kill everyone on that planet in a matter of minutes. Or even just one, if it was left alone long enough.

Hunter was furious. At himself. At the situation. At the cosmos. It seemed no matter what he did, he just wasn't going to win this fight. He'd come back from Paradise, he'd traveled across the Galaxy. He'd been tempted with promises to return to the best parts of his life . . . and for what? An outcome like this?

Maybe this was how it was supposed to happen, he thought darkly. Maybe the bad side was *supposed* to win all the time. And maybe the rest of them had got it wrong a long time ago.

But no sooner had the thought traveled through his head when something very strange happened. . . .

He was trailing behind the mob of REF ships, trying to

figure out how he could possibly ping them all before they busted up the entire planet, when suddenly there was a tremendous burst of light and energy. It came from behind him, and he swore he could feel the light particles going right through him. It was more intense than any prop-core explosion, more intense than when he saw the portal to Hell open up. It was blinding, even though his eyes were turned away from it.

Though the Great Flash—as it would come to be known—lasted just a billionth of a second, at the same time, it seemed to last forever. In fact, it was one of those things that did not even happen within the illusion of ordinary time. It had happened on a different plane entirely.

At the same moment it hit, Hunter saw an REF ship directly in front of him falter and slide off to the side. It was as if its prop core had suddenly gone off-line. Yet he had not fired on it. It was going down on its own.

This wasn't so strange, he thought for an instant. After all, Starcrashers broke down, too. But then he saw the REF ship right beside it slide away as well. Its lights went out, its exhaust nozzles went black. Then the ship in front of these two shut down. Then the one in front of that. And the one in front of that . . .

In the next instant it became very clear: *all* the REF ships were faltering. They weren't blowing up. Their prop cores weren't going south and taking the entire ships with them. They were just running out of power. And there was only one way that could happen. Somehow, the Big Generator had just shut down.

And with no juice from the Big Generator, Hunter knew the REF ships could not fly. And that they were defenseless.

But so was he.

This was getting serious now.

The mob of huge but powerless REF ships was falling through the thin atmosphere of *Doomsday 212*, and Hunter was falling right behind them.

The surface was rushing up to meet him very quickly, and a few of the fifteen enormous Starcrashers in front of him were beginning to tumble out of control. They all hit the top of the planet's atmosphere at about the same time, causing a gigantic sonic boom. Seconds later, the bottom of his ship started to smolder; he was beginning to burn up on reentry. With all his strength, Hunter yanked back on his ship's controls and tried to flatten it out. But he was moving a dead stick.

He had only one option here.

He had to eject.

Below him, the REF ships were going down much quicker than he. Gravity and the movement of mass had taken over. But then the ships began purging themselves of the tons of superhydraulics that were the lifeblood of any Starcrasher. In doing so, at just the right time, it slowed their descent just enough that they were able to stabilize slightly before slamming into the surface below. So, instead of crashing, they came down extremely hard but in one piece. And as luck would have it, the first few to hit landed very close to a long stream of refugees that were making their way toward one of the evacuation sites. Even more incredibly, Hunter could see REF soldiers jumping out of their wrecked ships just seconds after they'd hit and starting to move toward the helpless and terrified refugees.

Hunter couldn't believe it. It seemed that no matter what happened, the bad side always came up with the advantage. At that moment a very disturbing thought went through his mind. Why not plow right into one of these ships? Aim his useless craft at one of the REF vessels and at least go out in a blaze of glory and take at least a few more of these bastards with him. If the bad side was fated to win all the time anyway—despite everything he and his friends sought to do—what was the point of it all? There was always going to be evil, and he and his friends were fools to think—to actually believe!—that they could ever change that.

So why not auger in? Then he could close his eyes and see the light and feel the warmth, and wake up on the beach again, and find Xara waiting for him.

He pondered all this for several long, painful seconds.

Then he thought, *Too dramatic.*

He yanked the ejection handle an instant later.

The canopy blew away in pieces; it shattered as opposed to

coming off whole. Hunter was suddenly going facedown in a roaring wind. His airspeed had to be three hundred knots or more, especially in this thin upper atmosphere. His seat blew out next. He felt like someone had hit him in the ass with a hammer. The violence associated with ejecting was incredible. He was tumbling now, just him, no warm ship to wrap around him anymore. Free-falling through the puny atmosphere of this long-lost, depleted planet. What a strange place to be!

He heard a ruffling sound and then was jerked in a motion almost as violent as the ejection. Suddenly it seemed like he was flying in the opposite direction. He looked up and saw his chute starting to blossom. But again, this atmosphere was so weak he wondered if there was really enough air, way up here, to fill the chute completely. If not, he might have that glorious last crash yet. But eventually the chute did billow out—and just like that, he was floating again.

He looked down now and saw his aircraft spiraling away from him. His eyes watered up. It was as if someone had reached into his chest and tore his heart out. His machine had been with him a very long time. He had traveled billions of miles in it, across thousands of years. To part with it on this craphole of a planet was especially painful. He soon lost sight of it in a cloud of smoke coming up from below. He never heard the impact, never saw the flash.

And that was good. Maybe the only good thing that would happen to him this very long day.

He started falling very slowly now, and things took on a sort of dreamy quality—but not in a good way. He could see the refugees below him scatter as the REF ships banged in, all fifteen of them, on the same vast plain, a very unglamorous arrival.

The REF soldiers were flowing out of all the crumpled ships now. Even from this height, he could tell that the blood-suited soldiers would be especially rabid in what they were about to do. As far as Hunter could tell, these were the last of the SG's renegade special ops outfit, and yet he could almost predict their dark future. He had no doubts that they would get off this planet somehow, after their bloodlust was finally sated. Then they would get more ships and go to other places and continue to spread their brand of evil throughout the Galaxy. They would win . . . and keep winning, because that's just the way it was.

He'd given up trying to believe anything else.

But just then, there was another tremendous explosion high above him. He looked up and nearly relieved himself, so astonishing was the sight he saw. Right over his head, the sky was literally opening up. Not in spewing fire this time but with an onrush of gloriously white clouds. Behind them was an incredibly bright light. Impossibly bright. Yet it did not hurt his eyes.

Hunter blinked once, twice. But still the vision was there. It seemed real yet so unreal at the same time.

Coming through this hole in the sky now he saw eleven streaks of light. Behind them the most brilliant sun was shining. And that's when he realized what was happening here. He was looking at Paradise. He knew that sky, that sun, so well. And when the eleven streaks of light suddenly turned solid, he nearly wet himself again. It was the UPF fleet.

They were finally crossing over!

The REF soldiers below saw all this, too . . . and that's when things got a little weird.

Hunter thought that maybe he'd hit his head somewhere during the ejection, because suddenly the horde of REF soldiers on the ground started *flying up* to meet the UPF ships. Flying . . . with wings. Then he looked up and saw UPF soldiers pouring out of the ships, which were right above him now. They, too, had wings and were flying down from space to meet the ascending devils.

Then he put his eyes level again and knew what was happening. The great battle everyone was expecting was indeed going to take place. Not at Zero Point but here in the skies above *Doomsday 212*.

And he was going to be right in the middle of it.

The first wave of devils went zooming by him a moment later. An instant after that, Hunter was surrounded by men in white uniforms. These were UPF soldiers; there was no doubt about that. But just as Tomm and Calandrx and the others had been transformed by their crossover, so, too, had these men.

They were flying without the aid of propulsion units, and they were armed with little more than huge swords.

The two sides met head-on, and the battle was joined all around him. It was as if he wasn't really there. The fighting was instantly fierce, hand-to-hand, and brutal. He got to see some of the REF soldiers up close, and as angelic as the UPF soldiers had become, the REF soldiers had become just as ugly and disgusting. Several flew very close to him, their faces hideously distorted, their eyes red and filled with rage and hate. Their hands seemed deformed, too, as if it was impossible now for them to hold any kind of weapon save a huge sword.

All of these beings were moving incredibly fast—seeing him but avoiding him at the same time. Meanwhile, he was twisting and turning in the chute, the cords were becoming tangled in the great whirlwind he'd found himself in. Great flashes of light were going off all around him, burning his already singed eyeballs. The flashes seemed both real and unreal, and it was only as he was passing out of the thick of the battle did he realize that each flash was created when one of the combatants was dispatched. A sword to the heart caused a silent, bright flare—and then there was nothing. No remains. No dust. Nothing.

There would be no bodies left after this battle.

Hunter finally hit the ground—hard. His arrival scattered a group of refugees who'd been watching the battle above, too astounded to move. They took one look at him, though, and their mass paralysis was cured. All of them ran as fast as they could to get away from him.

He'd come down on top of a plateau of sorts, and it was windy up here. His chute dragged him for hundreds of feet, banging him up against many of the rocks strewn about the forbidding terrain. He finally released the straps, and the chute blew away. He fell backward, absolutely stunned, and watched in awe as the strange combat went on above him unabated. The white-suited soldiers continued to battle fiercely with the devils. He thought he could even see faces of people he recognized. Some of the combat was happening no more than 100 feet above him, or so it seemed.

He struggled to get to his feet. But then came another bright flash. It was so strong that it picked him up like a doll and blew him backward. He went flying over the edge of the plateau and fell for what seemed like a mile or two to the hard plain below. He hit with a great *thud*. Had he not been wearing his helmet, he would have surely cracked his skull open. As it was, he had a huge welt right in the middle of his forehead.

He rolled over and was flat out on his back again.

Dizzy.

Dazed.

Maybe even seeing things.

The ethereal fighting went on. Hunter saw it all—or at least he thought he did. At one point it seemed to be taking place just a few dozen feet above him. At other times, the combatants were battling each other in outer space. But for some reason, he could see that close up, too.

Then, for a little while, it seemed that he, too, was an angel and that he was in the middle of the great battle. That his friends Tomm, Calandrx, Erx, Berx, Klaaz, and Gordon were right beside him, and together they were battling furiously. Hunter and the others were fighting with huge swords, Tomm with his famous blackjack. And as they were slaying the REF soldiers, who really did look like devils now, Tomm and the others were telling him all kinds of things—infusing his brain with centuries' worth of knowledge. They finally told him how Zarex had died at the hands of the REF, and how by doing so, he'd really saved them all, but this Hunter did not understand, at least not yet. They told him how many people that day had simply done the right thing, and how that would help in the eventual victory. They even told him names of some of these people: SF officers, the anonymous arms dealers, even the guy Hunter had buried near the first evacuation site. Many heroes *were* made this day.

Then somehow they returned him to the ground and said their good-byes—final ones this time. And he watched the last of the great battle, the sky filled with flashes, as the devils were finally vanquished with the angels, triumphant, disappearing right along with them. And he knew, in that moment, that he would never see his friends again. That Tomm, and Calandrx, and Gordon, and Klaaz, and his two oldest friends,

Erx and Berx, were *really* gone this time. That their spirits had moved on forever.

And then there was one last great flash, and the sky above him was empty again. He lay there for a very long time, unable to move. Not because of his injuries, which were many but small. But simply because he was exhausted. He hadn't slept in weeks—or was it years? He didn't know. So he closed his eyes and started to drift. And of all the things that floated through his mind, it was the visions of men with wings that lingered the longest. From that, the strangest but strongest memory of his previous life came back to him.

Men . . . with wings.

He used to be something like them. Not exactly, but close.

He used to be . . . *The Wingman*.

And remembering that, he smiled, for the first time in a long time.

Then he finally went to sleep.

It wasn't until much later the next day that Hunter woke up.

But where was he? He'd fallen asleep on hard, rocky ground, but now he was lying on a grassy plain. Beside him was a stream, running quick with cold, fresh water. It was the sound of this water that eventually caused him to stir. He opened battered eyes to see not just miles of grass everywhere, but mountains and trees and lakes. For one very long moment he was convinced that he had died and gone to Heaven—again.

But then he looked up and knew, sadly, that this was not the case. High above, he could see the huge planetary rings, which he recognized, and that's when he knew he was still on *Doomsday 212*.

Yet the planet had changed radically in just a short time. How?

He looked off in the distance and saw six enormous Sky Chiefs moving slowly just above the landscape, beams of golden light shining down from their nose cones.

Then one word came to mind: *Puffing*.

The Sky Chiefs were puffing the planet.

No surprise, the Third Empire held the secrets of the Ancient Engineers, too.

He got to his feet and tried to remember what had happened. The original UPF ships finally did cross over, of that much he was certain. Their appearance had been delayed, though, almost as if on purpose—but that had been a good thing. If they had crossed over at the expected time, the REF would have blasted them to nothingness. By appearing when they did, they'd saved many lives and had won the day.

How then did they know to delay the arrival?

Just as the thought came to him, an image was standing in front of him. Huge. Smiling. But transparent. There, but not really there.

It was Zarex.

And at that moment, Hunter recalled what Tomm and the others had told him about Zarex's death. Then, at least one part of what happened became clearer.

"You let them kill you . . ." Hunter said to him now, "so you could go back to Paradise and warn the fleet."

Zarex just nodded. "I knew our ships had to cross over," he said. "The Vanex Door was breaking down, so it was essential that they leave. But I also knew the devils would be waiting for them and that all of you would be trying to prevent the ambush. So I had them delay exactly thirty-three minutes on the other side—and I guess that equaled about three minutes and thirty-three seconds over here. I was hoping it would be enough to catch the REF off guard. It was a gamble. But somehow it worked."

Hunter was astonished by Zarex's tale. And also by his appearance. *Spooky* was the only word for it.

Zarex tried to hand something to him. It was a bright green apple.

"This is from Xara," he said. "She's cried every day since you left. I didn't think tears in Heaven were possible. But . . ."

Hunter reached out and tried to take the apple—but couldn't. His hand went right through it. He and Zarex were in the same place but not the same plane. He tried again. At that moment he would have given anything to have that apple, that gift from Xara. But it was not to be. Hunter felt a very bad sensation in his chest. He knew what this meant. His last connection to Paradise was broken.

"Xara does have something to be happy about, though," Zarex revealed.

"How so?" Hunter asked.

Zarex took out a viz-screen device and studied it for a moment. "I'm not sure this will still work," he said. "But here goes."

He pushed the button, and a screen appeared out of nowhere. Hunter's breath caught in his throat. It was displaying a scene he was very familiar with. The beach with the diamond sands. The bright blue skies. The cobalt sea.

And walking on the beach was his precious Xara.

Hunter felt like a knife had been plunged into his heart, a pain of both sadness and guilt. Here she was, this beautiful girl with whom he'd spent so much time in the Garden of Eden, in Heaven, and she was so close—literally a missed heartbeat away—and yet, so very far away. He couldn't bear not being with her.

But there was guilt, too, because just days before, back on Far Planet, he was ready to give it all up, his quest, his flag, Xara herself, for a simpler life forever with his former love, the equally beautiful Dominique.

"A pleasant problem to have," Zarex said with a thin smile, knowing his thoughts. "Two beautiful women living in your heart."

"Don't be so sure," Hunter said.

The viz image started moving, and Hunter saw that someone had materialized beside Xara on the beach. They were walking along the sands together. Hunter took a closer look. Amazing . . .

"The Empress?" he gasped. "She's dead?"

Zarex nodded solemnly. "Do you recall that Great Flash?" he asked.

"When everything lost power?"

"Yes, temporarily," Zarex replied. "That was the Empress's doing. Tomm and Calandrx gave her the idea to do the right thing, and she did it, and just in time for our side. She was able to disable the Big Generator just long enough to give our ships time to cross over—and finally defeat the REF."

"And for that they killed her?"

"It's not clear what happened," Zarex said. "But she did lose her life, and now she is with her daughter in Paradise. Can you imagine that? Another Special who actually made it over! They may have a lifetime to catch up on, but they'll have eternity to do it in."

Zarex collapsed the viz image, and the device itself faded away.

"But what about you?" Hunter asked Zarex. "What has happened to you?"

"This is the price for crossing over the second time," Zarex replied, his voice halting. "Going back was not a problem. But coming back again? Well, you're not an angel anymore. You're not even a soul, either. You become a . . ."

He tried, but he just couldn't say the word.

So Hunter said it for him. "A ghost?"

Zarex nodded somberly.

"We'll figure out a way to—" Hunter started to say, but Zarex just shook his head. "There *is* no way, Hawk," he said. "This is just how it is and how it will always be. I'll always know I did the right thing—along with a lot of other souls. I mean, our side won; in the long run, this *was* a victory. And it will save a lot of people a lot of grief. So, take my advice: start up your quest again. Now is the time to make the next move. The most righteous thing *you* can do is to get Earth back into the hands of its rightful owners. I'm sorry none of us will be there with you to see it in the end, but I'm sure you'll find others to help along the way."

Hunter suddenly felt a wash of sadness go right through him. It was beginning to sink in now. All of his friends were gone.

"But you," he said to Zarex. "*Where* are you, exactly?"

The image shrugged. "Caught somewhere in between," he said. "Life and death? Heaven and Hell? Somewhere in the middle, I guess. It's all right, though. At least I have good company."

At that moment, another image started materializing. Hunter felt the nasty bump on his forehead. Was there anyway he was just imagining all this?

The image finally focused.

It was another ghost.

Hunter was shocked. He stared at the apparition for a moment. But then another piece of the puzzle fit together.

"So, it was you who was helping me all along," he said to the second ghost. "You let me out of Joxx's jail cell. You pulled me out of my crash on Far Planet. You've been at my side since I crossed over."

The second image nodded. It was Gym Bonz.

"I had to do my part, too," he said. "I couldn't let you guys do it all alone. But now . . ."

He, too, had trouble speaking.

So Zarex did it for him. "Now, he can't go back either," he said. "His wife . . . his kids . . ."

Hunter was crushed. These two had given up so much. And by trying to manipulate the cosmos, they'd wound up costing themselves an eternity in Paradise.

"Goddamn," Hunter cursed. "Was it all worth it? *Really?* I mean, just look at how many people died today—and every other day since all this craziness began."

Zarex smiled again. His image was fading. So was Bonz.

"But just think, Hawk," Zarex said. "If they did the right thing just one time in their lives, they'll all wind up in Happy Valley. That's all it takes. And we all know that's a better place than this one."

Hunter was still angry, though—and frustrated.

"But if that's true, then what the hell is all this for?" he asked, sweeping his arms, indicating his side of reality. "The pain, the struggle, the inhumanity? Why do we have to go through *all this?*"

Zarex just shrugged again. So did Bonz.

"*That's* the mystery of life, Hawk," Zarex said. "One of them, anyway. And it will all become clearer to you someday soon."

Both Spirits smiled sadly.
"Good-bye Hawk," Zarex said. "Be well, my brother . . ."
They both saluted him.
Then they slowly faded away.

MACK MALONEY

Don't miss the first three books in the hot
science fiction series from the author of the *Wingman* and
Chopper Ops series

STARHAWK

0-441-00868-2

In a state-sponsored gladiatorial contest—pitting pilot against
pilot—one man will not only test the limits of his endurance, but
he'll begin to learn the truth of his
identity.

STARHAWK: PLANET AMERICA

0441-00878-X

Rogue Imperial pilot Hawk Hunter goes AWOL, searching for the
mythical Home Planets. Battling across the galaxy, Hunter finds his
goal—Planet America—possible birthplace of humanity. His cele-
bration is short-lived, however, for an alien armada has targeted
America for destruction, and Hawk will have to summon all of his
inborn warrior skills to stop them.

STARHAWK: THE FOURTH EMPIRE

0-441-00878-X

Lead by Hawk Hunter, the freedom fighters have brought revolution
to the Emperor's door. But those who rule the galatic empire under
militaristic oppression will do anything to maintain power—and the
billion-years-old secret that lies beind it.

Available wherever books are sold or
to order call:
1-800-788-6262

(Ad #B262)

WILLIAM C. DIETZ

IMPERIAL BOUNTY   0-441-36697-X

Since her brother's absence, Princess Claudia has seized the throne and
brought the Empire to the brink of war with the Il Ronn. Only the missing
Prince Alexander can stop Claudi's plans. And McCade has only three
months to find him.

GALACTIC BOUNTY   0-441-87346-4

A traitor is on the loose. A treacherous navy captain plans to sell military
secrets to the alien Il Ronn. The only man who can stop him is Sam
McCade—an interstellar bounty hunter with a score to settle.

WHERE THE SHIPS DIE   0-441-00354-0

There are only four known wormholes in existence. But the location of
one of them is hidden in a veil of mystery, lost in a conspiracy of murder.
And its power belongs to the first human who finds it—or the alien race
who would kill for it...

THE FINAL BATTLE   0-441-00217-X

Defeated at the hands of the Legion, the alien Hudathans plan to fight fire
with fire. Using copycat technology, they create their own corps of
cyborgs and target the heart of the Confederacy, once and for all.

BODYGUARD   0-441-00105-X

In a future where violence, corruption, and murder grow as rapidly as
technology and corporations, there is always room for the Bodyguard.
He's hired muscle for a wired future—and he's the best money can buy.

LEGION OF THE DAMNED   0-441-48040-3

When all hope is lost—for the terminally ill, for the condemned criminal,
for the victim who can't be saved—there is one final choice. Life...as a
cyborg soldier.

AVAILABLE WHEREVER BOOKS ARE SOLD OR
TO ORDER CALL: 1-800-788-6262

(Ad # B170)

NOW AVAILABLE IN HARDCOVER

WILLIAM C. DIETZ

EARTHRISE

THE SEQUEL TO *DEATHDAY*

AVAILABLE WHEREVER BOOKS ARE SOLD OR TO ORDER CALL 1-800-788-6262

B025

From national bestselling author

RICK SHELLEY

The thrilling adventures of the Dirigent Mercenary Corps:
For them, war isn't just a duty and an honor, but a way of life...

☐ **OFFICER-CADET**   0-441-00526-8

☐ **LIEUTENANT**   0-441-00568-3

☐ **CAPTAIN**   0-441-00605-1

☐ **MAJOR**   0-441-00680-9

☐ **LIEUTENANT COLONEL**   0-441-00722-8

☐ **COLONEL**   0-441-00782-1

Also by Rick Shelley:

☐ **THE BUCHANAN CAMPAIGN**   0-441-00292-7
A battle for control between the Federation and the Second
Commonwealth explodes—with the planet Buchanan and
Sergeant David Spencer caught in the crossfire.

☐ **THE FIRES OF COVENTRY**   0-441-00385-0
This powerful follow-up to *The Buchanan Campaign* continues
the epic story of Sergeant David Spencer's fight to liberate
occupied worlds from an unrelenting enemy.

☐ **RETURN TO CAMEREIN**   0-441-00496-2
Captain David Spencer leads a daring rescue to find the
Commonwealth's hostage prince—and escape from under the
noses of the Federation troops.

☐ **SPEC OPS SQUAD:**
    HOLDING THE LINE   0-441-00834-8
By joining the Alliance of Light, Earth has found allies with
whom to explore universe—and an enemy that will never rest
until the Alliance lays in ruins.

AVAILABLE WHEREVER BOOKS ARE SOLD OR
TO ORDER CALL:

1-800-788-6262

(Ad # B256)

PENGUIN GROUP (USA) INC.
Online

Your Internet gateway to a virtual environment with
hundreds of entertaining and enlightening books
from Penguin Group (USA) Inc.

*While you're there, get the latest buzz on
the best authors and books around—*

Tom Clancy, Patricia Cornwell, W.E.B. Griffin,
Nora Roberts, William Gibson, Robin Cook,
Brian Jacques, Catherine Coulter, Stephen King,
Ken Follett, Terry McMillan, and many more!

**Penguin Group (USA) Inc. Online is located at
http://www.penguin.com**

PENGUIN GROUP (USA) Inc.
NEWS

Every month you'll get an inside look at our upcom-
ing books and new features on our site. This is an
ongoing effort to provide you with the most
up-to-date information about
our books and authors.

**Subscribe to Penguin Group (USA) Inc. News at
http://www.penguin.com/newsletters**